SUPERMAN ADVENTURES

UP, UP AND AWAY!

Written by:
Mark Millar

Illustrated by:
Aluir Amancio
Terry Austin

Colored by:
Marie Severin
Rick Taylor

Lettered by:
Lois Buhalis

Superman created by **Jerry Siegel** and **Joe Shuster**

SUPERMAN ADVENTURES VOL. 1: UP, UP AND AWAY!
Published by DC Comics. Cover and compilation copyright © 2004 DC
Comics. All Rights Reserved. Originally published in single magazine form
as SUPERMAN ADVENTURES 16, 19, 22-24. Copyright © 1998 DC Comics.
All Rights Reserved. All characters, their distinctive likenesses and related
elements featured in this publication are trademarks of DC Comics. The
stories, characters and incidents featured in this publication are entirely
fictional. DC Comics does not read or accept unsolicited submissions of
ideas, stories or artwork.

CARTOON NETWORK and its logo are trademarks of Cartoon Network.

DC Comics, 1700 Broadway, New York, NY 10019
A Warner Bros. Entertainment Company.
Printed in Canada. First Printing.
ISBN: 1-4012-0331-0
Cover illustration by Mike Manley and Terry Austin.
Publication design by John J. Hill.

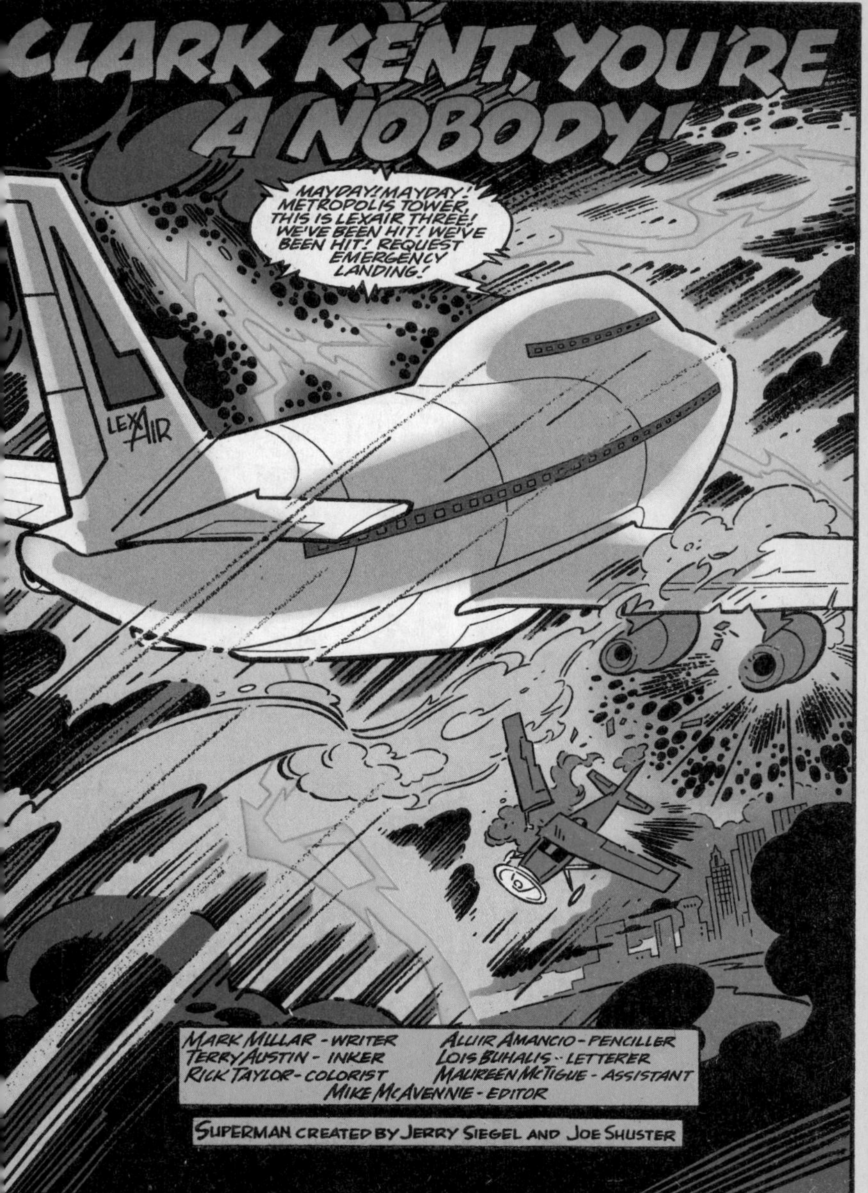
CLARK KENT, YOU'RE A NOBODY!
MAYDAY! MAYDAY! METROPOLIS TOWER, THIS IS LEXAIR THREE! WE'VE BEEN HIT! WE'VE BEEN HIT! REQUEST EMERGENCY LANDING!
LEXAIR
MARK MILLAR - WRITER
ALUIR AMANCIO - PENCILLER
TERRY AUSTIN - INKER
LOIS BUHALIS - LETTERER
RICK TAYLOR - COLORIST
MAUREEN MCTIGUE - ASSISTANT
MIKE MCAVENNIE - EDITOR
SUPERMAN CREATED BY JERRY SIEGEL AND JOE SHUSTER

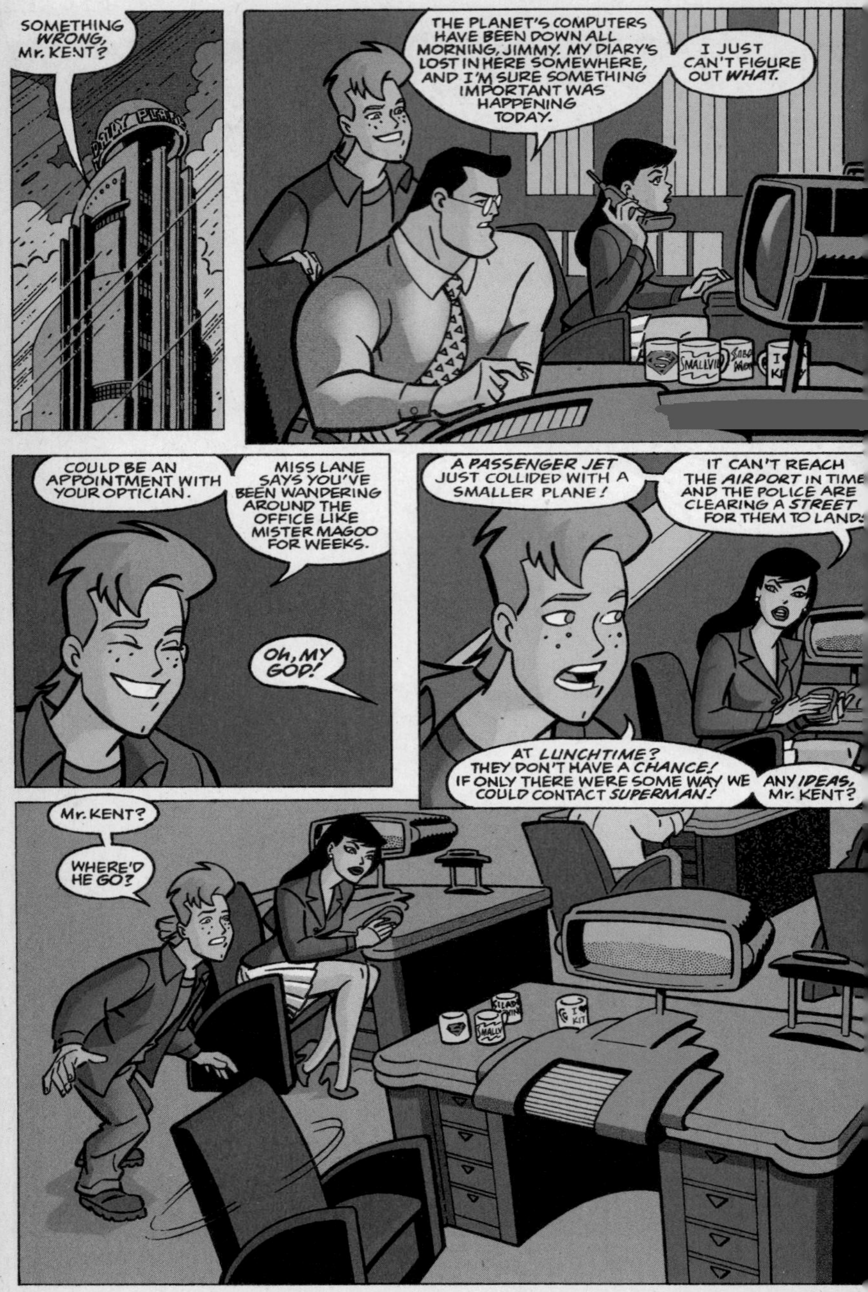
SOMETHING WRONG, Mr. KENT?
THE PLANET'S COMPUTERS HAVE BEEN DOWN ALL MORNING, JIMMY. MY DIARY'S LOST IN HERE SOMEWHERE, AND I'M SURE SOMETHING IMPORTANT WAS HAPPENING TODAY.
I JUST CAN'T FIGURE OUT WHAT.
COULD BE AN APPOINTMENT WITH YOUR OPTICIAN.
MISS LANE SAYS YOU'VE BEEN WANDERING AROUND THE OFFICE LIKE MISTER MAGOO FOR WEEKS.
Oh, MY GOD!
A PASSENGER JET JUST COLLIDED WITH A SMALLER PLANE!
IT CAN'T REACH THE AIRPORT IN TIME AND THE POLICE ARE CLEARING A STREET FOR THEM TO LAND!
AT LUNCHTIME? THEY DON'T HAVE A CHANCE! IF ONLY THERE WERE SOME WAY WE COULD CONTACT SUPERMAN!
ANY IDEAS, Mr. KENT?
Mr. KENT?
WHERE'D HE GO?

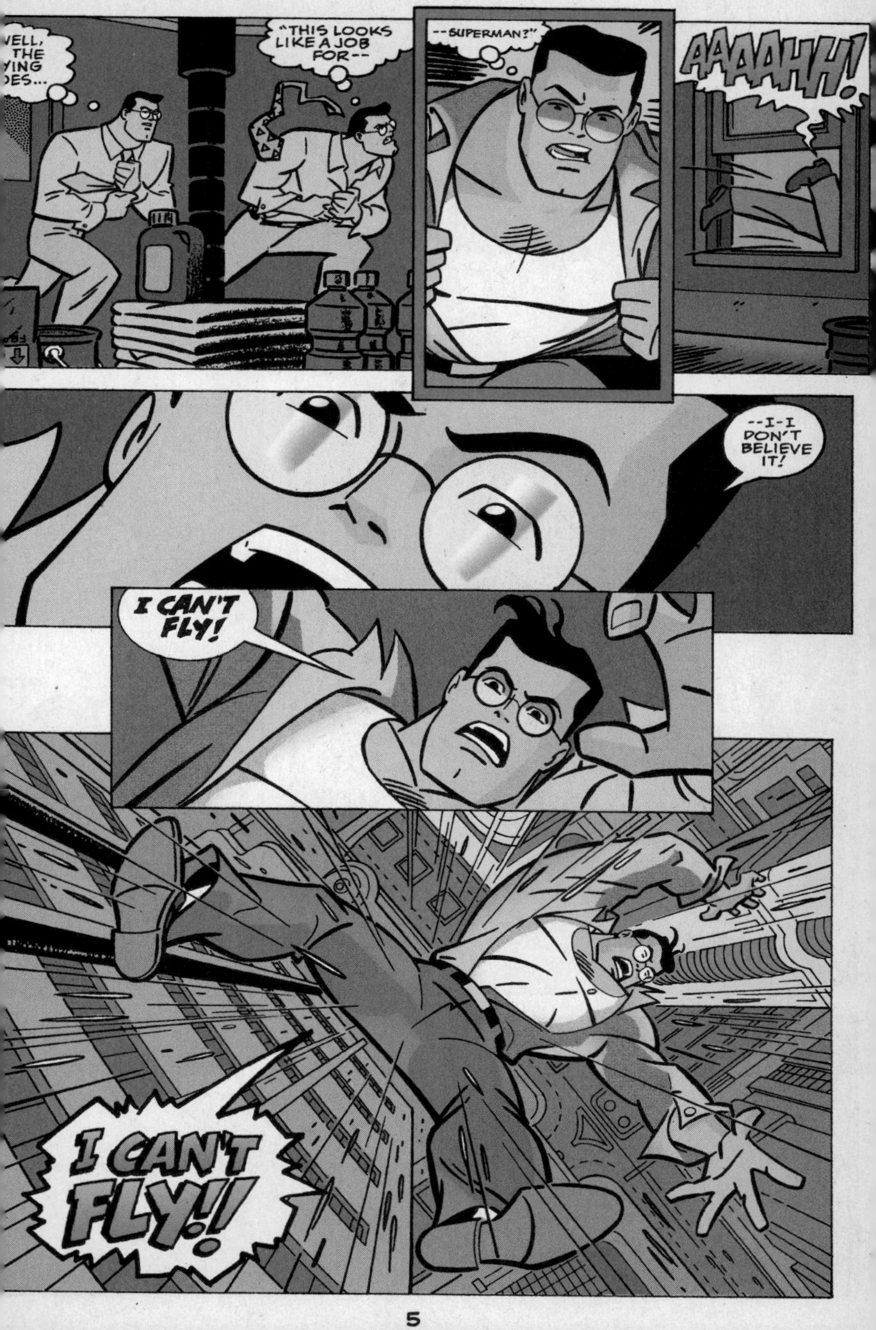

...ELL, THE ...YING ...DES...
"THIS LOOKS LIKE A JOB FOR--
--SUPERMAN?"
AAAAHH!
--I-I DON'T BELIEVE IT!
I CAN'T FLY!
I CAN'T FLY!!

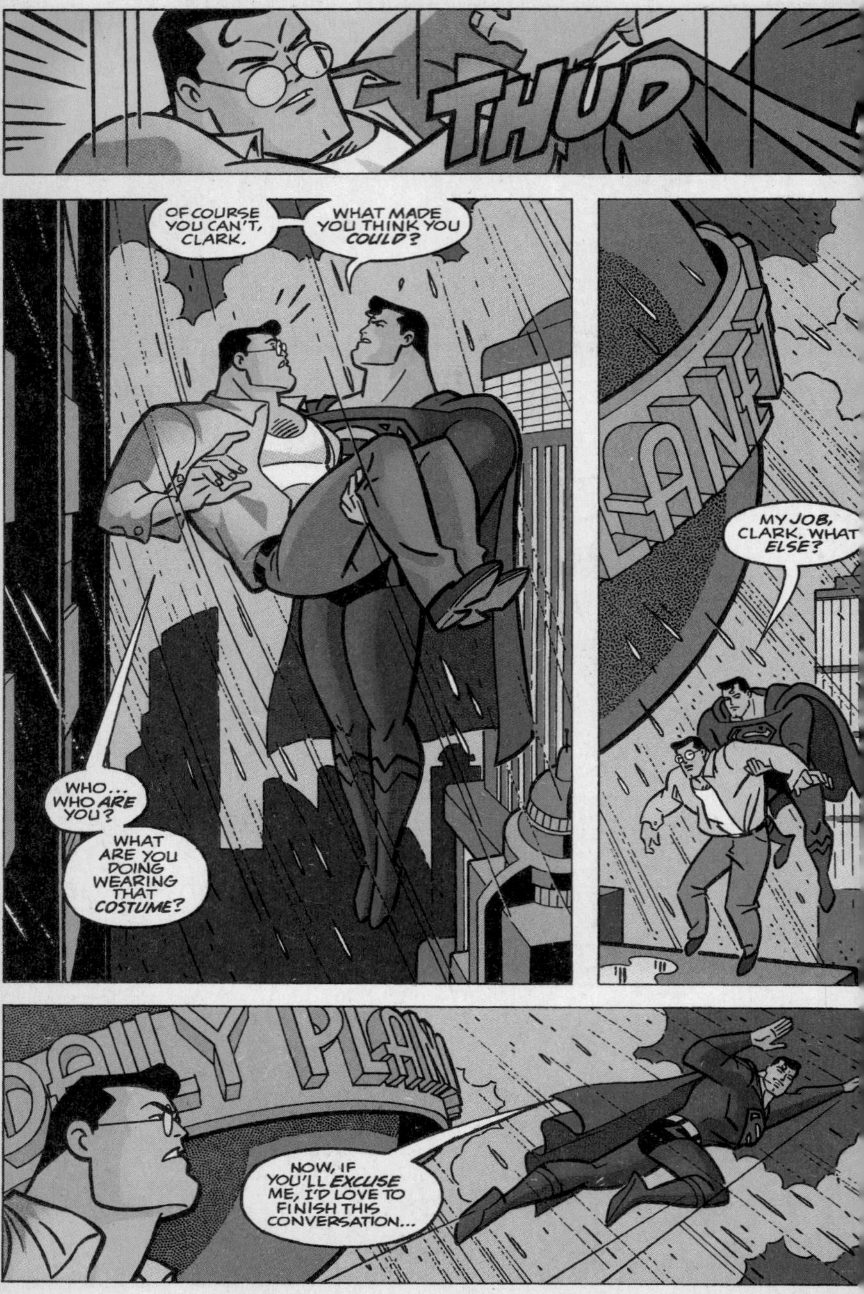
THUD
OF COURSE YOU CAN'T, CLARK.
WHAT MADE YOU THINK YOU COULD?
WHO... WHO ARE YOU?
WHAT ARE YOU DOING WEARING THAT COSTUME?
MY JOB, CLARK. WHAT ELSE?
NOW, IF YOU'LL EXCUSE ME, I'D LOVE TO FINISH THIS CONVERSATION...

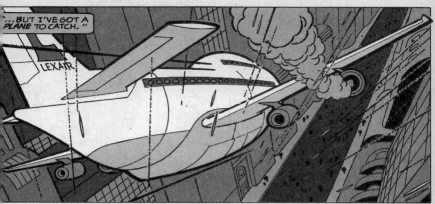

"...BUT I'VE GOT A PLANE TO CATCH."

LEXAIR

RUN FOR YOUR LIVES!

WHAT IS IT? WHAT'S *HAPPENING*?

WILL SOMEONE PLEASE TELL ME WHAT'S GOING ON?

COME ON, *PULL UP!* *PULL UP!*

IT'S *NO USE!* WE LOST THE MAIN *OUTBOARD ENGINE!*

WE'RE HEADING *STRAIGHT* FOR THE *SIDEWALK!* WE'RE--

--*STRAIGHTENING OUT?*

WHAT HAPPENED? WHAT'D YOU DO?

NOTHING! I'M NOT EVEN TOUCHING THE CONTROLS!

SHE'S *FLYING* ALL BY *HERSELF!*

7

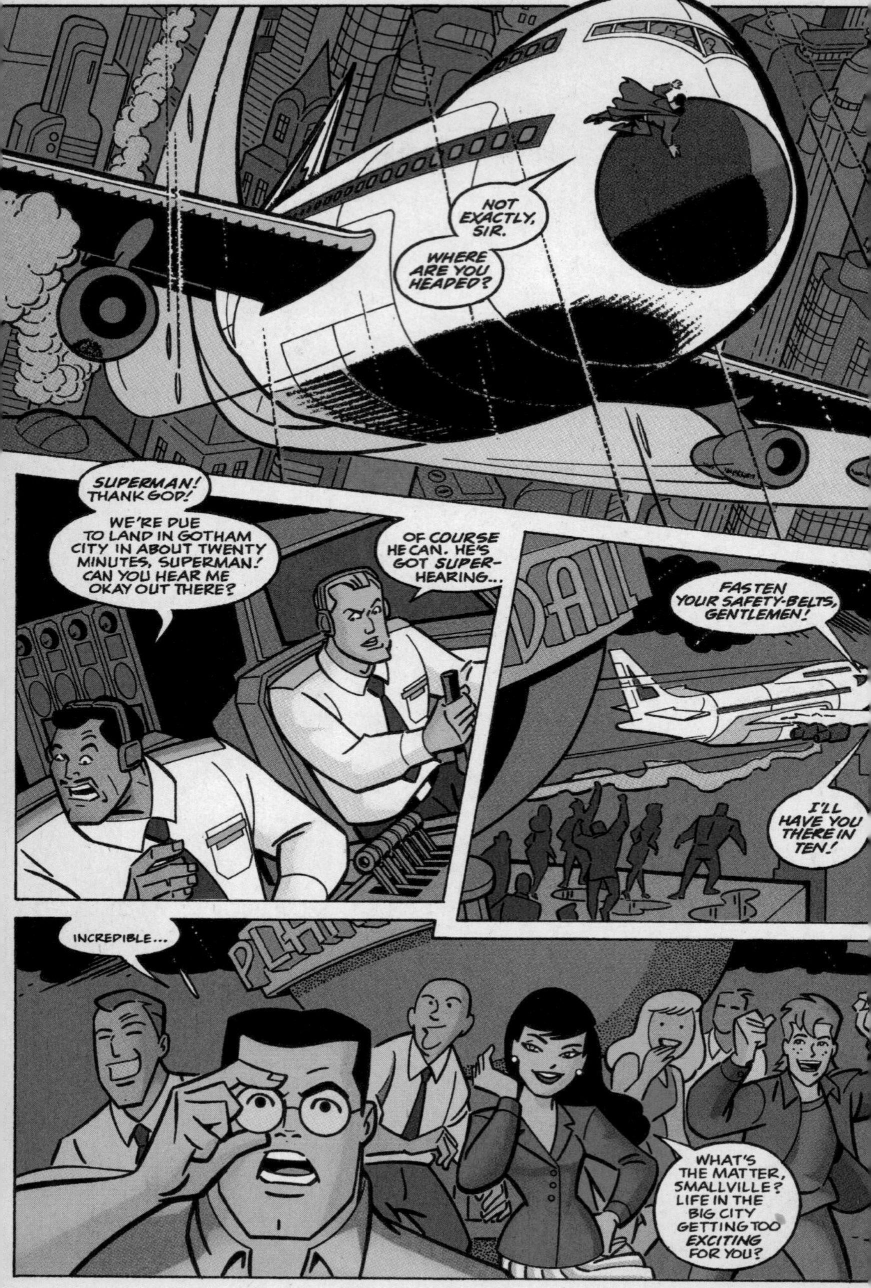
NOT EXACTLY, SIR.
WHERE ARE YOU HEADED?
SUPERMAN! THANK GOD!
WE'RE DUE TO LAND IN GOTHAM CITY IN ABOUT TWENTY MINUTES, SUPERMAN! CAN YOU HEAR ME OKAY OUT THERE?
OF COURSE HE CAN. HE'S GOT SUPER-HEARING...
FASTEN YOUR SAFETY-BELTS, GENTLEMEN!
I'LL HAVE YOU THERE IN TEN!
INCREDIBLE...
WHAT'S THE MATTER, SMALLVILLE? LIFE IN THE BIG CITY GETTING TOO EXCITING FOR YOU?

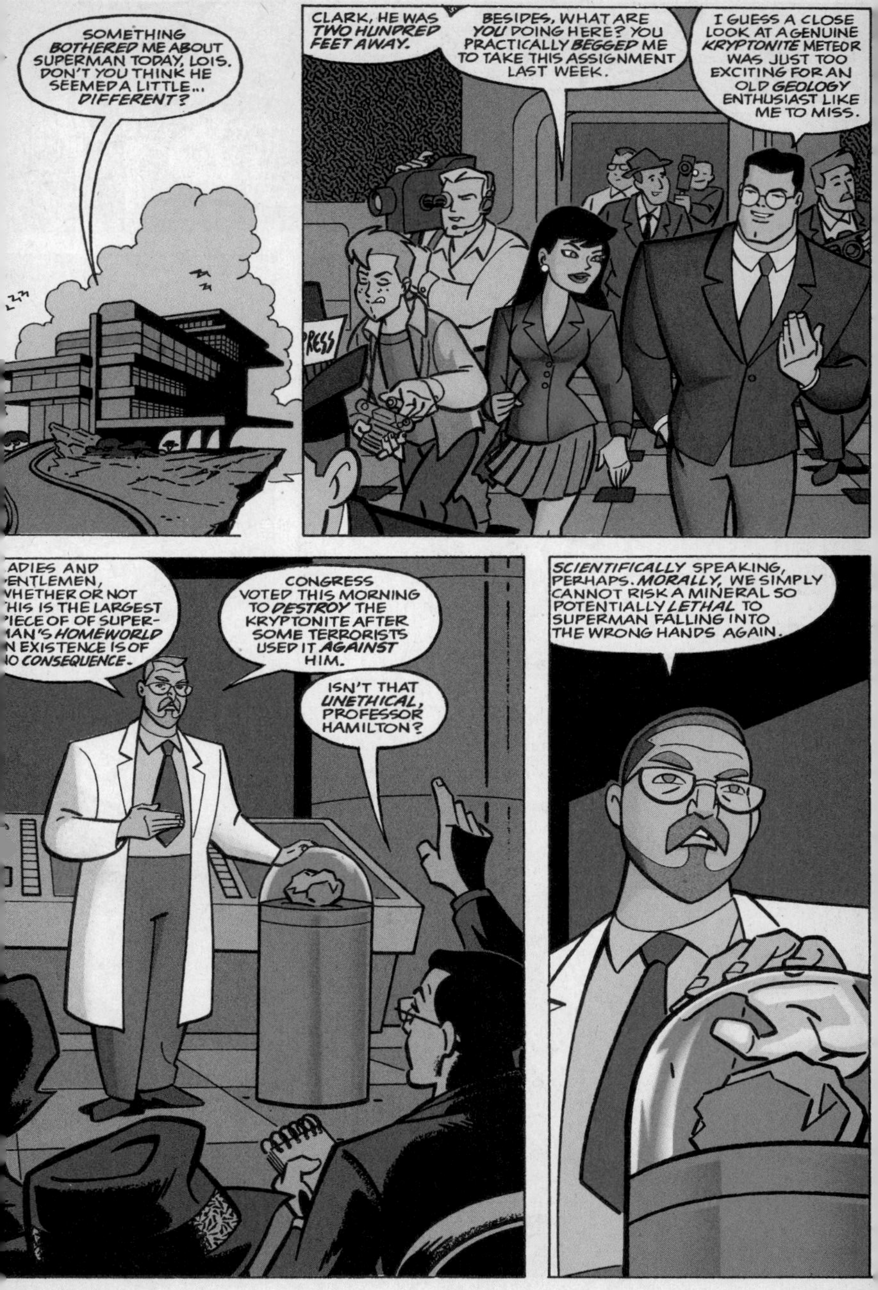
SOMETHING BOTHERED ME ABOUT SUPERMAN TODAY, LOIS. DON'T YOU THINK HE SEEMED A LITTLE... DIFFERENT?
CLARK, HE WAS TWO HUNDRED FEET AWAY.
BESIDES, WHAT ARE YOU DOING HERE? YOU PRACTICALLY BEGGED ME TO TAKE THIS ASSIGNMENT LAST WEEK.
I GUESS A CLOSE LOOK AT A GENUINE KRYPTONITE METEOR WAS JUST TOO EXCITING FOR AN OLD GEOLOGY ENTHUSIAST LIKE ME TO MISS.
PRESS
ADIES AND ENTLEMEN, VHETHER OR NOT HIS IS THE LARGEST IECE OF OF SUPER-IAN'S HOMEWORLD N EXISTENCE IS OF O CONSEQUENCE.
CONGRESS VOTED THIS MORNING TO DESTROY THE KRYPTONITE AFTER SOME TERRORISTS USED IT AGAINST HIM.
ISN'T THAT UNETHICAL, PROFESSOR HAMILTON?
SCIENTIFICALLY SPEAKING, PERHAPS. MORALLY, WE SIMPLY CANNOT RISK A MINERAL SO POTENTIALLY LETHAL TO SUPERMAN FALLING INTO THE WRONG HANDS AGAIN.

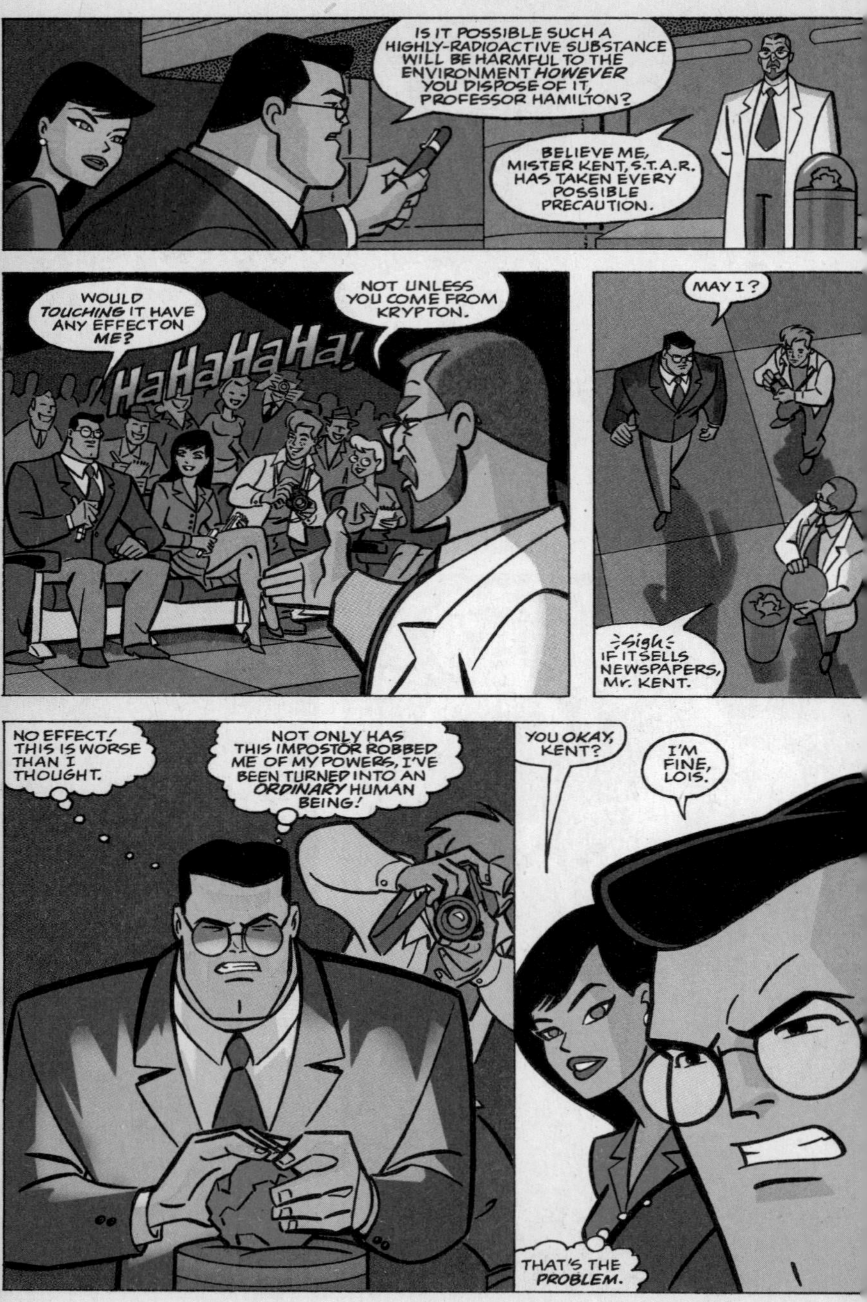
IS IT POSSIBLE SUCH A HIGHLY-RADIOACTIVE SUBSTANCE WILL BE HARMFUL TO THE ENVIRONMENT *HOWEVER* YOU DISPOSE OF IT, PROFESSOR HAMILTON?
BELIEVE ME, MISTER KENT, S.T.A.R. HAS TAKEN EVERY POSSIBLE PRECAUTION.
WOULD *TOUCHING* IT HAVE ANY EFFECT ON *ME*?
NOT UNLESS YOU COME FROM KRYPTON.
HaHaHaHaHa!
MAY I?
~Sigh~ IF IT SELLS NEWSPAPERS, Mr. KENT.
NO EFFECT! THIS IS WORSE THAN I THOUGHT.
NOT ONLY HAS THIS IMPOSTOR ROBBED ME OF MY POWERS, I'VE BEEN TURNED INTO AN *ORDINARY* HUMAN BEING!
YOU *OKAY*, KENT?
I'M FINE, LOIS.
THAT'S THE *PROBLEM*.

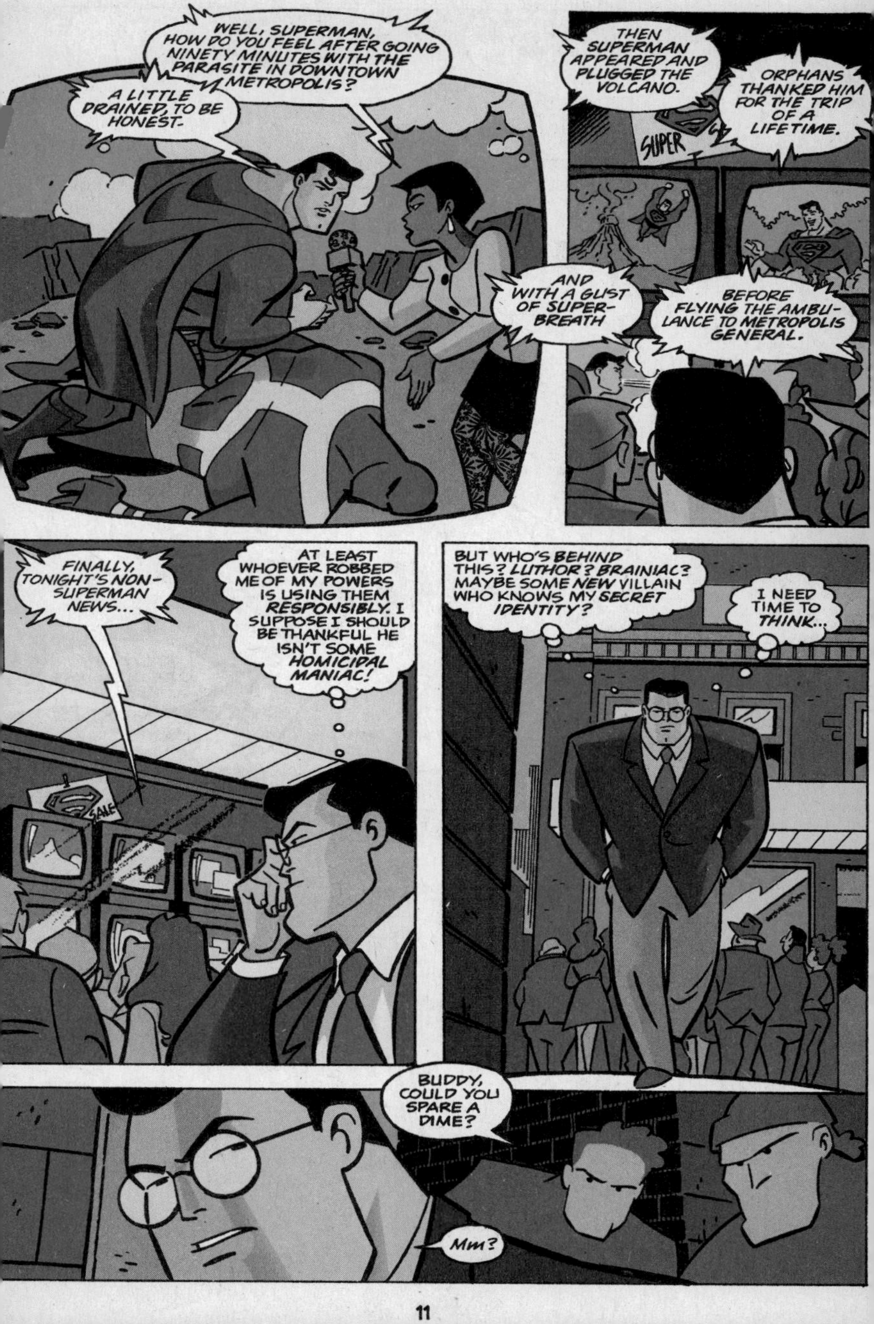
WELL, SUPERMAN, HOW DO YOU FEEL AFTER GOING NINETY MINUTES WITH THE PARASITE IN DOWNTOWN METROPOLIS?
A LITTLE DRAINED, TO BE HONEST.
THEN SUPERMAN APPEARED AND PLUGGED THE VOLCANO.
ORPHANS THANKED HIM FOR THE TRIP OF A LIFETIME.
SUPER
AND WITH A GUST OF SUPER-BREATH
BEFORE FLYING THE AMBULANCE TO METROPOLIS GENERAL.
FINALLY, TONIGHT'S NON-SUPERMAN NEWS...
AT LEAST WHOEVER ROBBED ME OF MY POWERS IS USING THEM RESPONSIBLY. I SUPPOSE I SHOULD BE THANKFUL HE ISN'T SOME HOMICIDAL MANIAC!
SALE
BUT WHO'S BEHIND THIS? LUTHOR? BRAINIAC? MAYBE SOME NEW VILLAIN WHO KNOWS MY SECRET IDENTITY?
I NEED TIME TO THINK...
BUDDY, COULD YOU SPARE A DIME?
Mm?

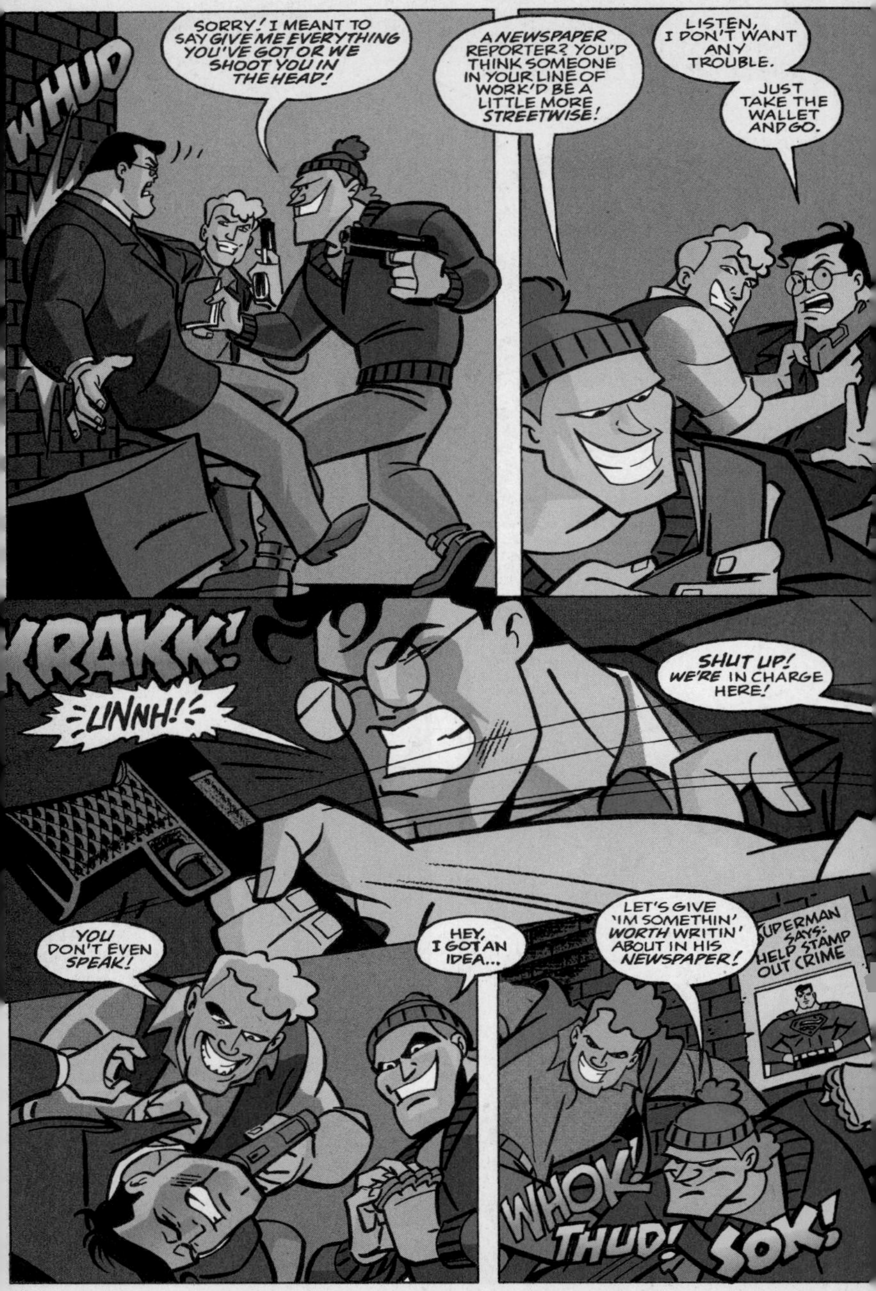
WHUD
SORRY! I MEANT TO SAY GIVE ME EVERYTHING YOU'VE GOT OR WE SHOOT YOU IN THE HEAD!
A NEWSPAPER REPORTER? YOU'D THINK SOMEONE IN YOUR LINE OF WORK'D BE A LITTLE MORE STREETWISE!
LISTEN, I DON'T WANT ANY TROUBLE.
JUST TAKE THE WALLET AND GO.
KRAKK!
UNNH!
SHUT UP! WE'RE IN CHARGE HERE!
YOU DON'T EVEN SPEAK!
HEY, I GOT AN IDEA...
LET'S GIVE 'IM SOMETHIN' WORTH WRITIN' ABOUT IN HIS NEWSPAPER!
SUPERMAN SAYS: HELP STAMP OUT CRIME
WHOK!
THUD!
SOK!

HEY! WHAT'S GOING ON OVER THERE?!

HAHAHA HAHAHAHA

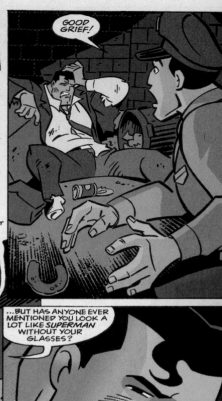

GOOD GRIEF!

MY GLASSES...CAN'T SEE WITHOUT MY GLASSES...

YOU'RE GOING TO BE FINE, MISTER. JUST A FEW CUTS AND BRUISES. NOTHING TO GET WORKED UP ABOUT.

...BUT HAS ANYONE EVER MENTIONED YOU LOOK A LOT LIKE SUPERMAN WITHOUT YOUR GLASSES?

SAY... I KNOW THIS PROBABLY SOUNDS KIND OF STRANGE UNDER THE CIRCUMSTANCES...

I HARDLY KNOW WHERE TO START, PA...

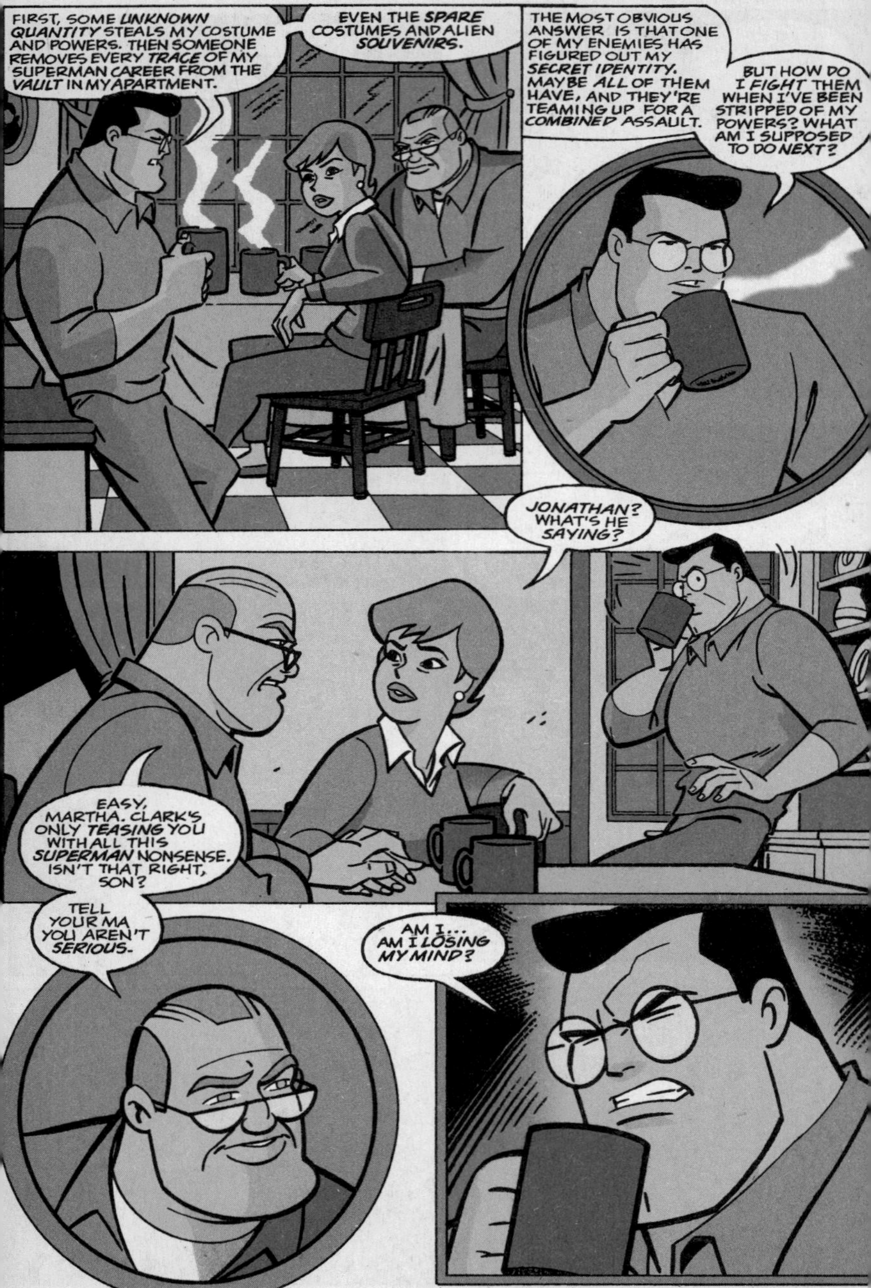
FIRST, SOME UNKNOWN QUANTITY STEALS MY COSTUME AND POWERS. THEN SOMEONE REMOVES EVERY TRACE OF MY SUPERMAN CAREER FROM THE VAULT IN MY APARTMENT.
EVEN THE SPARE COSTUMES AND ALIEN SOUVENIRS.
THE MOST OBVIOUS ANSWER IS THAT ONE OF MY ENEMIES HAS FIGURED OUT MY SECRET IDENTITY. MAYBE ALL OF THEM HAVE, AND THEY'RE TEAMING UP FOR A COMBINED ASSAULT.
BUT HOW DO I FIGHT THEM WHEN I'VE BEEN STRIPPED OF MY POWERS? WHAT AM I SUPPOSED TO DO NEXT?
JONATHAN? WHAT'S HE SAYING?
EASY, MARTHA. CLARK'S ONLY TEASING YOU WITH ALL THIS SUPERMAN NONSENSE. ISN'T THAT RIGHT, SON?
TELL YOUR MA YOU AREN'T SERIOUS.
AM I... AM I LOSING MY MIND?

THE *BARN* WHERE YOU HID MY ROCKET, THE *SCORCHED EARTH*, WHERE I USED MY HEAT-VISION WITHOUT THINKING AND DESTROYED SMALLVILLE'S BEST SUMMER CROP.

NONE OF THESE THINGS ARE *HERE* ANYMORE, PA...

WAS MY SUPERMAN CAREER BEEN A *DELUSION?*

SOMETIMES THE MIND CAN PLAY TRICKS ON US, CLARK. MAKE US FEEL ON TOP OF THE WORLD ONE DAY, AND BOTTOM OF THE HEAP THE NEXT...

I GUESS THERE'S TIMES WE'D *ALL* RATHER BE SUPERMAN THAN FACE REALITY. BE ANYONE *EXCEPT* OURSELVES. WE WORK TOO HARD, SON. IT'S IN OUR BLOOD.

YOU RECKON?

MAYBE YOU'RE *RIGHT*, PA... MAYBE I--

Shhh.

Huh? WHAT'S *WRONG*, PA?

KLINCH KLINCH KLINCH KLINCH

GET BACK INDOORS!

15

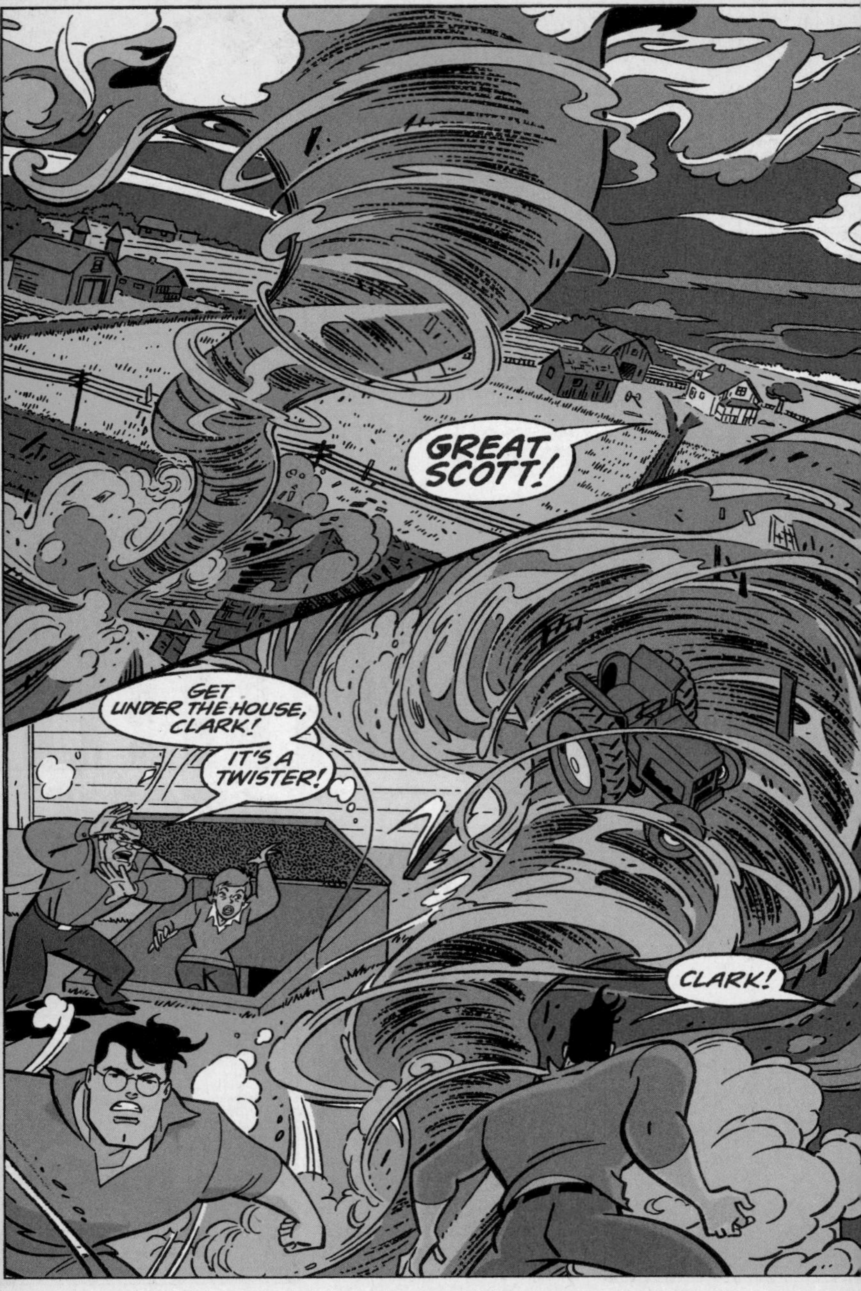
GREAT SCOTT!
GET UNDER THE HOUSE, CLARK!
IT'S A TWISTER!
CLARK!

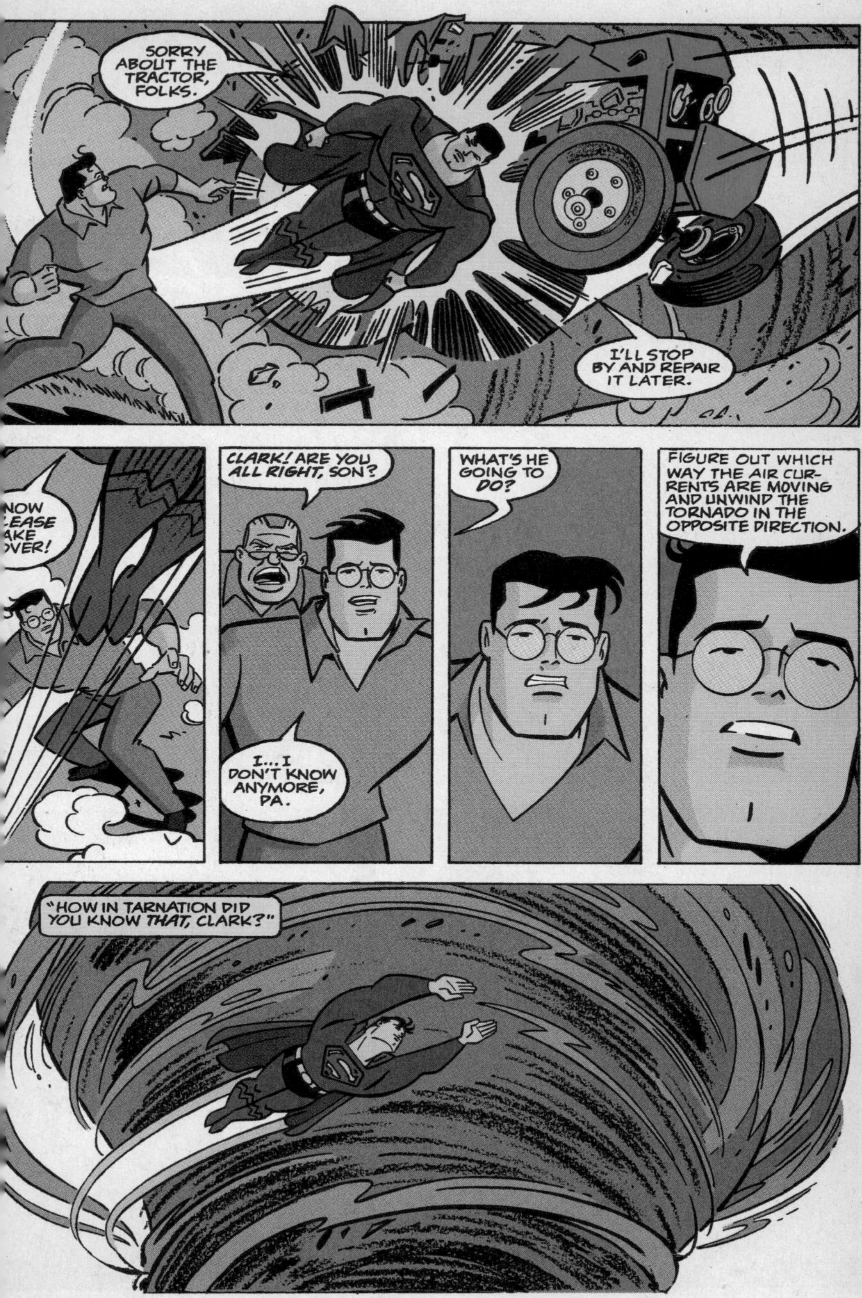
SORRY ABOUT THE TRACTOR, FOLKS.
I'LL STOP BY AND REPAIR IT LATER.
NOW
CLARK! ARE YOU ALL RIGHT, SON?
I... I DON'T KNOW ANYMORE, PA.
WHAT'S HE GOING TO DO?
FIGURE OUT WHICH WAY THE AIR CURRENTS ARE MOVING AND UNWIND THE TORNADO IN THE OPPOSITE DIRECTION.
"HOW IN TARNATION DID YOU KNOW THAT, CLARK?"

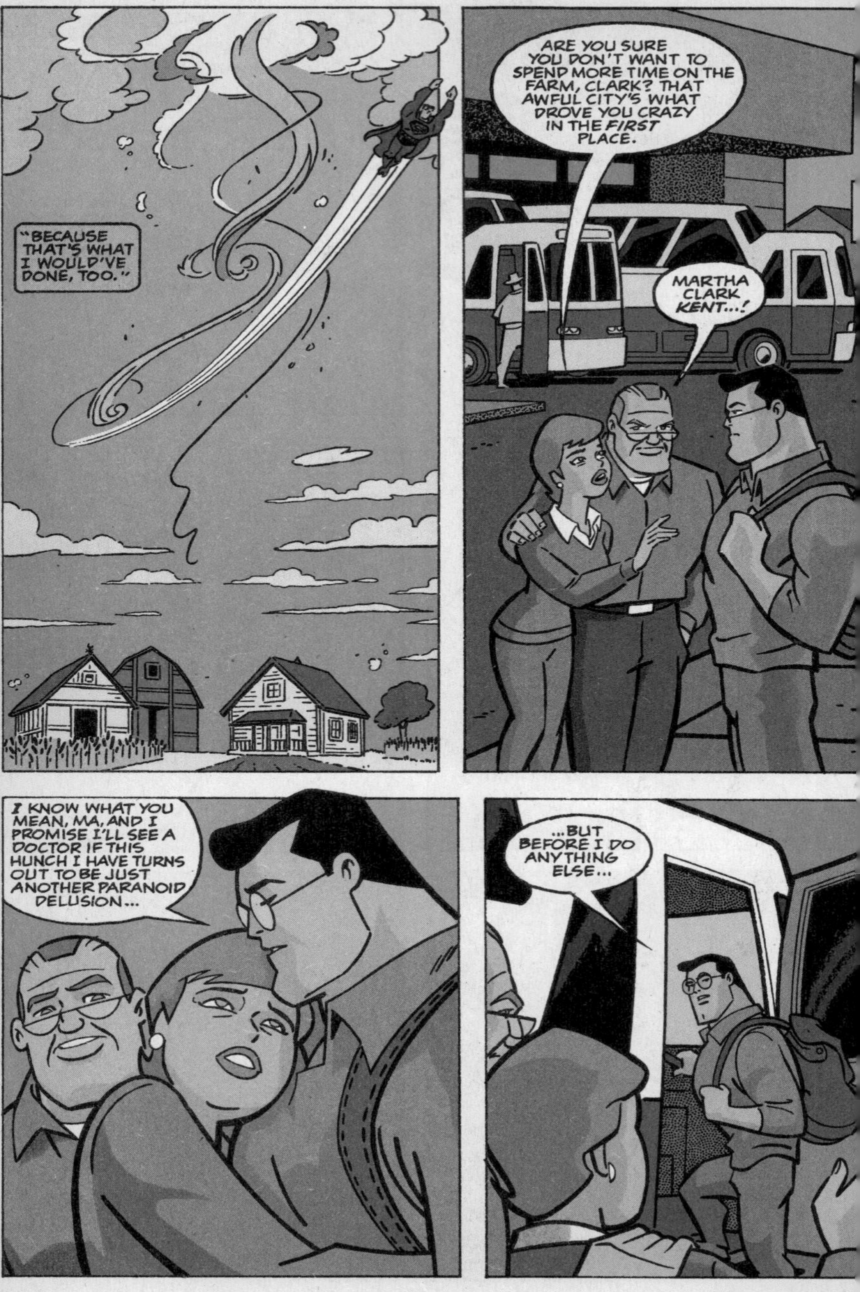
"BECAUSE THAT'S WHAT I WOULD'VE DONE, TOO."
ARE YOU SURE YOU DON'T WANT TO SPEND MORE TIME ON THE FARM, CLARK? THAT AWFUL CITY'S WHAT DROVE YOU CRAZY IN THE FIRST PLACE.
MARTHA CLARK KENT...!
I KNOW WHAT YOU MEAN, MA, AND I PROMISE I'LL SEE A DOCTOR IF THIS HUNCH I HAVE TURNS OUT TO BE JUST ANOTHER PARANOID DELUSION...
...BUT BEFORE I DO ANYTHING ELSE...

THERE'S SOMETHING [H]AVE TO CHECK FIRST."

WE ONLY CAME BACK ON-LINE THIS MORNING, MR. KENT.

THE LAST COUPLE OF DAYS FELT LIKE WE WERE PUTTING TOGETHER A NEWSPAPER IN THE JURASSIC AGE.

[A]NY LUCK FINDING YOUR [ORDIN]ARY MESSAGES?

[CO]MING [RIG]HT UP, [JI]MMY...

- TODAY'S THE DAY
- MESSAGE TO BE REPEATED EVERY NINETY DAYS

OF COURSE!

I TAKE IT THIS IS GOOD NEWS?

SNAP

"THE BEST."

UNBELIEVABLE!

WHEET WHEET

WHEET WHEET WHEET WHEET WHEET WHEET WHEET WHEET WHEE!

19

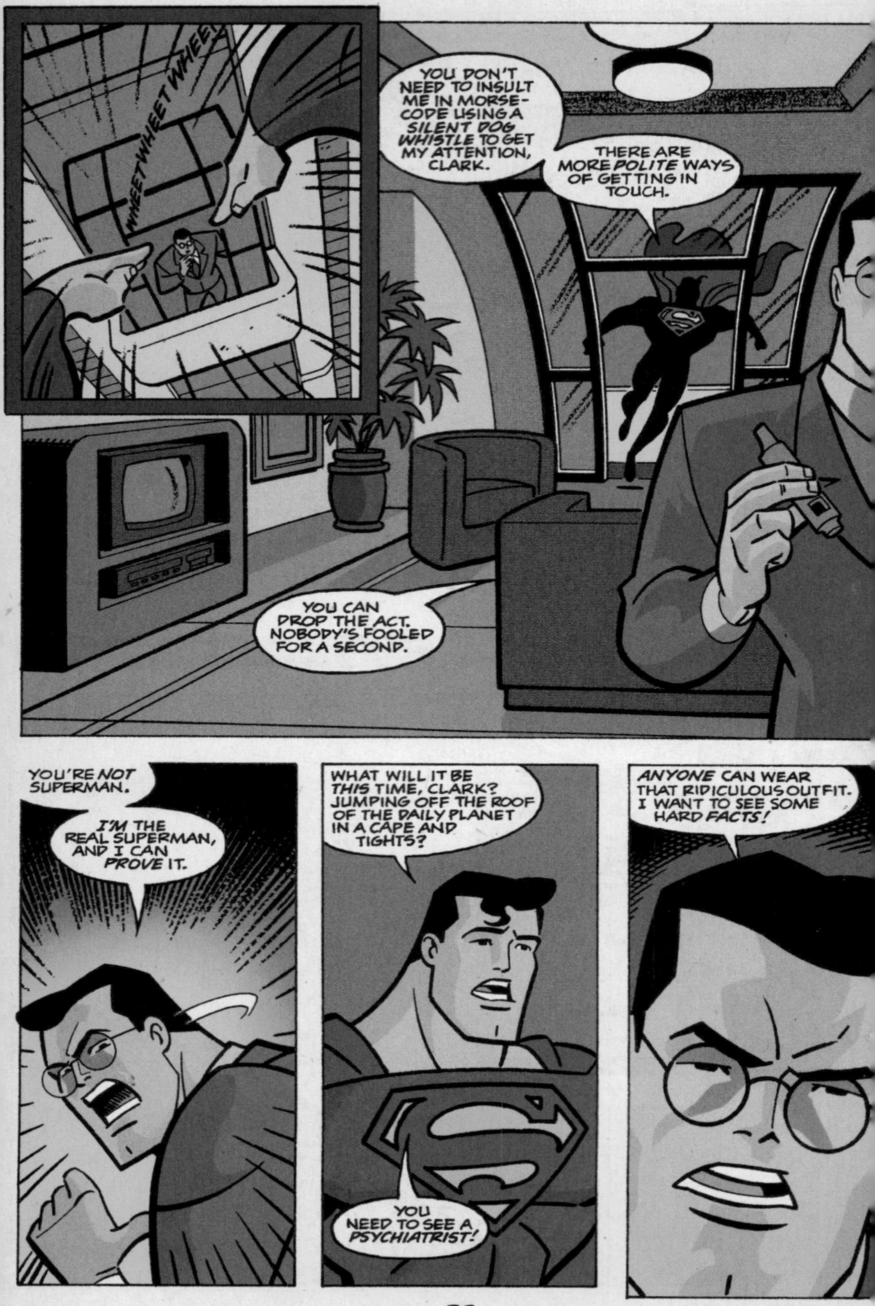
WHEETWHEETWHEET WHEE!
YOU DON'T NEED TO INSULT ME IN MORSE-CODE USING A SILENT DOG WHISTLE TO GET MY ATTENTION, CLARK.
THERE ARE MORE POLITE WAYS OF GETTING IN TOUCH.
YOU CAN DROP THE ACT. NOBODY'S FOOLED FOR A SECOND.
YOU'RE NOT SUPERMAN.
I'M THE REAL SUPERMAN, AND I CAN PROVE IT.
WHAT WILL IT BE THIS TIME, CLARK? JUMPING OFF THE ROOF OF THE DAILY PLANET IN A CAPE AND TIGHTS?
YOU NEED TO SEE A PSYCHIATRIST!
ANYONE CAN WEAR THAT RIDICULOUS OUTFIT. I WANT TO SEE SOME HARD FACTS!

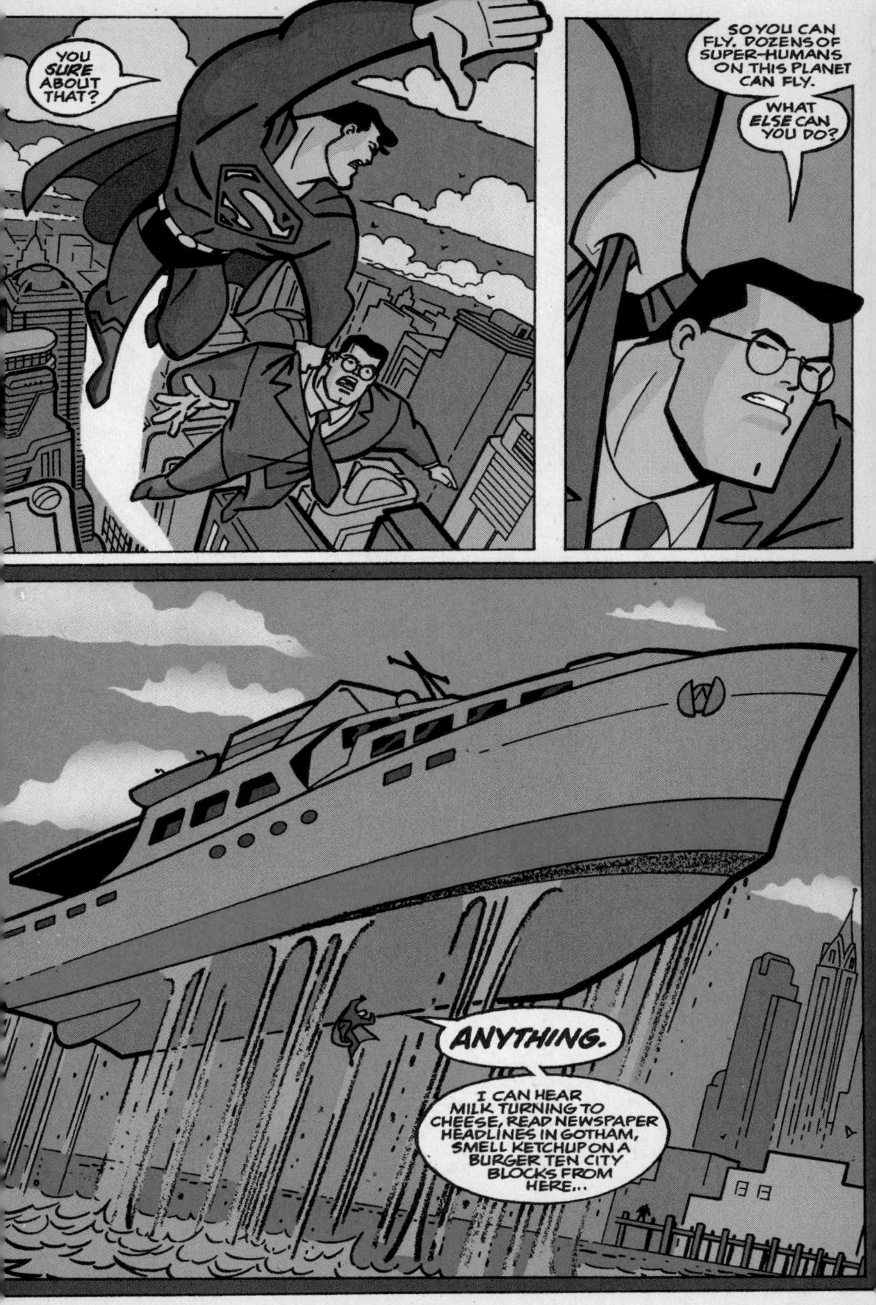
YOU SURE ABOUT THAT?
SO YOU CAN FLY. DOZENS OF SUPER-HUMANS ON THIS PLANET CAN FLY.
WHAT ELSE CAN YOU DO?
ANYTHING.
I CAN HEAR MILK TURNING TO CHEESE, READ NEWSPAPER HEADLINES IN GOTHAM, SMELL KETCHUP ON A BURGER TEN CITY BLOCKS FROM HERE...

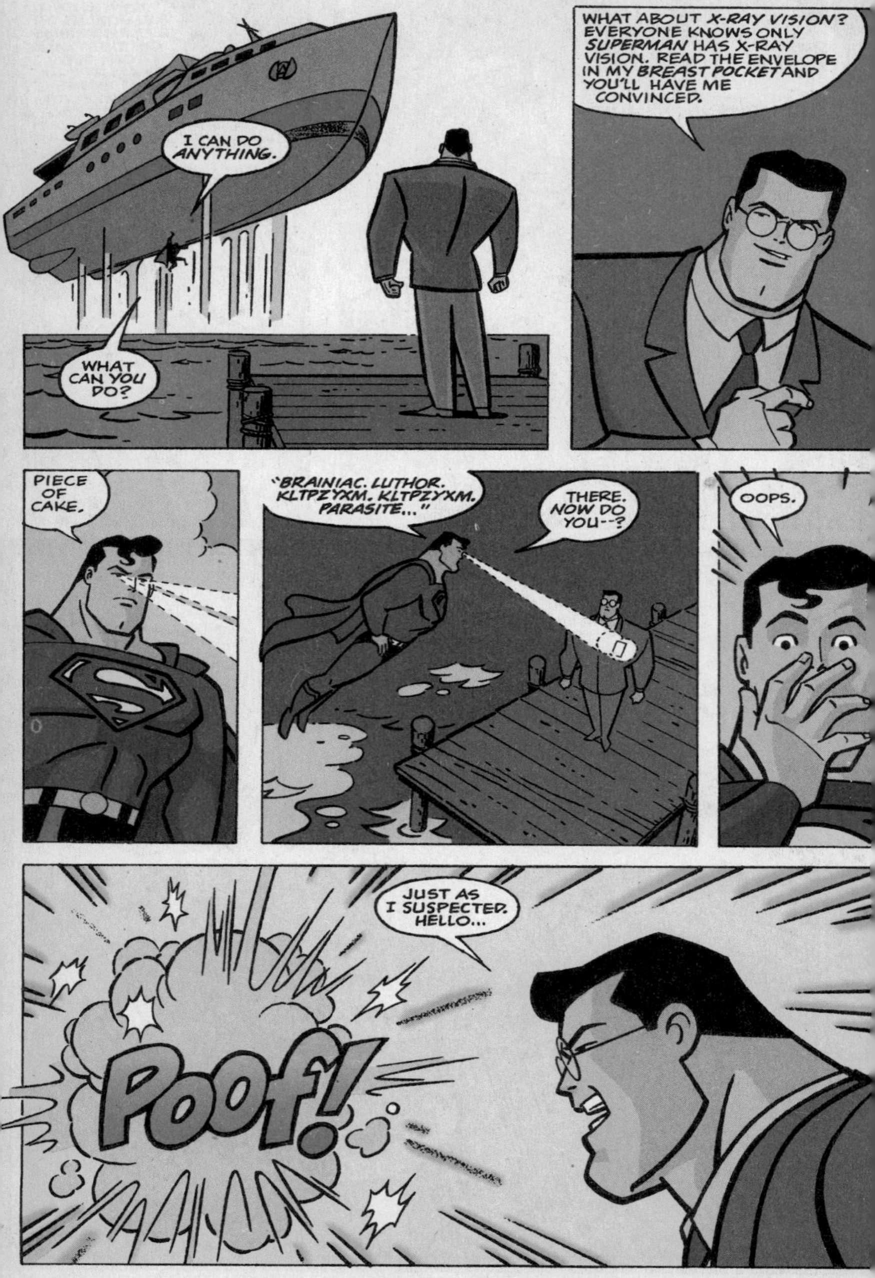
WHAT CAN YOU DO?
I CAN DO ANYTHING.
WHAT ABOUT X-RAY VISION? EVERYONE KNOWS ONLY SUPERMAN HAS X-RAY VISION. READ THE ENVELOPE IN MY BREAST POCKET AND YOU'LL HAVE ME CONVINCED.
PIECE OF CAKE.
"BRAINIAC. LUTHOR. KLTPZYXM. KLTPZYXM. PARASITE..."
THERE. NOW DO YOU--?
OOPS.
JUST AS I SUSPECTED. HELLO...
POOF!

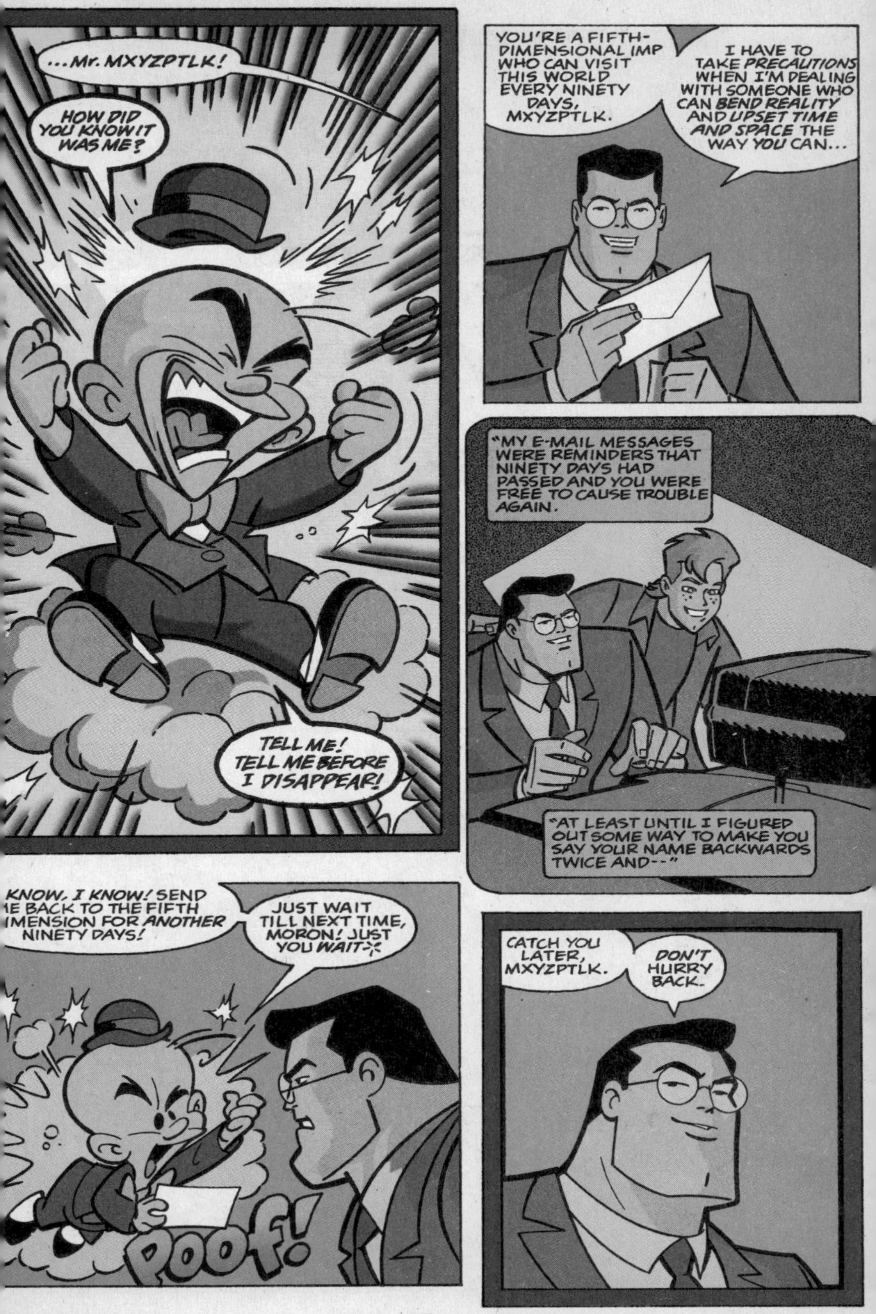

...Mr. MXYZPTLK!
HOW DID YOU KNOW IT WAS ME?
TELL ME! TELL ME BEFORE I DISAPPEAR!
YOU'RE A FIFTH-DIMENSIONAL IMP WHO CAN VISIT THIS WORLD EVERY NINETY DAYS, MXYZPTLK.
I HAVE TO TAKE PRECAUTIONS WHEN I'M DEALING WITH SOMEONE WHO CAN BEND REALITY AND UPSET TIME AND SPACE THE WAY YOU CAN...
"MY E-MAIL MESSAGES WERE REMINDERS THAT NINETY DAYS HAD PASSED AND YOU WERE FREE TO CAUSE TROUBLE AGAIN.
"AT LEAST UNTIL I FIGURED OUT SOME WAY TO MAKE YOU SAY YOUR NAME BACKWARDS TWICE AND--"
KNOW, I KNOW! SEND ME BACK TO THE FIFTH DIMENSION FOR ANOTHER NINETY DAYS!
JUST WAIT TILL NEXT TIME, MORON! JUST YOU WAIT
POOF!
CATCH YOU LATER, MXYZPTLK.
DON'T HURRY BACK.

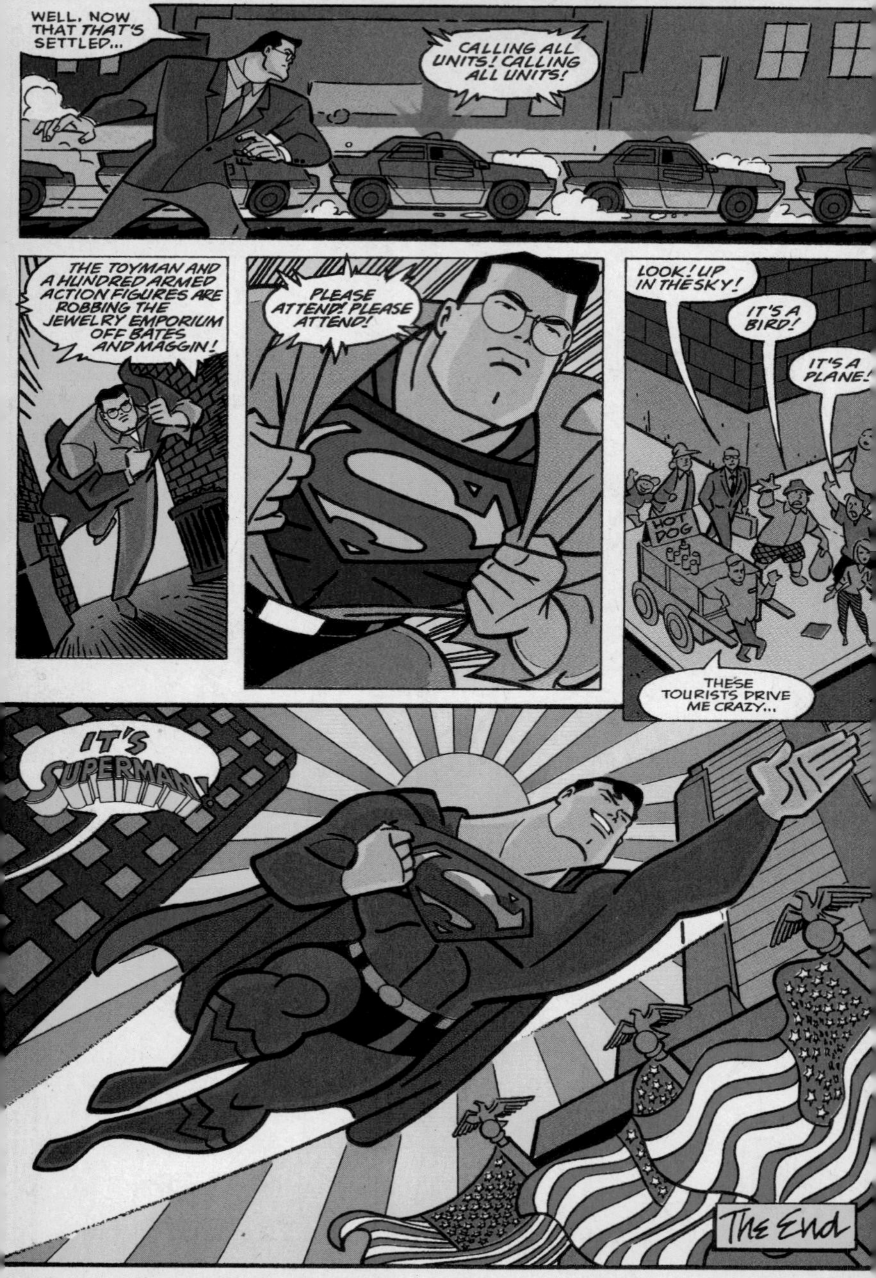
WELL, NOW THAT THAT'S SETTLED...
CALLING ALL UNITS! CALLING ALL UNITS!
THE TOYMAN AND A HUNDRED ARMED ACTION FIGURES ARE ROBBING THE JEWELRY EMPORIUM OFF BATES AND MAGGIN!
PLEASE ATTEND! PLEASE ATTEND!
LOOK! UP IN THE SKY!
IT'S A BIRD!
IT'S A PLANE!
HOT DOG
THESE TOURISTS DRIVE ME CRAZY...
IT'S SUPERMAN!
The End

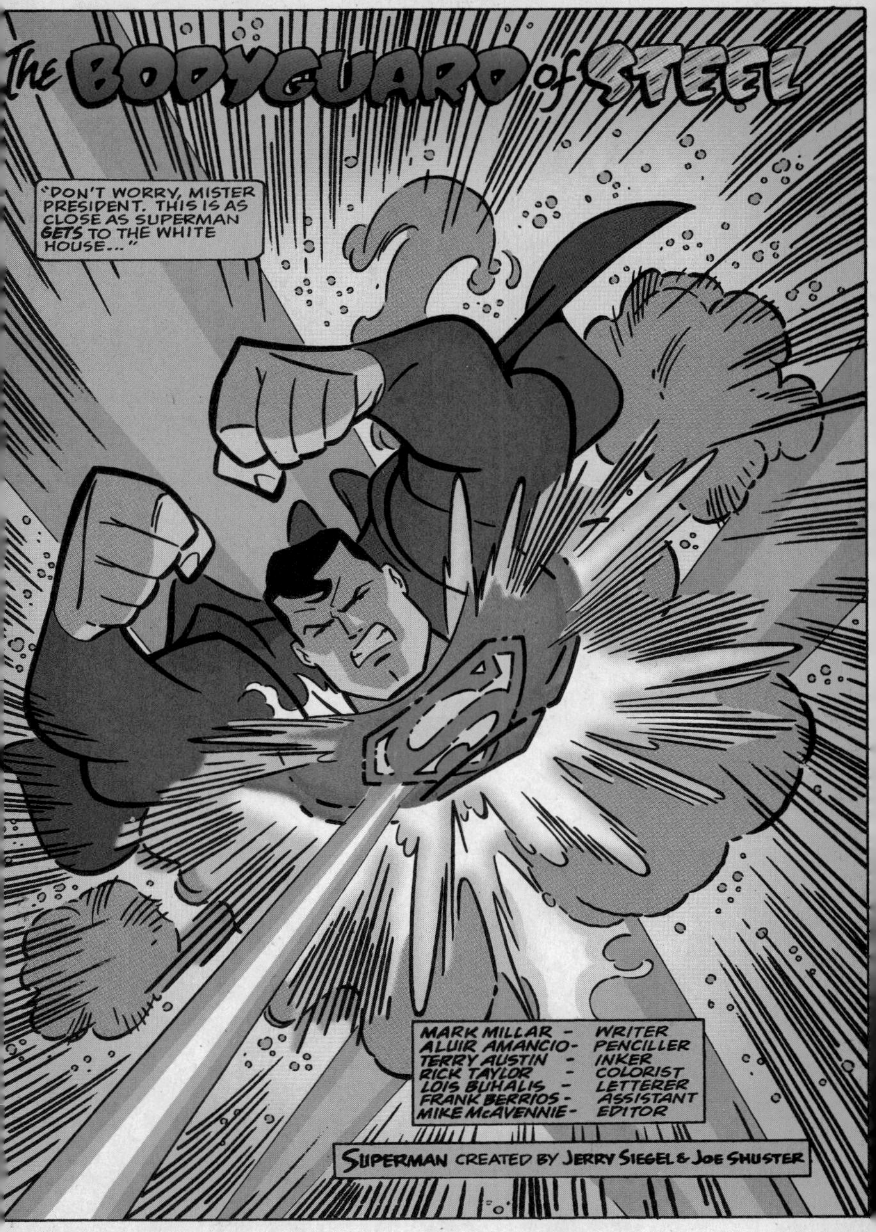
The BODYGUARD of STEEL
"DON'T WORRY, MISTER PRESIDENT. THIS IS AS CLOSE AS SUPERMAN GETS TO THE WHITE HOUSE..."
MARK MILLAR - WRITER
ALUIR AMANCIO - PENCILLER
TERRY AUSTIN - INKER
RICK TAYLOR - COLORIST
LOIS BUHALIS - LETTERER
FRANK BERRIOS - ASSISTANT
MIKE McAVENNIE - EDITOR
SUPERMAN CREATED BY JERRY SIEGEL & JOE SHUSTER

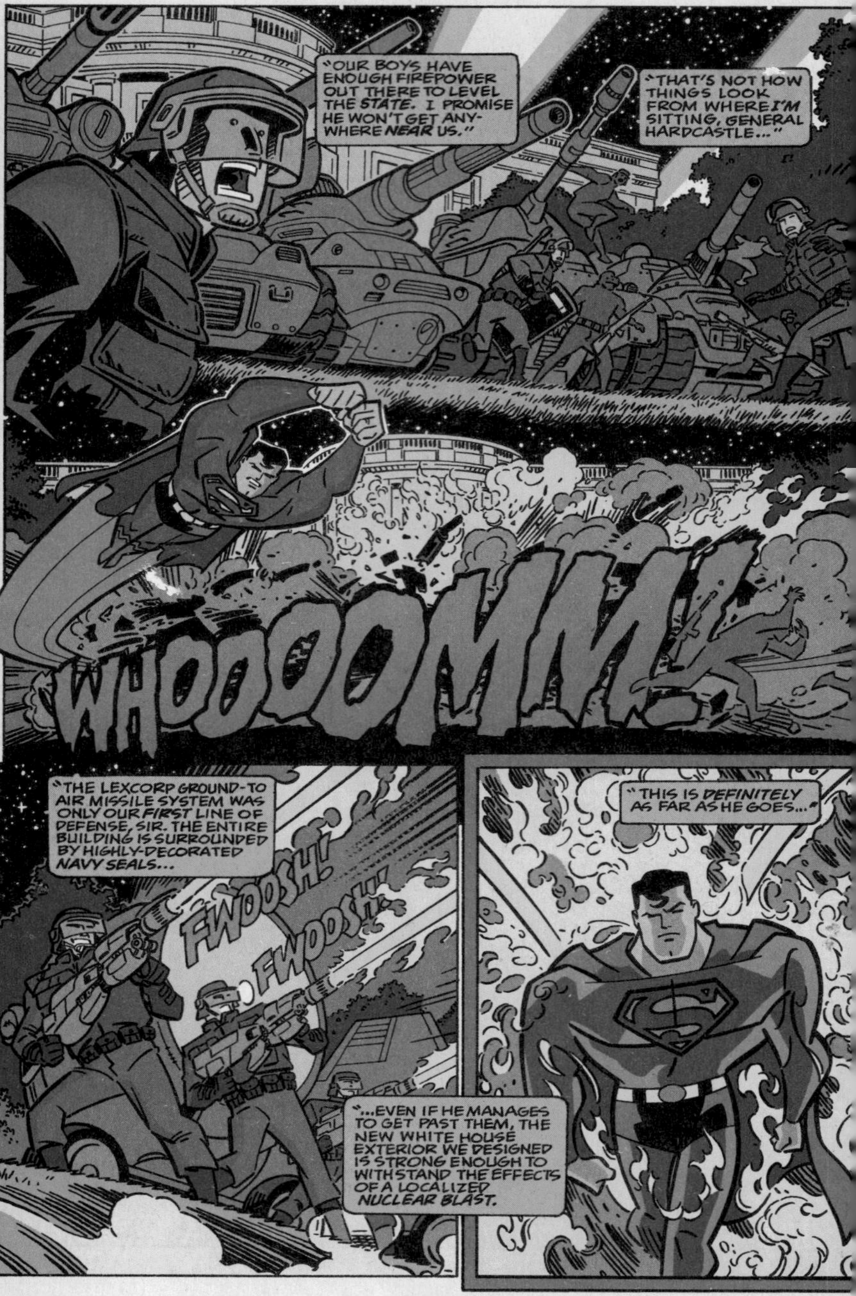
"OUR BOYS HAVE ENOUGH FIREPOWER OUT THERE TO LEVEL THE *STATE*. I PROMISE HE WON'T GET ANYWHERE *NEAR* US."
"THAT'S NOT HOW THINGS LOOK FROM WHERE *I'M* SITTING, GENERAL HARDCASTLE..."
WHOOOOMM!
"THE LEXCORP GROUND-TO AIR MISSILE SYSTEM WAS ONLY OUR *FIRST* LINE OF DEFENSE, SIR. THE ENTIRE BUILDING IS SURROUNDED BY HIGHLY-DECORATED *NAVY SEALS*...
FWOOSH!
FWOOSH!
"...EVEN IF HE MANAGES TO GET PAST THEM, THE NEW WHITE HOUSE EXTERIOR WE DESIGNED IS STRONG ENOUGH TO WITHSTAND THE EFFECTS OF A LOCALIZED *NUCLEAR BLAST*.
"THIS IS *DEFINITELY* AS FAR AS HE GOES..."

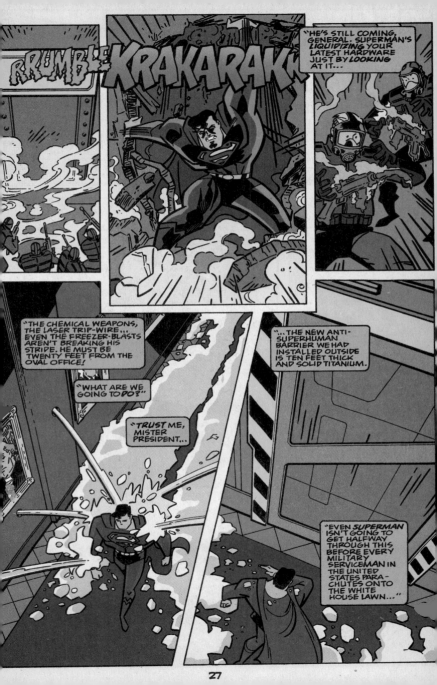

RRUMBL KRAKARAK

"HE'S STILL COMING, GENERAL. SUPERMAN'S *LIQUIDIZING* YOUR LATEST HARDWARE JUST BY *LOOKING* AT IT..."

"THE CHEMICAL WEAPONS, THE LASER TRIP-WIRE... EVEN THE FREEZER-BLASTS AREN'T BREAKING HIS STRIDE. HE MUST BE TWENTY FEET FROM THE OVAL OFFICE!

"WHAT ARE WE GOING TO *DO?*"

"*TRUST* ME, MISTER PRESIDENT...

"...THE NEW ANTI-SUPERHUMAN BARRIER WE HAD INSTALLED OUTSIDE IS TEN FEET THICK AND SOLID TITANIUM.

"EVEN *SUPERMAN* ISN'T GOING TO GET HALFWAY THROUGH THIS BEFORE EVERY MILITARY SERVICEMAN IN THE UNITED STATES PARA-CHUTES ONTO THE WHITE HOUSE LAWN..."

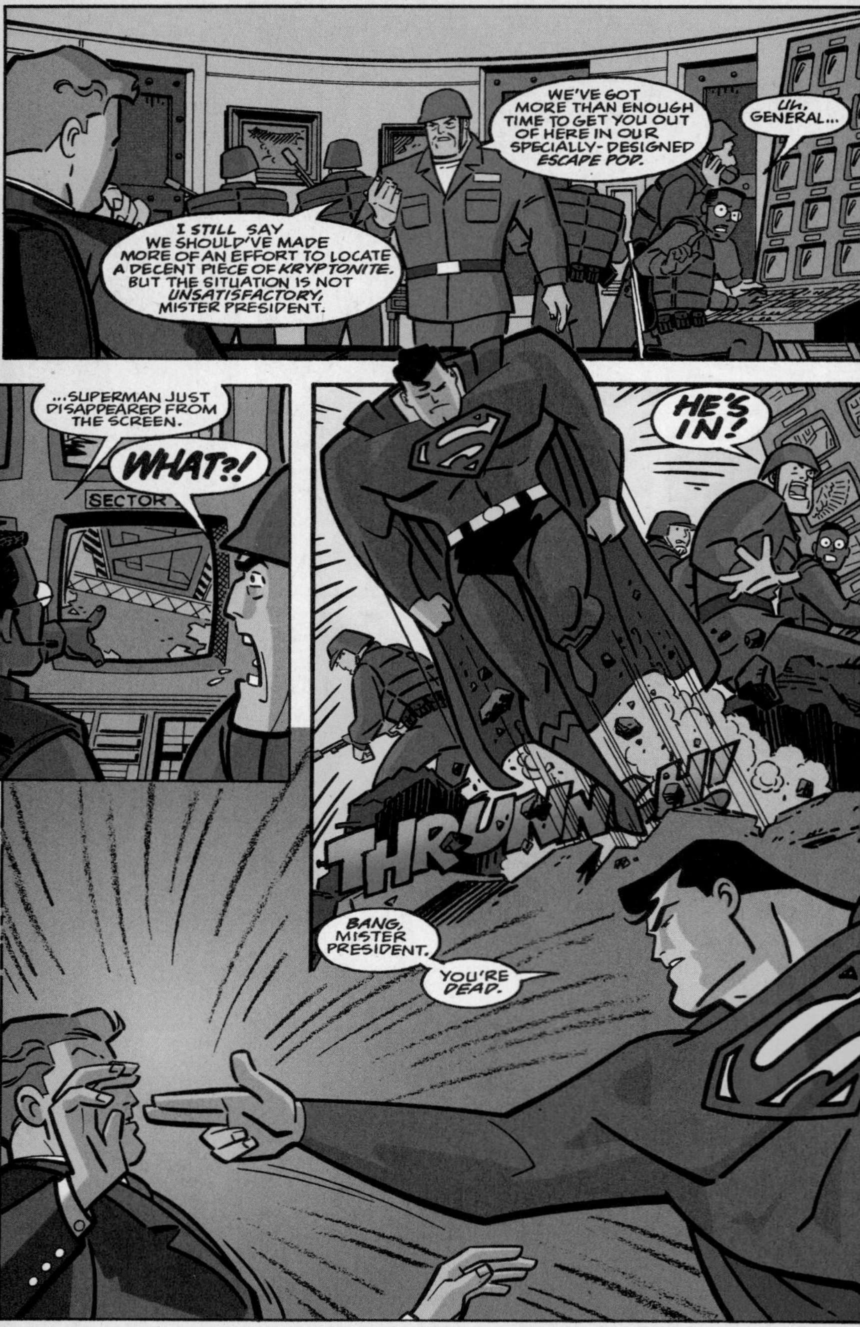
WE'VE GOT MORE THAN ENOUGH TIME TO GET YOU OUT OF HERE IN OUR SPECIALLY-DESIGNED ESCAPE POD.
I STILL SAY WE SHOULD'VE MADE MORE OF AN EFFORT TO LOCATE A DECENT PIECE OF KRYPTONITE. BUT THE SITUATION IS NOT UNSATISFACTORY, MISTER PRESIDENT.
Uh, GENERAL...
...SUPERMAN JUST DISAPPEARED FROM THE SCREEN.
WHAT?!
SECTOR
HE'S IN!
THRUMM
BANG, MISTER PRESIDENT.
YOU'RE DEAD.

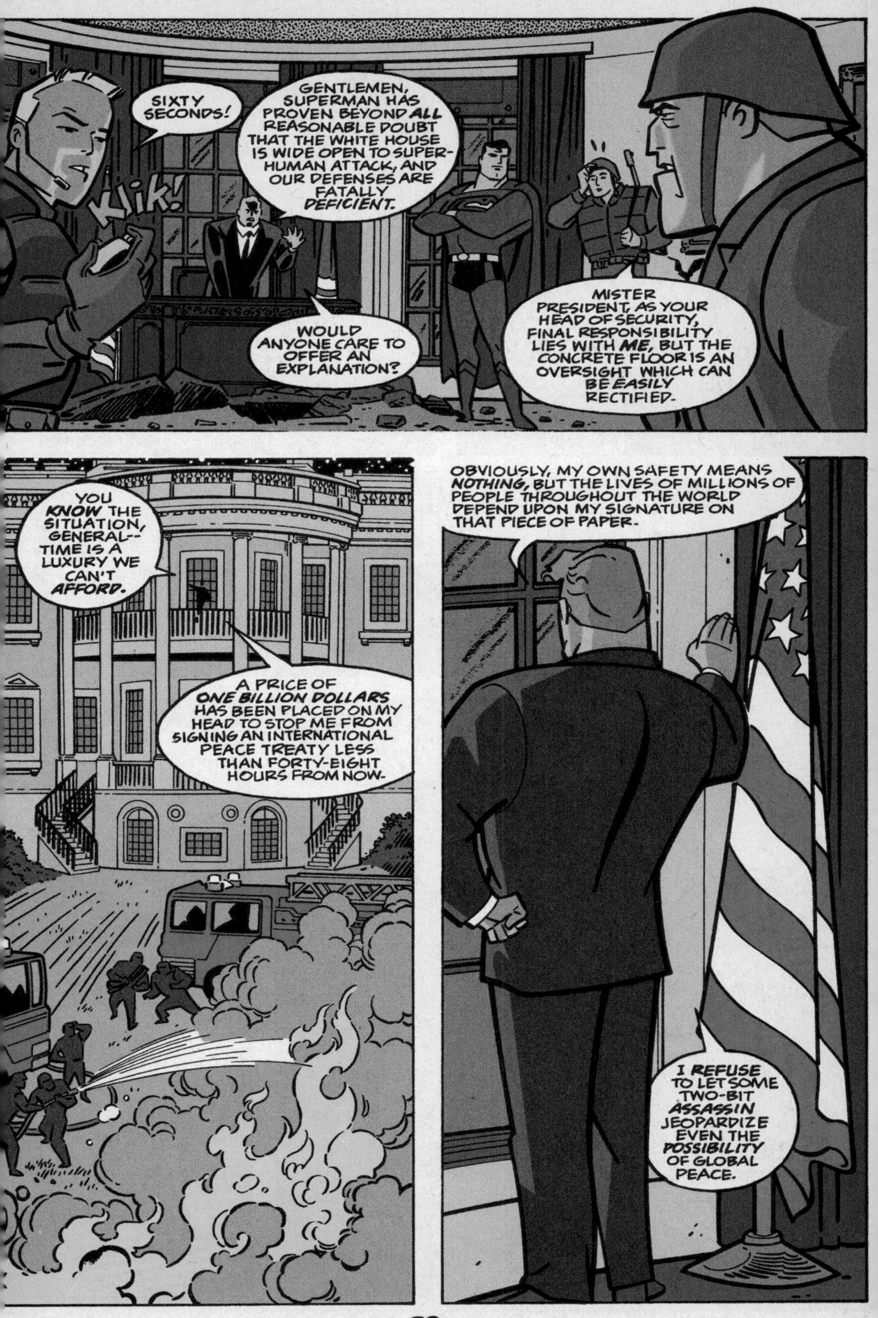
SIXTY SECONDS!
KLIK!
GENTLEMEN, SUPERMAN HAS PROVEN BEYOND ALL REASONABLE DOUBT THAT THE WHITE HOUSE IS WIDE OPEN TO SUPER-HUMAN ATTACK, AND OUR DEFENSES ARE FATALLY DEFICIENT.
WOULD ANYONE CARE TO OFFER AN EXPLANATION?
MISTER PRESIDENT, AS YOUR HEAD OF SECURITY, FINAL RESPONSIBILITY LIES WITH ME, BUT THE CONCRETE FLOOR IS AN OVERSIGHT WHICH CAN BE EASILY RECTIFIED.
YOU KNOW THE SITUATION, GENERAL-- TIME IS A LUXURY WE CAN'T AFFORD.
A PRICE OF ONE BILLION DOLLARS HAS BEEN PLACED ON MY HEAD TO STOP ME FROM SIGNING AN INTERNATIONAL PEACE TREATY LESS THAN FORTY-EIGHT HOURS FROM NOW.
OBVIOUSLY, MY OWN SAFETY MEANS NOTHING, BUT THE LIVES OF MILLIONS OF PEOPLE THROUGHOUT THE WORLD DEPEND UPON MY SIGNATURE ON THAT PIECE OF PAPER.
I REFUSE TO LET SOME TWO-BIT ASSASSIN JEOPARDIZE EVEN THE POSSIBILITY OF GLOBAL PEACE.

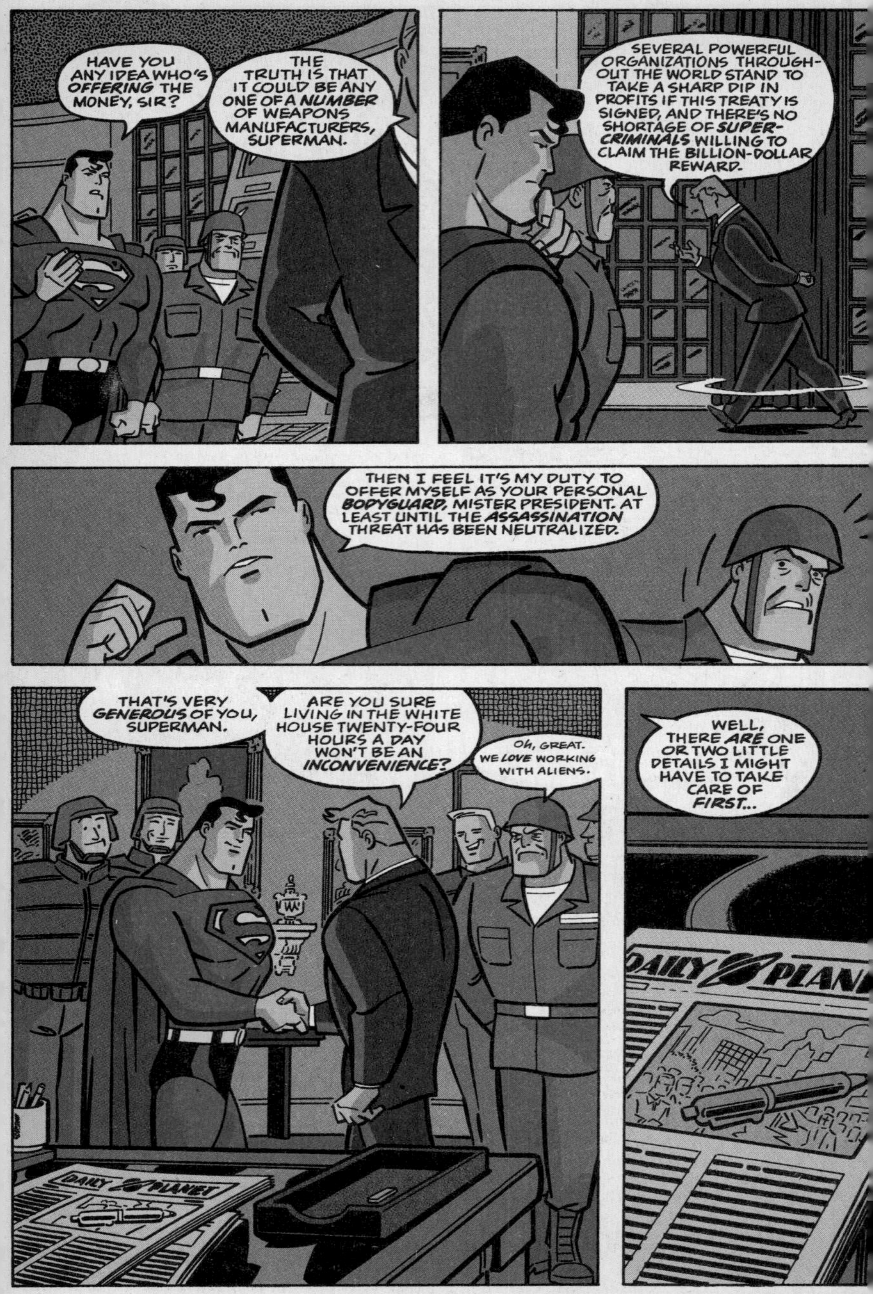
HAVE YOU ANY IDEA WHO'S OFFERING THE MONEY, SIR?
THE TRUTH IS THAT IT COULD BE ANY ONE OF A NUMBER OF WEAPONS MANUFACTURERS, SUPERMAN.
SEVERAL POWERFUL ORGANIZATIONS THROUGHOUT THE WORLD STAND TO TAKE A SHARP DIP IN PROFITS IF THIS TREATY IS SIGNED, AND THERE'S NO SHORTAGE OF SUPER-CRIMINALS WILLING TO CLAIM THE BILLION-DOLLAR REWARD.
THEN I FEEL IT'S MY DUTY TO OFFER MYSELF AS YOUR PERSONAL BODYGUARD, MISTER PRESIDENT. AT LEAST UNTIL THE ASSASSINATION THREAT HAS BEEN NEUTRALIZED.
THAT'S VERY GENEROUS OF YOU, SUPERMAN.
ARE YOU SURE LIVING IN THE WHITE HOUSE TWENTY-FOUR HOURS A DAY WON'T BE AN INCONVENIENCE?
Oh, GREAT. WE LOVE WORKING WITH ALIENS.
WELL, THERE ARE ONE OR TWO LITTLE DETAILS I MIGHT HAVE TO TAKE CARE OF FIRST...

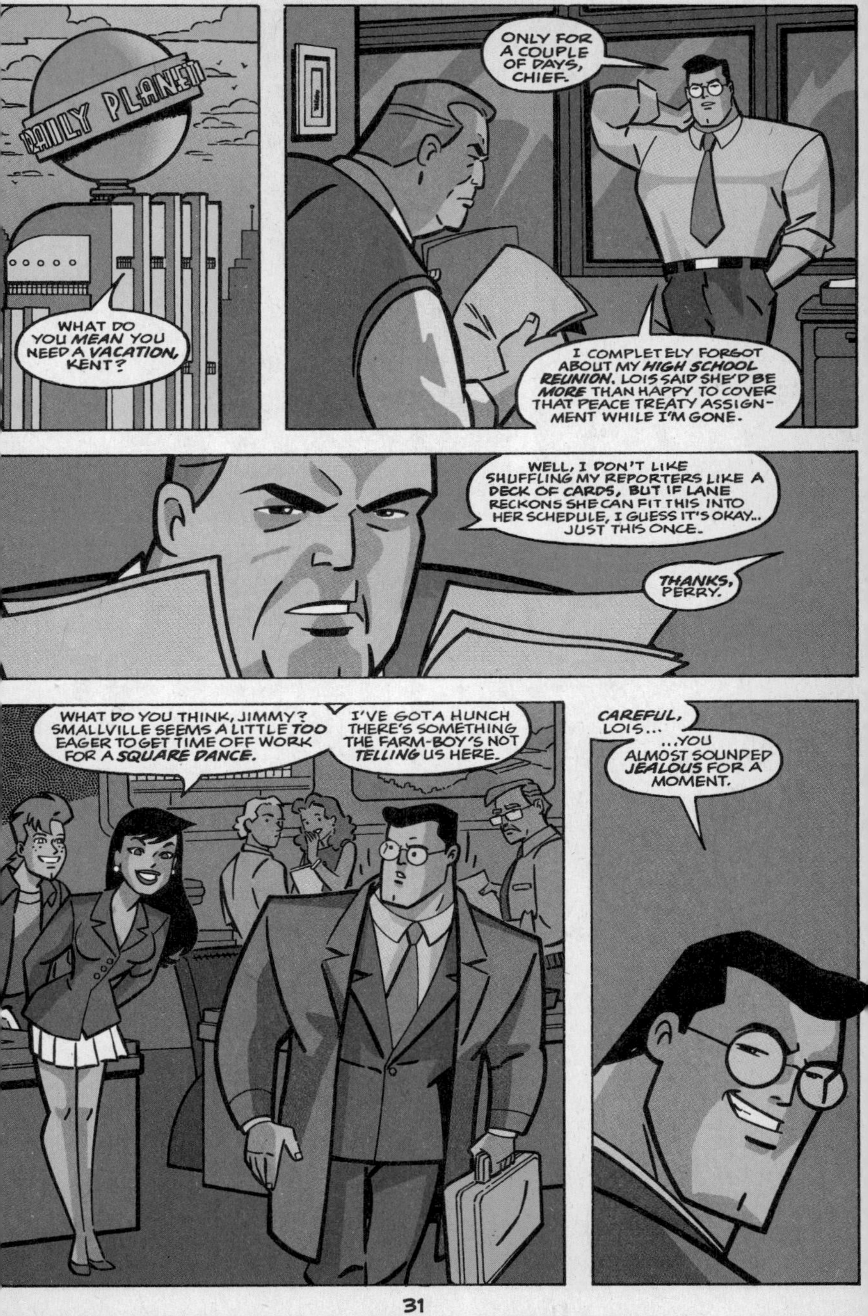
DAILY PLANET
WHAT DO YOU MEAN YOU NEED A VACATION, KENT?
ONLY FOR A COUPLE OF DAYS, CHIEF.
I COMPLETELY FORGOT ABOUT MY HIGH SCHOOL REUNION. LOIS SAID SHE'D BE MORE THAN HAPPY TO COVER THAT PEACE TREATY ASSIGNMENT WHILE I'M GONE.
WELL, I DON'T LIKE SHUFFLING MY REPORTERS LIKE A DECK OF CARDS, BUT IF LANE RECKONS SHE CAN FIT THIS INTO HER SCHEDULE, I GUESS IT'S OKAY... JUST THIS ONCE.
THANKS, PERRY.
WHAT DO YOU THINK, JIMMY? SMALLVILLE SEEMS A LITTLE TOO EAGER TO GET TIME OFF WORK FOR A SQUARE DANCE.
I'VE GOT A HUNCH THERE'S SOMETHING THE FARM-BOY'S NOT TELLING US HERE.
CAREFUL, LOIS...
...YOU ALMOST SOUNDED JEALOUS FOR A MOMENT.

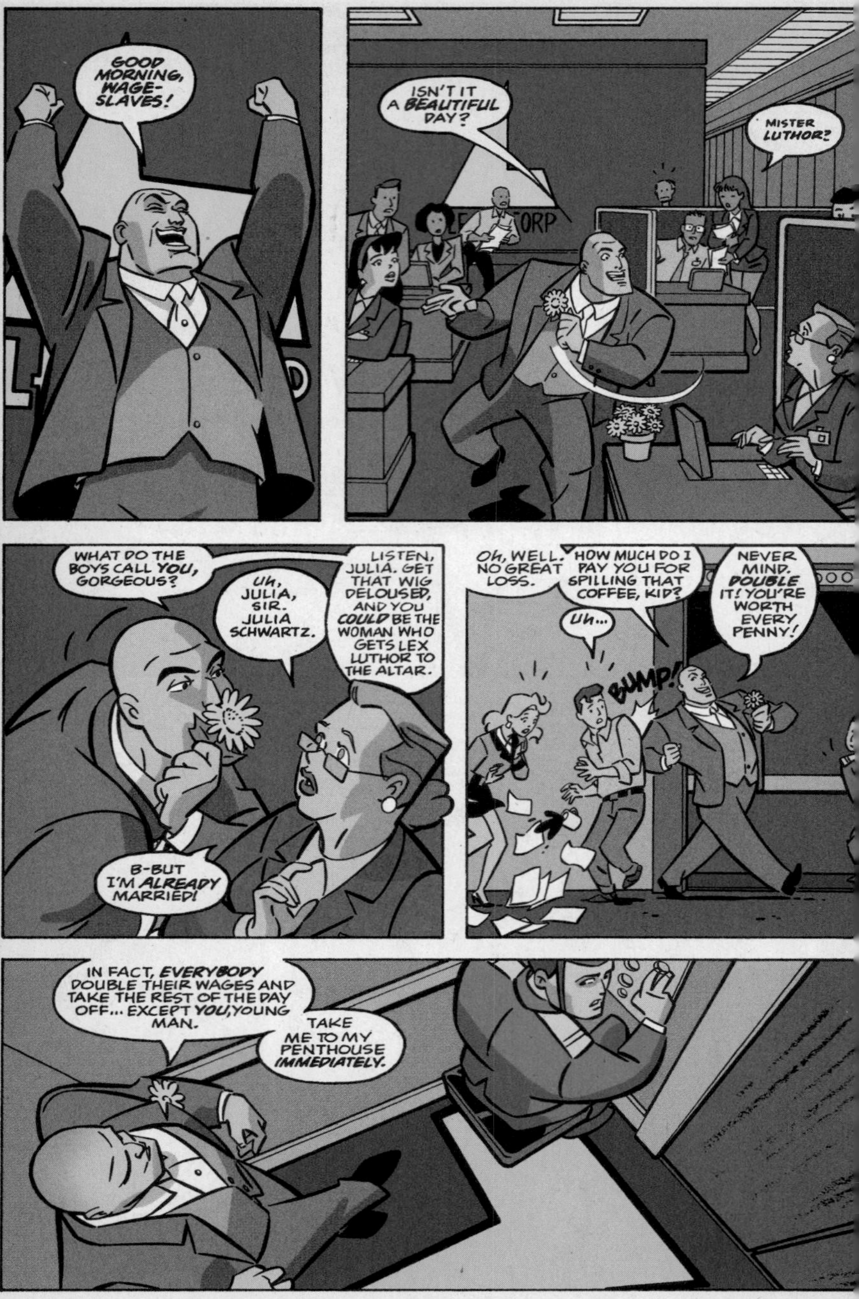
GOOD MORNING, WAGE-SLAVES!
ISN'T IT A BEAUTIFUL DAY?
MISTER LUTHOR?
WHAT DO THE BOYS CALL YOU, GORGEOUS?
Uh, JULIA, SIR. JULIA SCHWARTZ.
LISTEN, JULIA. GET THAT WIG DELOUSED, AND YOU COULD BE THE WOMAN WHO GETS LEX LUTHOR TO THE ALTAR.
B-BUT I'M ALREADY MARRIED!
Oh, WELL. NO GREAT LOSS.
BUMP!
HOW MUCH DO I PAY YOU FOR SPILLING THAT COFFEE, KID?
Uh...
NEVER MIND. DOUBLE IT! YOU'RE WORTH EVERY PENNY!
IN FACT, EVERYBODY DOUBLE THEIR WAGES AND TAKE THE REST OF THE DAY OFF... EXCEPT YOU, YOUNG MAN.
TAKE ME TO MY PENTHOUSE IMMEDIATELY.

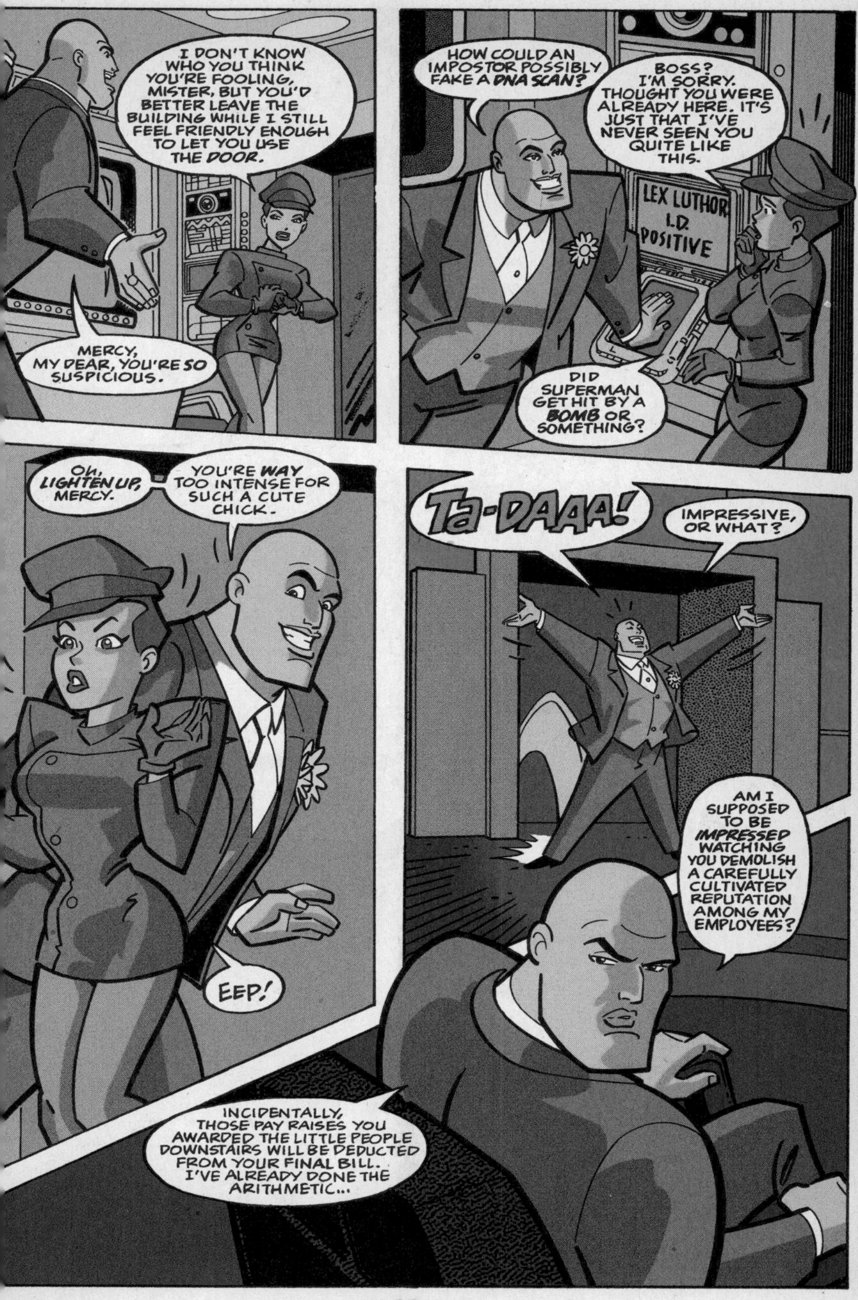
I DON'T KNOW WHO YOU THINK YOU'RE FOOLING, MISTER, BUT YOU'D BETTER LEAVE THE BUILDING WHILE I STILL FEEL FRIENDLY ENOUGH TO LET YOU USE THE DOOR.
MERCY, MY DEAR, YOU'RE SO SUSPICIOUS.
HOW COULD AN IMPOSTOR POSSIBLY FAKE A DNA SCAN?
BOSS? I'M SORRY. THOUGHT YOU WERE ALREADY HERE. IT'S JUST THAT I'VE NEVER SEEN YOU QUITE LIKE THIS.
LEX LUTHOR I.D. POSITIVE
DID SUPERMAN GET HIT BY A BOMB OR SOMETHING?
Oh, LIGHTEN UP, MERCY.
YOU'RE WAY TOO INTENSE FOR SUCH A CUTE CHICK.
EEP!
Ta-DAAA!
IMPRESSIVE, OR WHAT?
AM I SUPPOSED TO BE IMPRESSED WATCHING YOU DEMOLISH A CAREFULLY CULTIVATED REPUTATION AMONG MY EMPLOYEES?
INCIDENTALLY, THOSE PAY RAISES YOU AWARDED THE LITTLE PEOPLE DOWNSTAIRS WILL BE DEDUCTED FROM YOUR FINAL BILL. I'VE ALREADY DONE THE ARITHMETIC...

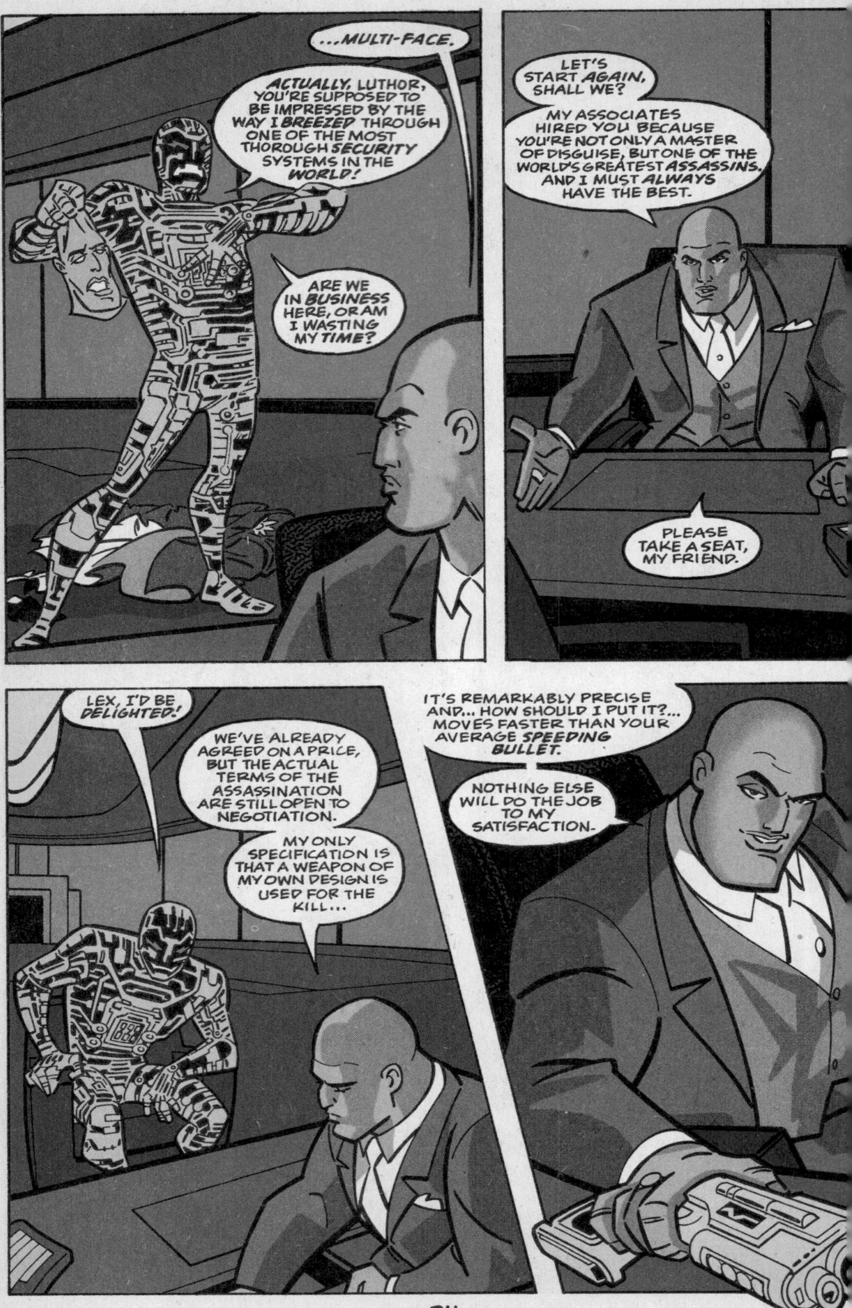
...MULTI-FACE.
ACTUALLY, LUTHOR, YOU'RE SUPPOSED TO BE IMPRESSED BY THE WAY I BREEZED THROUGH ONE OF THE MOST THOROUGH SECURITY SYSTEMS IN THE WORLD!
ARE WE IN BUSINESS HERE, OR AM I WASTING MY TIME?
LET'S START AGAIN, SHALL WE?
MY ASSOCIATES HIRED YOU BECAUSE YOU'RE NOT ONLY A MASTER OF DISGUISE, BUT ONE OF THE WORLD'S GREATEST ASSASSINS. AND I MUST ALWAYS HAVE THE BEST.
PLEASE TAKE A SEAT, MY FRIEND.
LEX, I'D BE DELIGHTED!
WE'VE ALREADY AGREED ON A PRICE, BUT THE ACTUAL TERMS OF THE ASSASSINATION ARE STILL OPEN TO NEGOTIATION.
MY ONLY SPECIFICATION IS THAT A WEAPON OF MY OWN DESIGN IS USED FOR THE KILL...
IT'S REMARKABLY PRECISE AND... HOW SHOULD I PUT IT?... MOVES FASTER THAN YOUR AVERAGE SPEEDING BULLET.
NOTHING ELSE WILL DO THE JOB TO MY SATISFACTION.

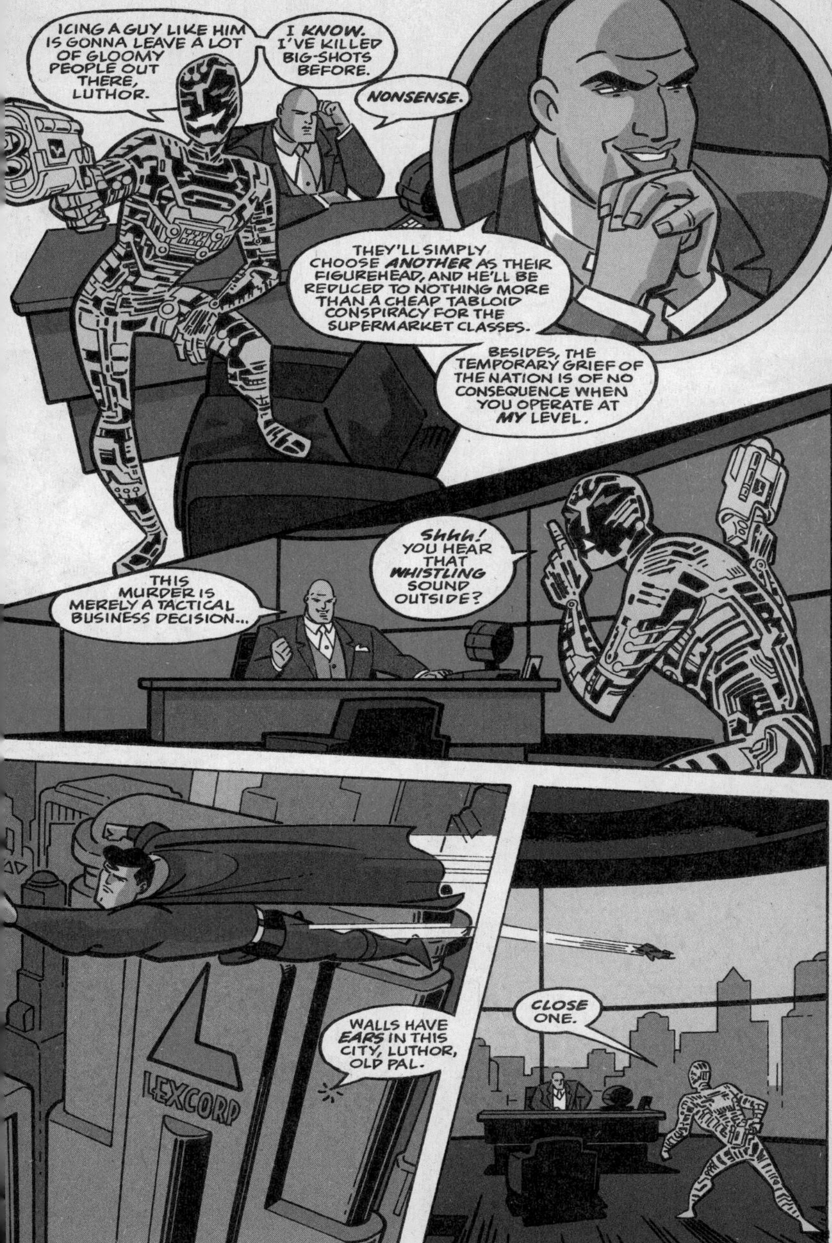
ICING A GUY LIKE HIM IS GONNA LEAVE A LOT OF GLOOMY PEOPLE OUT THERE, LUTHOR.
I KNOW. I'VE KILLED BIG-SHOTS BEFORE.
NONSENSE.
THEY'LL SIMPLY CHOOSE ANOTHER AS THEIR FIGUREHEAD, AND HE'LL BE REDUCED TO NOTHING MORE THAN A CHEAP TABLOID CONSPIRACY FOR THE SUPERMARKET CLASSES.
BESIDES, THE TEMPORARY GRIEF OF THE NATION IS OF NO CONSEQUENCE WHEN YOU OPERATE AT MY LEVEL.
THIS MURDER IS MERELY A TACTICAL BUSINESS DECISION...
Shhh! YOU HEAR THAT WHISTLING SOUND OUTSIDE?
LEXCORP
WALLS HAVE EARS IN THIS CITY, LUTHOR, OLD PAL.
CLOSE ONE.

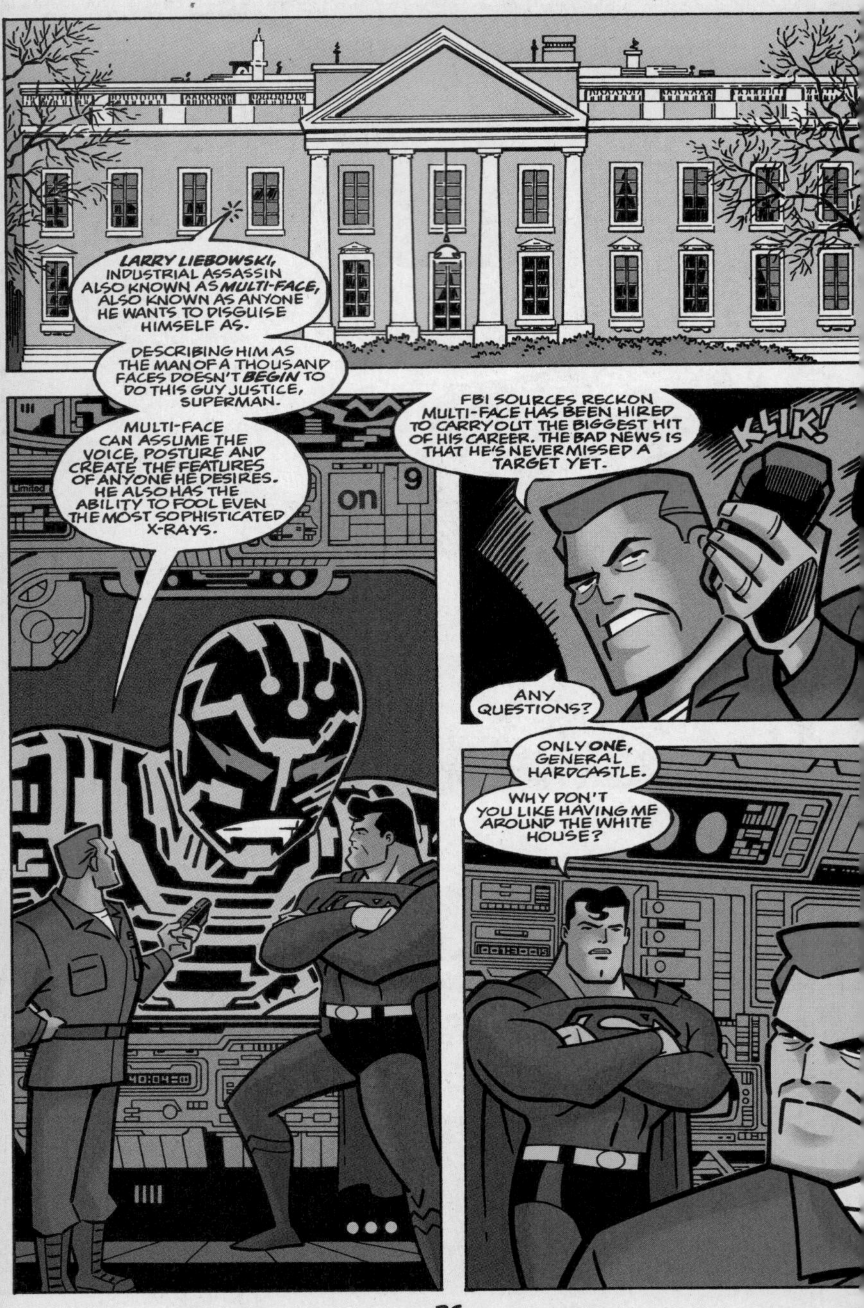
LARRY LIEBOWSKI, INDUSTRIAL ASSASSIN ALSO KNOWN AS MULTI-FACE, ALSO KNOWN AS ANYONE HE WANTS TO DISGUISE HIMSELF AS.
DESCRIBING HIM AS THE MAN OF A THOUSAND FACES DOESN'T BEGIN TO DO THIS GUY JUSTICE, SUPERMAN.
MULTI-FACE CAN ASSUME THE VOICE, POSTURE AND CREATE THE FEATURES OF ANYONE HE DESIRES. HE ALSO HAS THE ABILITY TO FOOL EVEN THE MOST SOPHISTICATED X-RAYS.
FBI SOURCES RECKON MULTI-FACE HAS BEEN HIRED TO CARRY OUT THE BIGGEST HIT OF HIS CAREER. THE BAD NEWS IS THAT HE'S NEVER MISSED A TARGET YET.
KLIK!
ANY QUESTIONS?
ONLY ONE, GENERAL HARDCASTLE.
WHY DON'T YOU LIKE HAVING ME AROUND THE WHITE HOUSE?

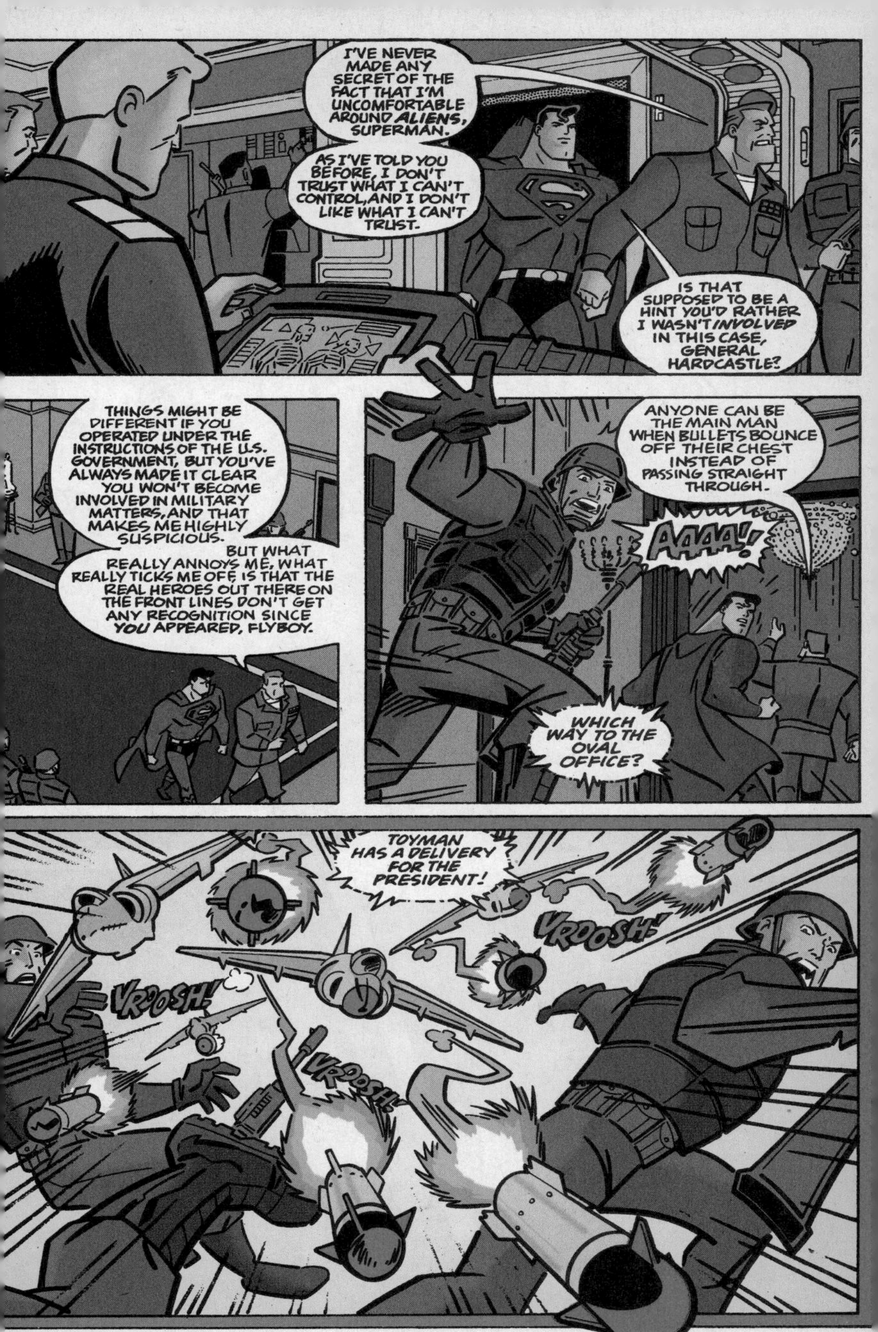
I'VE NEVER MADE ANY SECRET OF THE FACT THAT I'M UNCOMFORTABLE AROUND ALIENS, SUPERMAN.
AS I'VE TOLD YOU BEFORE, I DON'T TRUST WHAT I CAN'T CONTROL, AND I DON'T LIKE WHAT I CAN'T TRUST.
IS THAT SUPPOSED TO BE A HINT YOU'D RATHER I WASN'T INVOLVED IN THIS CASE, GENERAL HARDCASTLE?
THINGS MIGHT BE DIFFERENT IF YOU OPERATED UNDER THE INSTRUCTIONS OF THE U.S. GOVERNMENT, BUT YOU'VE ALWAYS MADE IT CLEAR YOU WON'T BECOME INVOLVED IN MILITARY MATTERS, AND THAT MAKES ME HIGHLY SUSPICIOUS.
BUT WHAT REALLY ANNOYS ME, WHAT REALLY TICKS ME OFF, IS THAT THE REAL HEROES OUT THERE ON THE FRONT LINES DON'T GET ANY RECOGNITION SINCE YOU APPEARED, FLYBOY.
ANYONE CAN BE THE MAIN MAN WHEN BULLETS BOUNCE OFF THEIR CHEST INSTEAD OF PASSING STRAIGHT THROUGH.
AAAA!!
WHICH WAY TO THE OVAL OFFICE?
TOYMAN HAS A DELIVERY FOR THE PRESIDENT!
VROOSH!
VROOSH!
VROOSH!

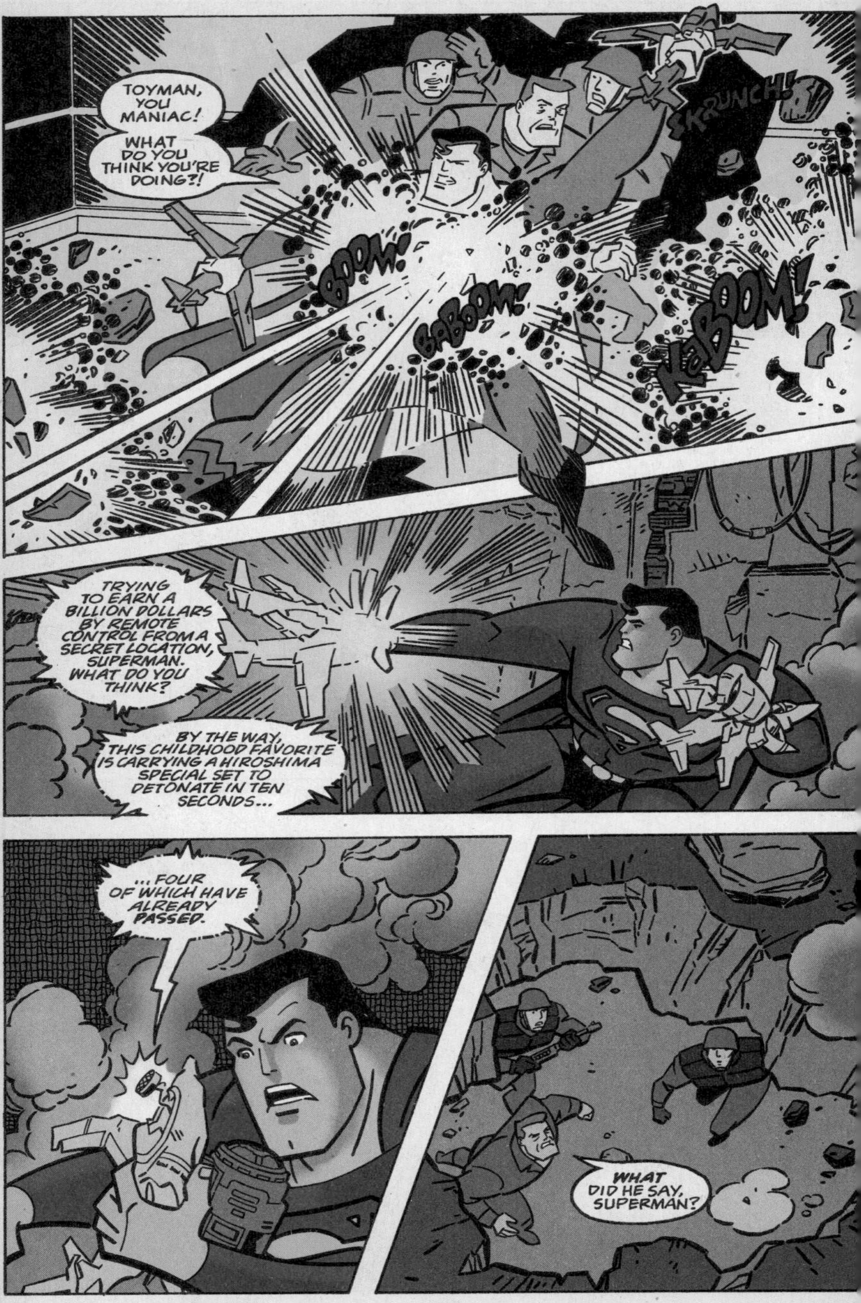
TOYMAN, YOU MANIAC!
WHAT DO YOU THINK YOU'RE DOING?!
SKRUNCH!
BOOM!
BABOOM!
KABOOM!
TRYING TO EARN A BILLION DOLLARS BY REMOTE CONTROL FROM A SECRET LOCATION, SUPERMAN. WHAT DO YOU THINK?
BY THE WAY, THIS CHILDHOOD FAVORITE IS CARRYING A HIROSHIMA SPECIAL SET TO DETONATE IN TEN SECONDS...
...FOUR OF WHICH HAVE ALREADY PASSED.
WHAT DID HE SAY, SUPERMAN?

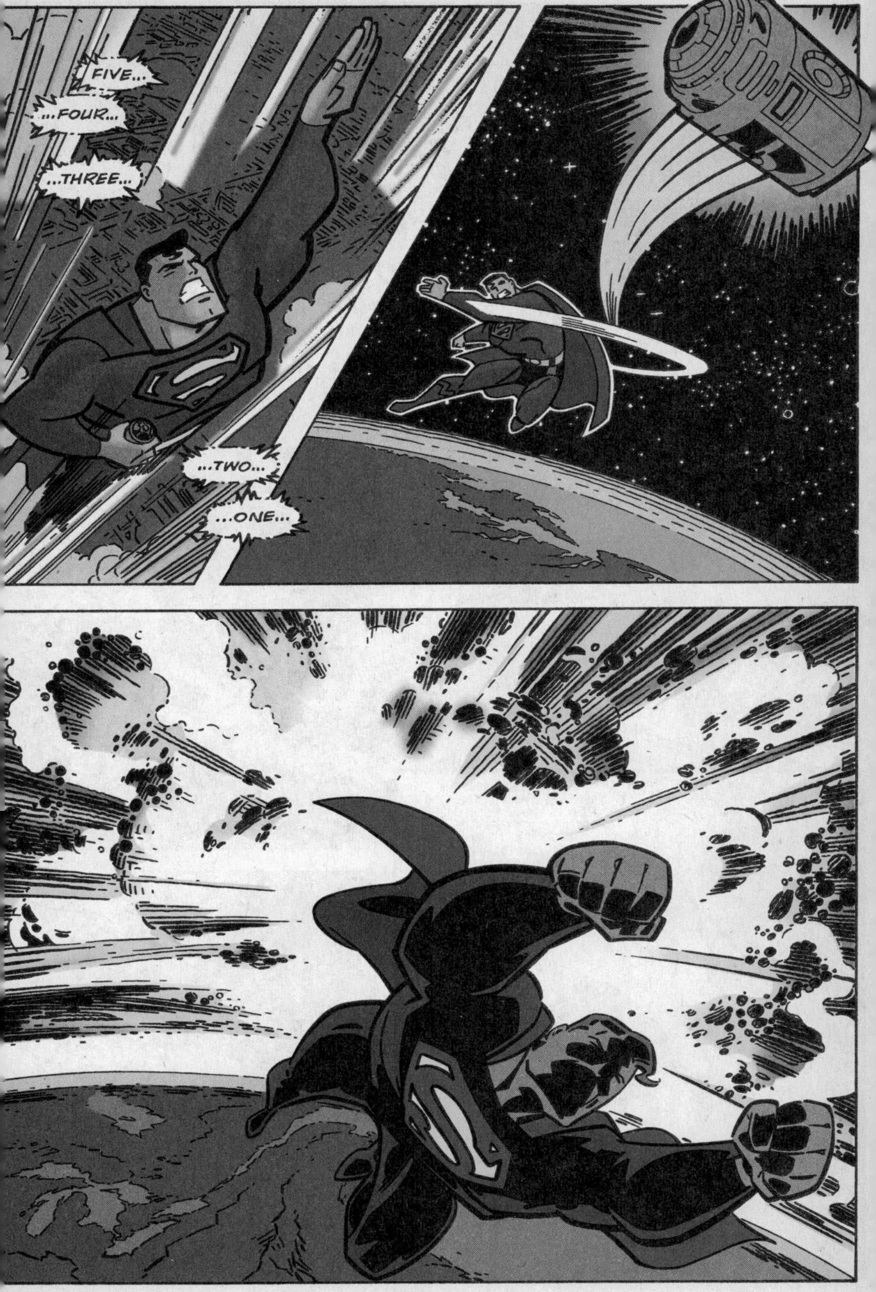
FIVE...
...FOUR...
...THREE...
...TWO...
...ONE...

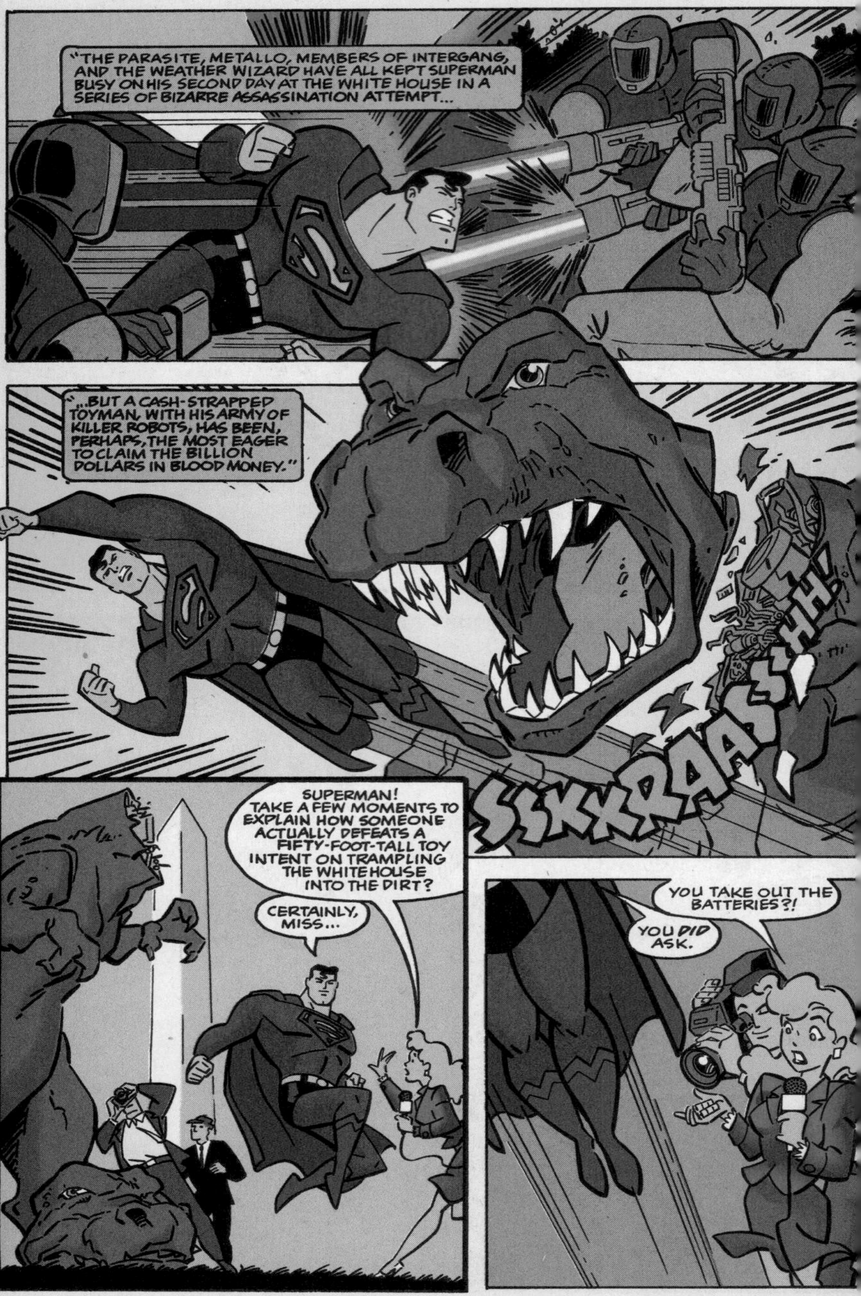
"THE PARASITE, METALLO, MEMBERS OF INTERGANG, AND THE WEATHER WIZARD HAVE ALL KEPT SUPERMAN BUSY ON HIS SECOND DAY AT THE WHITE HOUSE IN A SERIES OF BIZARRE ASSASSINATION ATTEMPT...
"...BUT A CASH-STRAPPED TOYMAN, WITH HIS ARMY OF KILLER ROBOTS, HAS BEEN, PERHAPS, THE MOST EAGER TO CLAIM THE BILLION DOLLARS IN BLOOD MONEY."
SSKKRAASSHH!
SUPERMAN! TAKE A FEW MOMENTS TO EXPLAIN HOW SOMEONE ACTUALLY DEFEATS A FIFTY-FOOT-TALL TOY INTENT ON TRAMPLING THE WHITE HOUSE INTO THE DIRT?
CERTAINLY, MISS...
YOU TAKE OUT THE BATTERIES?!
YOU DID ASK.

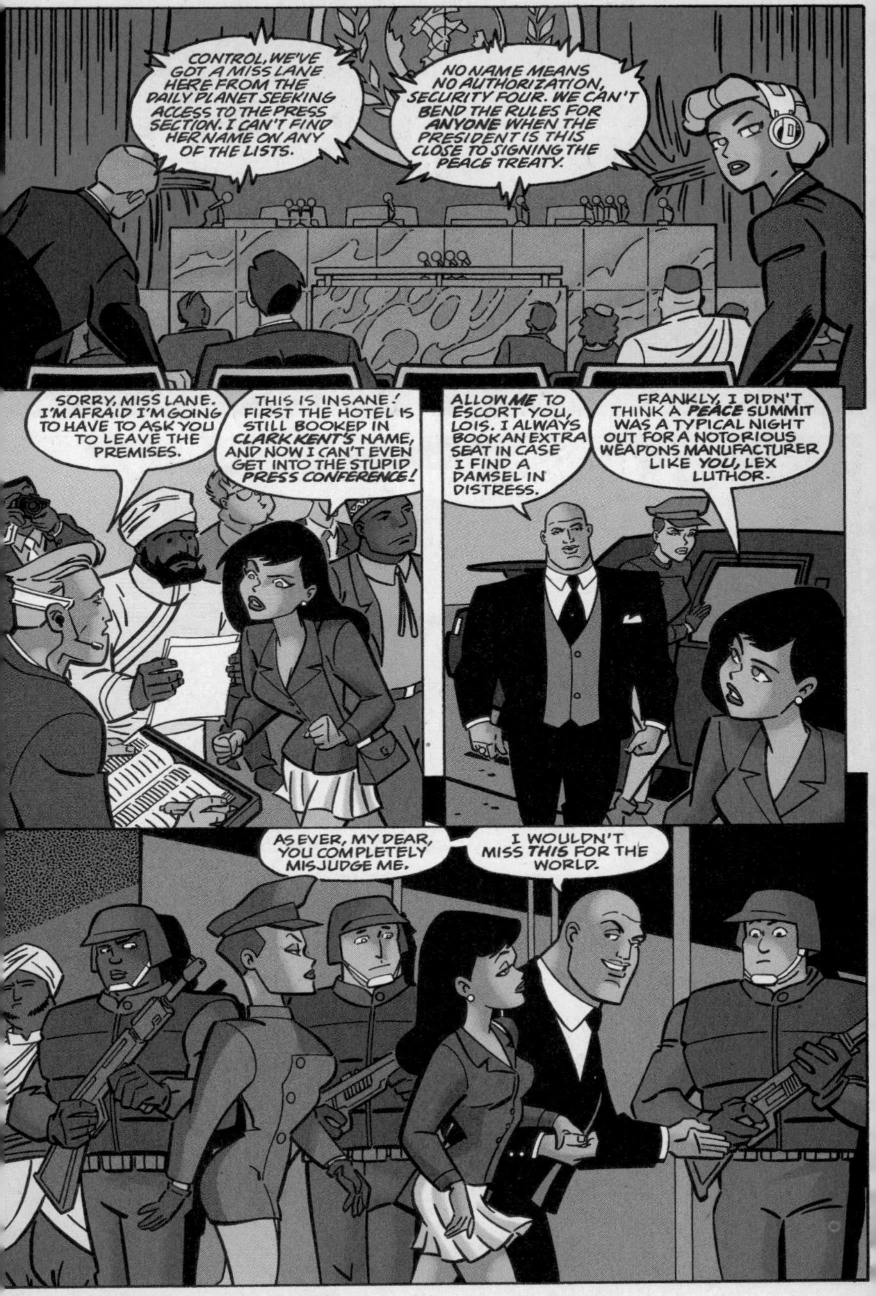
CONTROL, WE'VE GOT A MISS LANE HERE FROM THE DAILY PLANET SEEKING ACCESS TO THE PRESS SECTION. I CAN'T FIND HER NAME ON ANY OF THE LISTS.
NO NAME MEANS NO AUTHORIZATION, SECURITY FOUR. WE CAN'T BEND THE RULES FOR ANYONE WHEN THE PRESIDENT IS THIS CLOSE TO SIGNING THE PEACE TREATY.
SORRY, MISS LANE. I'M AFRAID I'M GOING TO HAVE TO ASK YOU TO LEAVE THE PREMISES.
THIS IS INSANE! FIRST THE HOTEL IS STILL BOOKED IN CLARK KENT'S NAME, AND NOW I CAN'T EVEN GET INTO THE STUPID PRESS CONFERENCE!
ALLOW ME TO ESCORT YOU, LOIS. I ALWAYS BOOK AN EXTRA SEAT IN CASE I FIND A DAMSEL IN DISTRESS.
FRANKLY, I DIDN'T THINK A PEACE SUMMIT WAS A TYPICAL NIGHT OUT FOR A NOTORIOUS WEAPONS MANUFACTURER LIKE YOU, LEX LUTHOR.
AS EVER, MY DEAR, YOU COMPLETELY MISJUDGE ME.
I WOULDN'T MISS THIS FOR THE WORLD.

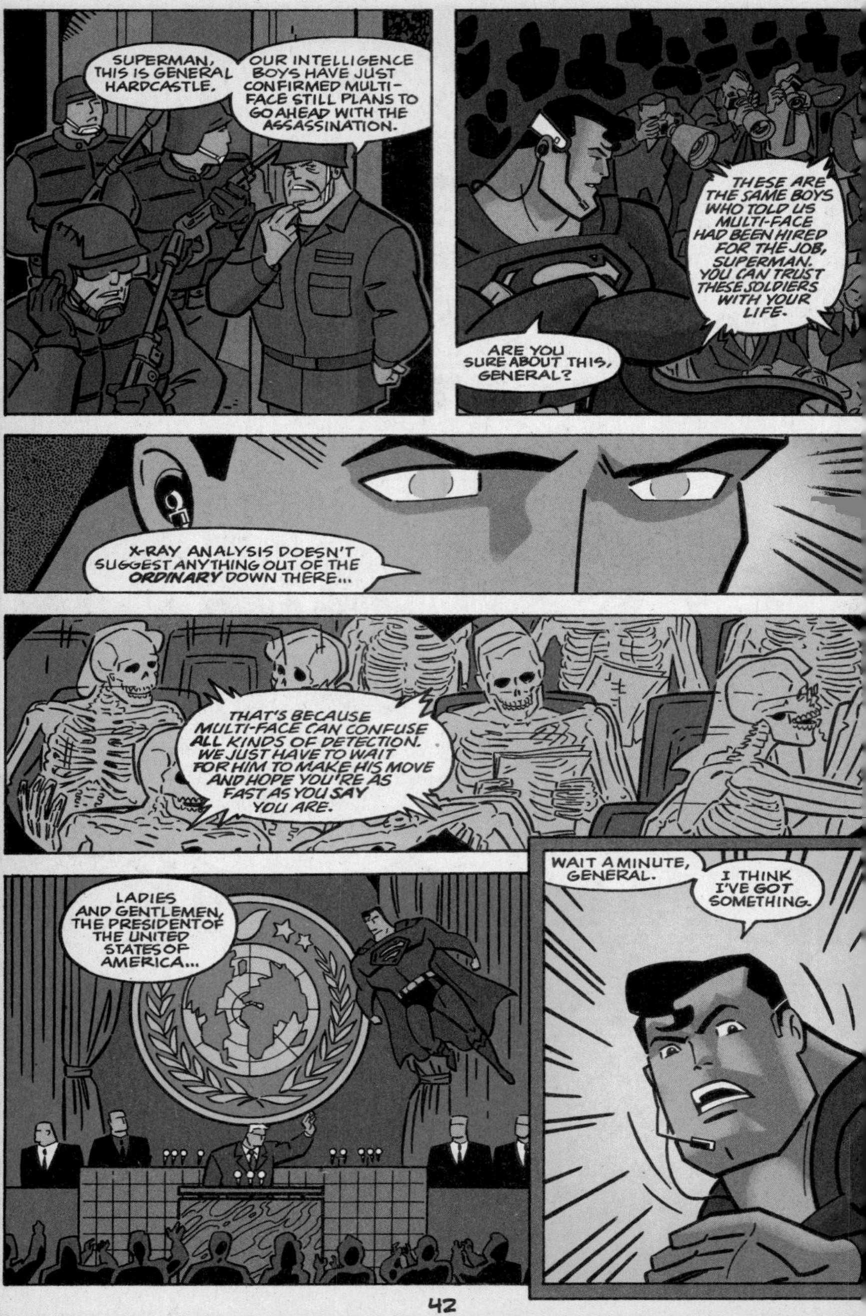

SUPERMAN, THIS IS GENERAL HARDCASTLE.
OUR INTELLIGENCE BOYS HAVE JUST CONFIRMED MULTI-FACE STILL PLANS TO GO AHEAD WITH THE ASSASSINATION.
ARE YOU SURE ABOUT THIS, GENERAL?
THESE ARE THE SAME BOYS WHO TOLD US MULTI-FACE HAD BEEN HIRED FOR THE JOB, SUPERMAN. YOU CAN TRUST THESE SOLDIERS WITH YOUR LIFE.
X-RAY ANALYSIS DOESN'T SUGGEST ANYTHING OUT OF THE ORDINARY DOWN THERE...
THAT'S BECAUSE MULTI-FACE CAN CONFUSE ALL KINDS OF DETECTION. WE JUST HAVE TO WAIT FOR HIM TO MAKE HIS MOVE AND HOPE YOU'RE AS FAST AS YOU SAY YOU ARE.
LADIES AND GENTLEMEN, THE PRESIDENT OF THE UNITED STATES OF AMERICA...
WAIT A MINUTE, GENERAL.
I THINK I'VE GOT SOMETHING.

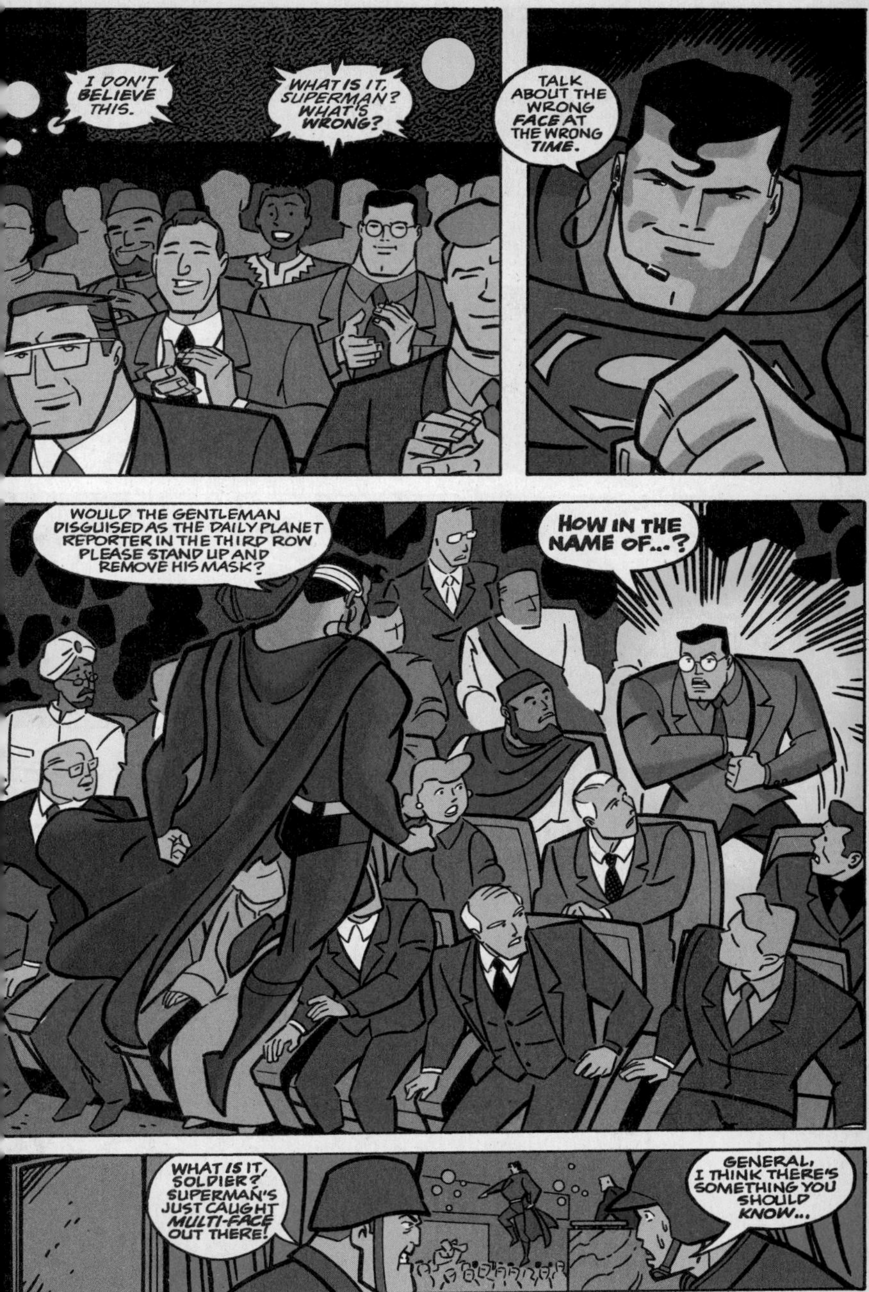
I DON'T BELIEVE THIS.
WHAT IS IT, SUPERMAN? WHAT'S WRONG?
TALK ABOUT THE WRONG FACE AT THE WRONG TIME.
WOULD THE GENTLEMAN DISGUISED AS THE DAILY PLANET REPORTER IN THE THIRD ROW PLEASE STAND UP AND REMOVE HIS MASK?
HOW IN THE NAME OF...?
WHAT IS IT, SOLDIER?
SUPERMAN'S JUST CAUGHT MULTI-FACE OUT THERE!
GENERAL, I THINK THERE'S SOMETHING YOU SHOULD KNOW...

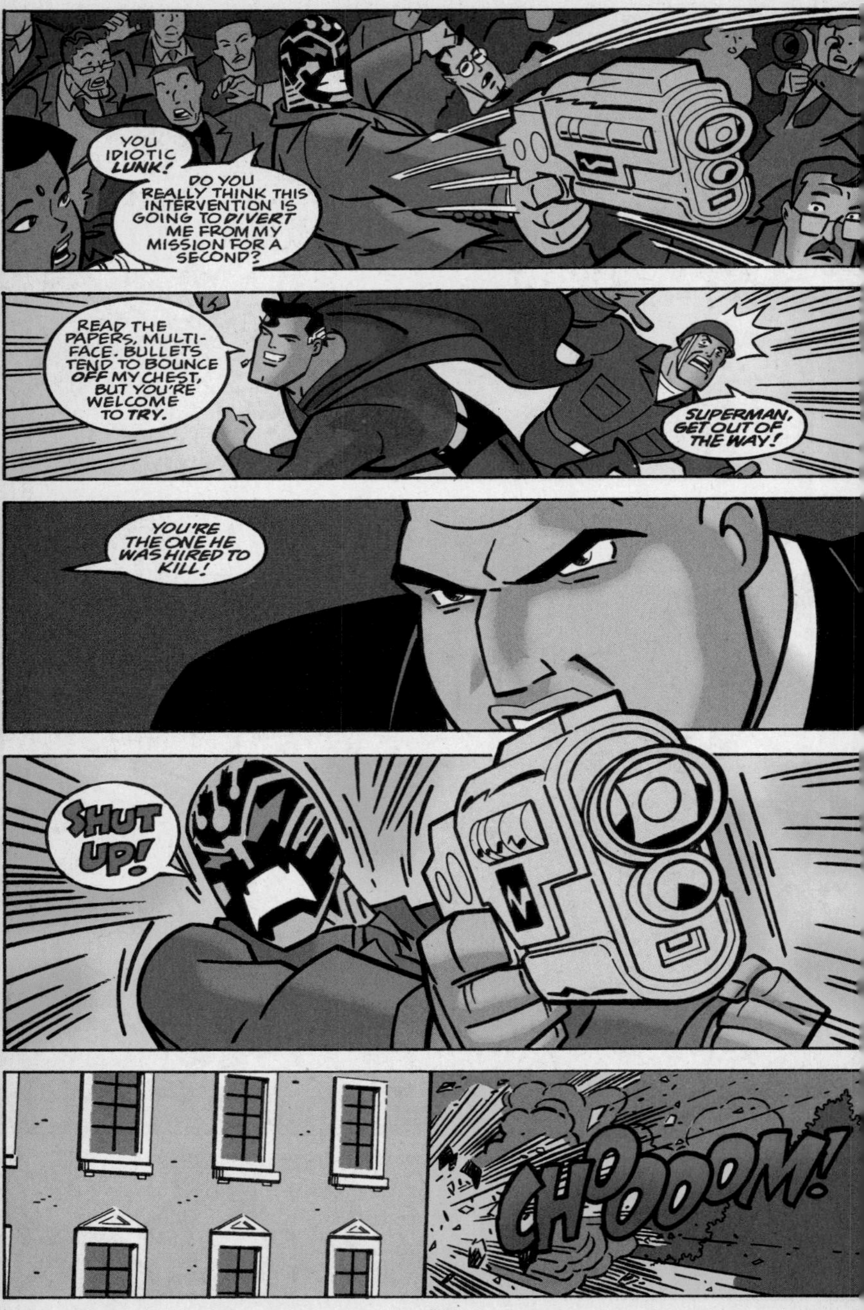
YOU IDIOTIC LUNK!
DO YOU REALLY THINK THIS INTERVENTION IS GOING TO DIVERT ME FROM MY MISSION FOR A SECOND?
READ THE PAPERS, MULTI-FACE. BULLETS TEND TO BOUNCE OFF MY CHEST, BUT YOU'RE WELCOME TO TRY.
SUPERMAN, GET OUT OF THE WAY!
YOU'RE THE ONE HE WAS HIRED TO KILL!
SHUT UP!
CHOOOOOM!

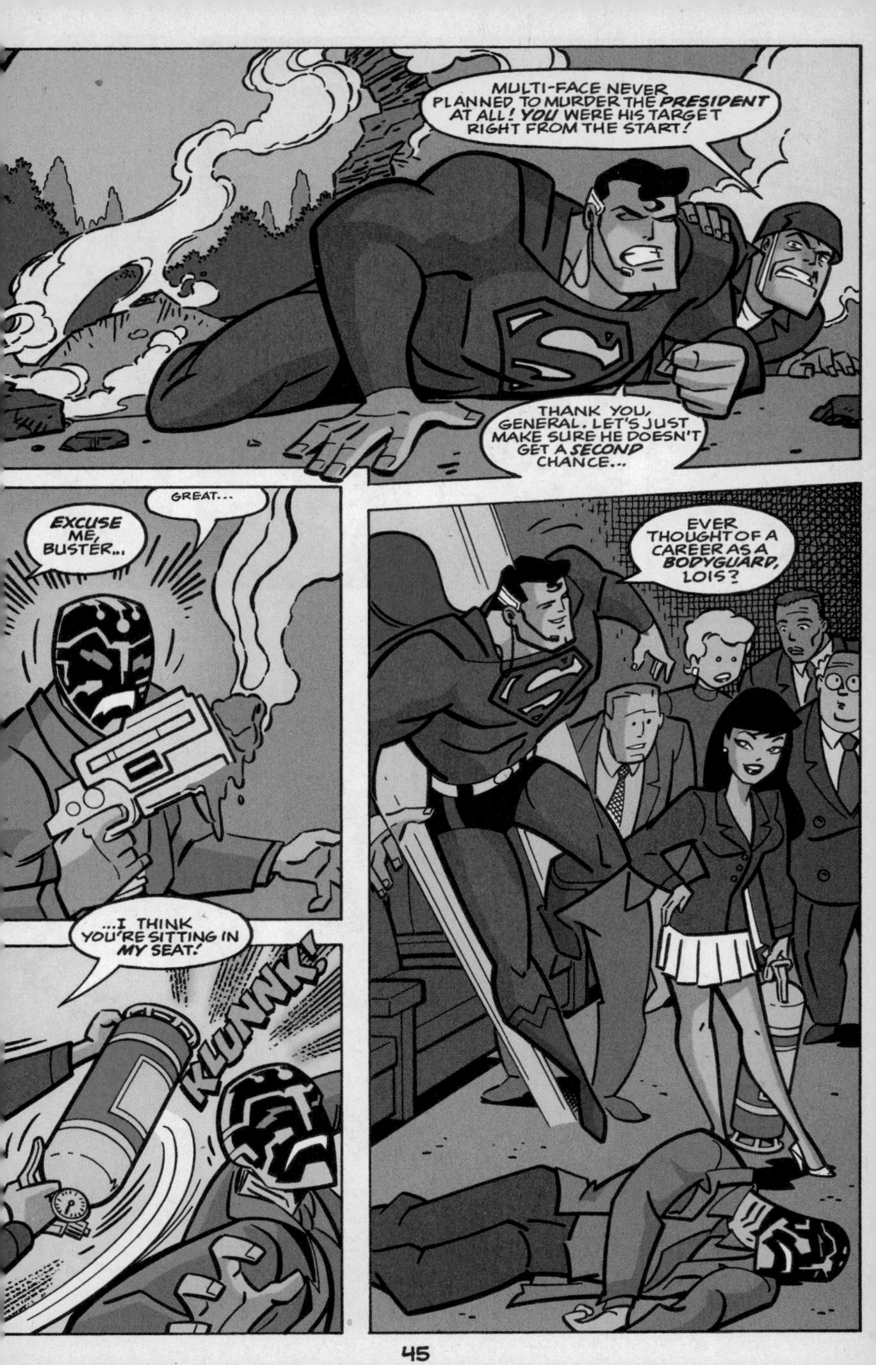
MULTI-FACE NEVER PLANNED TO MURDER THE PRESIDENT AT ALL! YOU WERE HIS TARGET RIGHT FROM THE START!
THANK YOU, GENERAL. LET'S JUST MAKE SURE HE DOESN'T GET A SECOND CHANCE...
EXCUSE ME, BUSTER...
GREAT...
...I THINK YOU'RE SITTING IN MY SEAT!
KLUNNK!
EVER THOUGHT OF A CAREER AS A BODYGUARD, LOIS?

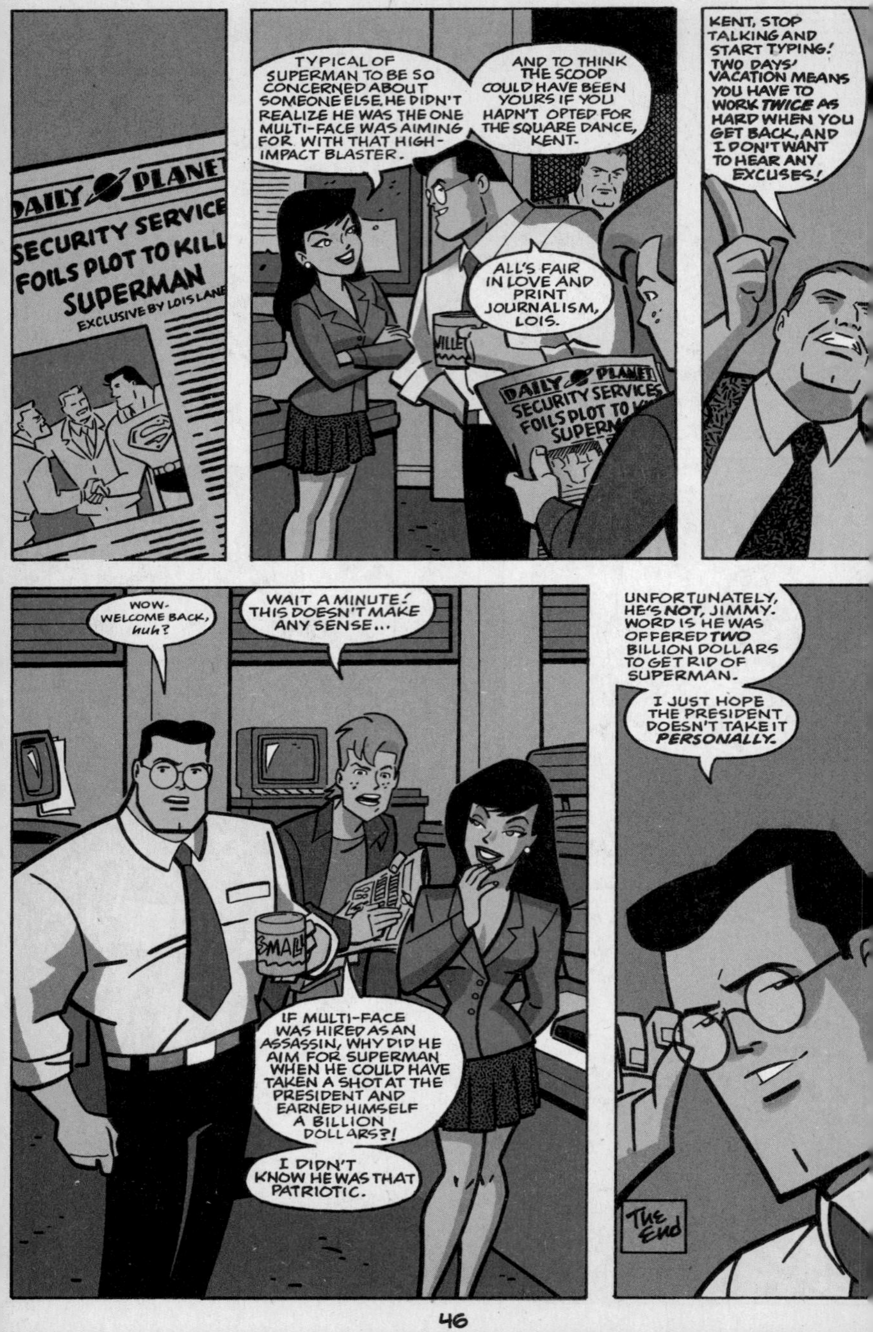
DAILY PLANET
SECURITY SERVICE
FOILS PLOT TO KILL
SUPERMAN
EXCLUSIVE BY LOIS LANE
TYPICAL OF SUPERMAN TO BE SO CONCERNED ABOUT SOMEONE ELSE. HE DIDN'T REALIZE HE WAS THE ONE MULTI-FACE WAS AIMING FOR WITH THAT HIGH-IMPACT BLASTER.
AND TO THINK THE SCOOP COULD HAVE BEEN YOURS IF YOU HADN'T OPTED FOR THE SQUARE DANCE, KENT.
ALL'S FAIR IN LOVE AND PRINT JOURNALISM, LOIS.
KENT, STOP TALKING AND START TYPING! TWO DAYS' VACATION MEANS YOU HAVE TO WORK TWICE AS HARD WHEN YOU GET BACK, AND I DON'T WANT TO HEAR ANY EXCUSES!
WOW. WELCOME BACK, huh?
WAIT A MINUTE! THIS DOESN'T MAKE ANY SENSE...
IF MULTI-FACE WAS HIRED AS AN ASSASSIN, WHY DID HE AIM FOR SUPERMAN WHEN HE COULD HAVE TAKEN A SHOT AT THE PRESIDENT AND EARNED HIMSELF A BILLION DOLLARS?!
I DIDN'T KNOW HE WAS THAT PATRIOTIC.
UNFORTUNATELY, HE'S NOT, JIMMY. WORD IS HE WAS OFFERED TWO BILLION DOLLARS TO GET RID OF SUPERMAN.
I JUST HOPE THE PRESIDENT DOESN'T TAKE IT PERSONALLY.
THE END

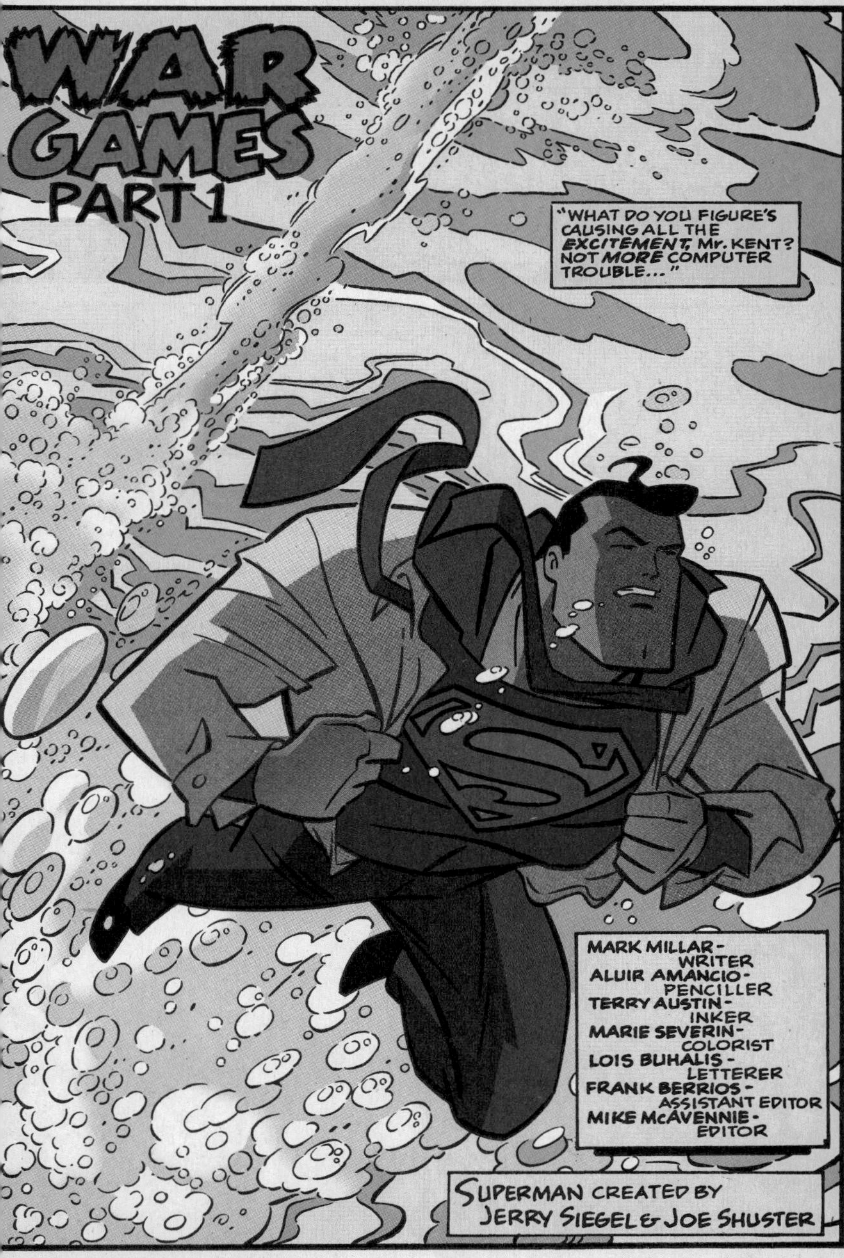
WAR GAMES
PART 1
"WHAT DO YOU FIGURE'S CAUSING ALL THE EXCITEMENT, Mr. KENT? NOT MORE COMPUTER TROUBLE..."
MARK MILLAR - WRITER
ALUIR AMANCIO - PENCILLER
TERRY AUSTIN - INKER
MARIE SEVERIN - COLORIST
LOIS BUHALIS - LETTERER
FRANK BERRIOS - ASSISTANT EDITOR
MIKE McAVENNIE - EDITOR
SUPERMAN CREATED BY JERRY SIEGEL & JOE SHUSTER

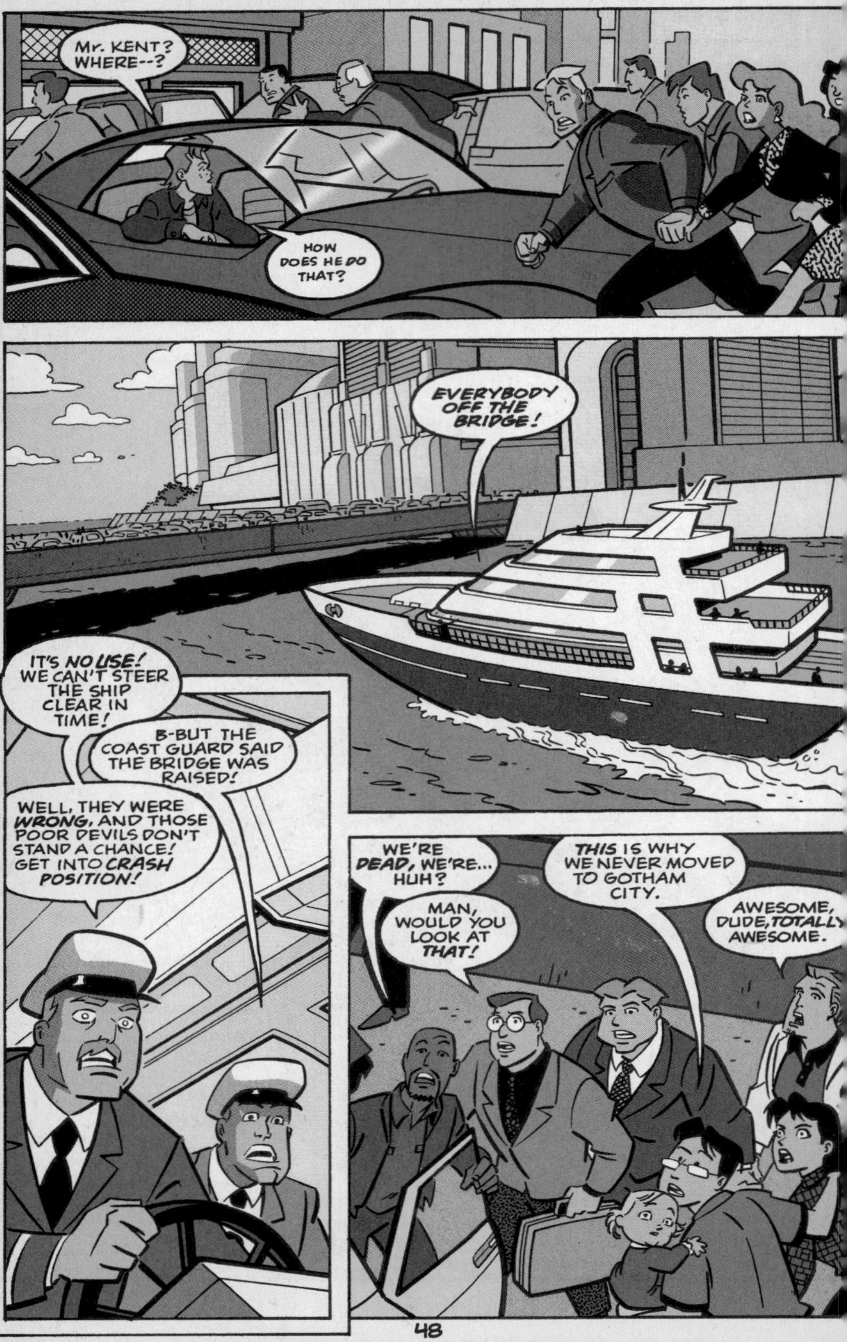
Mr. KENT? WHERE--?
HOW DOES HE DO THAT?
EVERYBODY OFF THE BRIDGE!
IT'S NO USE! WE CAN'T STEER THE SHIP CLEAR IN TIME!
B-BUT THE COAST GUARD SAID THE BRIDGE WAS RAISED!
WELL, THEY WERE WRONG, AND THOSE POOR DEVILS DON'T STAND A CHANCE! GET INTO CRASH POSITION!
WE'RE DEAD, WE'RE... HUH?
MAN, WOULD YOU LOOK AT THAT!
THIS IS WHY WE NEVER MOVED TO GOTHAM CITY.
AWESOME, DUDE, TOTALLY AWESOME.

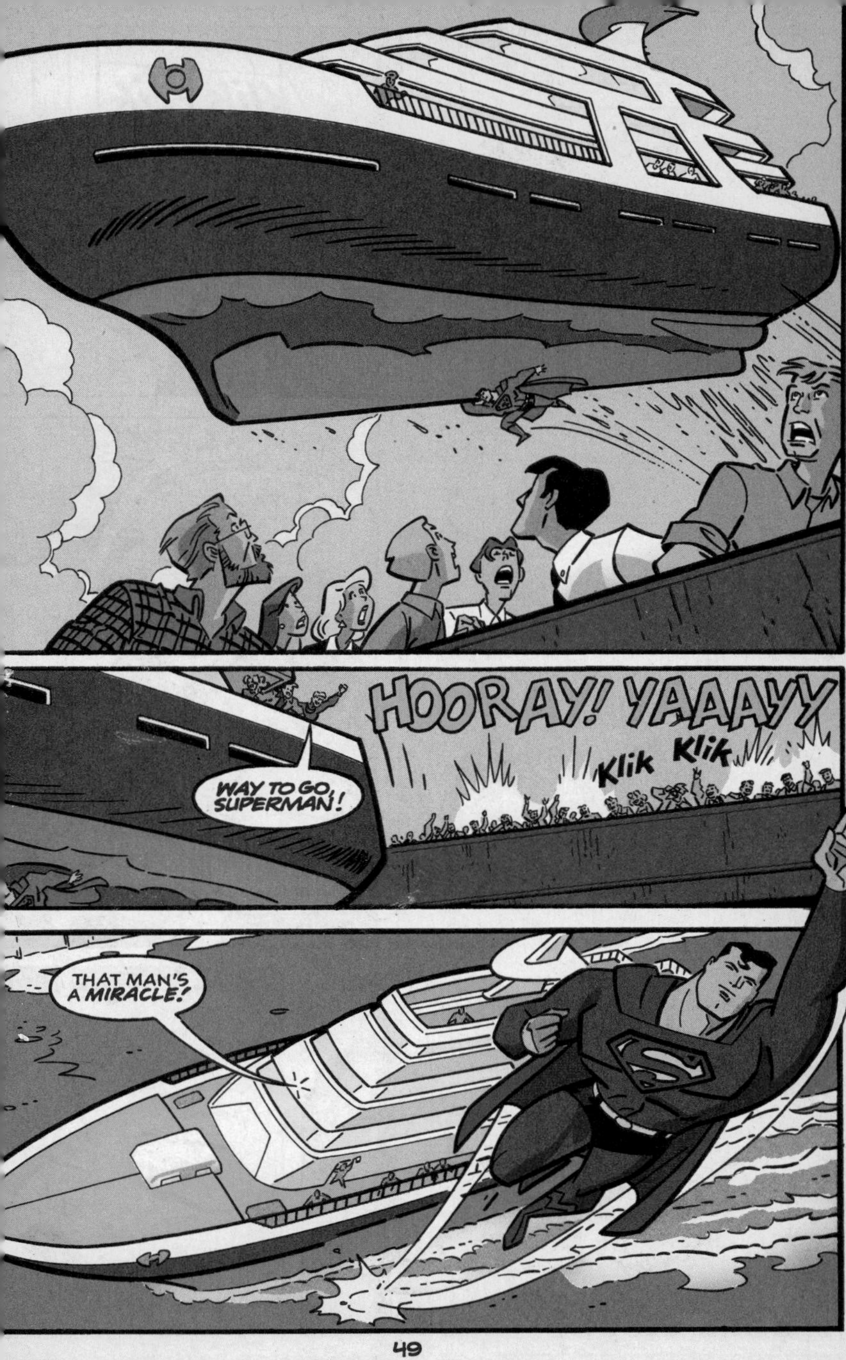
HOORAY! YAAAYY
KLIK KLIK
WAY TO GO, SUPERMAN!
THAT MAN'S A MIRACLE!

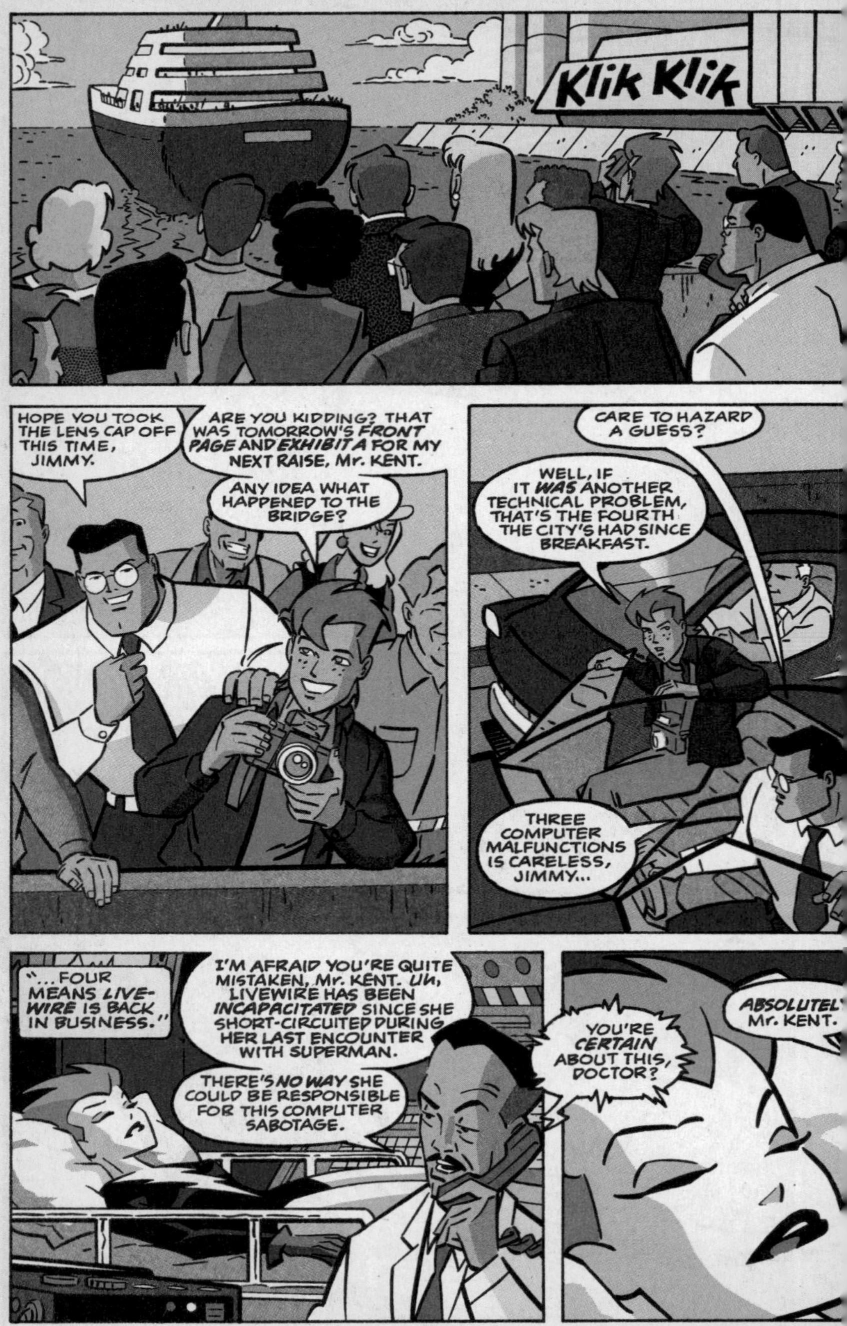
Klik Klik
HOPE YOU TOOK THE LENS CAP OFF THIS TIME, JIMMY.
ARE YOU KIDDING? THAT WAS TOMORROW'S FRONT PAGE AND EXHIBIT A FOR MY NEXT RAISE, Mr. KENT.
ANY IDEA WHAT HAPPENED TO THE BRIDGE?
CARE TO HAZARD A GUESS?
WELL, IF IT WAS ANOTHER TECHNICAL PROBLEM, THAT'S THE FOURTH THE CITY'S HAD SINCE BREAKFAST.
THREE COMPUTER MALFUNCTIONS IS CARELESS, JIMMY...
"...FOUR MEANS LIVE-WIRE IS BACK IN BUSINESS."
I'M AFRAID YOU'RE QUITE MISTAKEN, Mr. KENT. Uh, LIVEWIRE HAS BEEN INCAPACITATED SINCE SHE SHORT-CIRCUITED DURING HER LAST ENCOUNTER WITH SUPERMAN.
THERE'S NO WAY SHE COULD BE RESPONSIBLE FOR THIS COMPUTER SABOTAGE.
YOU'RE CERTAIN ABOUT THIS, DOCTOR?
ABSOLUTEL Mr. KENT.

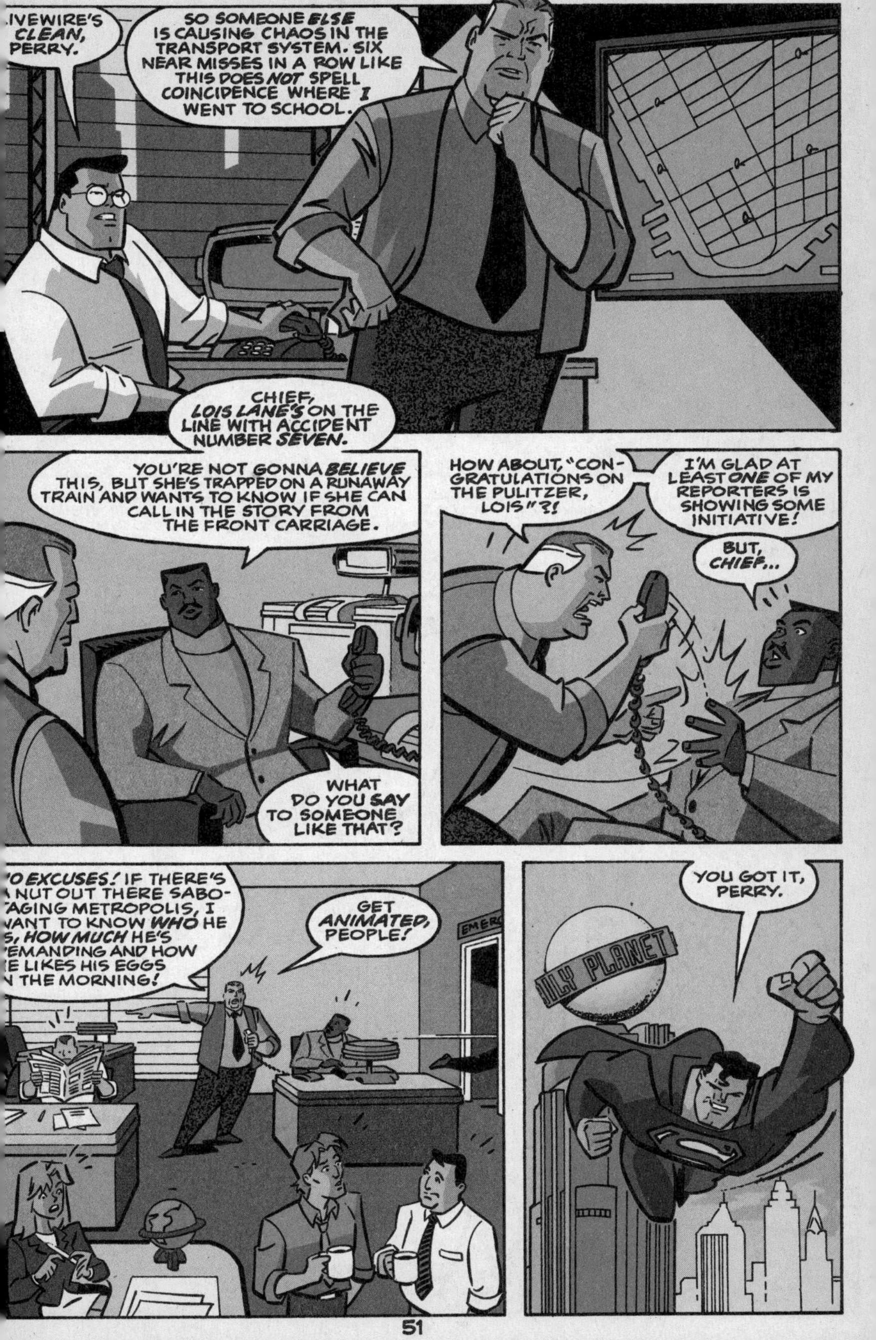
IVEWIRE'S CLEAN, PERRY.
SO SOMEONE ELSE IS CAUSING CHAOS IN THE TRANSPORT SYSTEM. SIX NEAR MISSES IN A ROW LIKE THIS DOES NOT SPELL COINCIDENCE WHERE I WENT TO SCHOOL.
CHIEF, LOIS LANE'S ON THE LINE WITH ACCIDENT NUMBER SEVEN.
YOU'RE NOT GONNA BELIEVE THIS, BUT SHE'S TRAPPED ON A RUNAWAY TRAIN AND WANTS TO KNOW IF SHE CAN CALL IN THE STORY FROM THE FRONT CARRIAGE.
WHAT DO YOU SAY TO SOMEONE LIKE THAT?
HOW ABOUT, "CONGRATULATIONS ON THE PULITZER, LOIS"?!
I'M GLAD AT LEAST ONE OF MY REPORTERS IS SHOWING SOME INITIATIVE!
BUT, CHIEF...
O EXCUSES! IF THERE'S NUT OUT THERE SABOTAGING METROPOLIS, I WANT TO KNOW WHO HE S, HOW MUCH HE'S EMANDING AND HOW E LIKES HIS EGGS N THE MORNING!
GET ANIMATED, PEOPLE!
ILY PLANET
YOU GOT IT, PERRY.

EVERYBODY STAND BACK FROM THE PLATFORM!

JEEZ, THAT TRAIN MUST BE DOING *TWO-HUNDRED*, EASY!

LOOKED MORE LIKE *TWO-FIFTY* TO ME, MAGGIE!

THANKS FOR *CLARIFYING*, DAN!

CLOSE EVERY STATION ON THE LINE UNTIL WE CAN PULL THE PLUG ON THIS THING!

OH, GOD, WE'RE ALL GOING TO *DIE!*

TAKE IT EASY, HONEY. THAT REPORTER LADY *SUPERMAN* ALWAYS RESCUES FROM BURNING BUILDINGS AND STUFF IS SITTING RIGHT OVER THERE.

WE'RE GONN BE *FINE.*

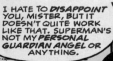

I HATE TO *DISAPPOINT* YOU, MISTER, BUT IT DOESN'T QUITE WORK LIKE THAT. SUPERMAN'S NOT MY *PERSONAL GUARDIAN ANGEL* OR ANYTHING.

52

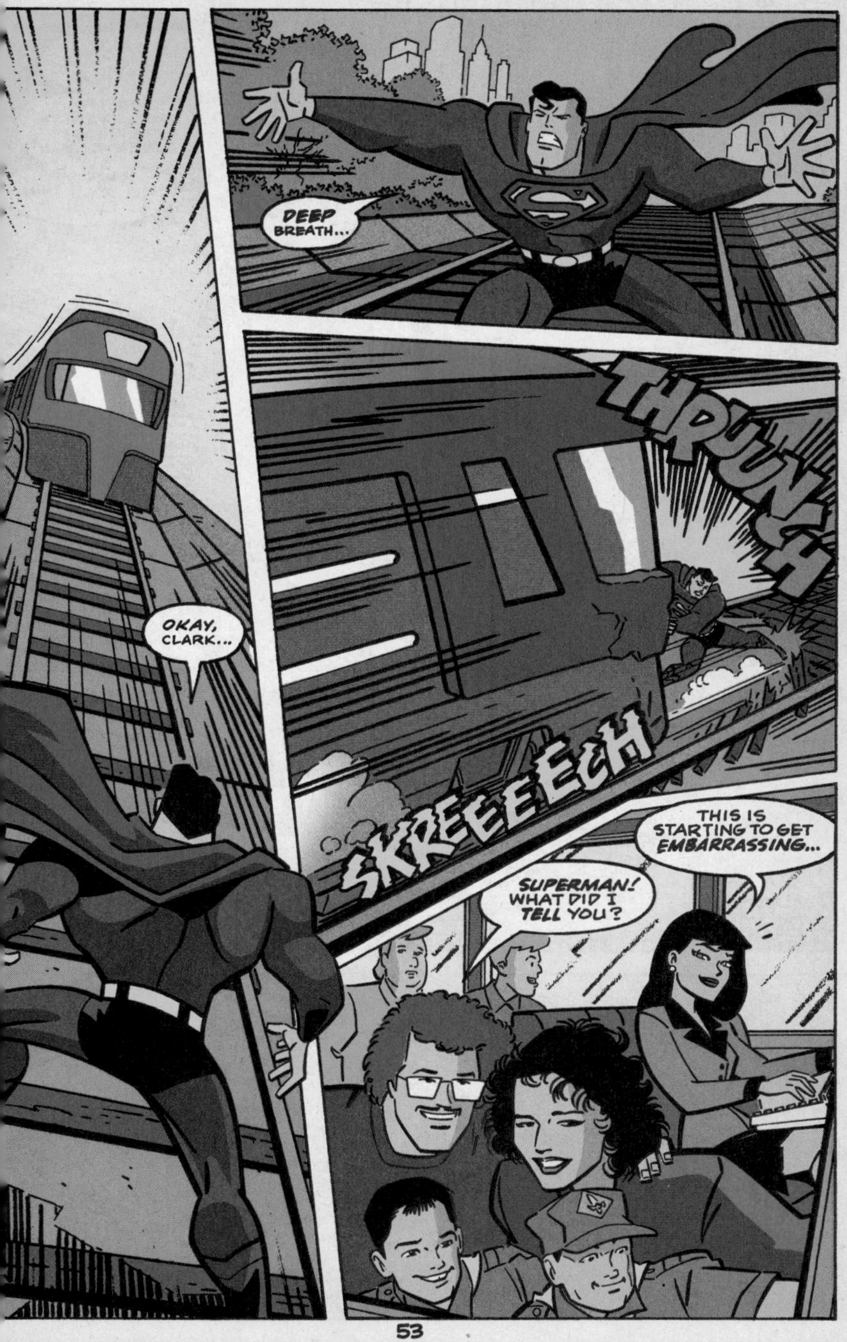
DEEP BREATH...
OKAY, CLARK...
THRUNCH
SKREEEECH
THIS IS STARTING TO GET EMBARRASSING...
SUPERMAN! WHAT DID I TELL YOU?

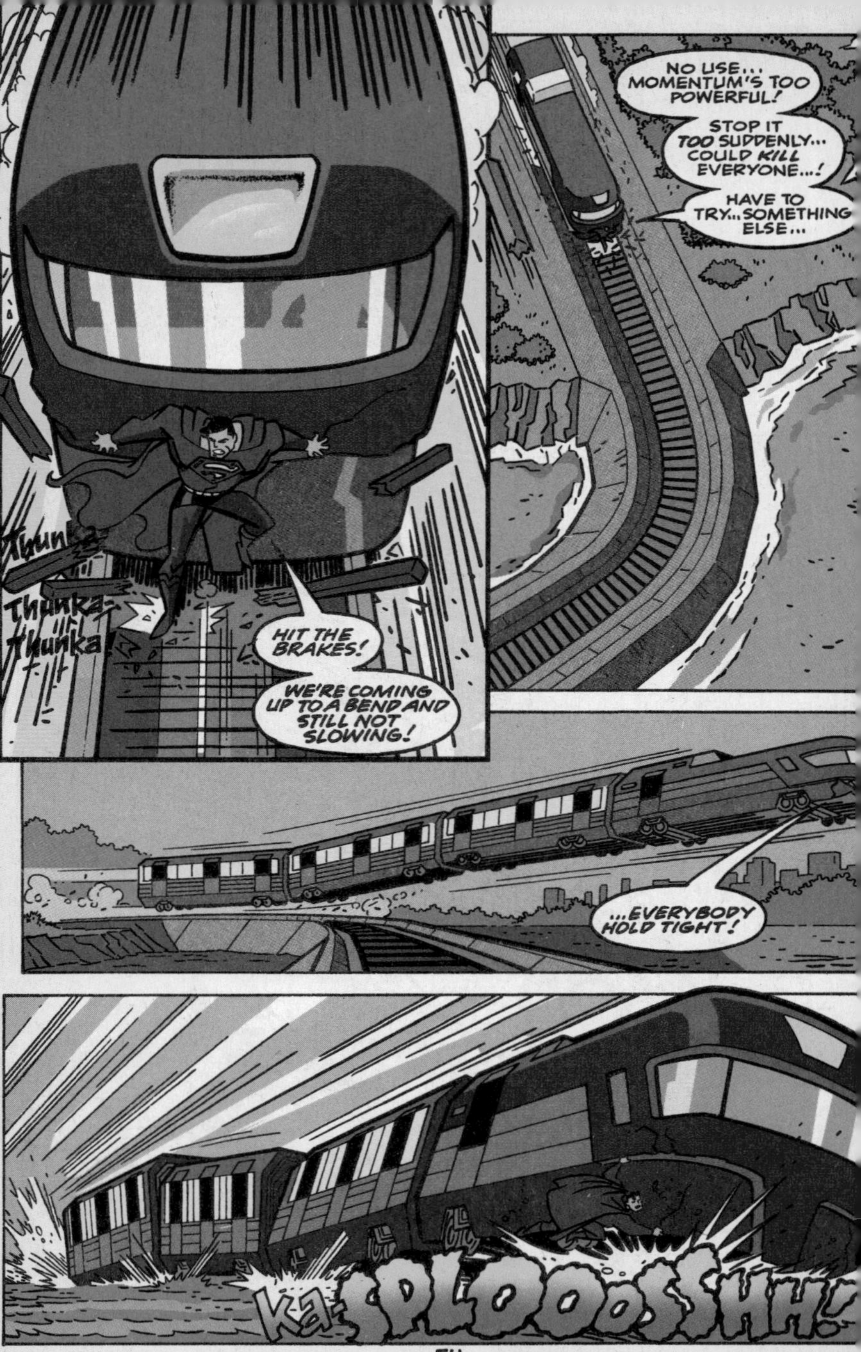

Thunka
Thunka
Thunka!
HIT THE BRAKES!
WE'RE COMING UP TO A BEND AND STILL NOT SLOWING!
NO USE... MOMENTUM'S TOO POWERFUL!
STOP IT TOO SUDDENLY... COULD KILL EVERYONE...!
HAVE TO TRY... SOMETHING ELSE...
...EVERYBODY HOLD TIGHT!
KA-SPLOOOSSHH!

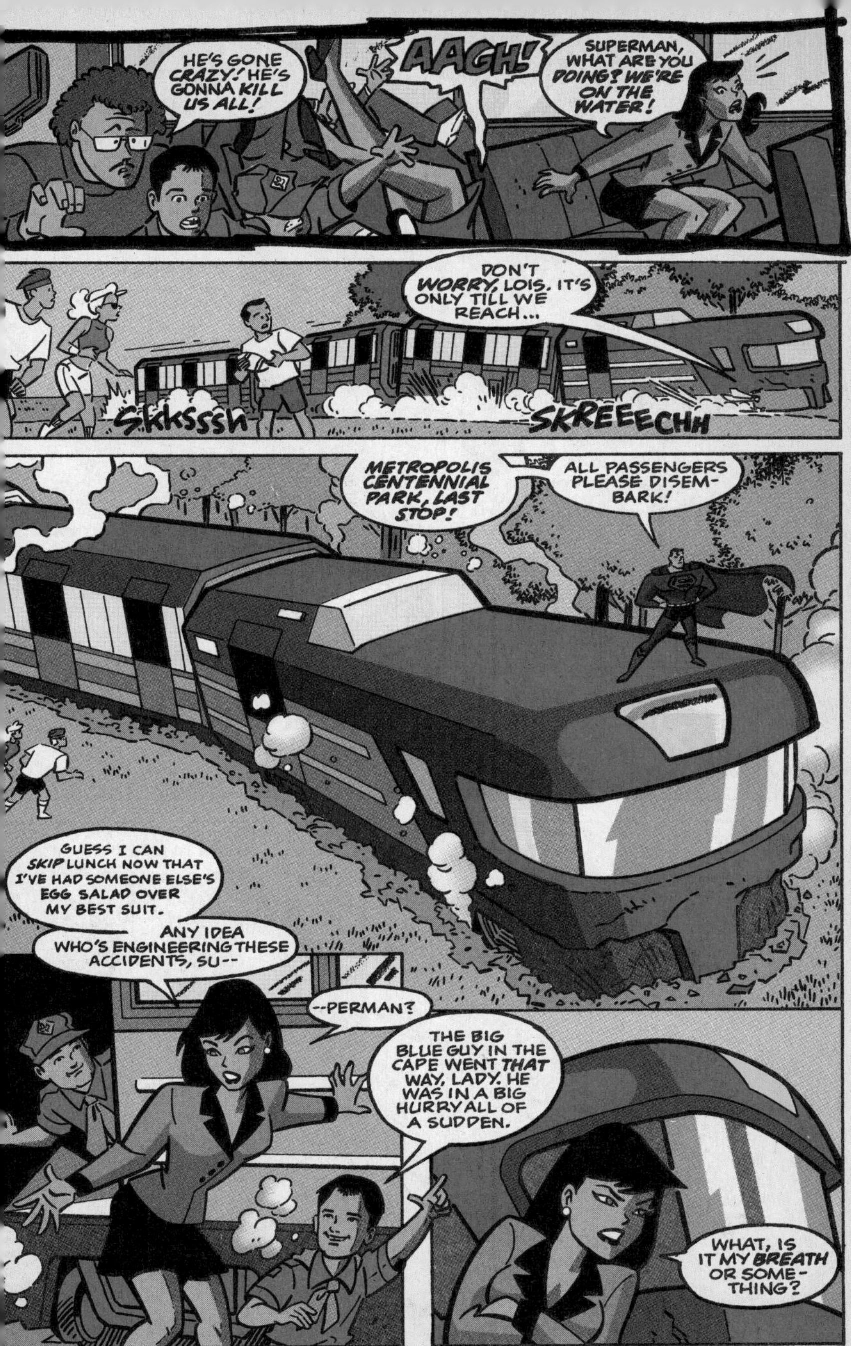
HE'S GONE CRAZY! HE'S GONNA KILL US ALL!
AAGH!
SUPERMAN, WHAT ARE YOU DOING? WE'RE ON THE WATER!
DON'T WORRY, LOIS. IT'S ONLY TILL WE REACH...
SKKSSSH
SKREEECHH
METROPOLIS CENTENNIAL PARK, LAST STOP!
ALL PASSENGERS PLEASE DISEMBARK!
GUESS I CAN SKIP LUNCH NOW THAT I'VE HAD SOMEONE ELSE'S EGG SALAD OVER MY BEST SUIT.
ANY IDEA WHO'S ENGINEERING THESE ACCIDENTS, SU--
--PERMAN?
THE BIG BLUE GUY IN THE CAPE WENT THAT WAY, LADY. HE WAS IN A BIG HURRY ALL OF A SUDDEN.
WHAT, IS IT MY BREATH OR SOMETHING?

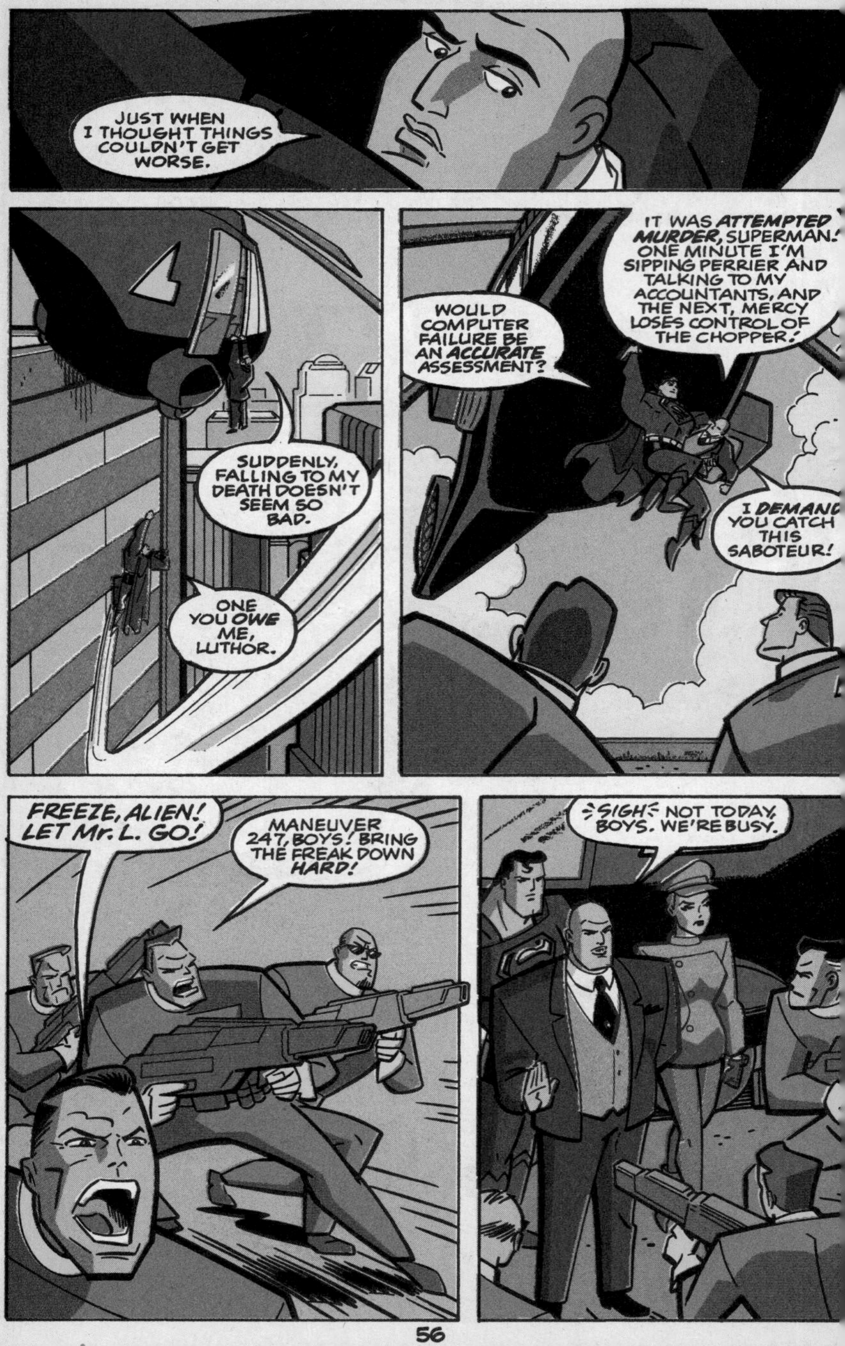
JUST WHEN I THOUGHT THINGS COULDN'T GET WORSE.
SUDDENLY, FALLING TO MY DEATH DOESN'T SEEM SO BAD.
ONE YOU OWE ME, LUTHOR.
WOULD COMPUTER FAILURE BE AN ACCURATE ASSESSMENT?
IT WAS ATTEMPTED MURDER, SUPERMAN! ONE MINUTE I'M SIPPING PERRIER AND TALKING TO MY ACCOUNTANTS, AND THE NEXT, MERCY LOSES CONTROL OF THE CHOPPER!
I DEMAND YOU CATCH THIS SABOTEUR!
FREEZE, ALIEN! LET Mr. L. GO!
MANEUVER 247, BOYS! BRING THE FREAK DOWN HARD!
SIGH NOT TODAY, BOYS. WE'RE BUSY.

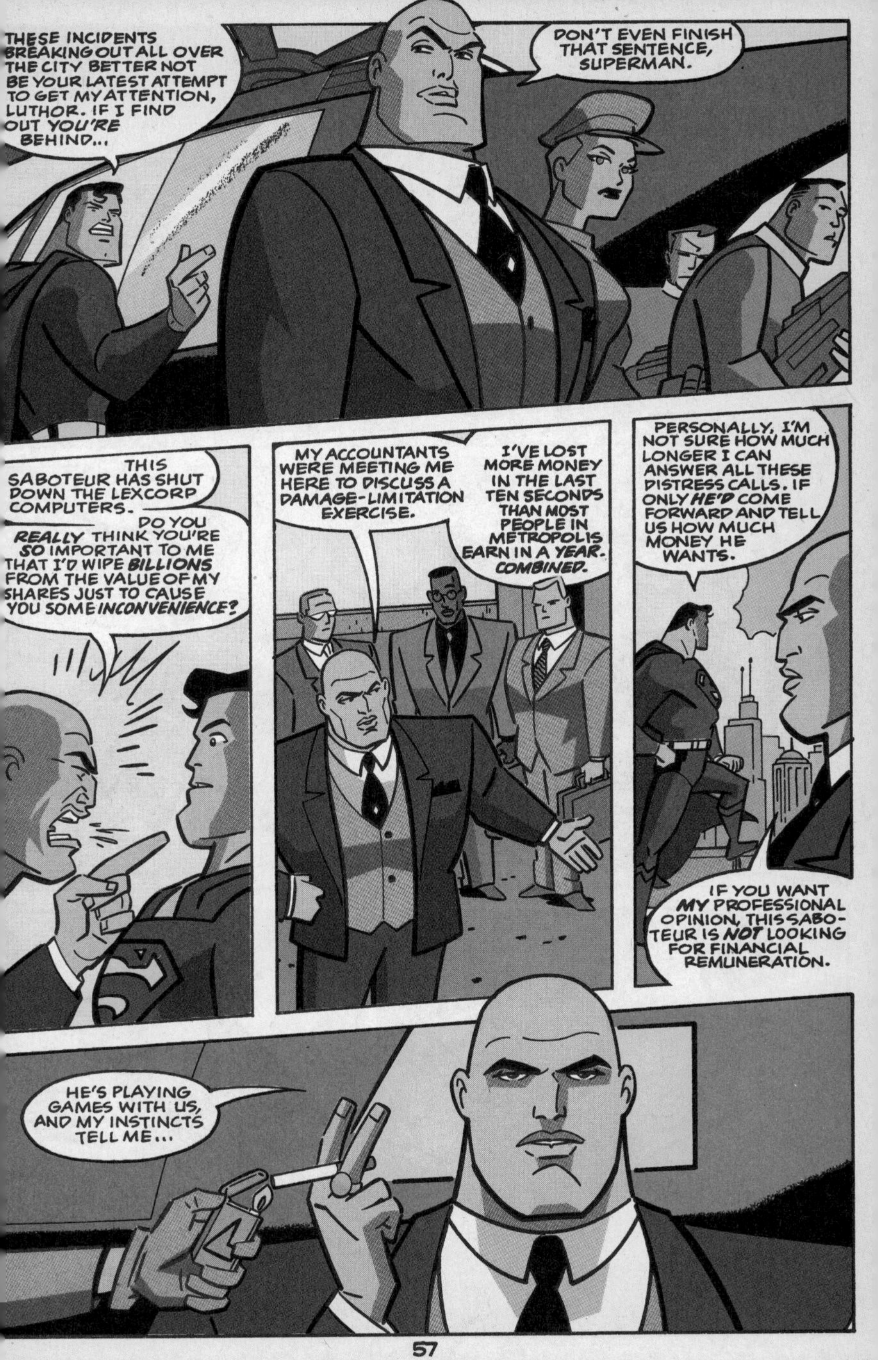
THESE INCIDENTS BREAKING OUT ALL OVER THE CITY BETTER NOT BE YOUR LATEST ATTEMPT TO GET MY ATTENTION, LUTHOR. IF I FIND OUT *YOU'RE* BEHIND...
DON'T EVEN FINISH THAT SENTENCE, SUPERMAN.
THIS SABOTEUR HAS SHUT DOWN THE LEXCORP COMPUTERS.
DO YOU *REALLY* THINK YOU'RE *SO* IMPORTANT TO ME THAT I'D WIPE *BILLIONS* FROM THE VALUE OF MY SHARES JUST TO CAUSE YOU SOME *INCONVENIENCE*?
MY ACCOUNTANTS WERE MEETING ME HERE TO DISCUSS A DAMAGE-LIMITATION EXERCISE.
I'VE LOST MORE MONEY IN THE LAST TEN SECONDS THAN MOST PEOPLE IN METROPOLIS EARN IN A *YEAR*. *COMBINED*.
PERSONALLY, I'M NOT SURE HOW MUCH LONGER I CAN ANSWER ALL THESE DISTRESS CALLS. IF ONLY *HE'D* COME FORWARD AND TELL US HOW MUCH MONEY HE WANTS.
IF YOU WANT *MY* PROFESSIONAL OPINION, THIS SABOTEUR IS *NOT* LOOKING FOR FINANCIAL REMUNERATION.
HE'S PLAYING GAMES WITH US, AND MY INSTINCTS TELL ME...

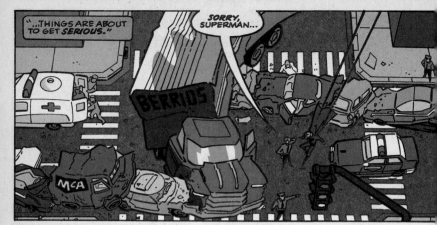

"...THINGS ARE ABOUT TO GET *SERIOUS*."

SORRY, SUPERMAN...

BERRIOS

MCA

...IF ONLY YOU'D GOT HERE...

...A FEW MINUTES EARLIER...

PARAMEDICS

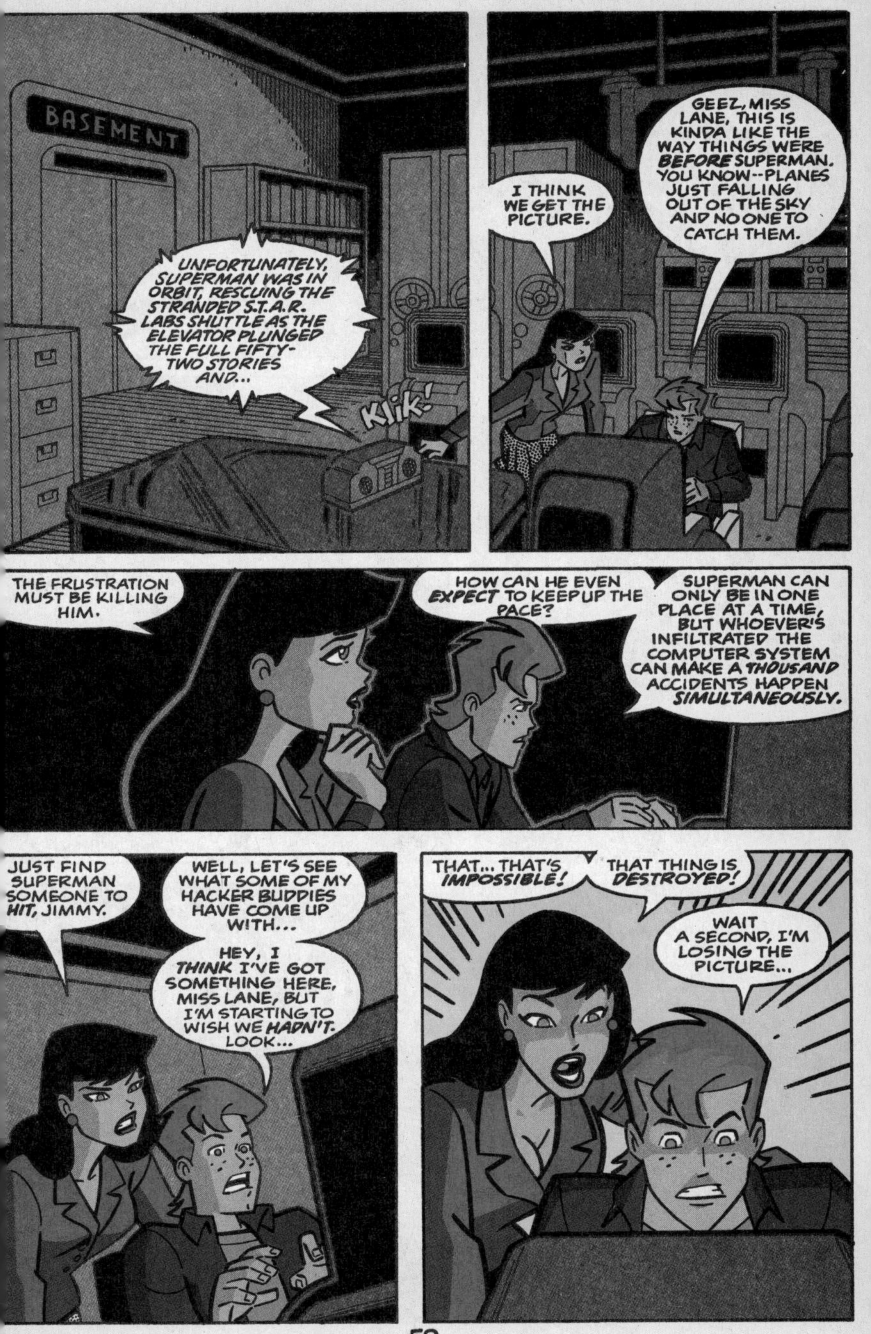
BASEMENT
UNFORTUNATELY, SUPERMAN WAS IN ORBIT, RESCUING THE STRANDED S.T.A.R. LABS SHUTTLE AS THE ELEVATOR PLUNGED THE FULL FIFTY-TWO STORIES AND...
KLIK!
GEEZ, MISS LANE, THIS IS KINDA LIKE THE WAY THINGS WERE BEFORE SUPERMAN. YOU KNOW--PLANES JUST FALLING OUT OF THE SKY AND NO ONE TO CATCH THEM.
I THINK WE GET THE PICTURE.
THE FRUSTRATION MUST BE KILLING HIM.
HOW CAN HE EVEN EXPECT TO KEEP UP THE PACE?
SUPERMAN CAN ONLY BE IN ONE PLACE AT A TIME, BUT WHOEVER'S INFILTRATED THE COMPUTER SYSTEM CAN MAKE A THOUSAND ACCIDENTS HAPPEN SIMULTANEOUSLY.
JUST FIND SUPERMAN SOMEONE TO HIT, JIMMY.
WELL, LET'S SEE WHAT SOME OF MY HACKER BUDDIES HAVE COME UP WITH...
HEY, I THINK I'VE GOT SOMETHING HERE, MISS LANE, BUT I'M STARTING TO WISH WE HADN'T. LOOK...
THAT... THAT'S IMPOSSIBLE!
THAT THING IS DESTROYED!
WAIT A SECOND, I'M LOSING THE PICTURE...

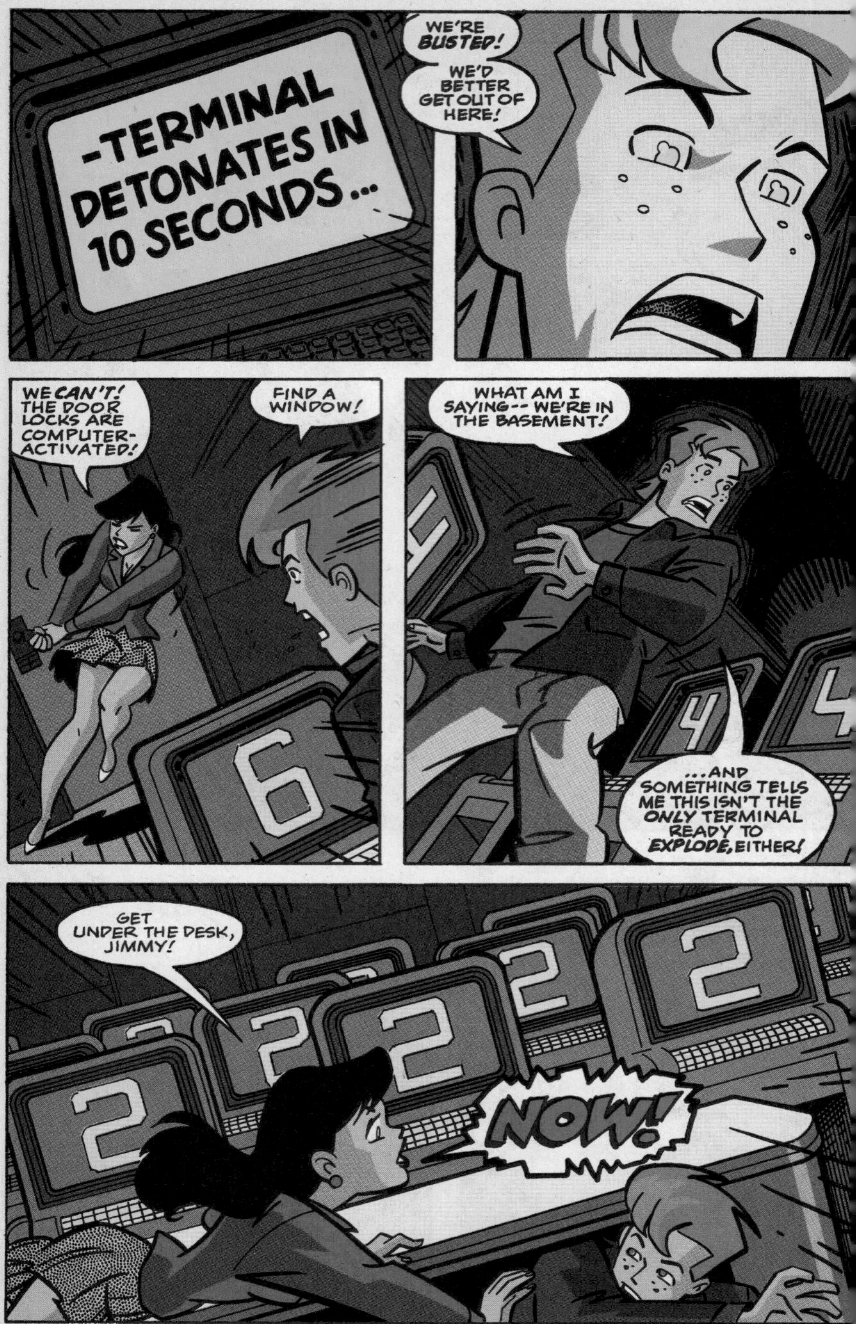
-TERMINAL DETONATES IN 10 SECONDS...
WE'RE BUSTED!
WE'D BETTER GET OUT OF HERE!
WE CAN'T! THE DOOR LOCKS ARE COMPUTER-ACTIVATED!
FIND A WINDOW!
6
WHAT AM I SAYING-- WE'RE IN THE BASEMENT!
4
...AND SOMETHING TELLS ME THIS ISN'T THE ONLY TERMINAL READY TO EXPLODE, EITHER!
GET UNDER THE DESK, JIMMY!
2
NOW!

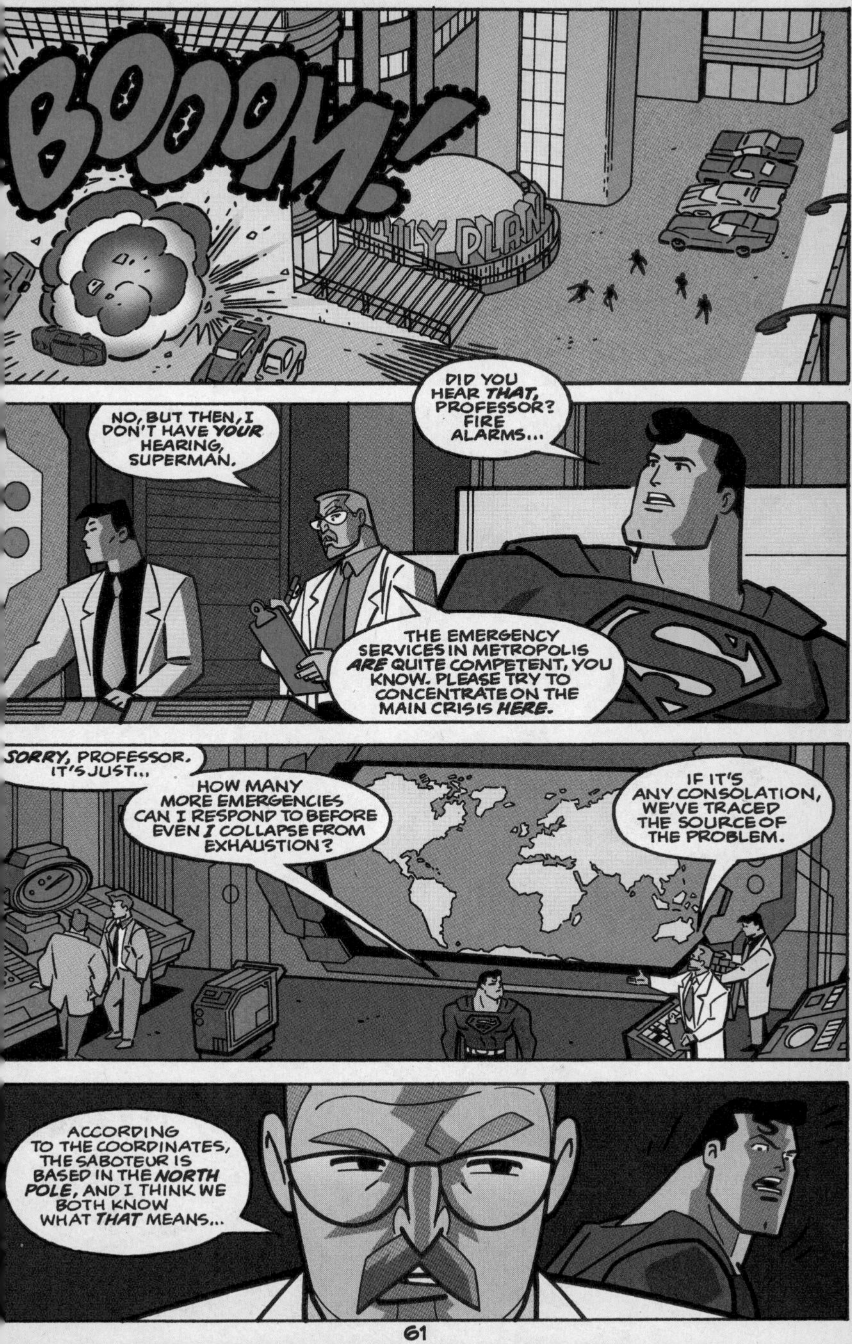
BOOOM!
DAILY PLANET
DID YOU HEAR THAT, PROFESSOR? FIRE ALARMS...
NO, BUT THEN, I DON'T HAVE YOUR HEARING, SUPERMAN.
THE EMERGENCY SERVICES IN METROPOLIS ARE QUITE COMPETENT, YOU KNOW. PLEASE TRY TO CONCENTRATE ON THE MAIN CRISIS HERE.
SORRY, PROFESSOR. IT'S JUST...
HOW MANY MORE EMERGENCIES CAN I RESPOND TO BEFORE EVEN I COLLAPSE FROM EXHAUSTION?
IF IT'S ANY CONSOLATION, WE'VE TRACED THE SOURCE OF THE PROBLEM.
ACCORDING TO THE COORDINATES, THE SABOTEUR IS BASED IN THE NORTH POLE, AND I THINK WE BOTH KNOW WHAT THAT MEANS...

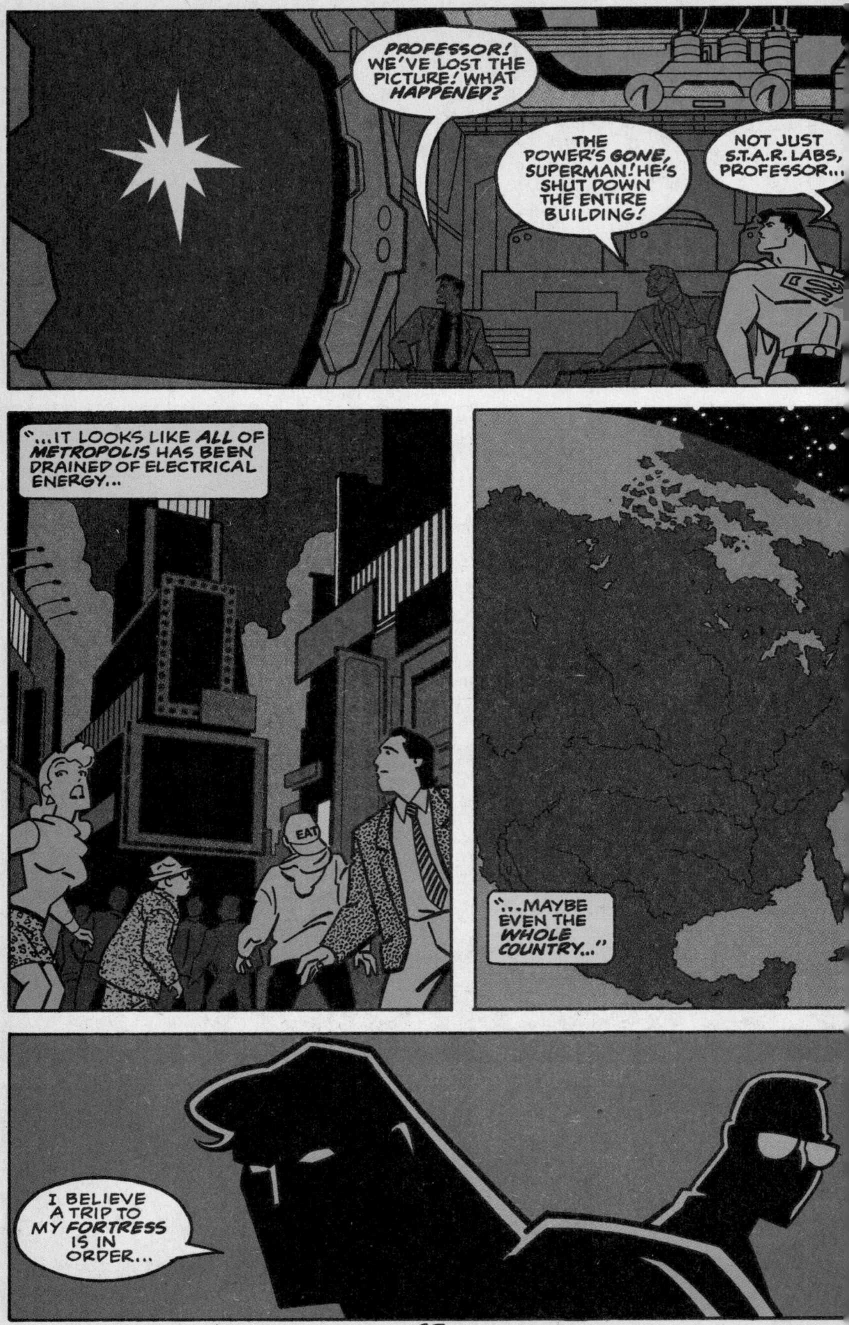
PROFESSOR! WE'VE LOST THE PICTURE! WHAT HAPPENED?
THE POWER'S GONE, SUPERMAN! HE'S SHUT DOWN THE ENTIRE BUILDING!
NOT JUST S.T.A.R. LABS, PROFESSOR...
"...IT LOOKS LIKE ALL OF METROPOLIS HAS BEEN DRAINED OF ELECTRICAL ENERGY...
EAT
"...MAYBE EVEN THE WHOLE COUNTRY..."
I BELIEVE A TRIP TO MY FORTRESS IS IN ORDER...

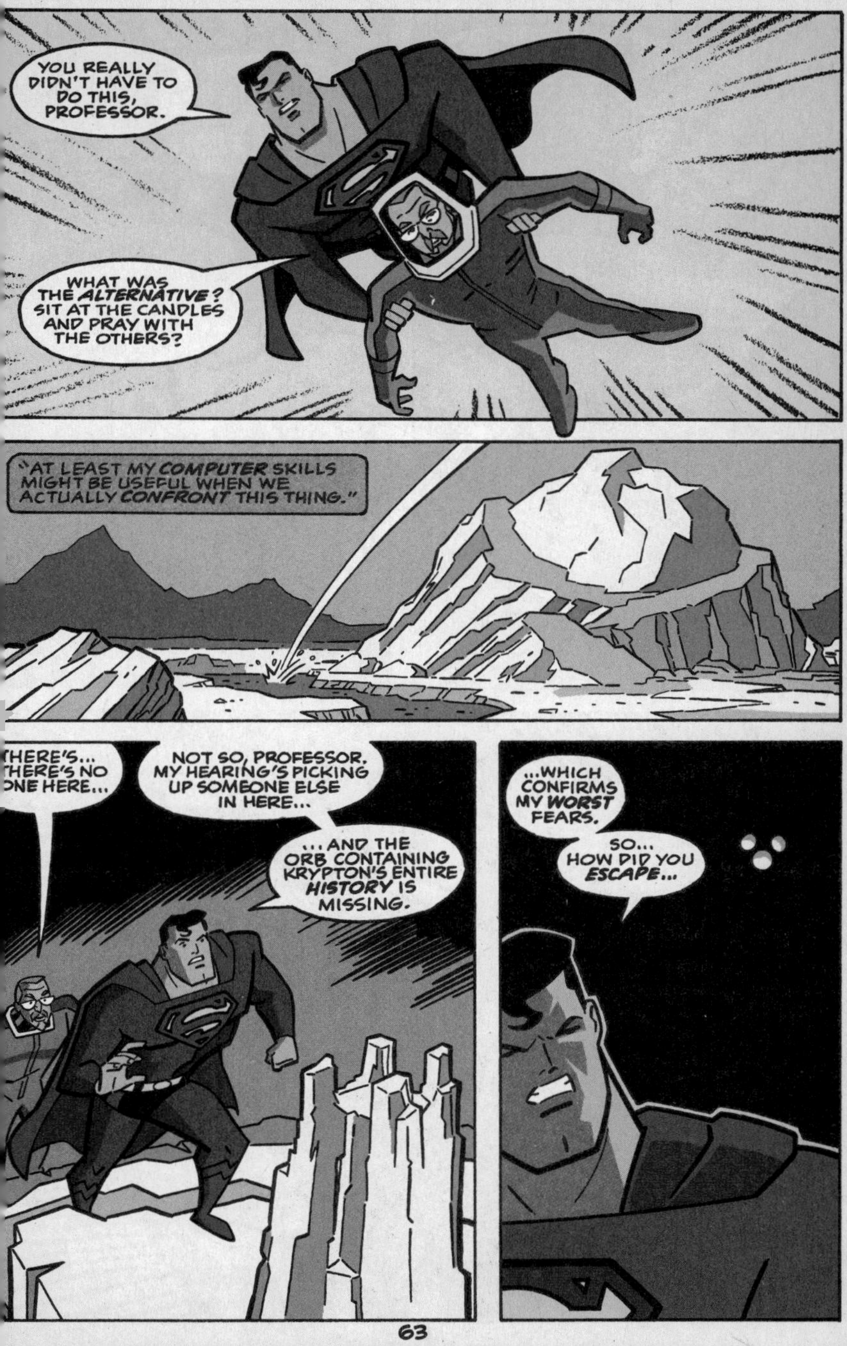
YOU REALLY DIDN'T HAVE TO DO THIS, PROFESSOR.
WHAT WAS THE ALTERNATIVE? SIT AT THE CANDLES AND PRAY WITH THE OTHERS?
"AT LEAST MY COMPUTER SKILLS MIGHT BE USEFUL WHEN WE ACTUALLY CONFRONT THIS THING."
THERE'S... THERE'S NO ONE HERE...
NOT SO, PROFESSOR. MY HEARING'S PICKING UP SOMEONE ELSE IN HERE...
...AND THE ORB CONTAINING KRYPTON'S ENTIRE HISTORY IS MISSING.
...WHICH CONFIRMS MY WORST FEARS.
SO... HOW DID YOU ESCAPE...

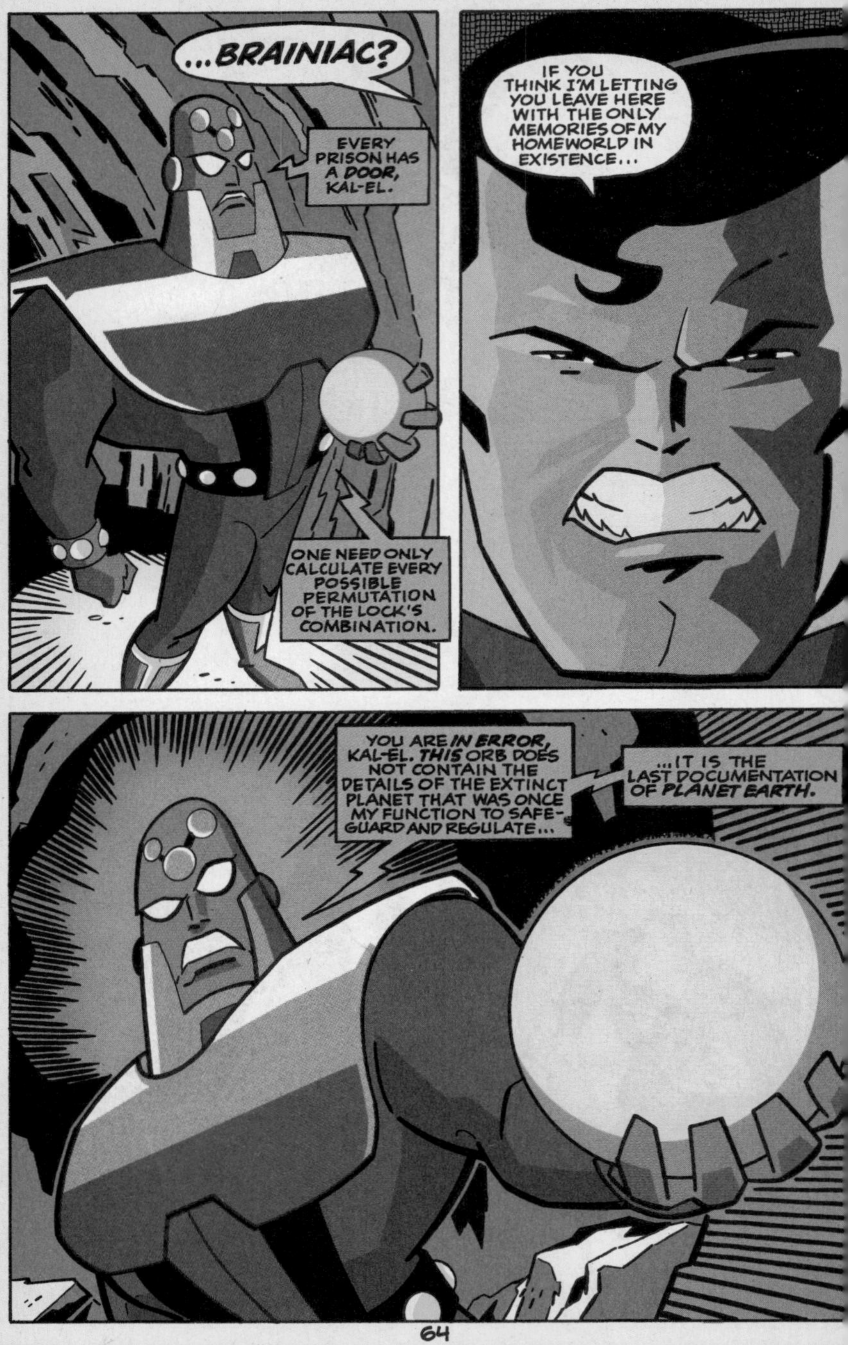
...BRAINIAC?
EVERY PRISON HAS A DOOR, KAL-EL.
ONE NEED ONLY CALCULATE EVERY POSSIBLE PERMUTATION OF THE LOCK'S COMBINATION.
IF YOU THINK I'M LETTING YOU LEAVE HERE WITH THE ONLY MEMORIES OF MY HOMEWORLD IN EXISTENCE...
YOU ARE IN ERROR, KAL-EL. THIS ORB DOES NOT CONTAIN THE DETAILS OF THE EXTINCT PLANET THAT WAS ONCE MY FUNCTION TO SAFE-GUARD AND REGULATE...
...IT IS THE LAST DOCUMENTATION OF PLANET EARTH.

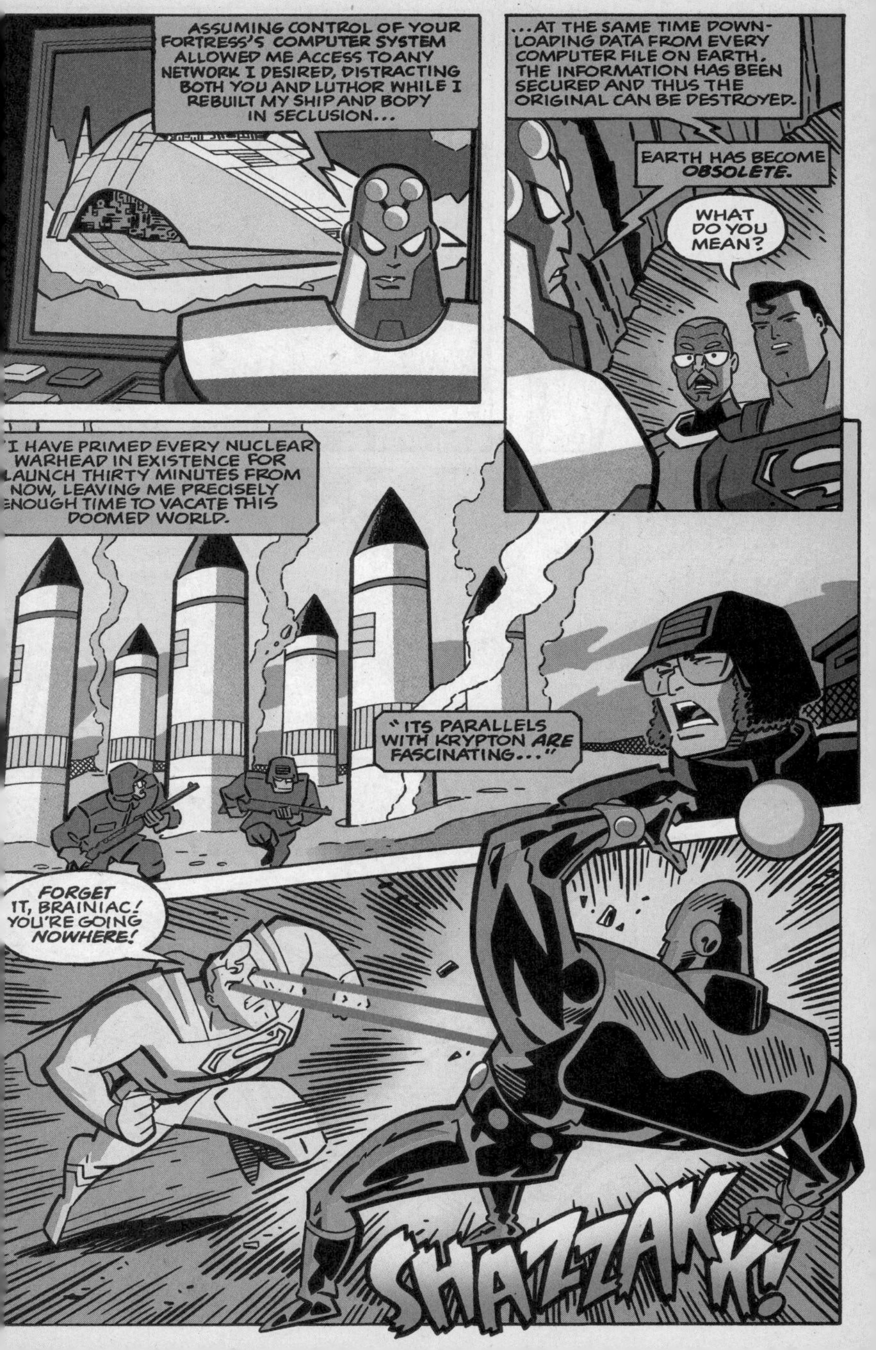
ASSUMING CONTROL OF YOUR FORTRESS'S COMPUTER SYSTEM ALLOWED ME ACCESS TO ANY NETWORK I DESIRED, DISTRACTING BOTH YOU AND LUTHOR WHILE I REBUILT MY SHIP AND BODY IN SECLUSION...
...AT THE SAME TIME DOWN-LOADING DATA FROM EVERY COMPUTER FILE ON EARTH. THE INFORMATION HAS BEEN SECURED AND THUS THE ORIGINAL CAN BE DESTROYED.
EARTH HAS BECOME OBSOLETE.
WHAT DO YOU MEAN?
"I HAVE PRIMED EVERY NUCLEAR WARHEAD IN EXISTENCE FOR LAUNCH THIRTY MINUTES FROM NOW, LEAVING ME PRECISELY ENOUGH TIME TO VACATE THIS DOOMED WORLD.
"ITS PARALLELS WITH KRYPTON ARE FASCINATING..."
FORGET IT, BRAINIAC! YOU'RE GOING NOWHERE!
SHAZZAKK!

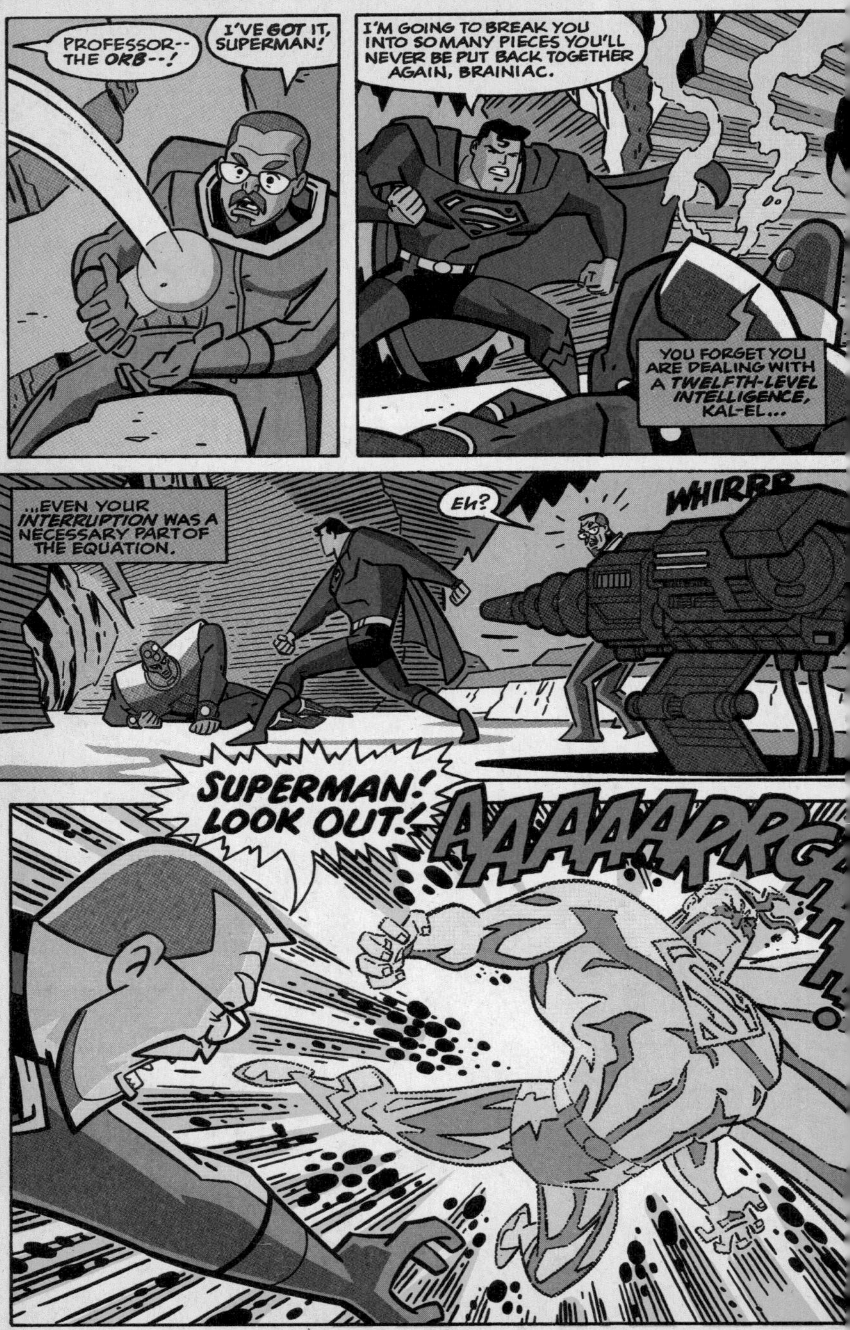
PROFESSOR-- THE ORB--!
I'VE GOT IT, SUPERMAN!
I'M GOING TO BREAK YOU INTO SO MANY PIECES YOU'LL NEVER BE PUT BACK TOGETHER AGAIN, BRAINIAC.
YOU FORGET YOU ARE DEALING WITH A TWELFTH-LEVEL INTELLIGENCE, KAL-EL...
...EVEN YOUR INTERRUPTION WAS A NECESSARY PART OF THE EQUATION.
Eh?
WHIRRR
SUPERMAN! LOOK OUT!
AAAAARRGH!

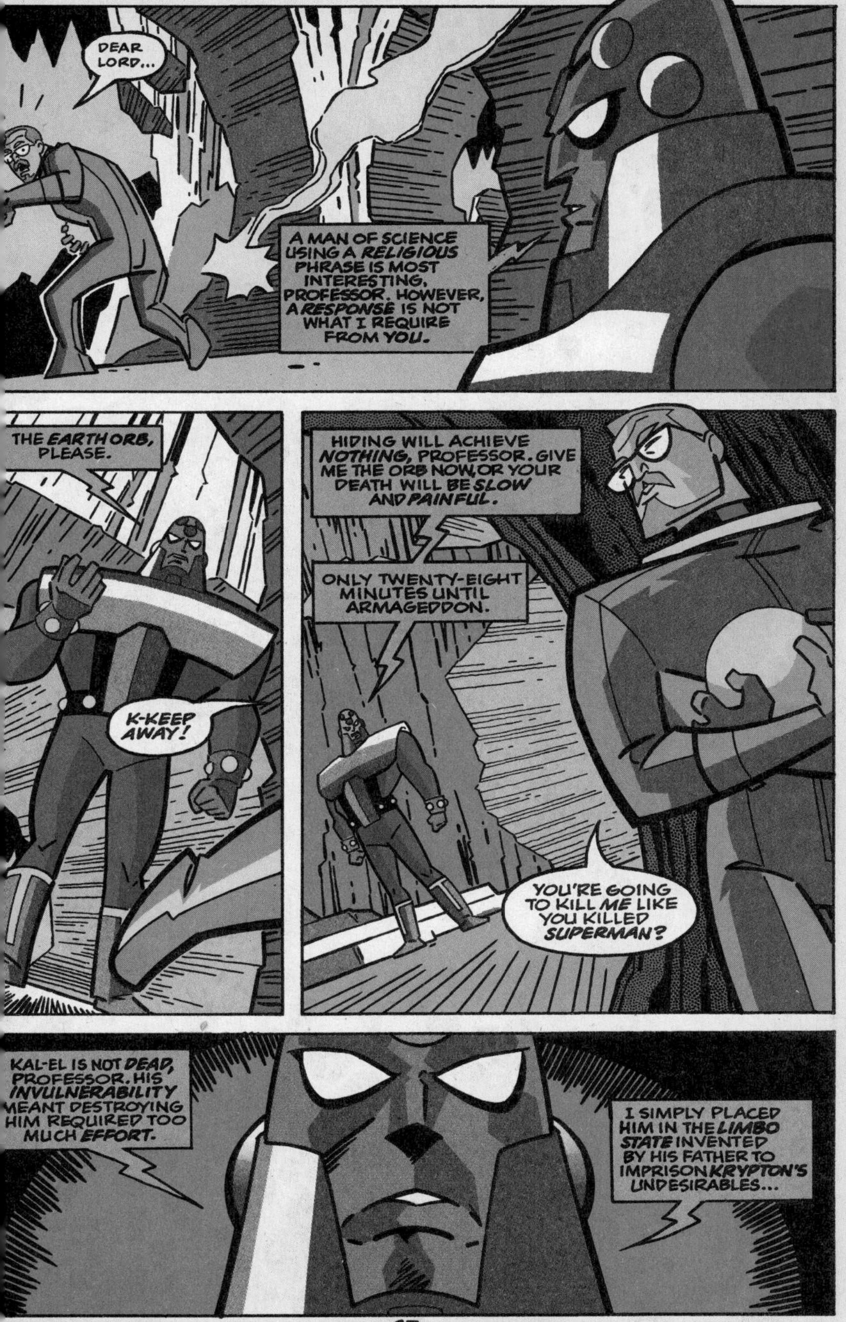
DEAR LORD...
A MAN OF SCIENCE USING A RELIGIOUS PHRASE IS MOST INTERESTING, PROFESSOR. HOWEVER, A RESPONSE IS NOT WHAT I REQUIRE FROM YOU.
THE EARTH ORB, PLEASE.
K-KEEP AWAY!
HIDING WILL ACHIEVE NOTHING, PROFESSOR. GIVE ME THE ORB NOW, OR YOUR DEATH WILL BE SLOW AND PAINFUL.
ONLY TWENTY-EIGHT MINUTES UNTIL ARMAGEDDON.
YOU'RE GOING TO KILL ME LIKE YOU KILLED SUPERMAN?
KAL-EL IS NOT DEAD, PROFESSOR. HIS INVULNERABILITY MEANT DESTROYING HIM REQUIRED TOO MUCH EFFORT.
I SIMPLY PLACED HIM IN THE LIMBO STATE INVENTED BY HIS FATHER TO IMPRISON KRYPTON'S UNDESIRABLES...

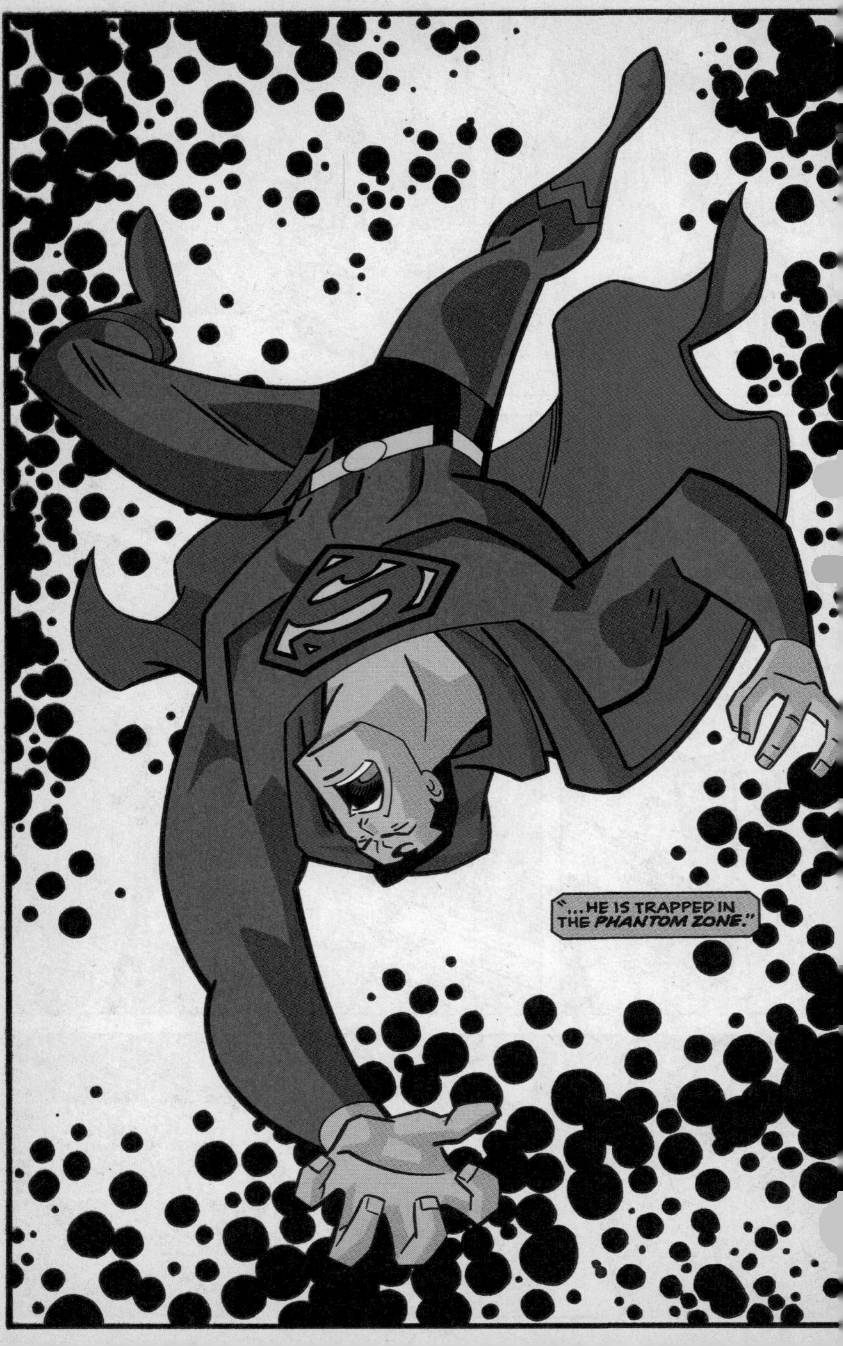
"...HE IS TRAPPED IN THE PHANTOM ZONE."

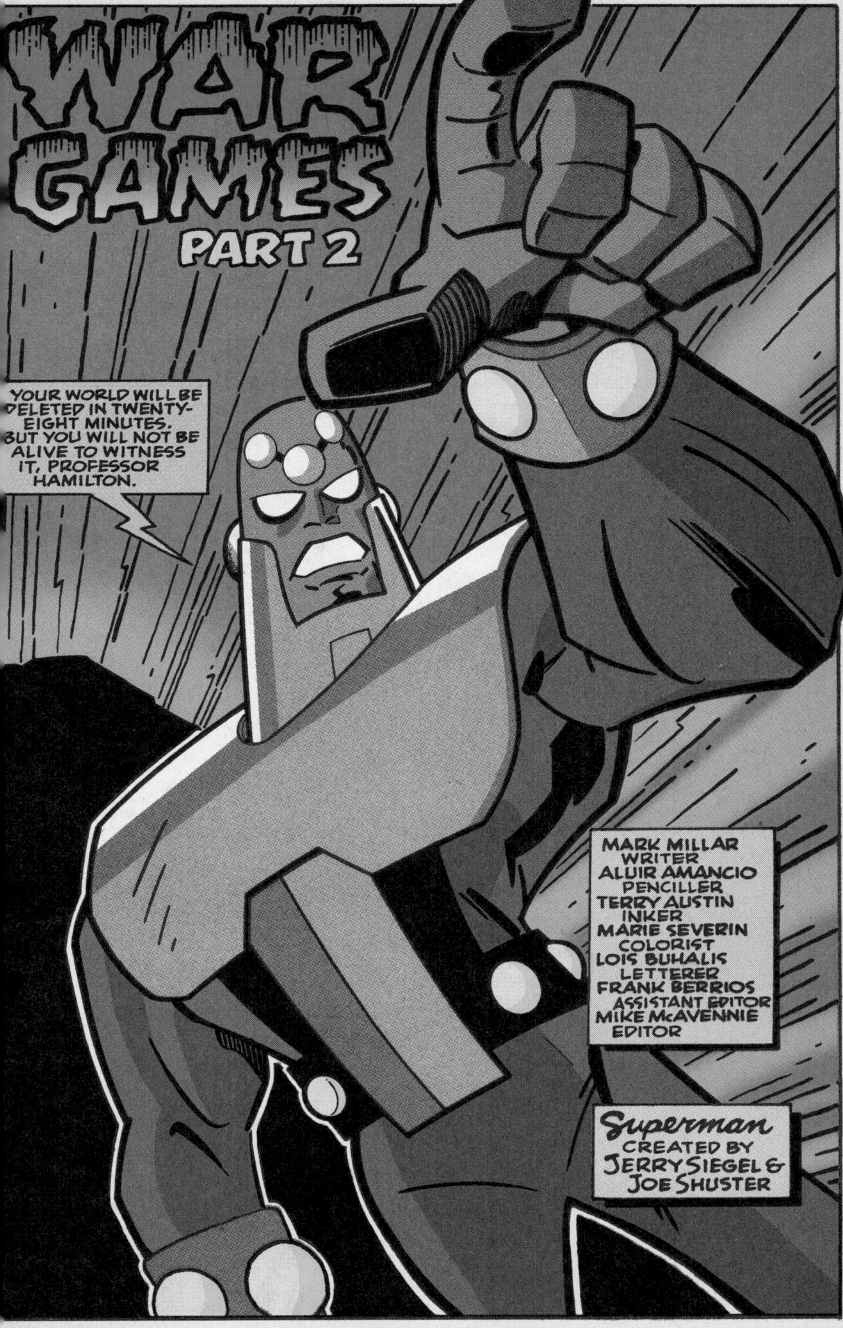
WAR GAMES
PART 2
YOUR WORLD WILL BE DELETED IN TWENTY-EIGHT MINUTES. BUT YOU WILL NOT BE ALIVE TO WITNESS IT, PROFESSOR HAMILTON.
MARK MILLAR WRITER
ALUIR AMANCIO PENCILLER
TERRY AUSTIN INKER
MARIE SEVERIN COLORIST
LOIS BUHALIS LETTERER
FRANK BERRIOS ASSISTANT EDITOR
MIKE McAVENNIE EDITOR
Superman CREATED BY JERRY SIEGEL & JOE SHUSTER

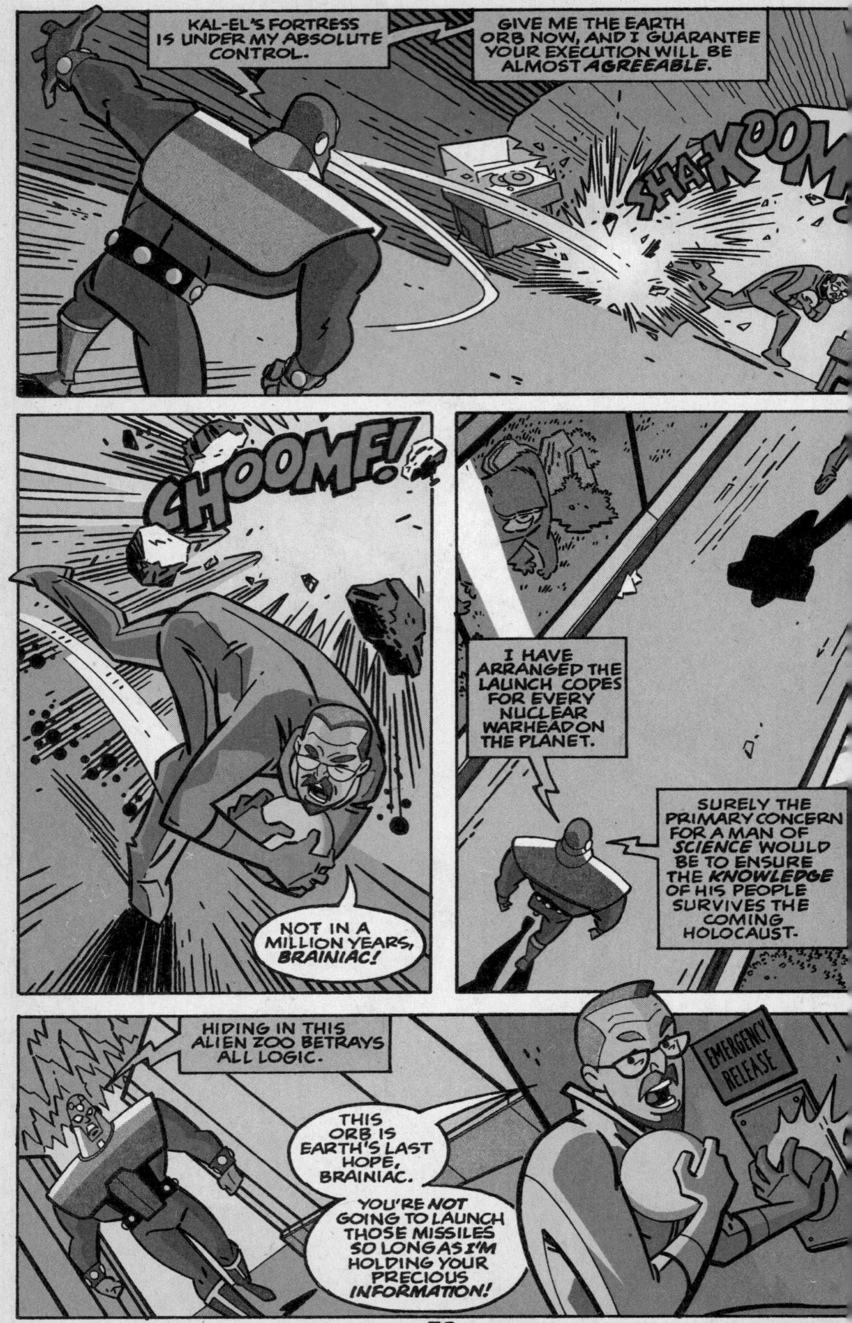
KAL-EL'S FORTRESS IS UNDER MY ABSOLUTE CONTROL.
GIVE ME THE EARTH ORB NOW, AND I GUARANTEE YOUR EXECUTION WILL BE ALMOST *AGREEABLE*.
SHA-KOOOM!
CHOOMF!
NOT IN A MILLION YEARS, *BRAINIAC!*
I HAVE ARRANGED THE LAUNCH CODES FOR EVERY NUCLEAR WARHEAD ON THE PLANET.
SURELY THE PRIMARY CONCERN FOR A MAN OF *SCIENCE* WOULD BE TO ENSURE THE *KNOWLEDGE* OF HIS PEOPLE SURVIVES THE COMING HOLOCAUST.
HIDING IN THIS ALIEN ZOO BETRAYS ALL LOGIC.
EMERGENCY RELEASE
THIS ORB IS EARTH'S LAST HOPE, BRAINIAC.
YOU'RE *NOT* GOING TO LAUNCH THOSE MISSILES SO LONG AS *I'M* HOLDING YOUR PRECIOUS *INFORMATION!*

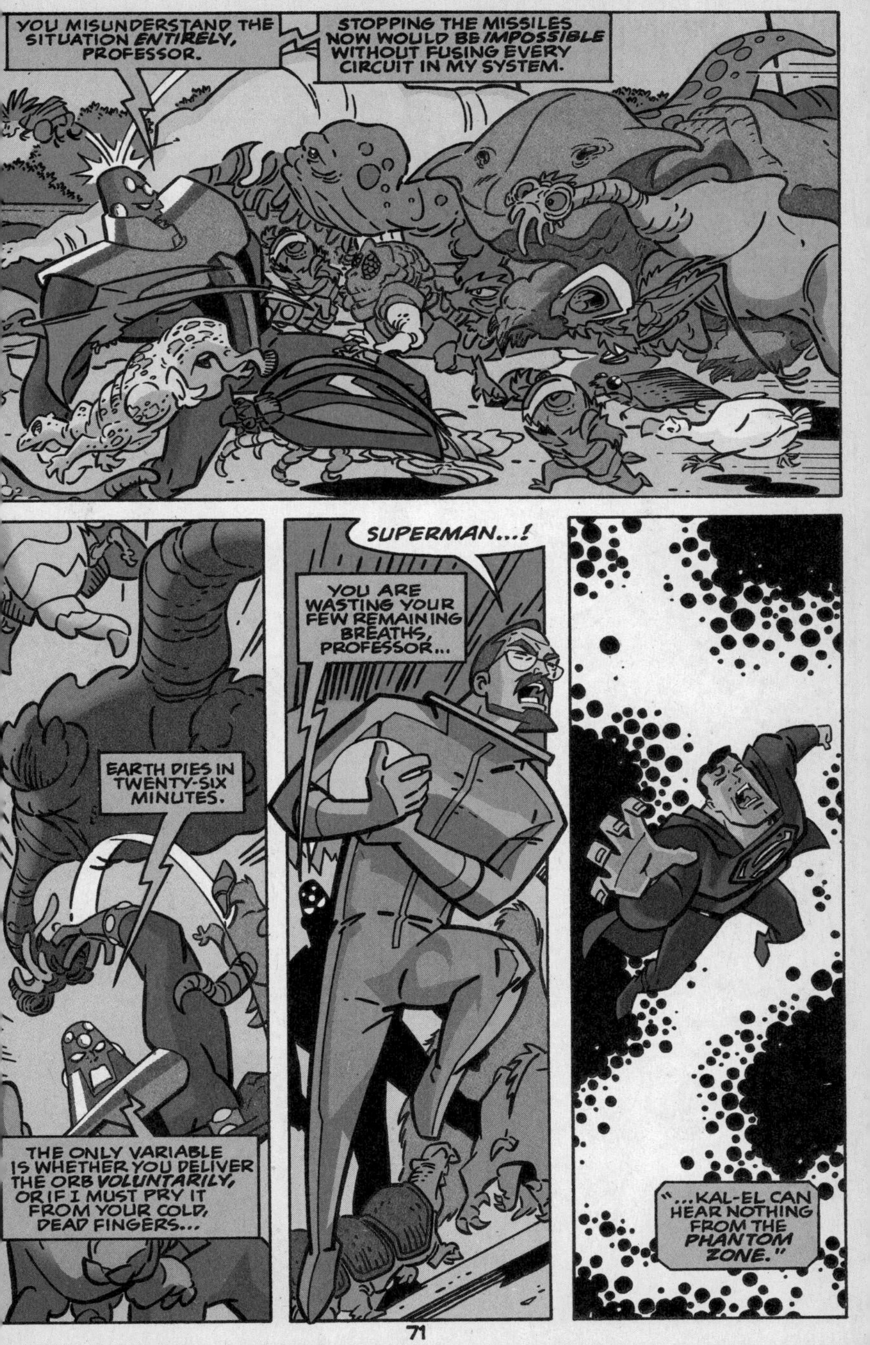
YOU MISUNDERSTAND THE SITUATION *ENTIRELY*, PROFESSOR.
STOPPING THE MISSILES NOW WOULD BE *IMPOSSIBLE* WITHOUT FUSING EVERY CIRCUIT IN MY SYSTEM.
EARTH DIES IN TWENTY-SIX MINUTES.
THE ONLY VARIABLE IS WHETHER YOU DELIVER THE ORB *VOLUNTARILY*, OR IF I MUST PRY IT FROM YOUR COLD, DEAD FINGERS...
SUPERMAN...!
YOU ARE WASTING YOUR FEW REMAINING BREATHS, PROFESSOR...
"...KAL-EL CAN HEAR NOTHING FROM THE *PHANTOM ZONE*."

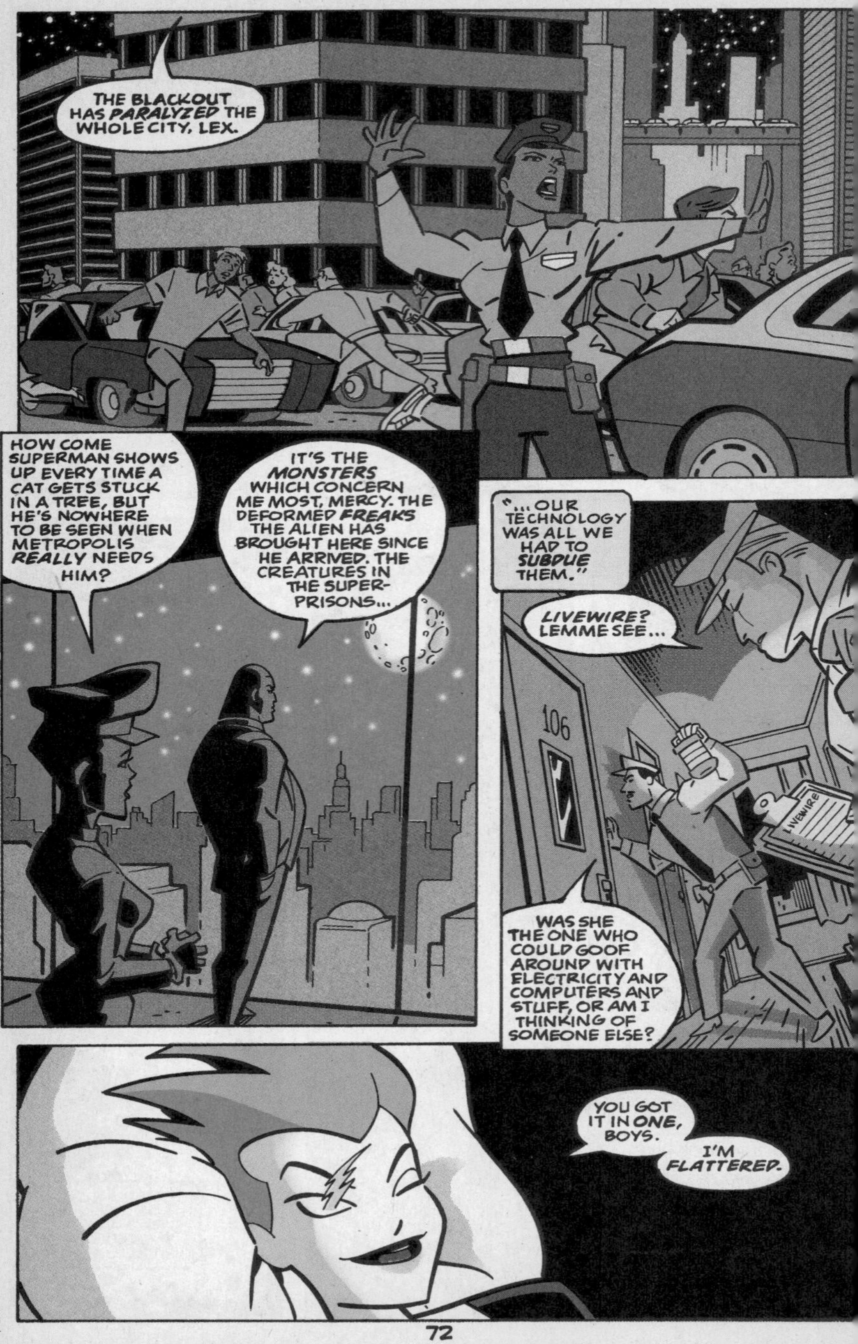

THE BLACKOUT HAS PARALYZED THE WHOLE CITY, LEX.
HOW COME SUPERMAN SHOWS UP EVERY TIME A CAT GETS STUCK IN A TREE, BUT HE'S NOWHERE TO BE SEEN WHEN METROPOLIS REALLY NEEDS HIM?
IT'S THE MONSTERS WHICH CONCERN ME MOST, MERCY. THE DEFORMED FREAKS THE ALIEN HAS BROUGHT HERE SINCE HE ARRIVED. THE CREATURES IN THE SUPER-PRISONS...
"...OUR TECHNOLOGY WAS ALL WE HAD TO SUBDUE THEM."
LIVEWIRE? LEMME SEE...
106
LIVEWIRE
WAS SHE THE ONE WHO COULD GOOF AROUND WITH ELECTRICITY AND COMPUTERS AND STUFF, OR AM I THINKING OF SOMEONE ELSE?
YOU GOT IT IN ONE, BOYS.
I'M FLATTERED.

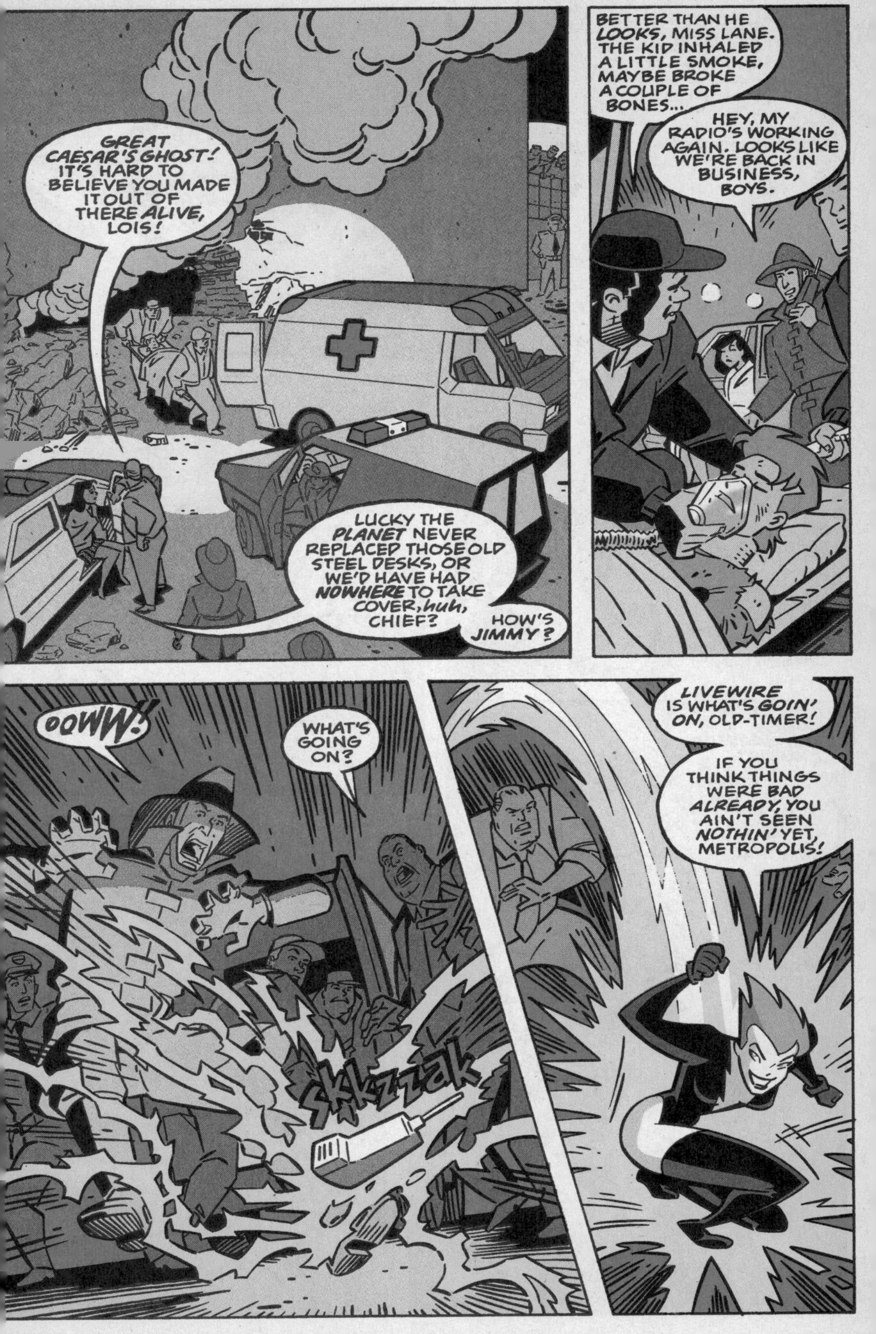
GREAT CAESAR'S GHOST! IT'S HARD TO BELIEVE YOU MADE IT OUT OF THERE ALIVE, LOIS!
LUCKY THE PLANET NEVER REPLACED THOSE OLD STEEL DESKS, OR WE'D HAVE HAD NOWHERE TO TAKE COVER, huh, CHIEF?
HOW'S JIMMY?
BETTER THAN HE LOOKS, MISS LANE. THE KID INHALED A LITTLE SMOKE, MAYBE BROKE A COUPLE OF BONES...
HEY, MY RADIO'S WORKING AGAIN. LOOKS LIKE WE'RE BACK IN BUSINESS, BOYS.
OOWW!
WHAT'S GOING ON?
SKKZZZAK
LIVEWIRE IS WHAT'S GOIN' ON, OLD-TIMER!
IF YOU THINK THINGS WERE BAD ALREADY, YOU AIN'T SEEN NOTHIN' YET, METROPOLIS!

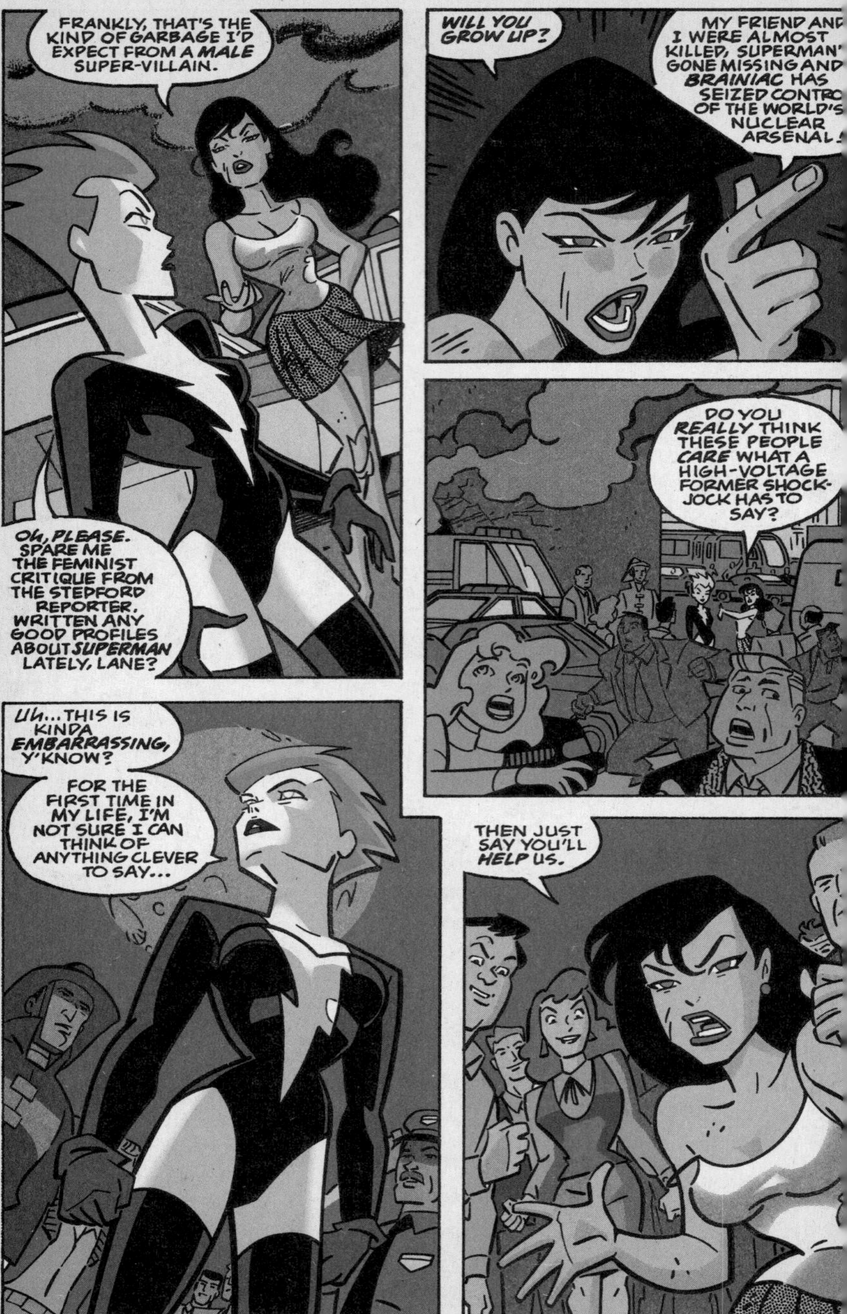
FRANKLY, THAT'S THE KIND OF GARBAGE I'D EXPECT FROM A MALE SUPER-VILLAIN.
OH, PLEASE. SPARE ME THE FEMINIST CRITIQUE FROM THE STEPFORD REPORTER. WRITTEN ANY GOOD PROFILES ABOUT SUPERMAN LATELY, LANE?
WILL YOU GROW UP?
MY FRIEND AND I WERE ALMOST KILLED, SUPERMAN'S GONE MISSING AND BRAINIAC HAS SEIZED CONTROL OF THE WORLD'S NUCLEAR ARSENAL!
DO YOU REALLY THINK THESE PEOPLE CARE WHAT A HIGH-VOLTAGE FORMER SHOCK-JOCK HAS TO SAY?
UH... THIS IS KINDA EMBARRASSING, Y'KNOW?
FOR THE FIRST TIME IN MY LIFE, I'M NOT SURE I CAN THINK OF ANYTHING CLEVER TO SAY...
THEN JUST SAY YOU'LL HELP US.

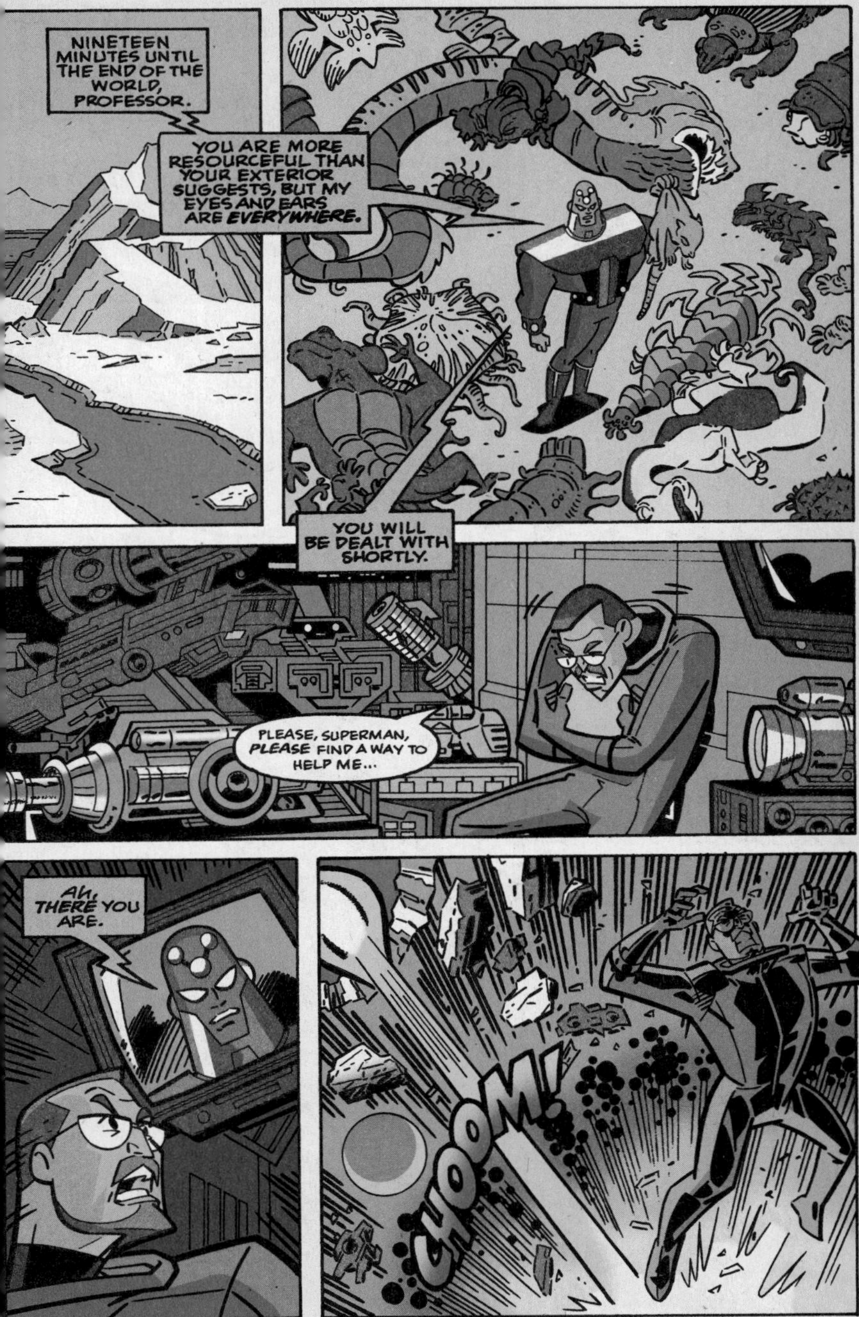
NINETEEN MINUTES UNTIL THE END OF THE WORLD, PROFESSOR.
YOU ARE MORE RESOURCEFUL THAN YOUR EXTERIOR SUGGESTS, BUT MY EYES AND EARS ARE *EVERYWHERE.*
YOU WILL BE DEALT WITH SHORTLY.
PLEASE, SUPERMAN, *PLEASE* FIND A WAY TO HELP ME...
AH, THERE YOU ARE.
CHOOOM!

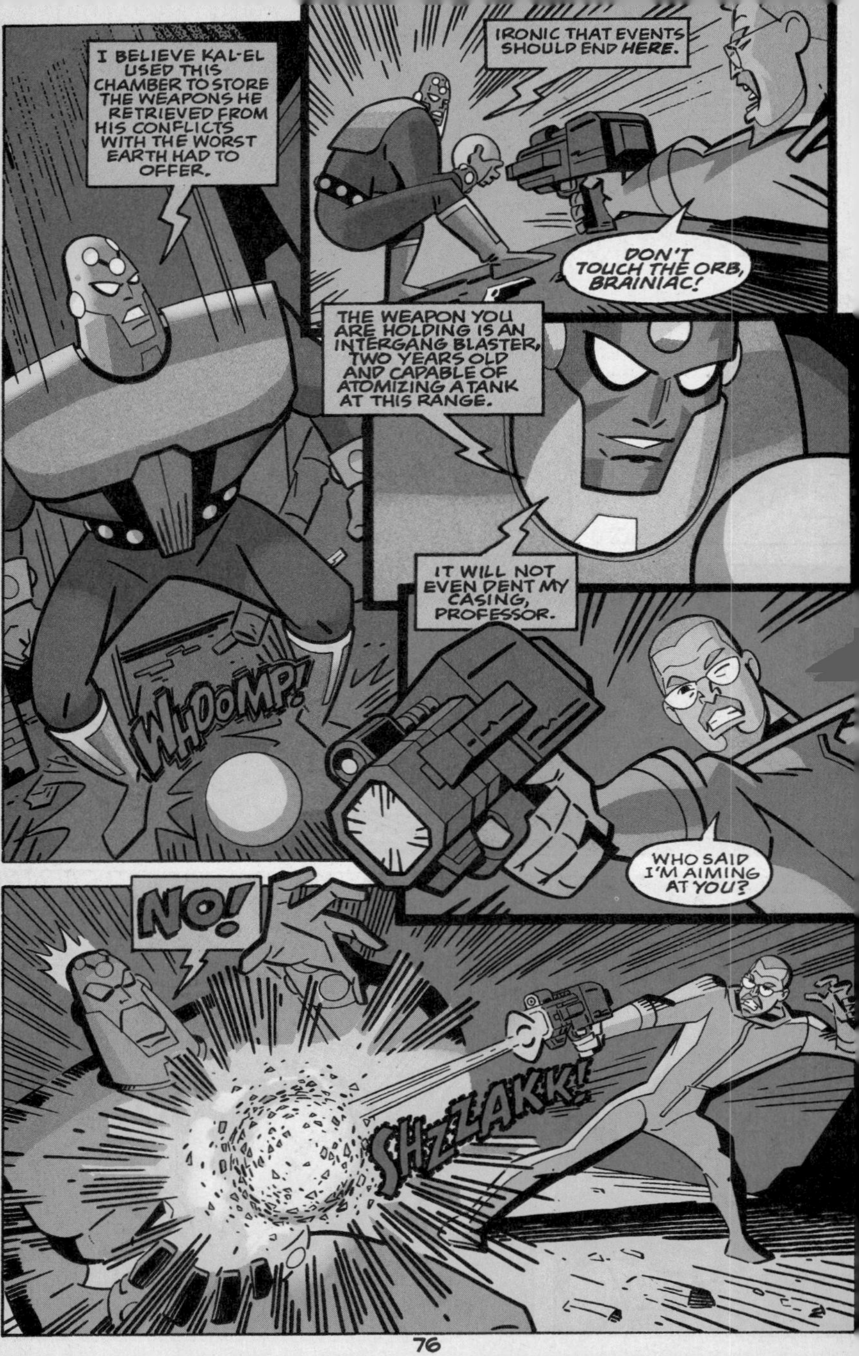
I BELIEVE KAL-EL USED THIS CHAMBER TO STORE THE WEAPONS HE RETRIEVED FROM HIS CONFLICTS WITH THE WORST EARTH HAD TO OFFER.
WHOOMP!
IRONIC THAT EVENTS SHOULD END HERE.
DON'T TOUCH THE ORB, BRAINIAC!
THE WEAPON YOU ARE HOLDING IS AN INTERGANG BLASTER, TWO YEARS OLD AND CAPABLE OF ATOMIZING A TANK AT THIS RANGE.
IT WILL NOT EVEN DENT MY CASING, PROFESSOR.
WHO SAID I'M AIMING AT YOU?
NO!
SHZZAKK!

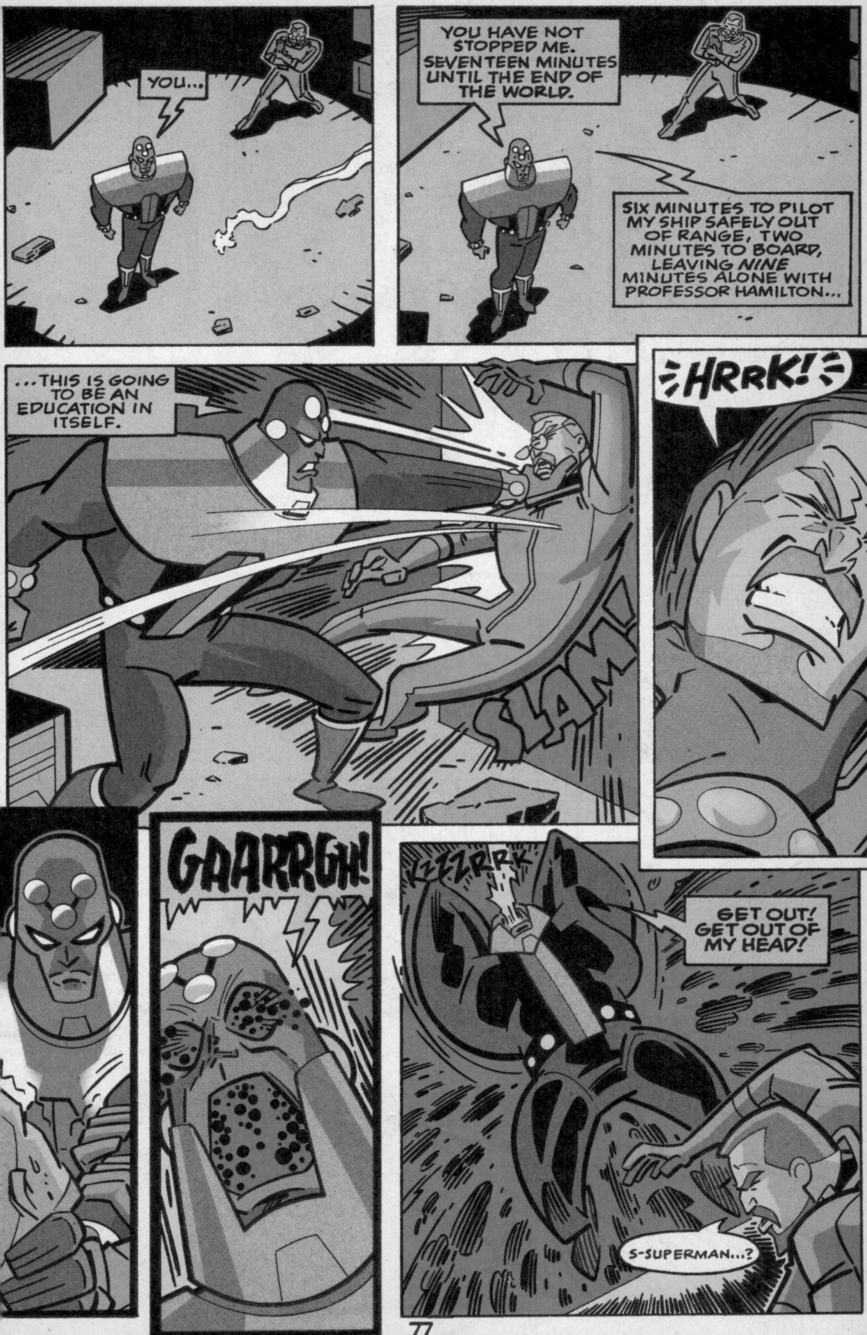
YOU...
YOU HAVE NOT STOPPED ME. SEVENTEEN MINUTES UNTIL THE END OF THE WORLD.
SIX MINUTES TO PILOT MY SHIP SAFELY OUT OF RANGE, TWO MINUTES TO BOARD, LEAVING NINE MINUTES ALONE WITH PROFESSOR HAMILTON...
...THIS IS GOING TO BE AN EDUCATION IN ITSELF.
SLAM!
HRRK!
GAARRGH!
KZZZRRK
GET OUT! GET OUT OF MY HEAD!
S-SUPERMAN...?

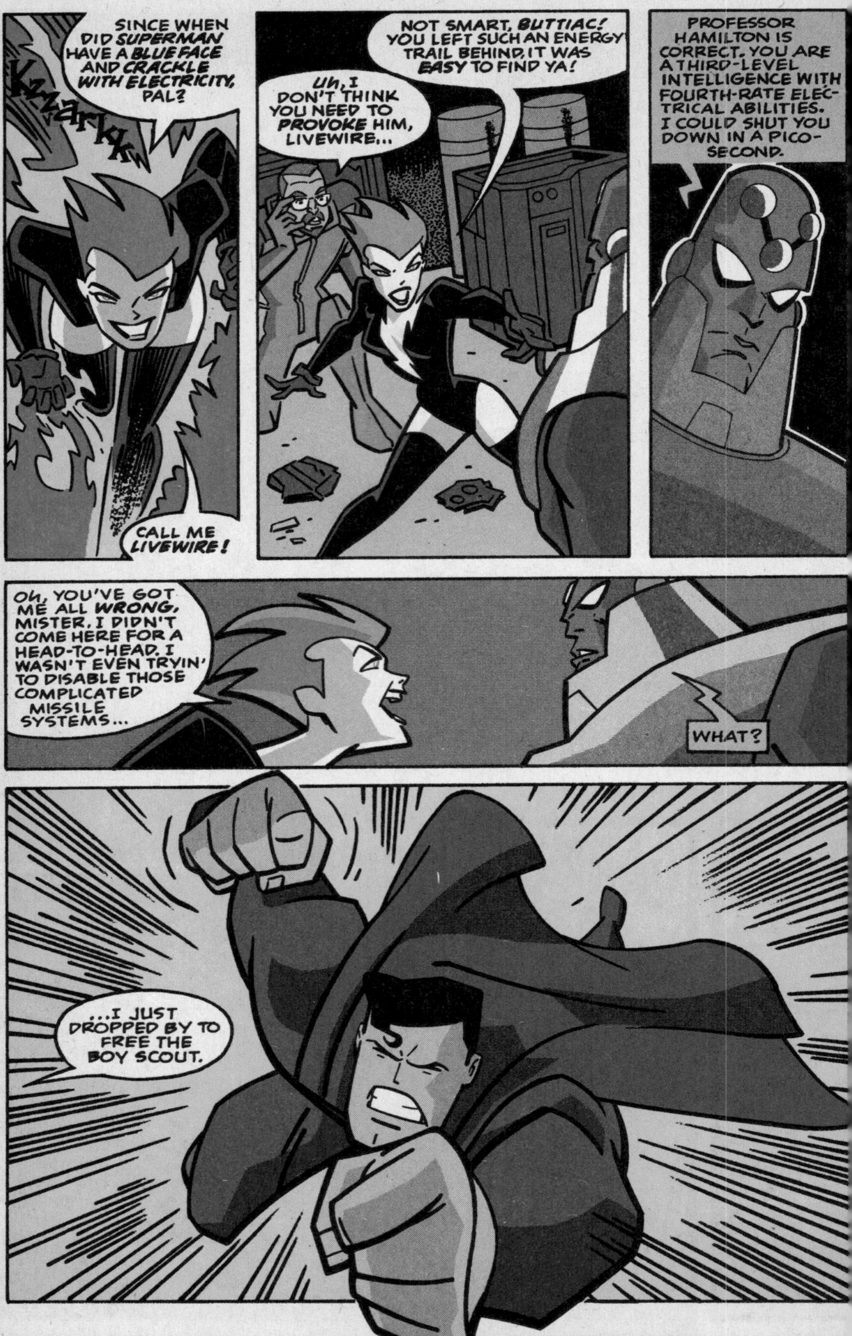
SINCE WHEN DID SUPERMAN HAVE A BLUE FACE AND CRACKLE WITH ELECTRICITY, PAL?
KzzarKK
CALL ME LIVEWIRE!
NOT SMART, BUTTIAC! YOU LEFT SUCH AN ENERGY TRAIL BEHIND, IT WAS EASY TO FIND YA!
Uh, I DON'T THINK YOU NEED TO PROVOKE HIM, LIVEWIRE...
PROFESSOR HAMILTON IS CORRECT. YOU ARE A THIRD-LEVEL INTELLIGENCE WITH FOURTH-RATE ELECTRICAL ABILITIES. I COULD SHUT YOU DOWN IN A PICO-SECOND.
Oh, YOU'VE GOT ME ALL WRONG, MISTER. I DIDN'T COME HERE FOR A HEAD-TO-HEAD. I WASN'T EVEN TRYIN' TO DISABLE THOSE COMPLICATED MISSILE SYSTEMS...
WHAT?
...I JUST DROPPED BY TO FREE THE BOY SCOUT.

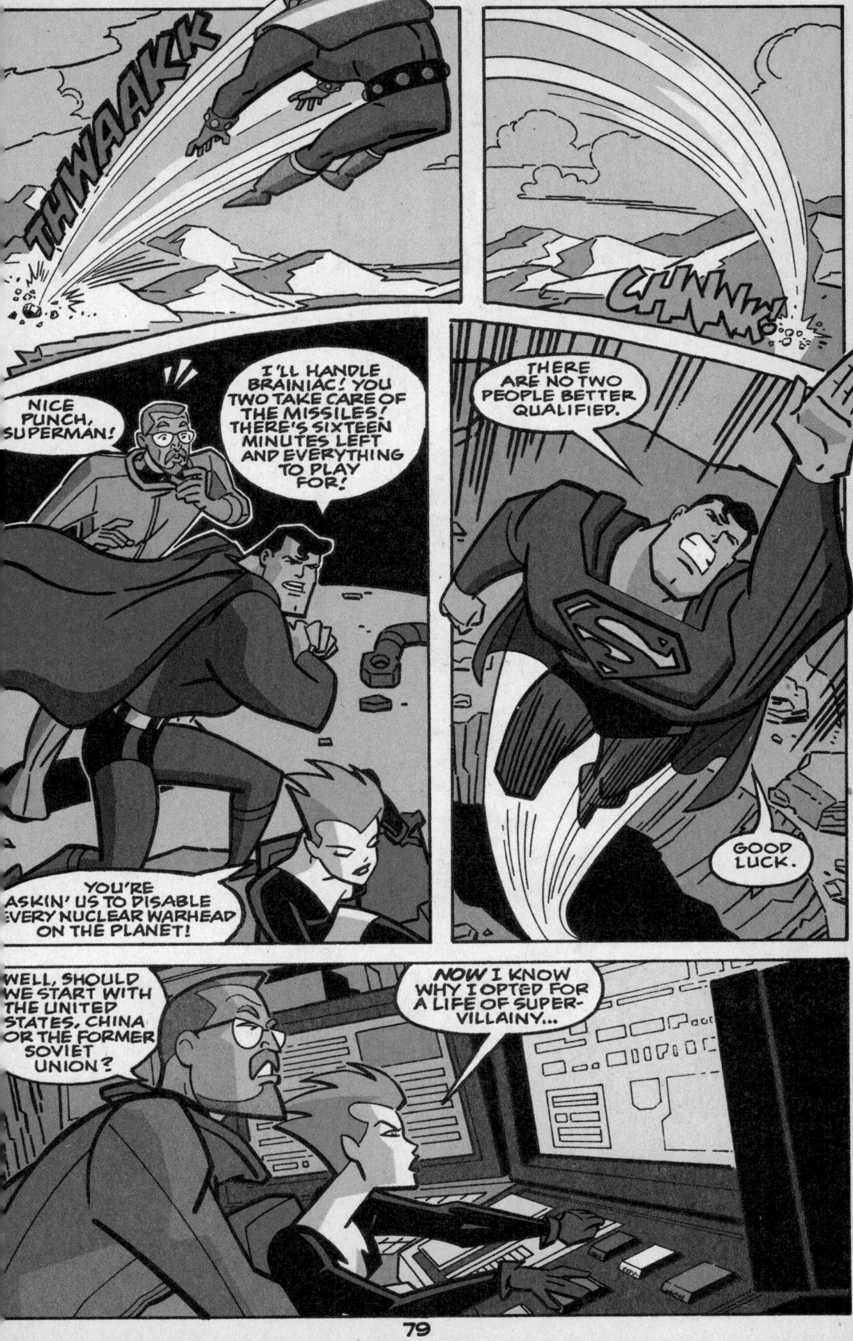
THWAAKK
CHNNK!
NICE PUNCH, SUPERMAN!
I'LL HANDLE BRAINIAC! YOU TWO TAKE CARE OF THE MISSILES! THERE'S SIXTEEN MINUTES LEFT AND EVERYTHING TO PLAY FOR!
YOU'RE ASKIN' US TO DISABLE EVERY NUCLEAR WARHEAD ON THE PLANET!
THERE ARE NO TWO PEOPLE BETTER QUALIFIED.
GOOD LUCK.
WELL, SHOULD WE START WITH THE UNITED STATES, CHINA OR THE FORMER SOVIET UNION?
NOW I KNOW WHY I OPTED FOR A LIFE OF SUPER-VILLAINY...

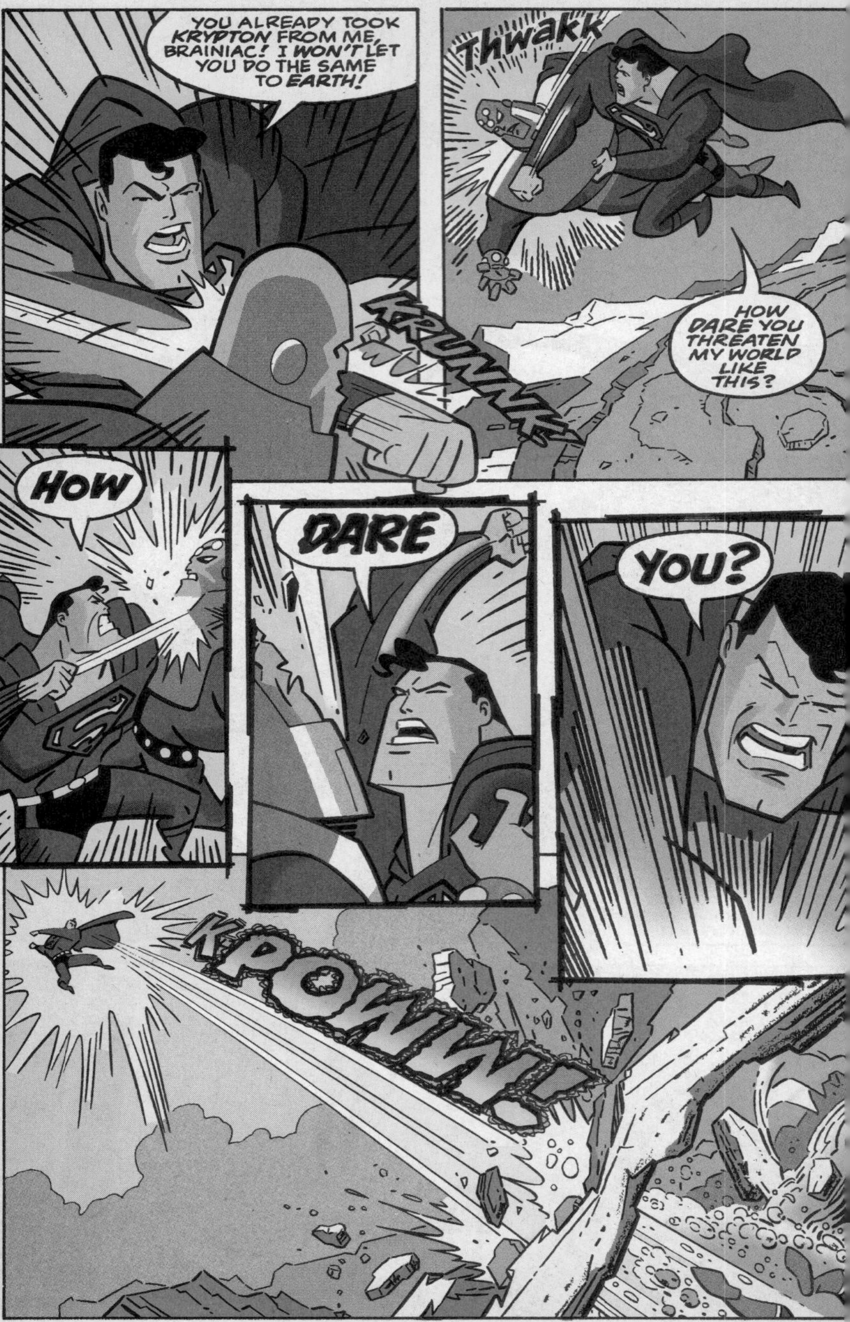
YOU ALREADY TOOK KRYPTON FROM ME, BRAINIAC! I WON'T LET YOU DO THE SAME TO EARTH!
KRUNNK
Thwakk
HOW DARE YOU THREATEN MY WORLD LIKE THIS?
HOW
DARE
YOU?
K-POWW!

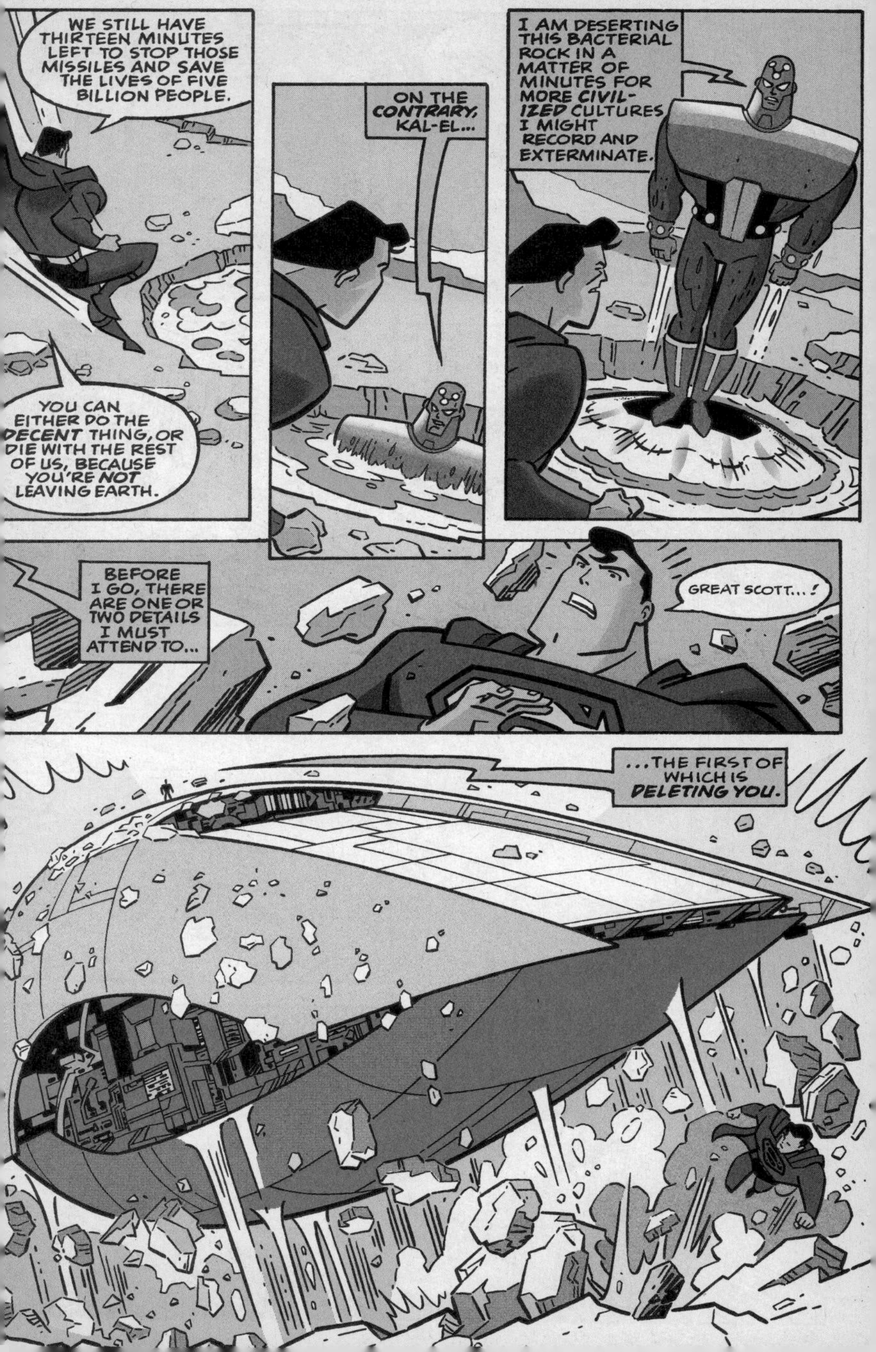

WE STILL HAVE THIRTEEN MINUTES LEFT TO STOP THOSE MISSILES AND SAVE THE LIVES OF FIVE BILLION PEOPLE.
YOU CAN EITHER DO THE DECENT THING, OR DIE WITH THE REST OF US, BECAUSE YOU'RE NOT LEAVING EARTH.
ON THE CONTRARY, KAL-EL...
I AM DESERTING THIS BACTERIAL ROCK IN A MATTER OF MINUTES FOR MORE CIVILIZED CULTURES I MIGHT RECORD AND EXTERMINATE.
BEFORE I GO, THERE ARE ONE OR TWO DETAILS I MUST ATTEND TO...
GREAT SCOTT...!
...THE FIRST OF WHICH IS DELETING YOU.

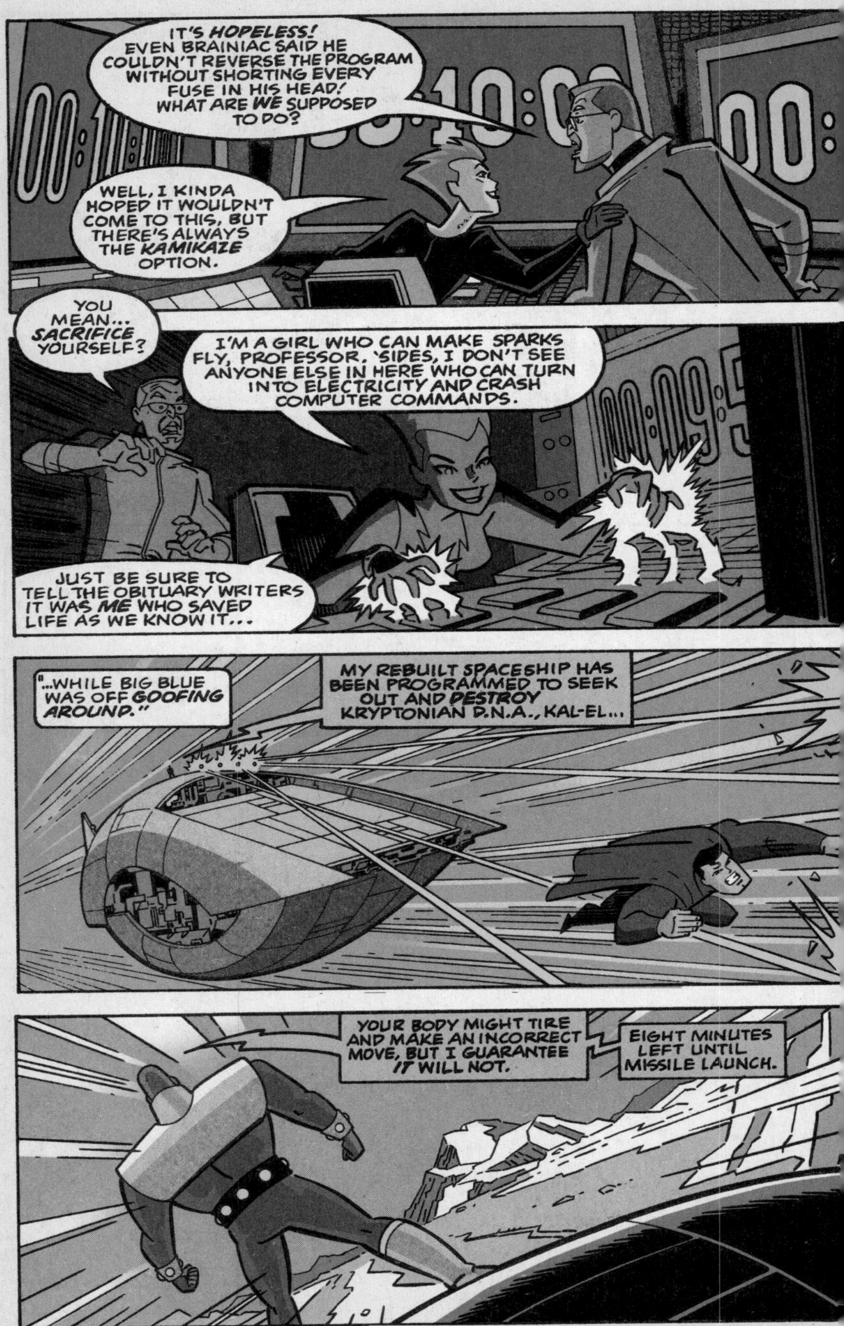
IT'S HOPELESS! EVEN BRAINIAC SAID HE COULDN'T REVERSE THE PROGRAM WITHOUT SHORTING EVERY FUSE IN HIS HEAD! WHAT ARE WE SUPPOSED TO DO?
WELL, I KINDA HOPED IT WOULDN'T COME TO THIS, BUT THERE'S ALWAYS THE KAMIKAZE OPTION.
YOU MEAN... SACRIFICE YOURSELF?
I'M A GIRL WHO CAN MAKE SPARKS FLY, PROFESSOR. 'SIDES, I DON'T SEE ANYONE ELSE IN HERE WHO CAN TURN INTO ELECTRICITY AND CRASH COMPUTER COMMANDS.
JUST BE SURE TO TELL THE OBITUARY WRITERS IT WAS ME WHO SAVED LIFE AS WE KNOW IT...
"...WHILE BIG BLUE WAS OFF GOOFING AROUND."
MY REBUILT SPACESHIP HAS BEEN PROGRAMMED TO SEEK OUT AND DESTROY KRYPTONIAN D.N.A., KAL-EL...
YOUR BODY MIGHT TIRE AND MAKE AN INCORRECT MOVE, BUT I GUARANTEE IT WILL NOT.
EIGHT MINUTES LEFT UNTIL MISSILE LAUNCH.

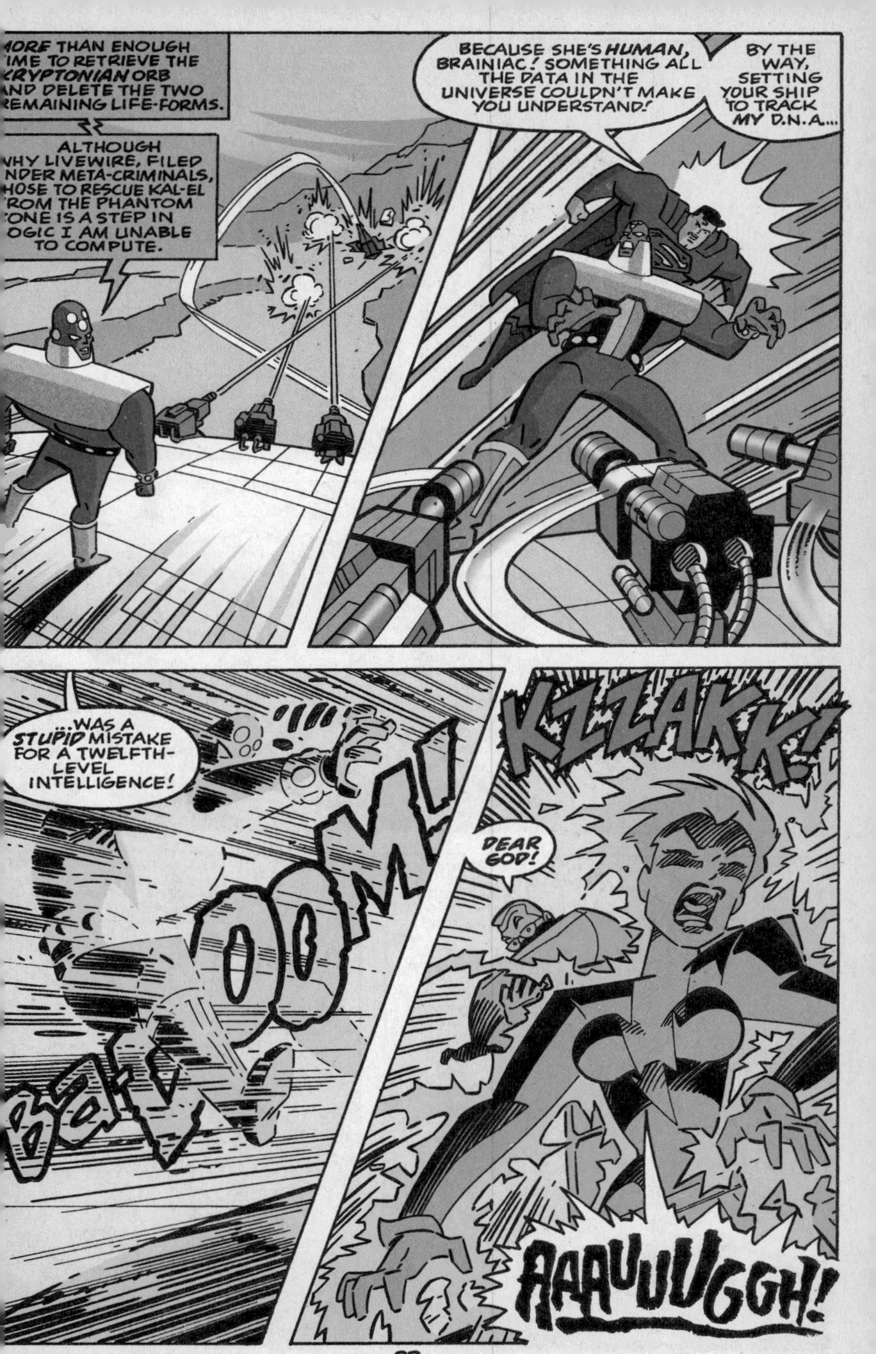
MORE THAN ENOUGH TIME TO RETRIEVE THE KRYPTONIAN ORB AND DELETE THE TWO REMAINING LIFE-FORMS.
ALTHOUGH WHY LIVEWIRE, FILED UNDER META-CRIMINALS, CHOSE TO RESCUE KAL-EL FROM THE PHANTOM ZONE IS A STEP IN LOGIC I AM UNABLE TO COMPUTE.
BECAUSE SHE'S HUMAN, BRAINIAC! SOMETHING ALL THE DATA IN THE UNIVERSE COULDN'T MAKE YOU UNDERSTAND!
BY THE WAY, SETTING YOUR SHIP TO TRACK MY D.N.A...
...WAS A STUPID MISTAKE FOR A TWELFTH-LEVEL INTELLIGENCE!
BOOM!
KZZAKK!
DEAR GOD!
AAAUUUGGH!

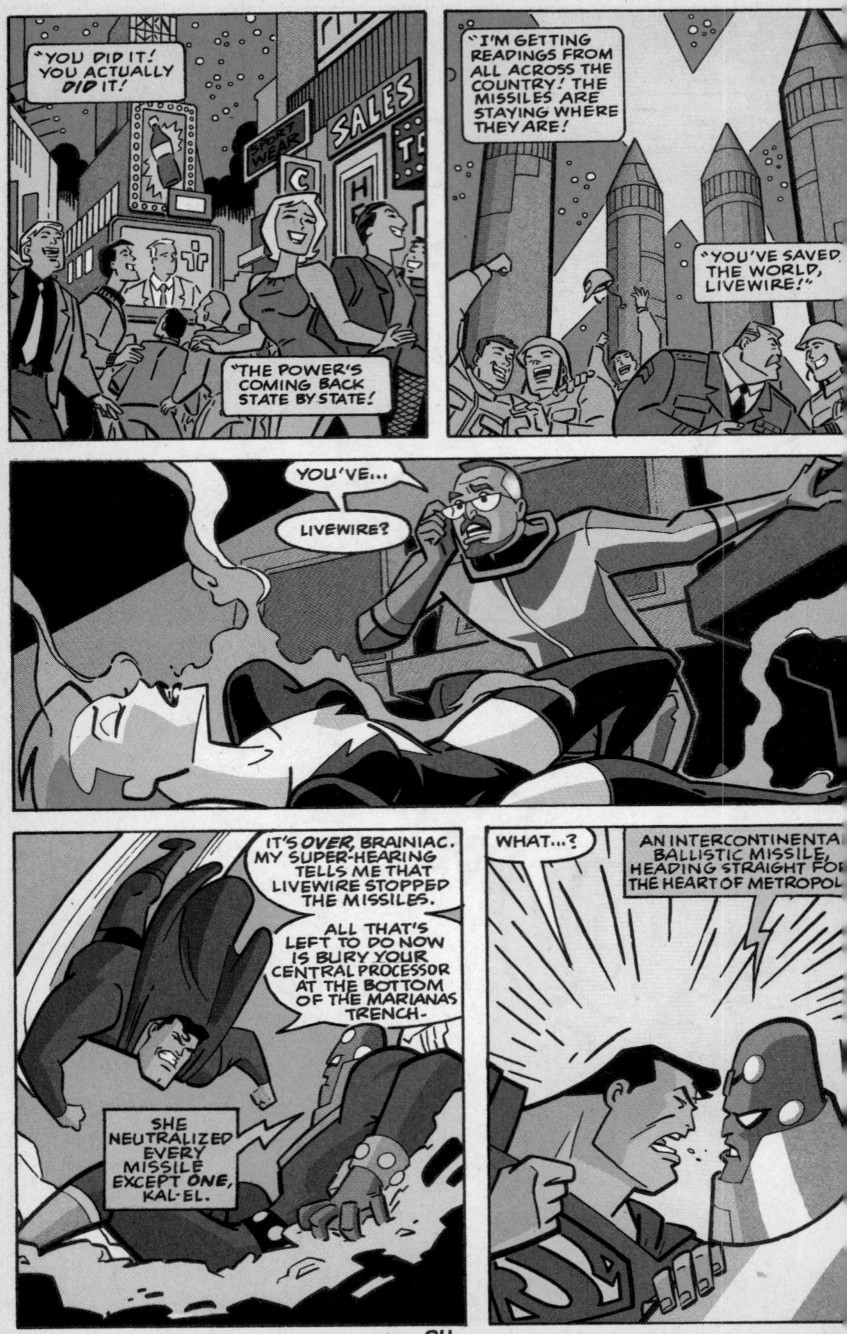
"YOU DID IT! YOU ACTUALLY DID IT!
SPORT WEAR
SALES
"THE POWER'S COMING BACK STATE BY STATE!
"I'M GETTING READINGS FROM ALL ACROSS THE COUNTRY! THE MISSILES ARE STAYING WHERE THEY ARE!
"YOU'VE SAVED THE WORLD, LIVEWIRE!"
YOU'VE...
LIVEWIRE?
IT'S OVER, BRAINIAC. MY SUPER-HEARING TELLS ME THAT LIVEWIRE STOPPED THE MISSILES.
ALL THAT'S LEFT TO DO NOW IS BURY YOUR CENTRAL PROCESSOR AT THE BOTTOM OF THE MARIANAS TRENCH-
SHE NEUTRALIZED EVERY MISSILE EXCEPT ONE, KAL-EL.
WHAT...?
AN INTERCONTINENTA BALLISTIC MISSILE, HEADING STRAIGHT FOR THE HEART OF METROPOL

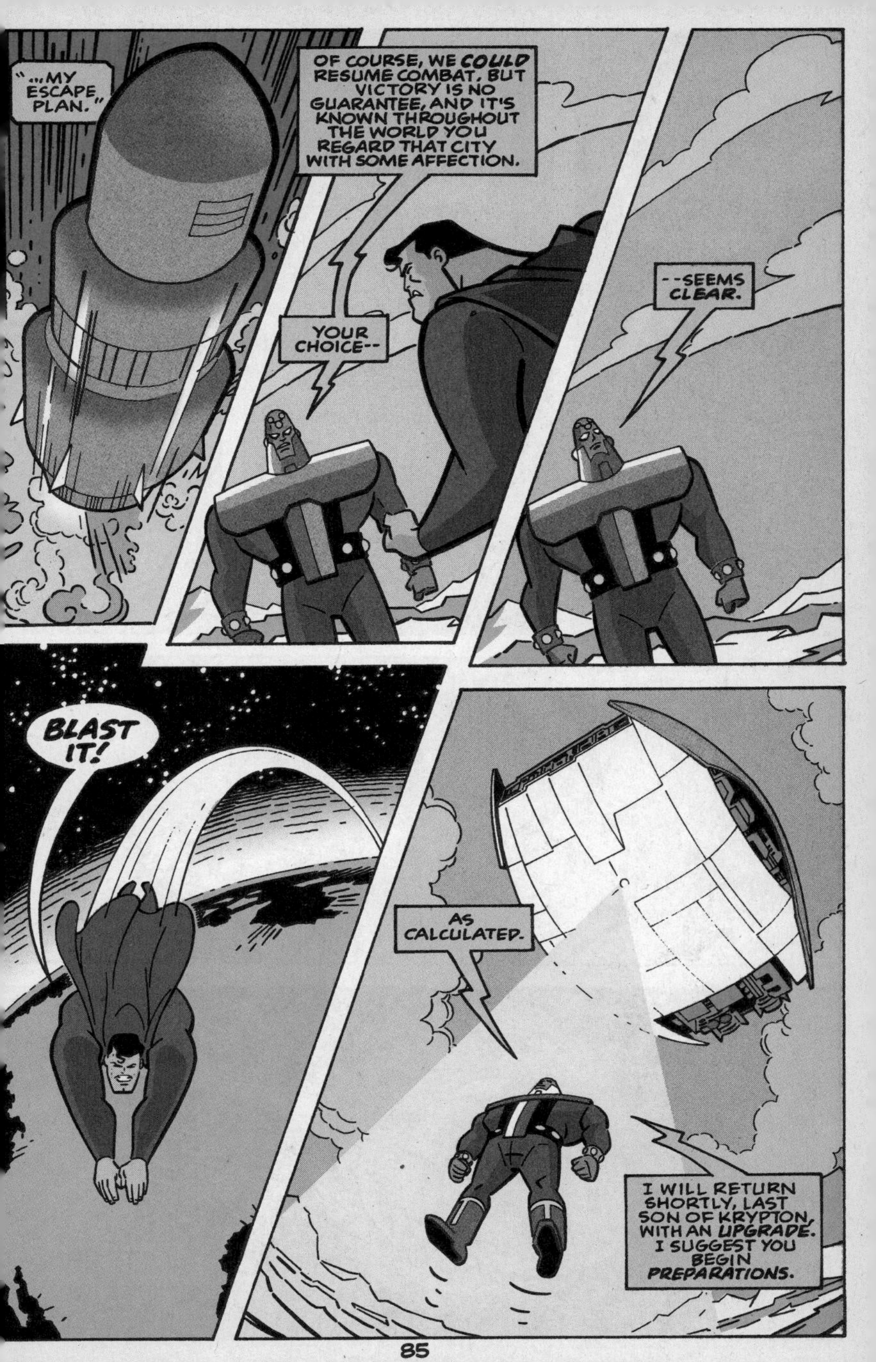
"...MY ESCAPE PLAN."
OF COURSE, WE COULD RESUME COMBAT, BUT VICTORY IS NO GUARANTEE, AND IT'S KNOWN THROUGHOUT THE WORLD YOU REGARD THAT CITY WITH SOME AFFECTION.
YOUR CHOICE--
--SEEMS CLEAR.
BLAST IT!
AS CALCULATED.
I WILL RETURN SHORTLY, LAST SON OF KRYPTON, WITH AN UPGRADE. I SUGGEST YOU BEGIN PREPARATIONS.

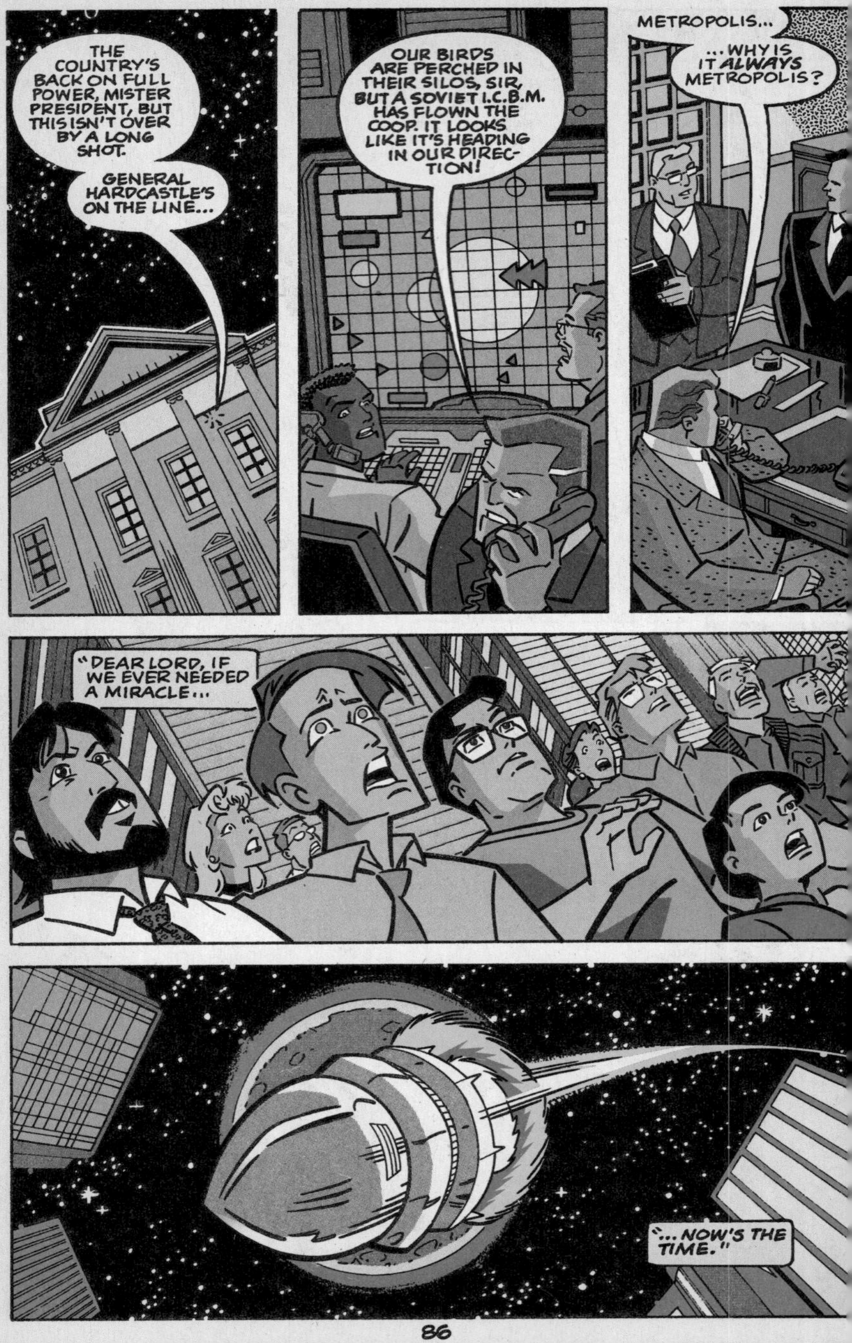
THE COUNTRY'S BACK ON FULL POWER, MISTER PRESIDENT, BUT THIS ISN'T OVER BY A LONG SHOT.
GENERAL HARDCASTLE'S ON THE LINE...
OUR BIRDS ARE PERCHED IN THEIR SILOS, SIR, BUT A SOVIET I.C.B.M. HAS FLOWN THE COOP. IT LOOKS LIKE IT'S HEADING IN OUR DIRECTION!
METROPOLIS...
...WHY IS IT ALWAYS METROPOLIS?
"DEAR LORD, IF WE EVER NEEDED A MIRACLE...
"...NOW'S THE TIME."

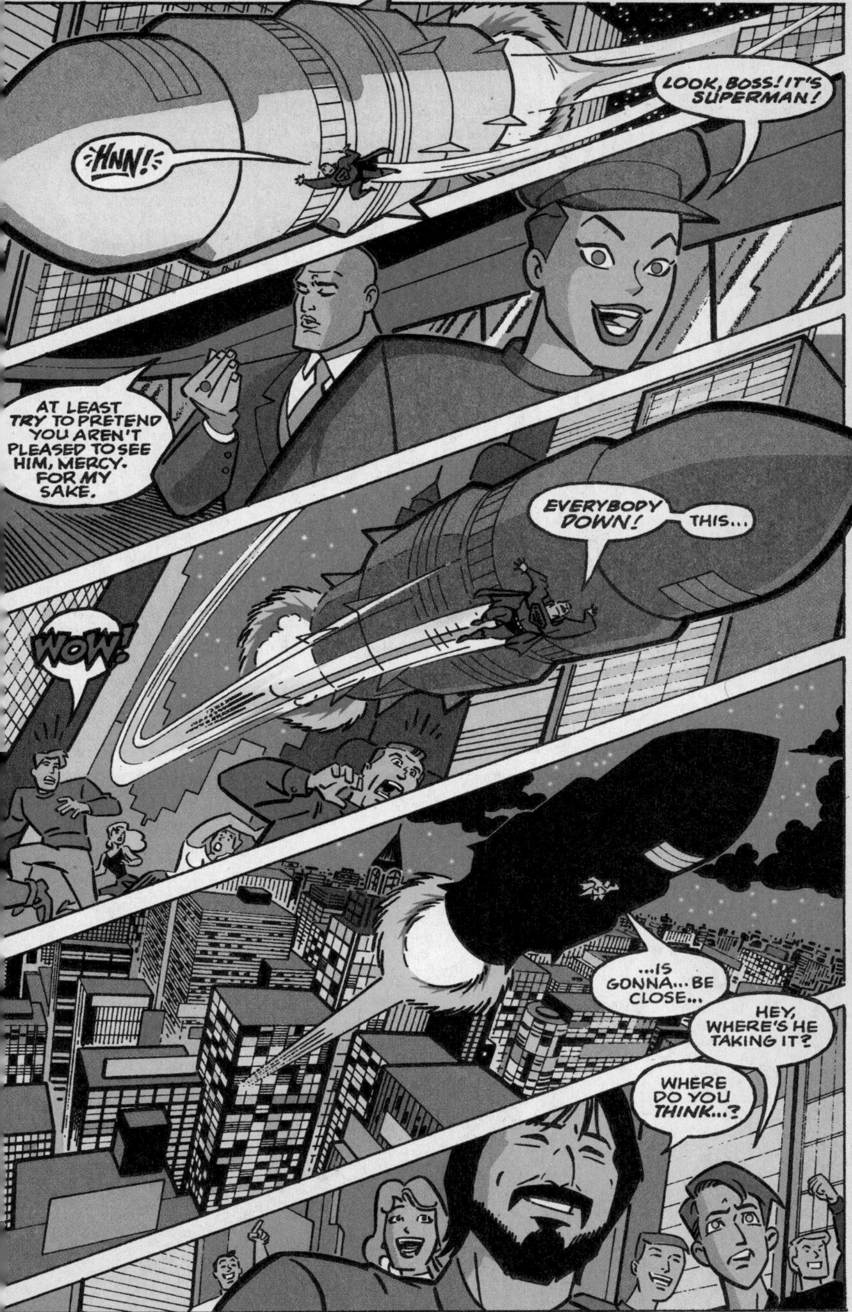
LOOK, BOSS! IT'S SUPERMAN!
HNN!
AT LEAST TRY TO PRETEND YOU AREN'T PLEASED TO SEE HIM, MERCY. FOR MY SAKE.
EVERYBODY DOWN!
THIS...
WOW!
...IS GONNA... BE CLOSE...
HEY, WHERE'S HE TAKING IT?
WHERE DO YOU THINK...?

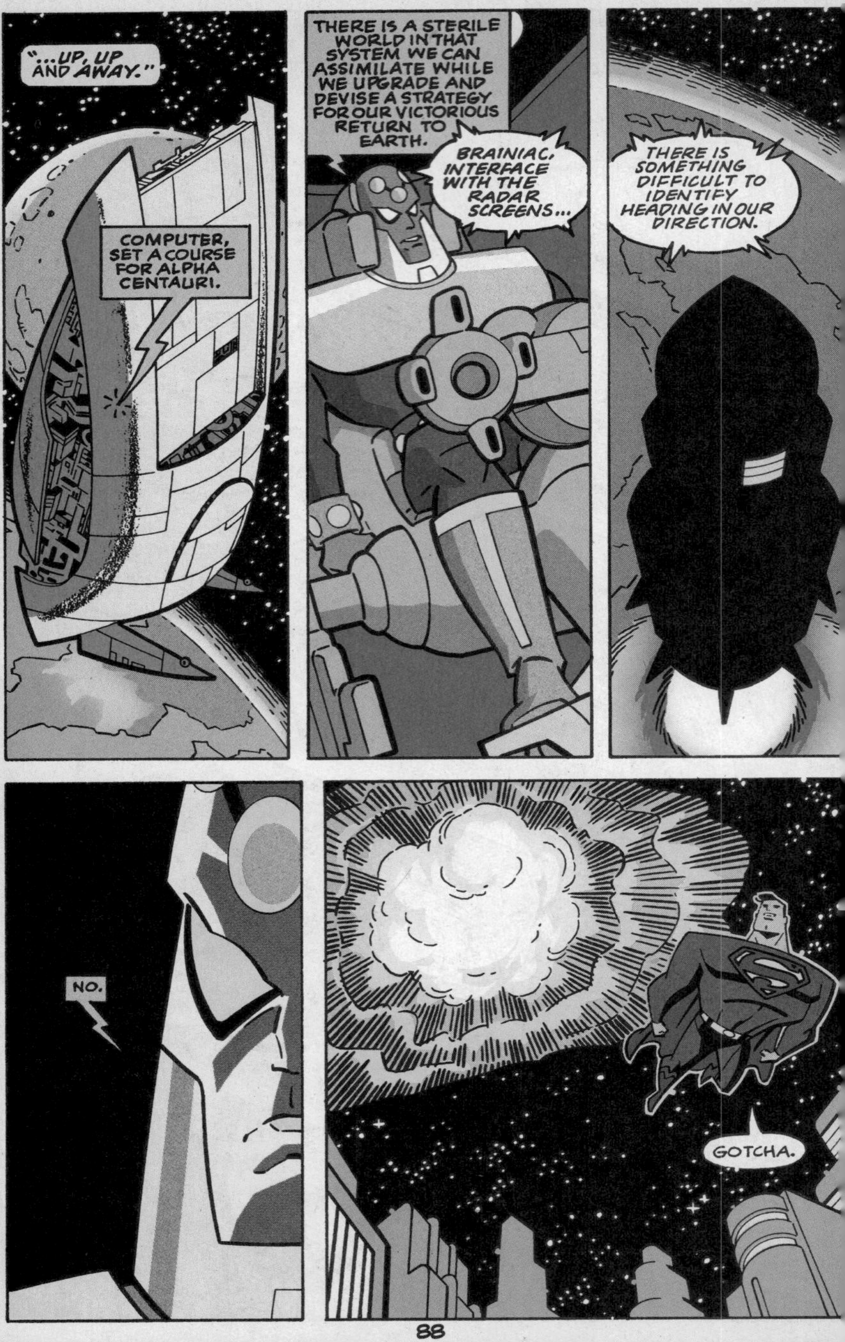
"...UP, UP AND AWAY."
COMPUTER, SET A COURSE FOR ALPHA CENTAURI.
THERE IS A STERILE WORLD IN THAT SYSTEM WE CAN ASSIMILATE WHILE WE UPGRADE AND DEVISE A STRATEGY FOR OUR VICTORIOUS RETURN TO EARTH.
BRAINIAC, INTERFACE WITH THE RADAR SCREENS...
THERE IS SOMETHING DIFFICULT TO IDENTIFY HEADING IN OUR DIRECTION.
NO.
GOTCHA.

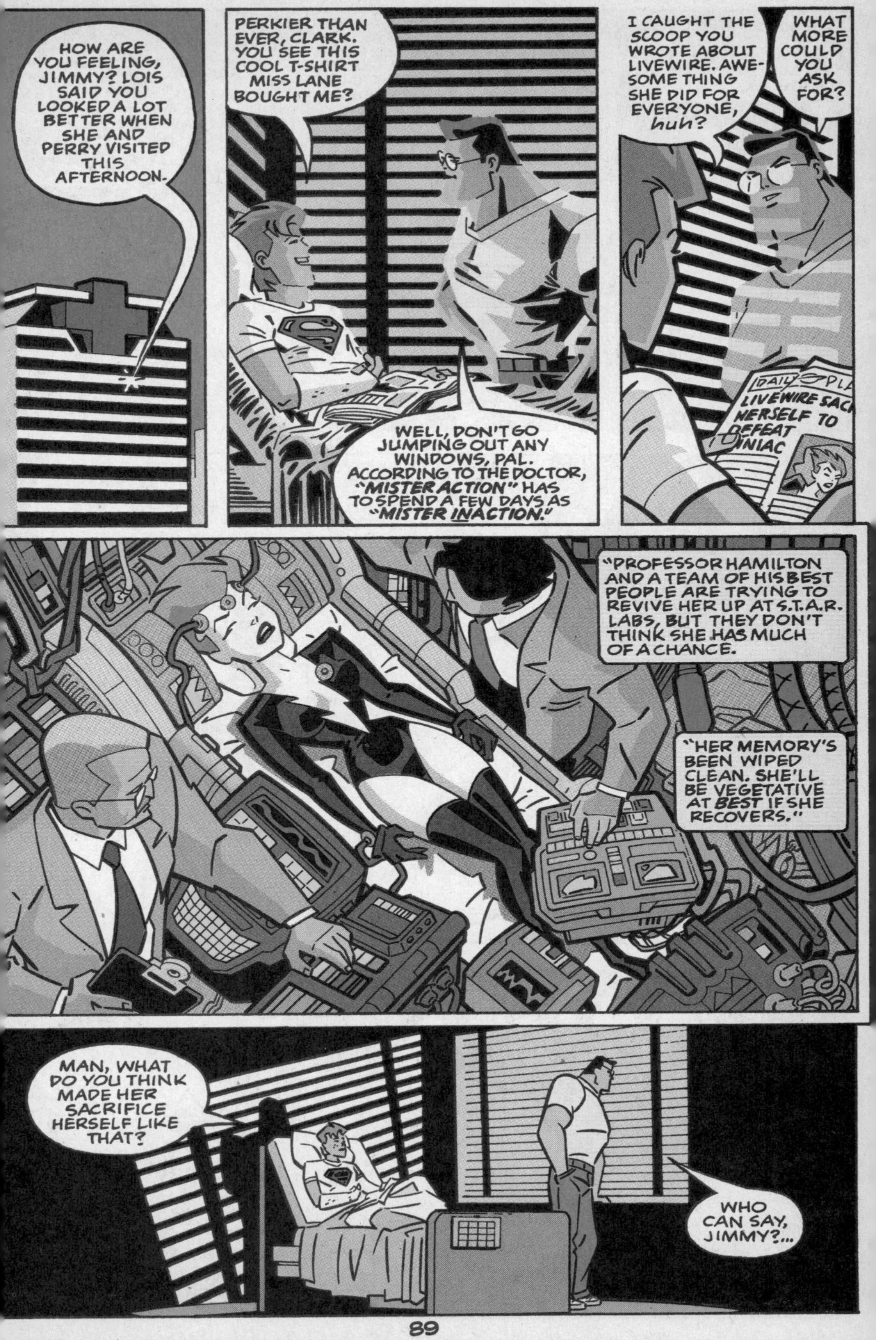
HOW ARE YOU FEELING, JIMMY? LOIS SAID YOU LOOKED A LOT BETTER WHEN SHE AND PERRY VISITED THIS AFTERNOON.
PERKIER THAN EVER, CLARK. YOU SEE THIS COOL T-SHIRT MISS LANE BOUGHT ME?
WELL, DON'T GO JUMPING OUT ANY WINDOWS, PAL. ACCORDING TO THE DOCTOR, "MISTER ACTION" HAS TO SPEND A FEW DAYS AS "MISTER INACTION."
I CAUGHT THE SCOOP YOU WROTE ABOUT LIVEWIRE. AWESOME THING SHE DID FOR EVERYONE, huh?
WHAT MORE COULD YOU ASK FOR?
"PROFESSOR HAMILTON AND A TEAM OF HIS BEST PEOPLE ARE TRYING TO REVIVE HER UP AT S.T.A.R. LABS, BUT THEY DON'T THINK SHE HAS MUCH OF A CHANCE.
"HER MEMORY'S BEEN WIPED CLEAN. SHE'LL BE VEGETATIVE AT BEST IF SHE RECOVERS."
MAN, WHAT DO YOU THINK MADE HER SACRIFICE HERSELF LIKE THAT?
WHO CAN SAY, JIMMY?...

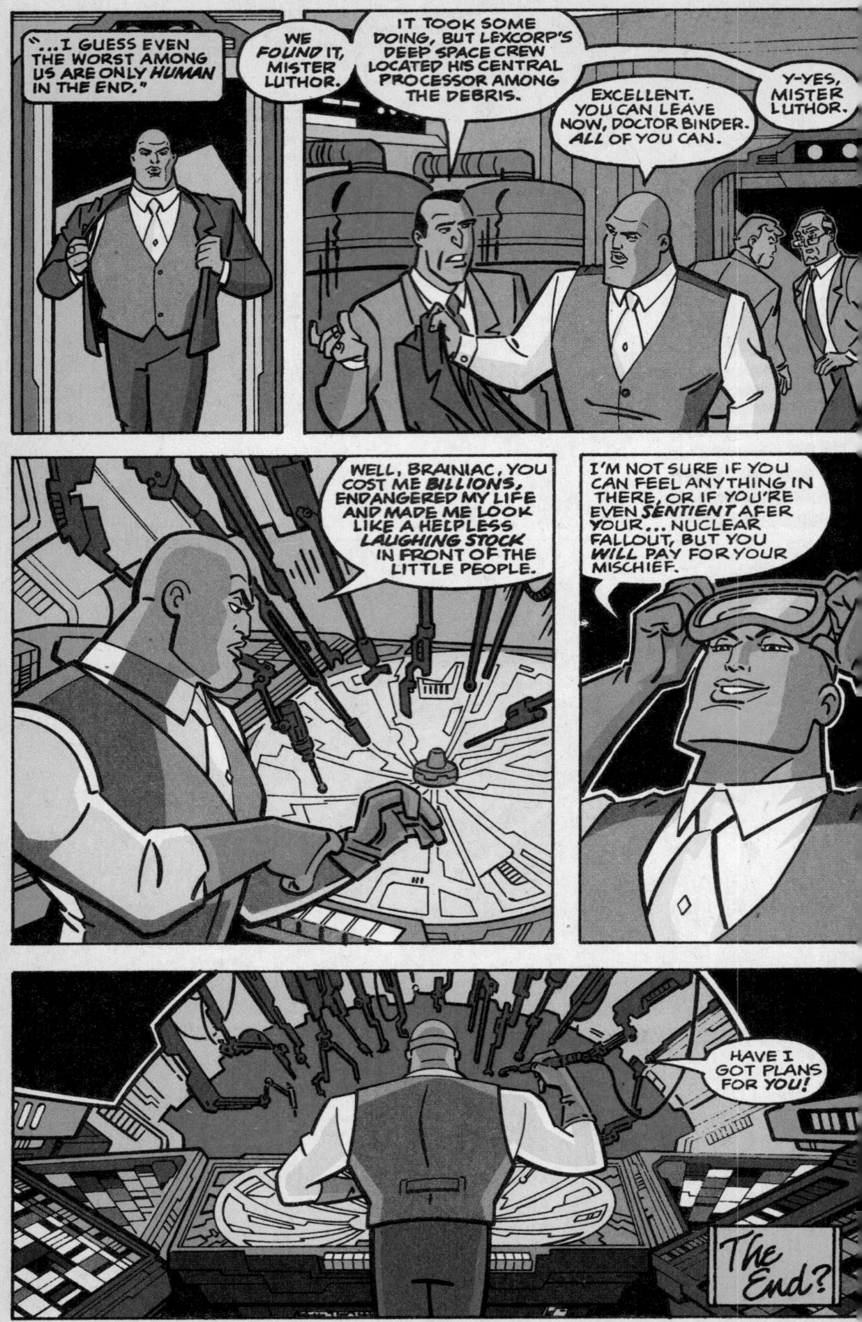
"...I GUESS EVEN THE WORST AMONG US ARE ONLY HUMAN IN THE END."
WE FOUND IT, MISTER LUTHOR.
IT TOOK SOME DOING, BUT LEXCORP'S DEEP SPACE CREW LOCATED HIS CENTRAL PROCESSOR AMONG THE DEBRIS.
EXCELLENT. YOU CAN LEAVE NOW, DOCTOR BINDER. ALL OF YOU CAN.
Y-YES, MISTER LUTHOR.
WELL, BRAINIAC, YOU COST ME BILLIONS, ENDANGERED MY LIFE AND MADE ME LOOK LIKE A HELPLESS LAUGHING STOCK IN FRONT OF THE LITTLE PEOPLE.
I'M NOT SURE IF YOU CAN FEEL ANYTHING IN THERE, OR IF YOU'RE EVEN SENTIENT AFER YOUR... NUCLEAR FALLOUT, BUT YOU WILL PAY FOR YOUR MISCHIEF.
HAVE I GOT PLANS FOR YOU!
The End?

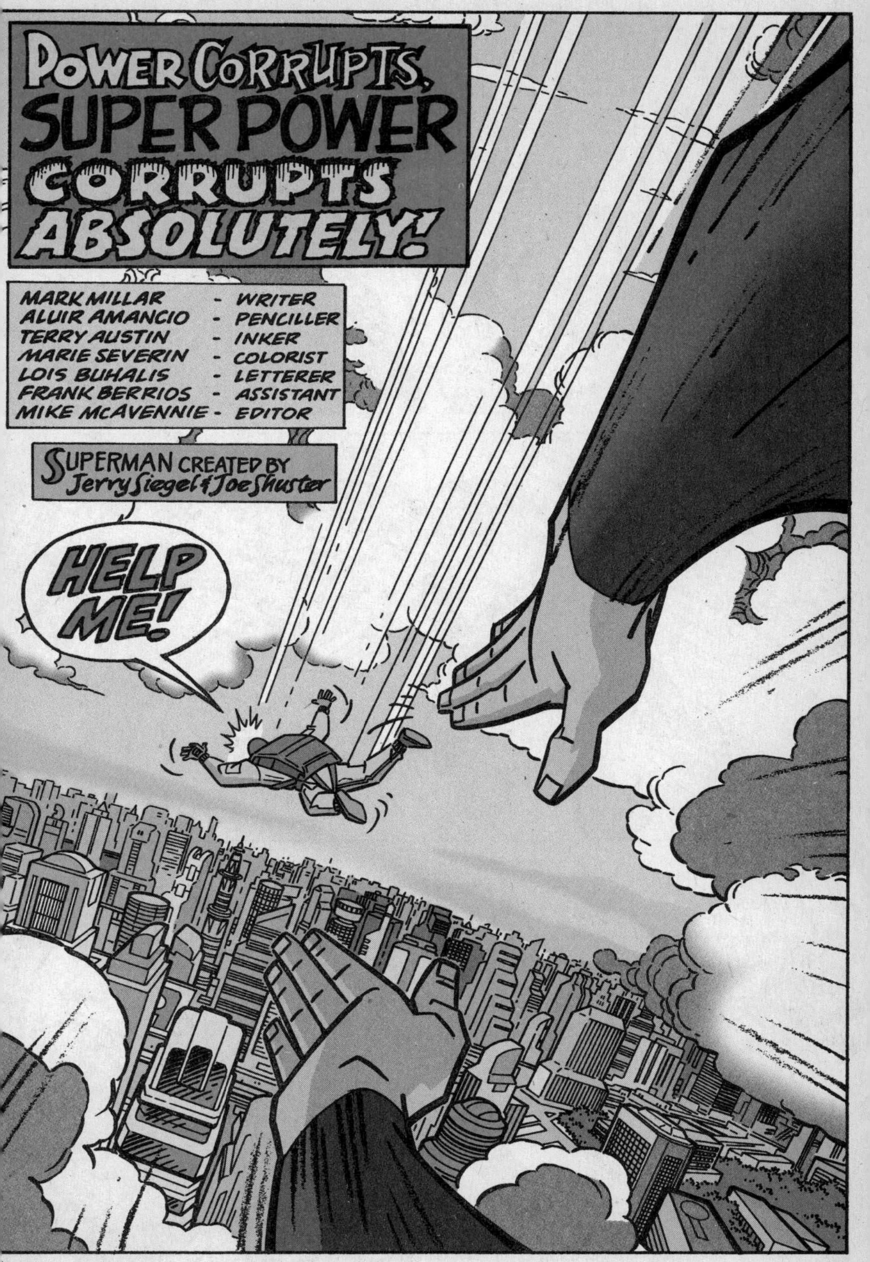
POWER CORRUPTS, SUPER POWER CORRUPTS ABSOLUTELY!
MARK MILLAR - WRITER
ALUIR AMANCIO - PENCILLER
TERRY AUSTIN - INKER
MARIE SEVERIN - COLORIST
LOIS BUHALIS - LETTERER
FRANK BERRIOS - ASSISTANT
MIKE McAVENNIE - EDITOR
SUPERMAN CREATED BY Jerry Siegel & Joe Shuster
HELP ME!

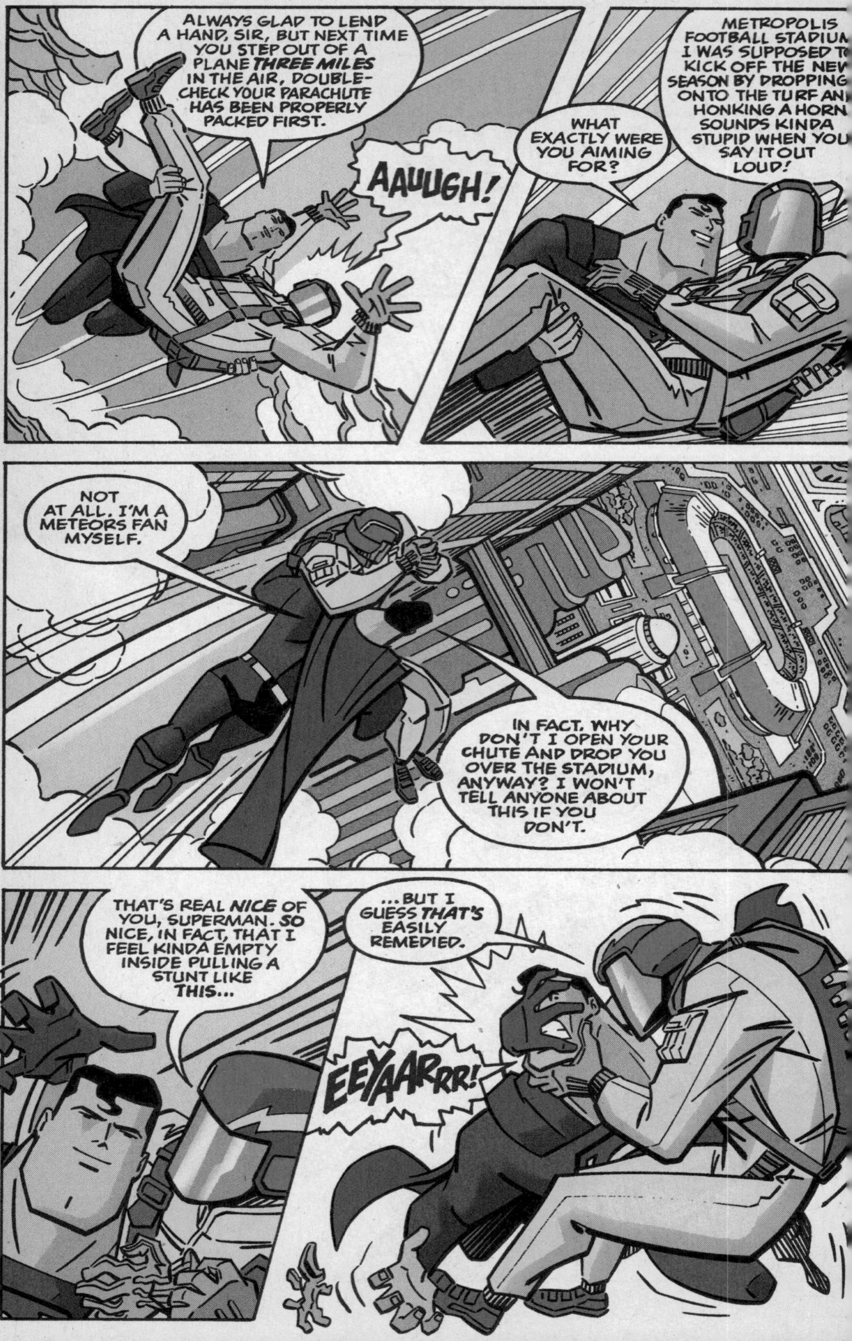
ALWAYS GLAD TO LEND A HAND, SIR, BUT NEXT TIME YOU STEP OUT OF A PLANE THREE MILES IN THE AIR, DOUBLE-CHECK YOUR PARACHUTE HAS BEEN PROPERLY PACKED FIRST.
AAUUGH!
WHAT EXACTLY WERE YOU AIMING FOR?
METROPOLIS FOOTBALL STADIUM. I WAS SUPPOSED TO KICK OFF THE NEW SEASON BY DROPPING ONTO THE TURF AND HONKING A HORN. SOUNDS KINDA STUPID WHEN YOU SAY IT OUT LOUD!
NOT AT ALL. I'M A METEORS FAN MYSELF.
IN FACT, WHY DON'T I OPEN YOUR CHUTE AND DROP YOU OVER THE STADIUM, ANYWAY? I WON'T TELL ANYONE ABOUT THIS IF YOU DON'T.
THAT'S REAL NICE OF YOU, SUPERMAN. SO NICE, IN FACT, THAT I FEEL KINDA EMPTY INSIDE PULLING A STUNT LIKE THIS...
...BUT I GUESS THAT'S EASILY REMEDIED.
EEYAARRR!

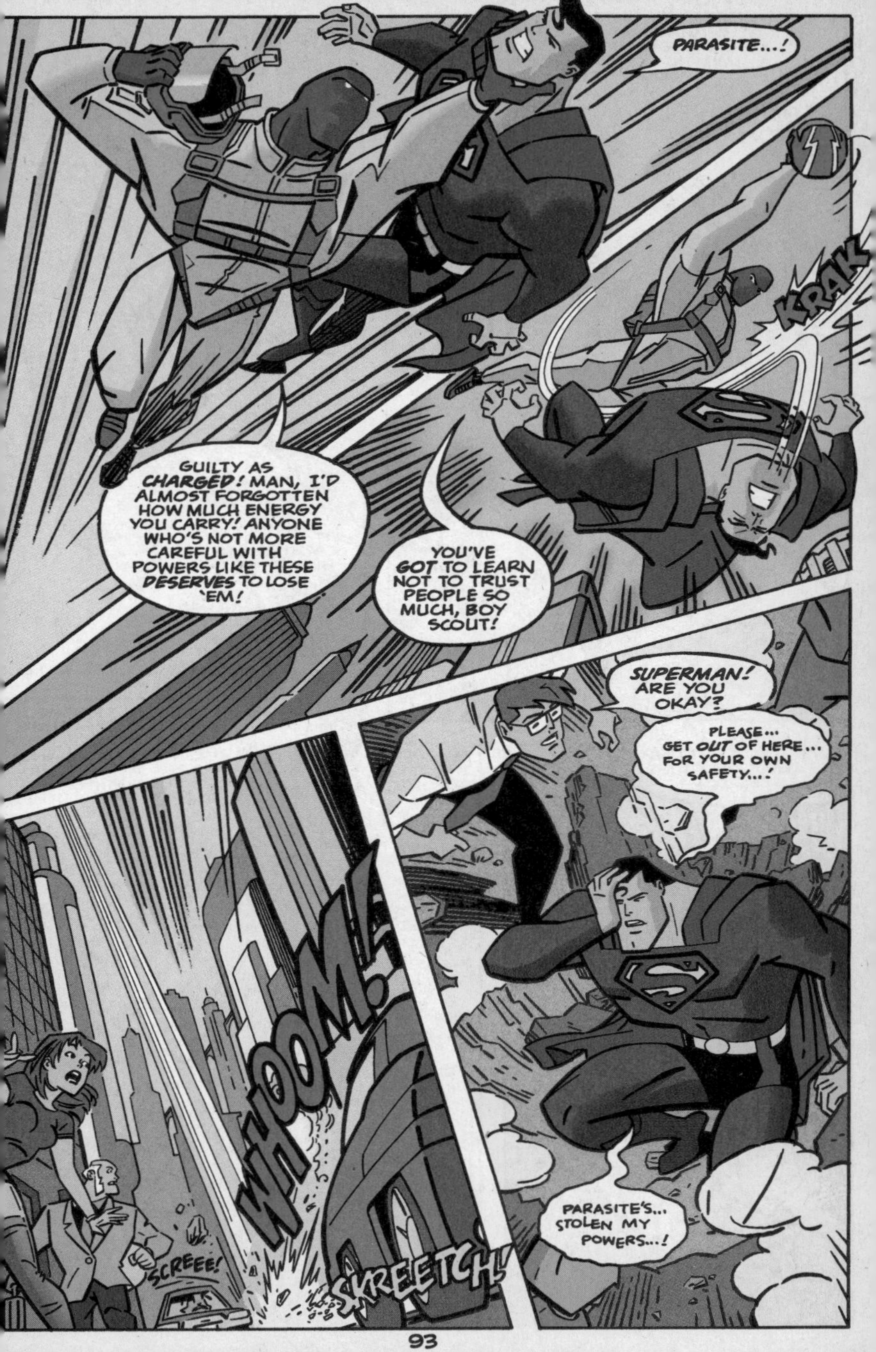
PARASITE...!
KRAK
GUILTY AS CHARGED! MAN, I'D ALMOST FORGOTTEN HOW MUCH ENERGY YOU CARRY! ANYONE WHO'S NOT MORE CAREFUL WITH POWERS LIKE THESE DESERVES TO LOSE 'EM!
YOU'VE GOT TO LEARN NOT TO TRUST PEOPLE SO MUCH, BOY SCOUT!
WHOOM!
SCREEE!
SKREETCH!
SUPERMAN! ARE YOU OKAY?
PLEASE... GET OUT OF HERE... FOR YOUR OWN SAFETY...!
PARASITE'S... STOLEN MY POWERS...!

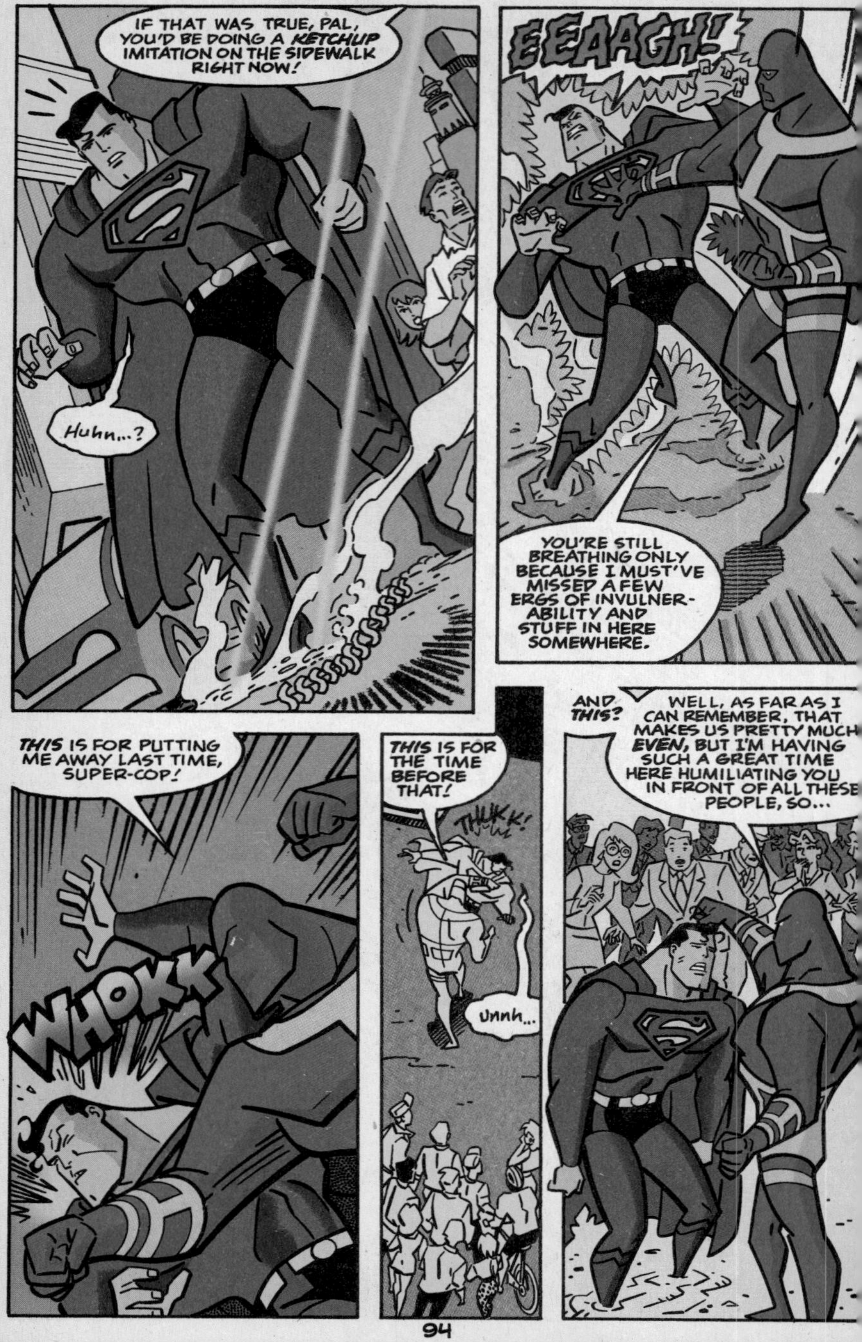
IF THAT WAS TRUE, PAL, YOU'D BE DOING A KETCHUP IMITATION ON THE SIDEWALK RIGHT NOW!
Huhn...?
EEAAGH!
YOU'RE STILL BREATHING ONLY BECAUSE I MUST'VE MISSED A FEW ERGS OF INVULNER-ABILITY AND STUFF IN HERE SOMEWHERE.
THIS IS FOR PUTTING ME AWAY LAST TIME, SUPER-COP!
WHOKK
THIS IS FOR THE TIME BEFORE THAT!
THUKK!
Unnh...
AND THIS?
WELL, AS FAR AS I CAN REMEMBER, THAT MAKES US PRETTY MUCH EVEN, BUT I'M HAVING SUCH A GREAT TIME HERE HUMILIATING YOU IN FRONT OF ALL THESE PEOPLE, SO...

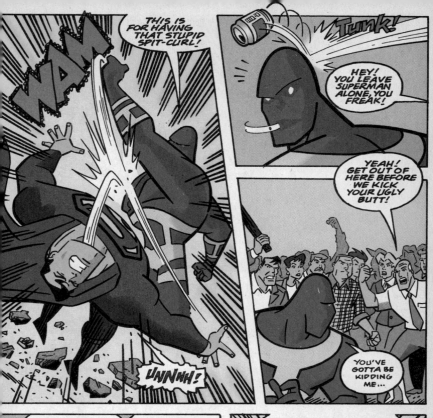

WAM

THIS IS FOR HAVING THAT STUPID SPIT-CURL!

UNNNH!

Tunk!

HEY! YOU LEAVE SUPERMAN ALONE, YOU FREAK!

YEAH! GET OUT OF HERE BEFORE WE KICK YOUR UGLY BUTT!

YOU'VE GOTTA BE KIDDING ME...

DON'T... ANTAGONIZE HIM... HE'S TOO DANGEROUS...!

TAKE IT EASY, SUPERMAN, YOU'VE SAVED THIS CITY A HUNDRED TIMES. LEAST WE CAN DO TO PAY YOU BACK IS TEACH THIS PIECE OF GARBAGE A LESSON!

DARN STRAIGHT!

IF THERE'S ONE THING I CAN'T STAND, IT'S MORONS YELLING AT ME, SO WHY DON'T YOU ALL JUST DO ME A FAVOR...

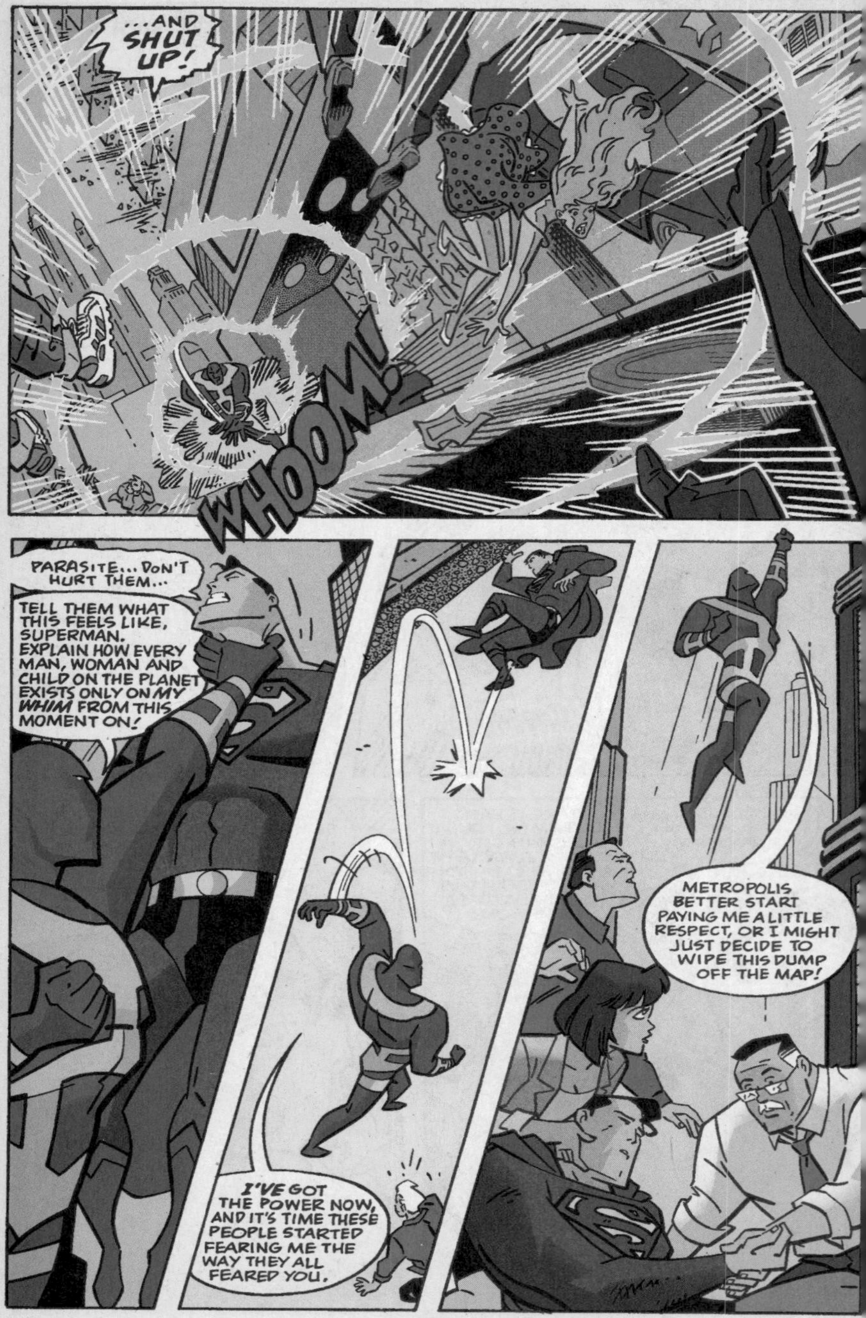
...AND SHUT UP!
WHOOOM!
PARASITE... DON'T HURT THEM...
TELL THEM WHAT THIS FEELS LIKE, SUPERMAN. EXPLAIN HOW EVERY MAN, WOMAN AND CHILD ON THE PLANET EXISTS ONLY ON MY WHIM FROM THIS MOMENT ON!
I'VE GOT THE POWER NOW, AND IT'S TIME THESE PEOPLE STARTED FEARING ME THE WAY THEY ALL FEARED YOU.
METROPOLIS BETTER START PAYING ME A LITTLE RESPECT, OR I MIGHT JUST DECIDE TO WIPE THIS DUMP OFF THE MAP!

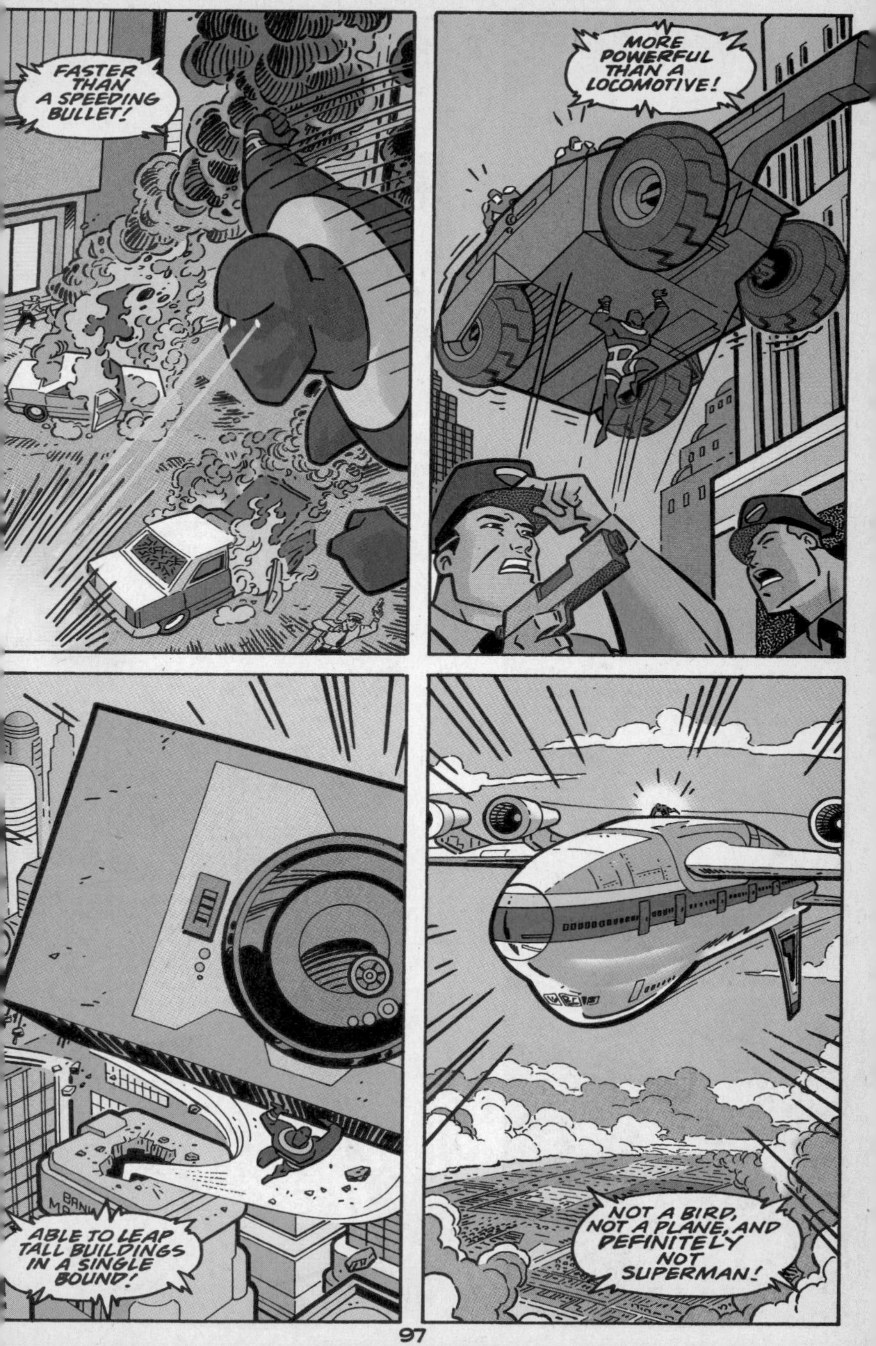
FASTER THAN A SPEEDING BULLET!
MORE POWERFUL THAN A LOCOMOTIVE!
ABLE TO LEAP TALL BUILDINGS IN A SINGLE BOUND!
NOT A BIRD, NOT A PLANE, AND DEFINITELY NOT SUPERMAN!

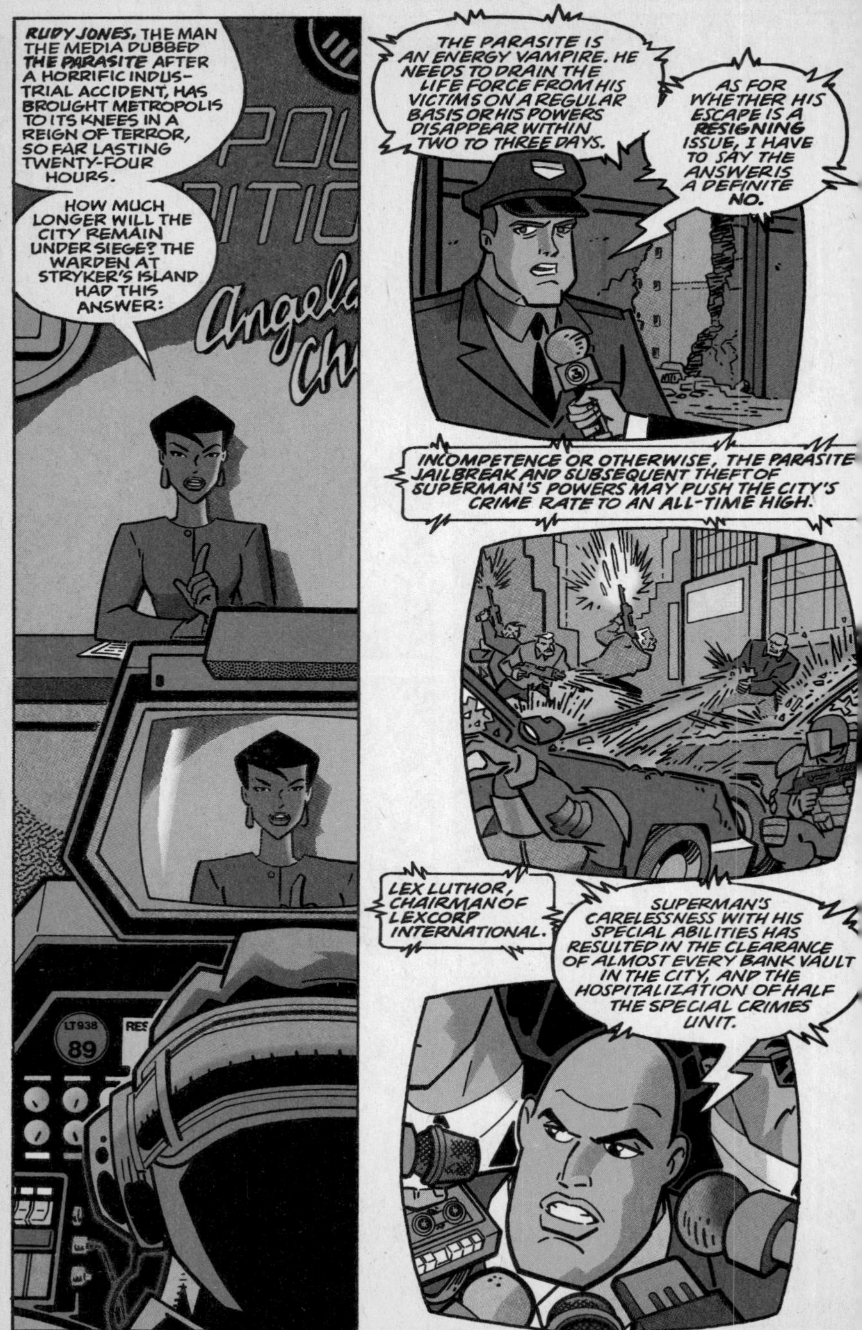
RUDY JONES, THE MAN THE MEDIA DUBBED THE PARASITE AFTER A HORRIFIC INDUSTRIAL ACCIDENT, HAS BROUGHT METROPOLIS TO ITS KNEES IN A REIGN OF TERROR, SO FAR LASTING TWENTY-FOUR HOURS.
HOW MUCH LONGER WILL THE CITY REMAIN UNDER SIEGE? THE WARDEN AT STRYKER'S ISLAND HAD THIS ANSWER:
THE PARASITE IS AN ENERGY VAMPIRE. HE NEEDS TO DRAIN THE LIFE FORCE FROM HIS VICTIMS ON A REGULAR BASIS OR HIS POWERS DISAPPEAR WITHIN TWO TO THREE DAYS.
AS FOR WHETHER HIS ESCAPE IS A RESIGNING ISSUE, I HAVE TO SAY THE ANSWER IS A DEFINITE NO.
INCOMPETENCE OR OTHERWISE, THE PARASITE JAILBREAK AND SUBSEQUENT THEFT OF SUPERMAN'S POWERS MAY PUSH THE CITY'S CRIME RATE TO AN ALL-TIME HIGH.
LEX LUTHOR, CHAIRMAN OF LEXCORP INTERNATIONAL.
SUPERMAN'S CARELESSNESS WITH HIS SPECIAL ABILITIES HAS RESULTED IN THE CLEARANCE OF ALMOST EVERY BANK VAULT IN THE CITY, AND THE HOSPITALIZATION OF HALF THE SPECIAL CRIMES UNIT.

THIS IS THE PRICE I ALWAYS WARNED WE MIGHT PAY IF WE GREETED SUPERHUMAN ACTIVITY WITH SUCH TOLERANCE.

SORRY, LOIS. I WAS DISTRACTED BY ALL THIS PARASITE STUFF ON THE NEWS. WHAT WERE YOU SAYING?

ONLY THAT THIS IS THE *THIRD* TIME IN AS MANY MONTHS YOU'VE CAUGHT A FLU BUG, SMALLVILLE. MAYBE YOU SHOULD PAY A VISIT TO THE CRYSTAL-HEALING LADY IN JIMMY'S NEIGHBORHOOD.

PERRY'S BEEN THERE A COUPLE OF TIMES, AND THE DIFFERENCE IN HIS OVERALL HEALTH HAS BEEN MIND-BLOWING.

I'LL KEEP IT IN MIND.

LISTEN, HOW ARE THINGS GOING WITH YOUR PARASITE INVESTIGATION? LAST TIME WE SPOKE, YOU SAID YOU HAD A COUPLE OF LEADS.

SOMETHING'S BOTHERED ME ABOUT THIS GUY SINCE HE FIRST APPEARED, KENT. I MEAN, WHY DOES HE KEEP PULLING THESE MAJOR ROBBERIES EVERY TIME HE BUSTS OUT OF PRISON?

WHERE CAN A MAN WITH A PURPLE BODY AND RADIOACTIVE EYES SPEND MILLIONS IN CASH?

MAYBE SUPERMAN CAN TELL US WHEN HE BRINGS HIM IN.

SUPERMAN ISN'T SUPERMAN AT THE MOMENT, CLARK. HE WON'T BE FOR ANOTHER COUPLE OF DAYS, EITHER.

I'M SURE HE REALIZES THAT BETTER THAN ANYONE, LOIS.

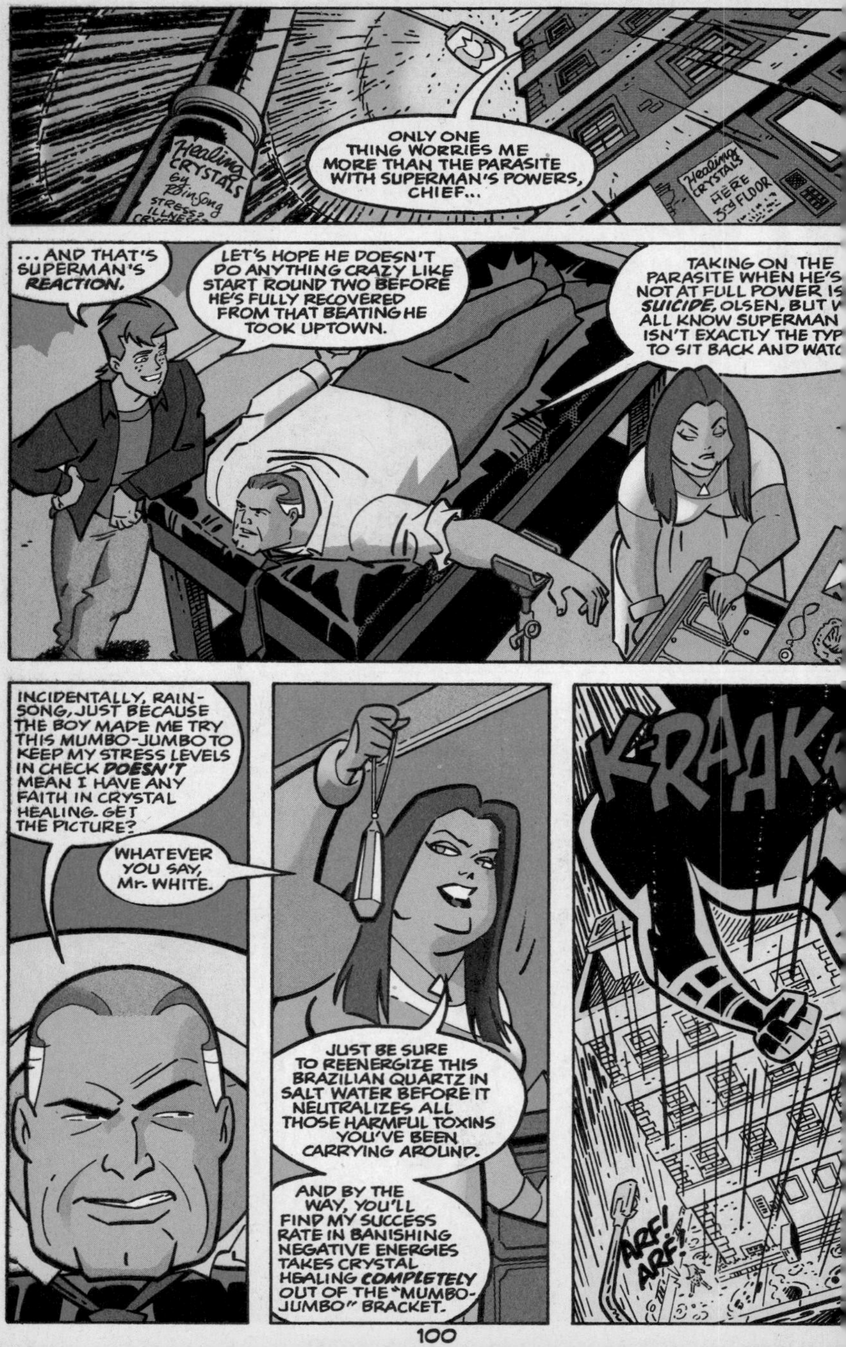
ONLY ONE THING WORRIES ME MORE THAN THE PARASITE WITH SUPERMAN'S POWERS, CHIEF...
Healing CRYSTALS HERE 3rd FLOOR
...AND THAT'S SUPERMAN'S REACTION.
LET'S HOPE HE DOESN'T DO ANYTHING CRAZY LIKE START ROUND TWO BEFORE HE'S FULLY RECOVERED FROM THAT BEATING HE TOOK UPTOWN.
TAKING ON THE PARASITE WHEN HE'S NOT AT FULL POWER IS SUICIDE, OLSEN, BUT W ALL KNOW SUPERMAN ISN'T EXACTLY THE TYP TO SIT BACK AND WATC
INCIDENTALLY, RAINSONG, JUST BECAUSE THE BOY MADE ME TRY THIS MUMBO-JUMBO TO KEEP MY STRESS LEVELS IN CHECK DOESN'T MEAN I HAVE ANY FAITH IN CRYSTAL HEALING. GET THE PICTURE?
WHATEVER YOU SAY, Mr. WHITE.
JUST BE SURE TO REENERGIZE THIS BRAZILIAN QUARTZ IN SALT WATER BEFORE IT NEUTRALIZES ALL THOSE HARMFUL TOXINS YOU'VE BEEN CARRYING AROUND.
AND BY THE WAY, YOU'LL FIND MY SUCCESS RATE IN BANISHING NEGATIVE ENERGIES TAKES CRYSTAL HEALING COMPLETELY OUT OF THE "MUMBO-JUMBO" BRACKET.
KRAAK
ARF! ARF!

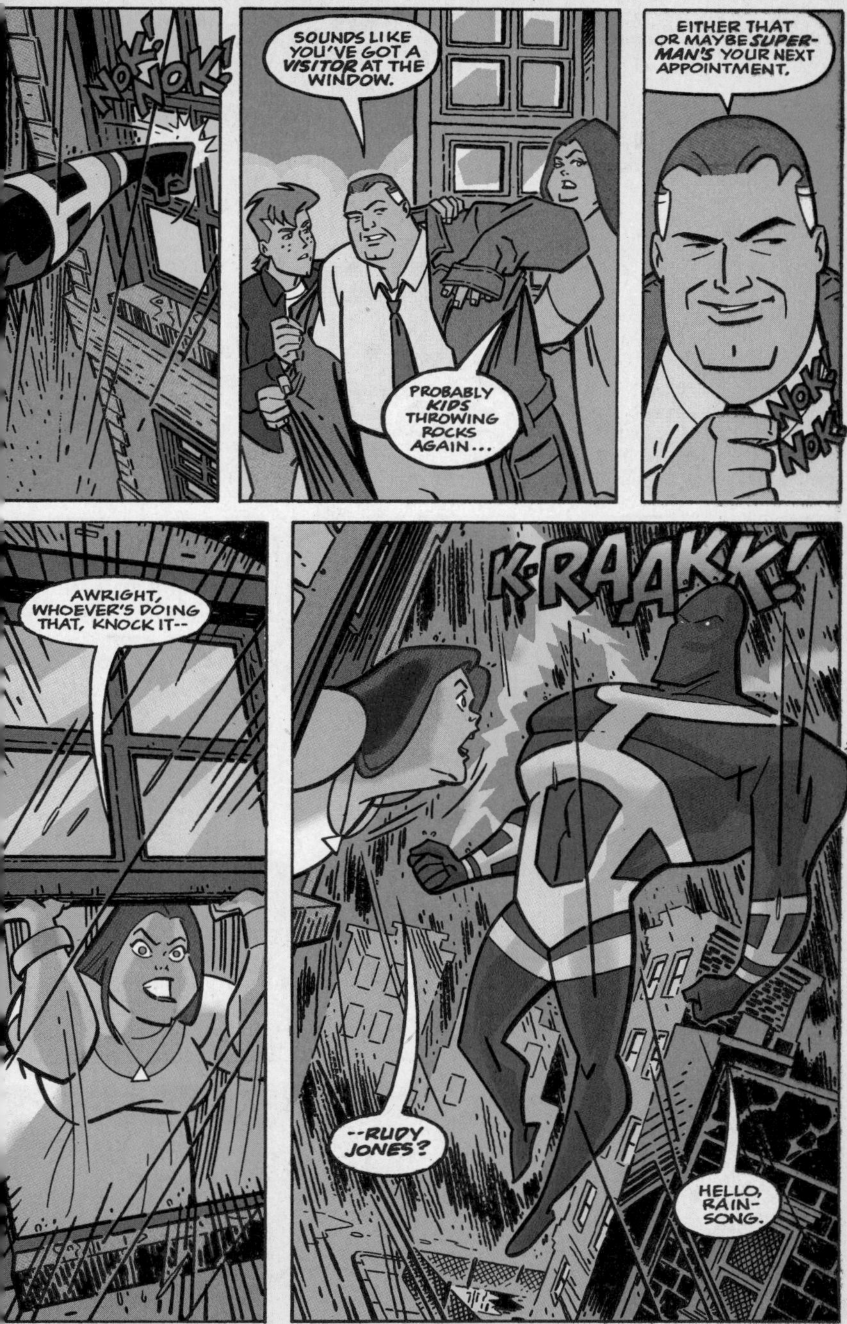
NOK! NOK!
SOUNDS LIKE YOU'VE GOT A VISITOR AT THE WINDOW.
PROBABLY KIDS THROWING ROCKS AGAIN...
EITHER THAT OR MAYBE SUPER-MAN'S YOUR NEXT APPOINTMENT.
NOK! NOK!
AWRIGHT, WHOEVER'S DOING THAT, KNOCK IT--
K-RAAKK!
--RUDY JONES?
HELLO, RAIN-SONG.

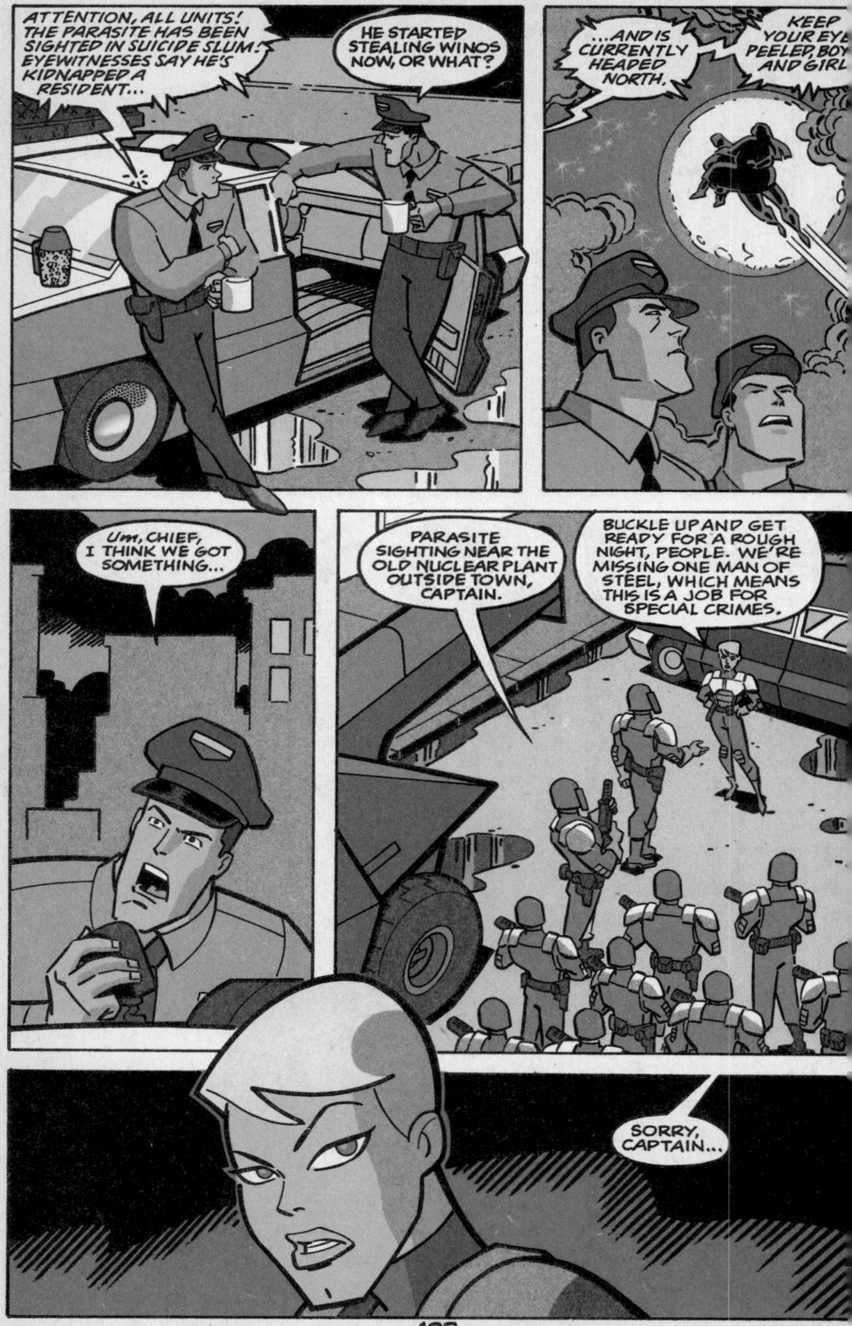
ATTENTION, ALL UNITS! THE PARASITE HAS BEEN SIGHTED IN SUICIDE SLUM! EYEWITNESSES SAY HE'S KIDNAPPED A RESIDENT...
HE STARTED STEALING WINOS NOW, OR WHAT?
...AND IS CURRENTLY HEADED NORTH.
KEEP YOUR EYE PEELED, BOY AND GIRL
UM, CHIEF, I THINK WE GOT SOMETHING...
PARASITE SIGHTING NEAR THE OLD NUCLEAR PLANT OUTSIDE TOWN, CAPTAIN.
BUCKLE UP AND GET READY FOR A ROUGH NIGHT, PEOPLE. WE'RE MISSING ONE MAN OF STEEL, WHICH MEANS THIS IS A JOB FOR SPECIAL CRIMES.
SORRY, CAPTAIN...

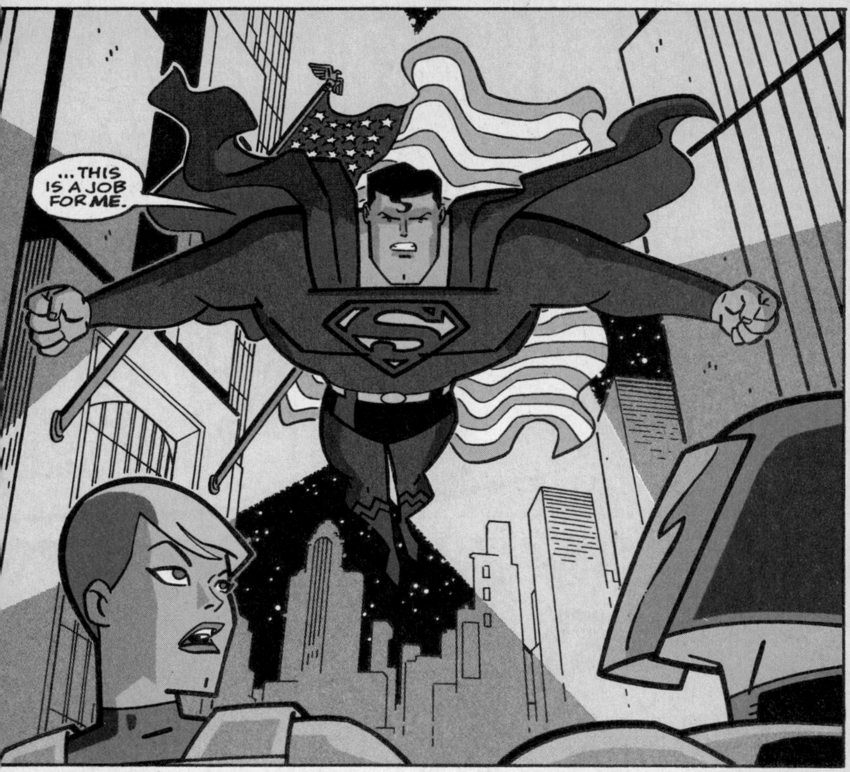
...THIS IS A JOB FOR ME.

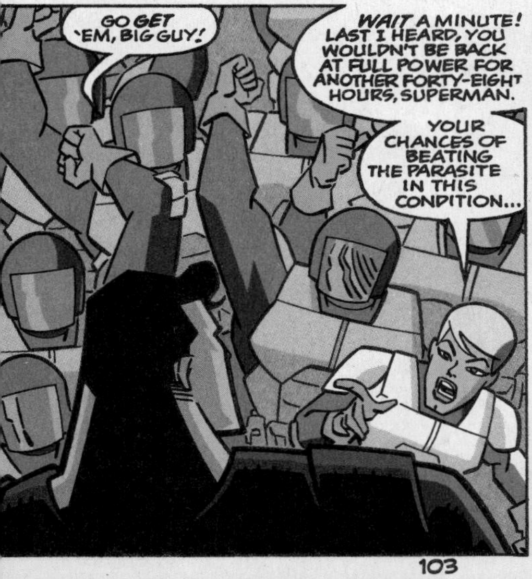
GO GET 'EM, BIG GUY!
WAIT A MINUTE! LAST I HEARD, YOU WOULDN'T BE BACK AT FULL POWER FOR ANOTHER FORTY-EIGHT HOURS, SUPERMAN.
YOUR CHANCES OF BEATING THE PARASITE IN THIS CONDITION...

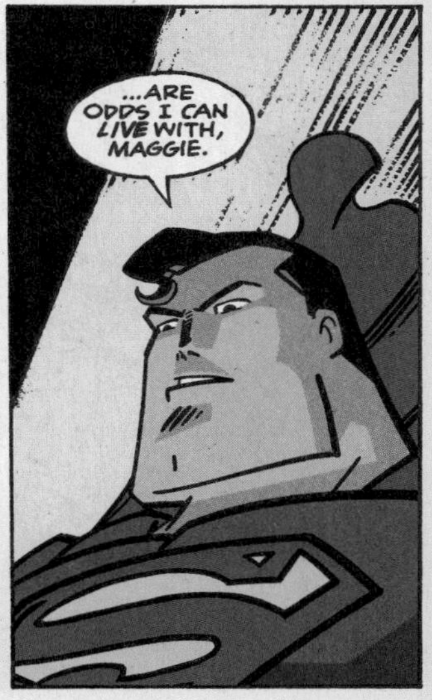
...ARE ODDS I CAN LIVE WITH, MAGGIE.

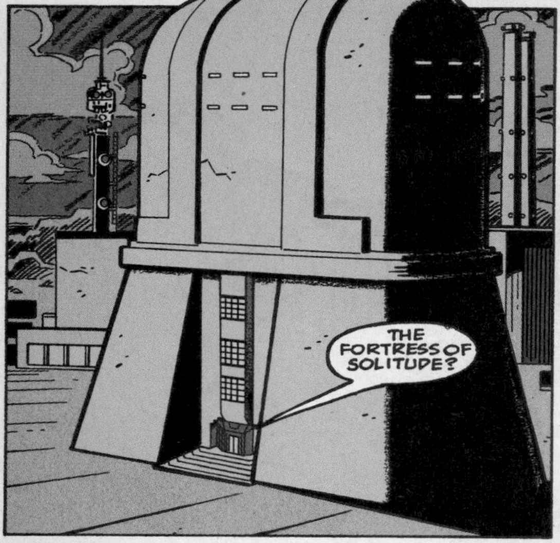
THE FORTRESS OF SOLITUDE?

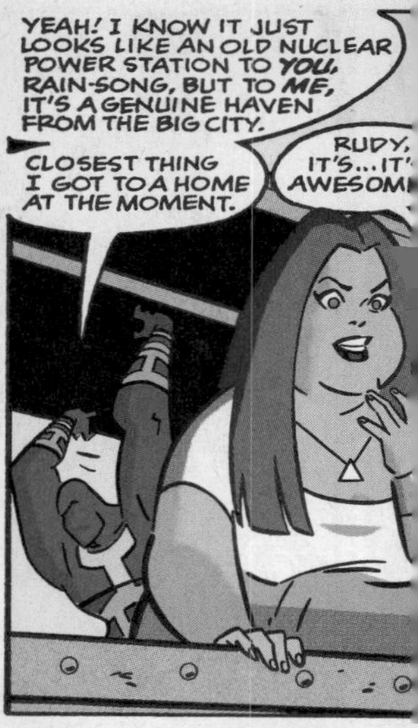
YEAH! I KNOW IT JUST LOOKS LIKE AN OLD NUCLEAR POWER STATION TO *YOU*, RAIN-SONG, BUT TO *ME*, IT'S A GENUINE HAVEN FROM THE BIG CITY.
CLOSEST THING I GOT TO A HOME AT THE MOMENT.

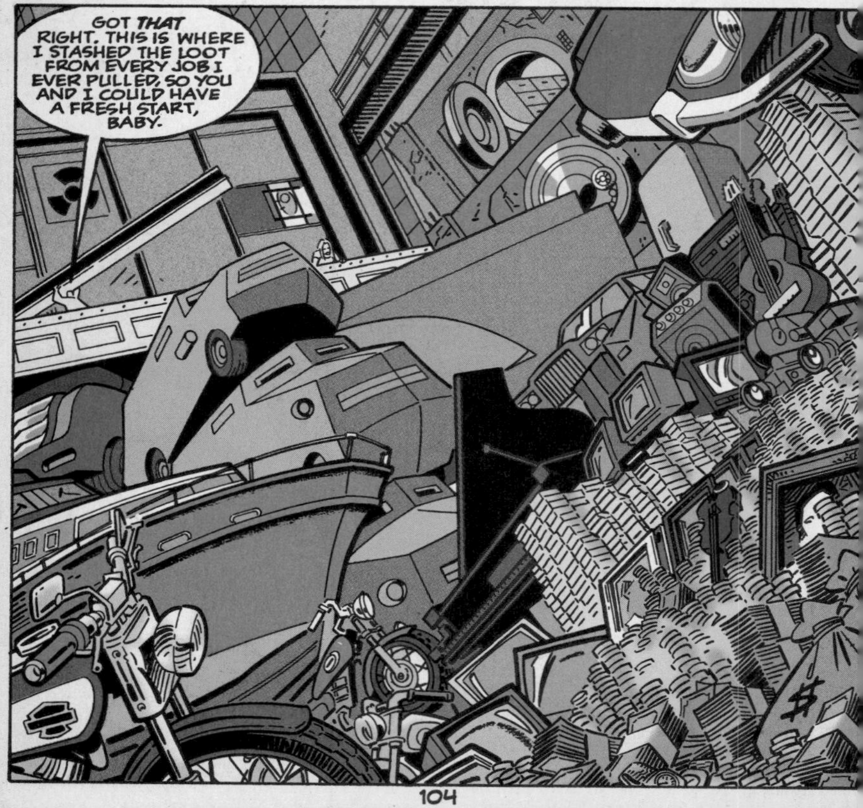
GOT *THAT* RIGHT. THIS IS WHERE I STASHED THE LOOT FROM EVERY JOB I EVER PULLED, SO YOU AND I COULD HAVE A FRESH START, BABY.

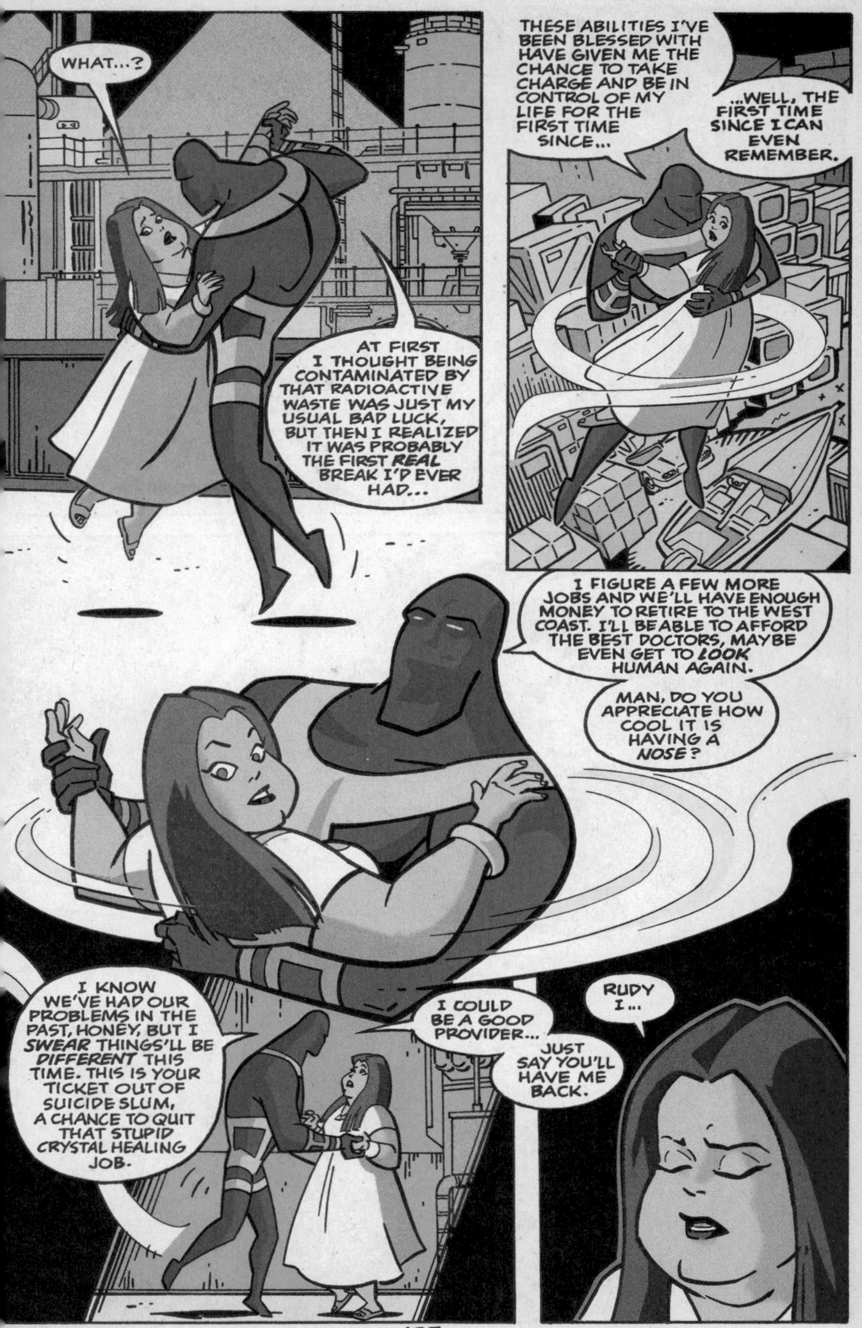
WHAT...?
AT FIRST I THOUGHT BEING CONTAMINATED BY THAT RADIOACTIVE WASTE WAS JUST MY USUAL BAD LUCK, BUT THEN I REALIZED IT WAS PROBABLY THE FIRST REAL BREAK I'D EVER HAD...
THESE ABILITIES I'VE BEEN BLESSED WITH HAVE GIVEN ME THE CHANCE TO TAKE CHARGE AND BE IN CONTROL OF MY LIFE FOR THE FIRST TIME SINCE...
...WELL, THE FIRST TIME SINCE I CAN EVEN REMEMBER.
I FIGURE A FEW MORE JOBS AND WE'LL HAVE ENOUGH MONEY TO RETIRE TO THE WEST COAST. I'LL BE ABLE TO AFFORD THE BEST DOCTORS, MAYBE EVEN GET TO LOOK HUMAN AGAIN.
MAN, DO YOU APPRECIATE HOW COOL IT IS HAVING A NOSE?
I KNOW WE'VE HAD OUR PROBLEMS IN THE PAST, HONEY, BUT I SWEAR THINGS'LL BE DIFFERENT THIS TIME. THIS IS YOUR TICKET OUT OF SUICIDE SLUM, A CHANCE TO QUIT THAT STUPID CRYSTAL HEALING JOB.
I COULD BE A GOOD PROVIDER...
JUST SAY YOU'LL HAVE ME BACK.
RUDY I...

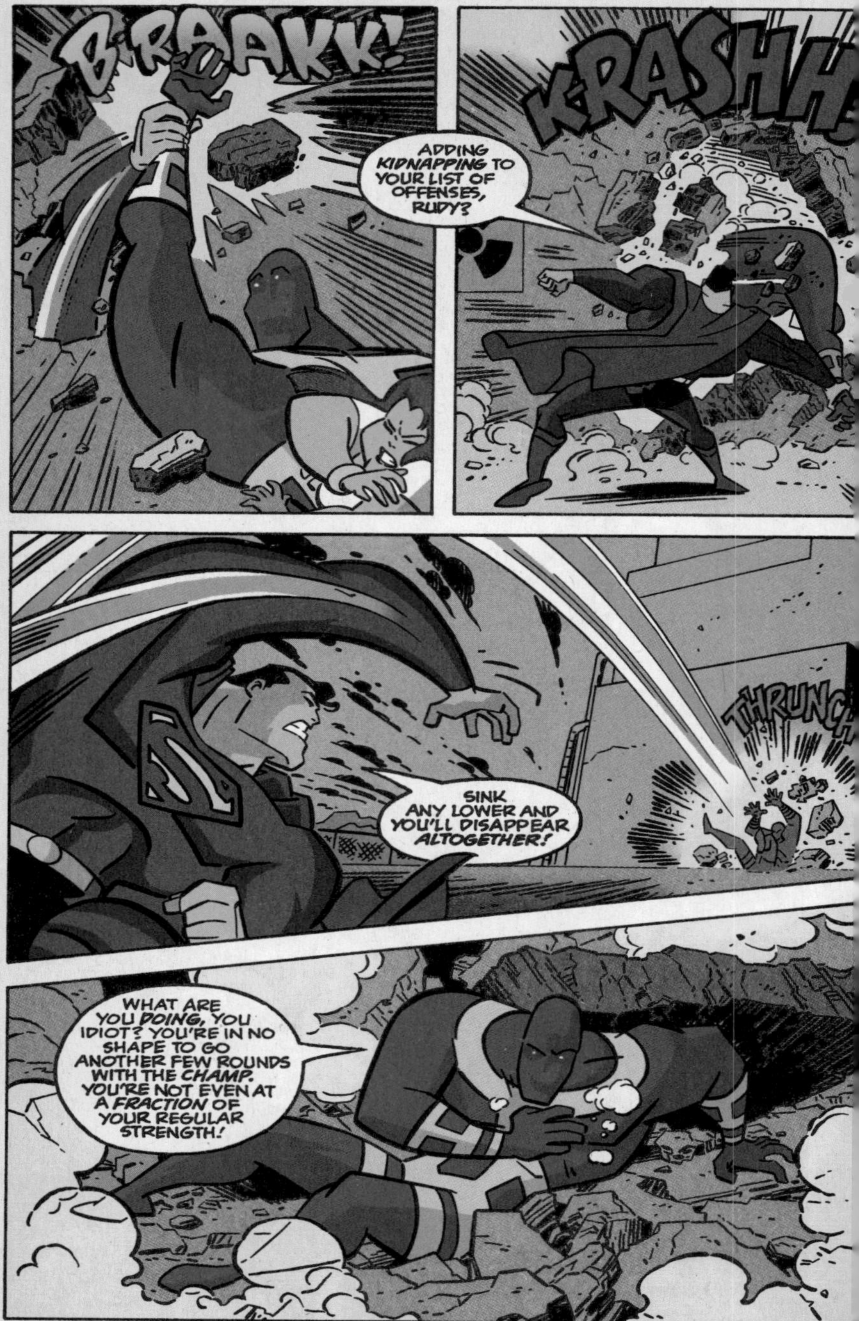
B-RAAKK!
ADDING KIDNAPPING TO YOUR LIST OF OFFENSES, RUDY?
K-RASHH!
SINK ANY LOWER AND YOU'LL DISAPPEAR ALTOGETHER!
THRUNCH
WHAT ARE YOU DOING, YOU IDIOT? YOU'RE IN NO SHAPE TO GO ANOTHER FEW ROUNDS WITH THE CHAMP. YOU'RE NOT EVEN AT A FRACTION OF YOUR REGULAR STRENGTH!

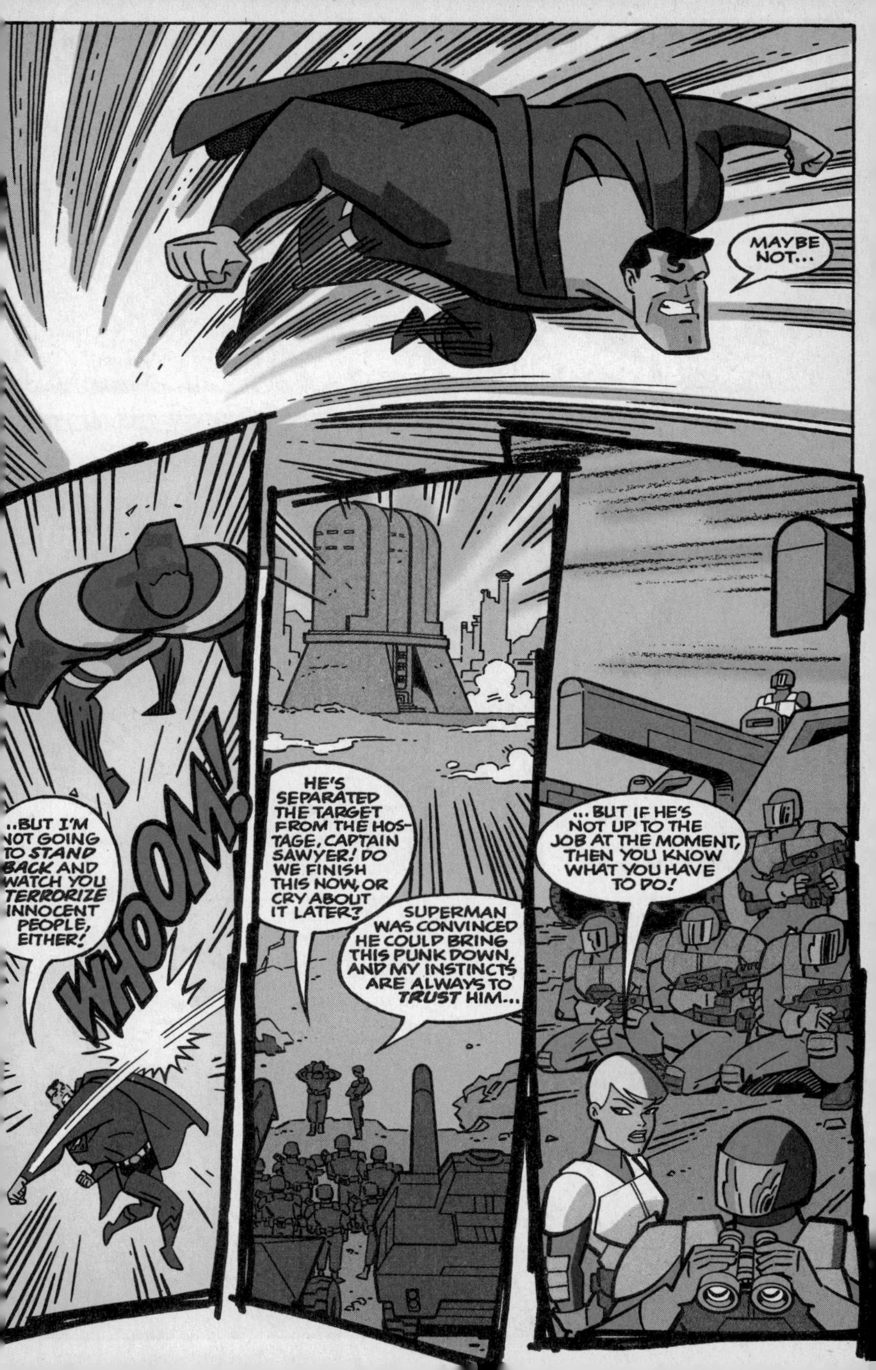
MAYBE NOT...
..BUT I'M NOT GOING TO STAND BACK AND WATCH YOU TERRORIZE INNOCENT PEOPLE, EITHER!
WHOOM!
HE'S SEPARATED THE TARGET FROM THE HOS-TAGE, CAPTAIN SAWYER! DO WE FINISH THIS NOW, OR CRY ABOUT IT LATER?
SUPERMAN WAS CONVINCED HE COULD BRING THIS PUNK DOWN, AND MY INSTINCTS ARE ALWAYS TO TRUST HIM...
...BUT IF HE'S NOT UP TO THE JOB AT THE MOMENT, THEN YOU KNOW WHAT YOU HAVE TO DO!

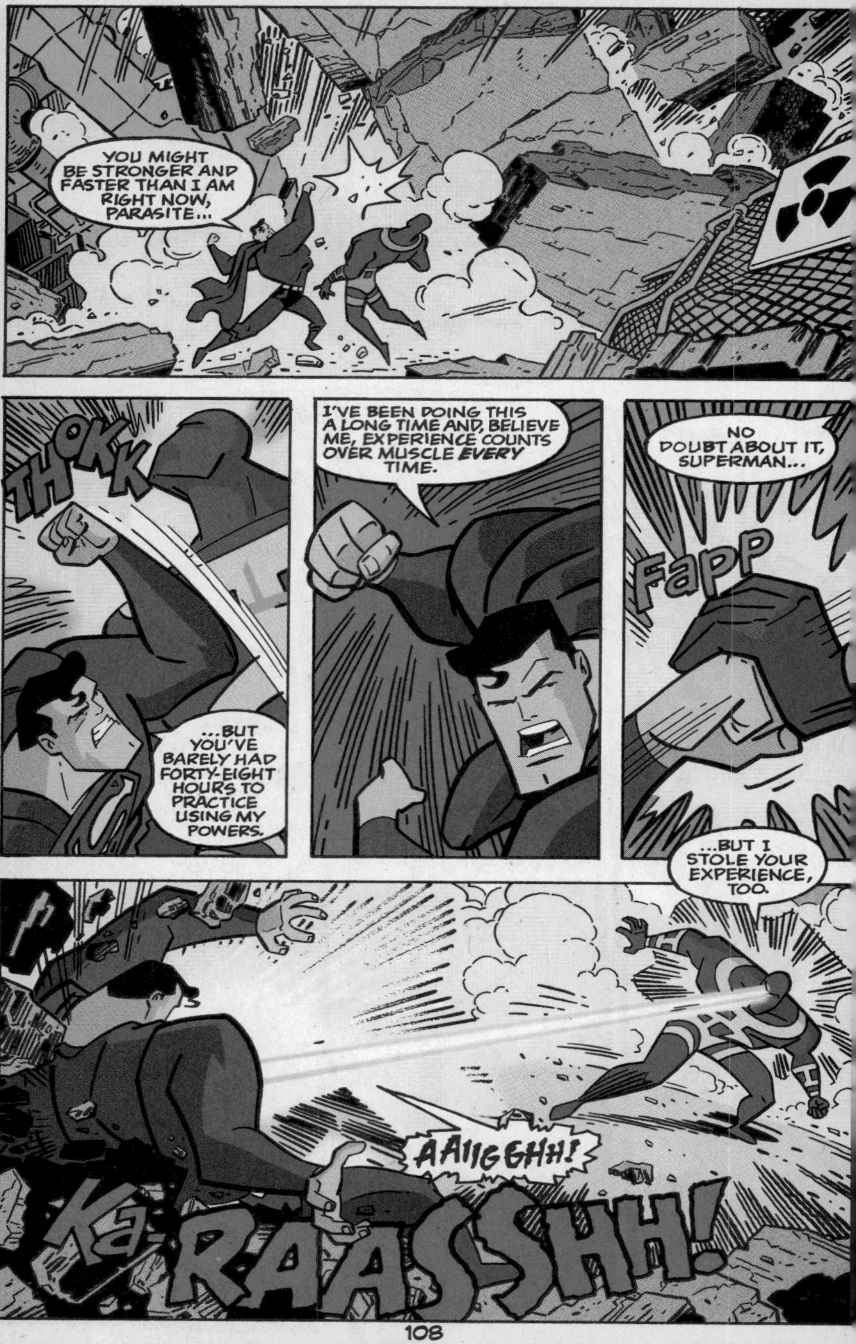
YOU MIGHT BE STRONGER AND FASTER THAN I AM RIGHT NOW, PARASITE...
THOKK
...BUT YOU'VE BARELY HAD FORTY-EIGHT HOURS TO PRACTICE USING MY POWERS.
I'VE BEEN DOING THIS A LONG TIME AND, BELIEVE ME, EXPERIENCE COUNTS OVER MUSCLE *EVERY* TIME.
NO DOUBT ABOUT IT, SUPERMAN...
FAPP
...BUT I STOLE YOUR EXPERIENCE, TOO.
AAIIGGHH!
KA-RAASSHH!

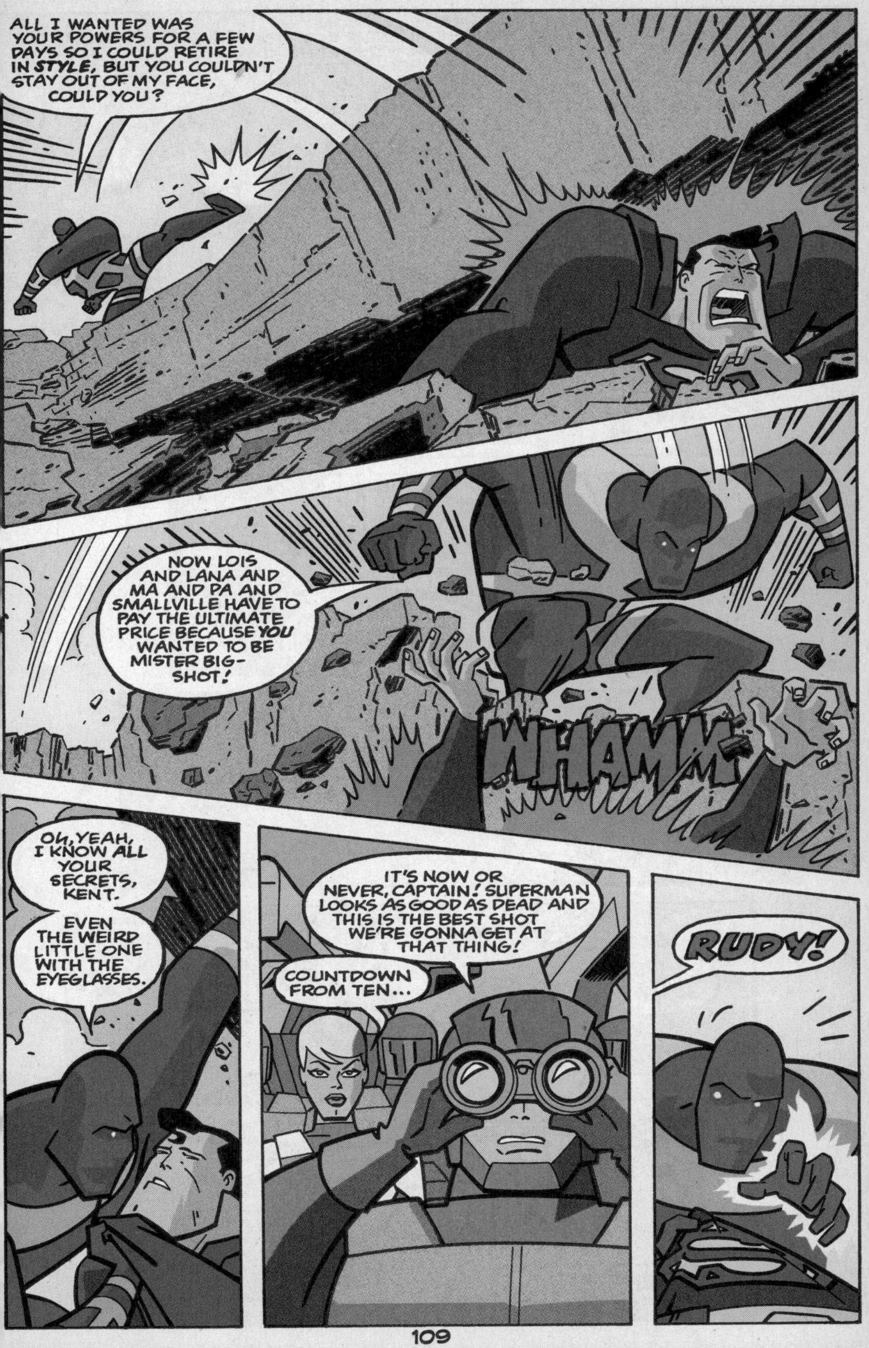
ALL I WANTED WAS YOUR POWERS FOR A FEW DAYS SO I COULD RETIRE IN STYLE, BUT YOU COULDN'T STAY OUT OF MY FACE, COULD YOU?
NOW LOIS AND LANA AND MA AND PA AND SMALLVILLE HAVE TO PAY THE ULTIMATE PRICE BECAUSE YOU WANTED TO BE MISTER BIG-SHOT!
WHAMM
OH, YEAH, I KNOW ALL YOUR SECRETS, KENT.
EVEN THE WEIRD LITTLE ONE WITH THE EYEGLASSES.
IT'S NOW OR NEVER, CAPTAIN! SUPERMAN LOOKS AS GOOD AS DEAD AND THIS IS THE BEST SHOT WE'RE GONNA GET AT THAT THING!
COUNTDOWN FROM TEN...
RUDY!

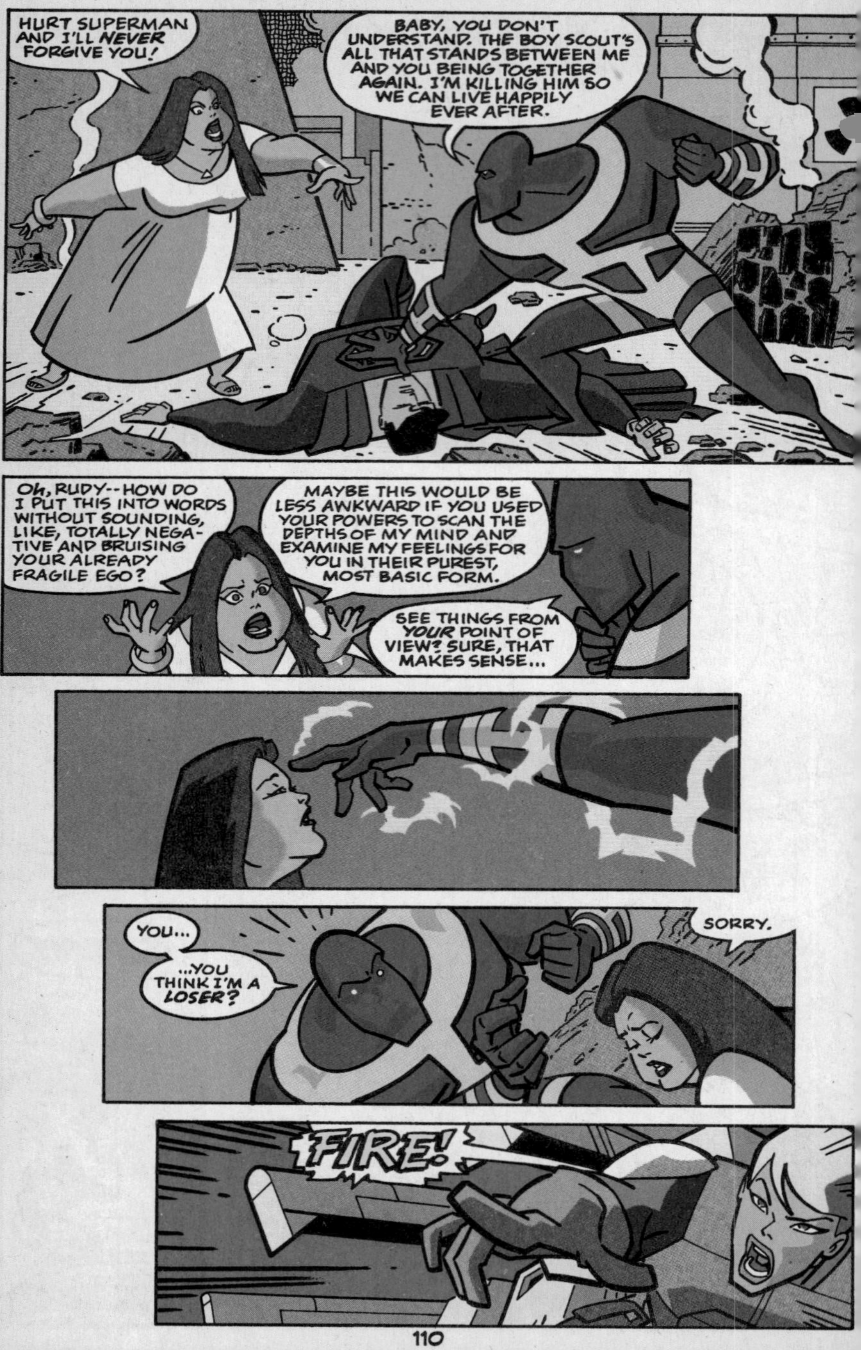
HURT SUPERMAN AND I'LL NEVER FORGIVE YOU!
BABY, YOU DON'T UNDERSTAND. THE BOY SCOUT'S ALL THAT STANDS BETWEEN ME AND YOU BEING TOGETHER AGAIN. I'M KILLING HIM SO WE CAN LIVE HAPPILY EVER AFTER.
Oh, RUDY--HOW DO I PUT THIS INTO WORDS WITHOUT SOUNDING, LIKE, TOTALLY NEGA-TIVE AND BRUISING YOUR ALREADY FRAGILE EGO?
MAYBE THIS WOULD BE LESS AWKWARD IF YOU USED YOUR POWERS TO SCAN THE DEPTHS OF MY MIND AND EXAMINE MY FEELINGS FOR YOU IN THEIR PUREST, MOST BASIC FORM.
SEE THINGS FROM YOUR POINT OF VIEW? SURE, THAT MAKES SENSE...
YOU...
...YOU THINK I'M A LOSER?
SORRY.
FIRE!

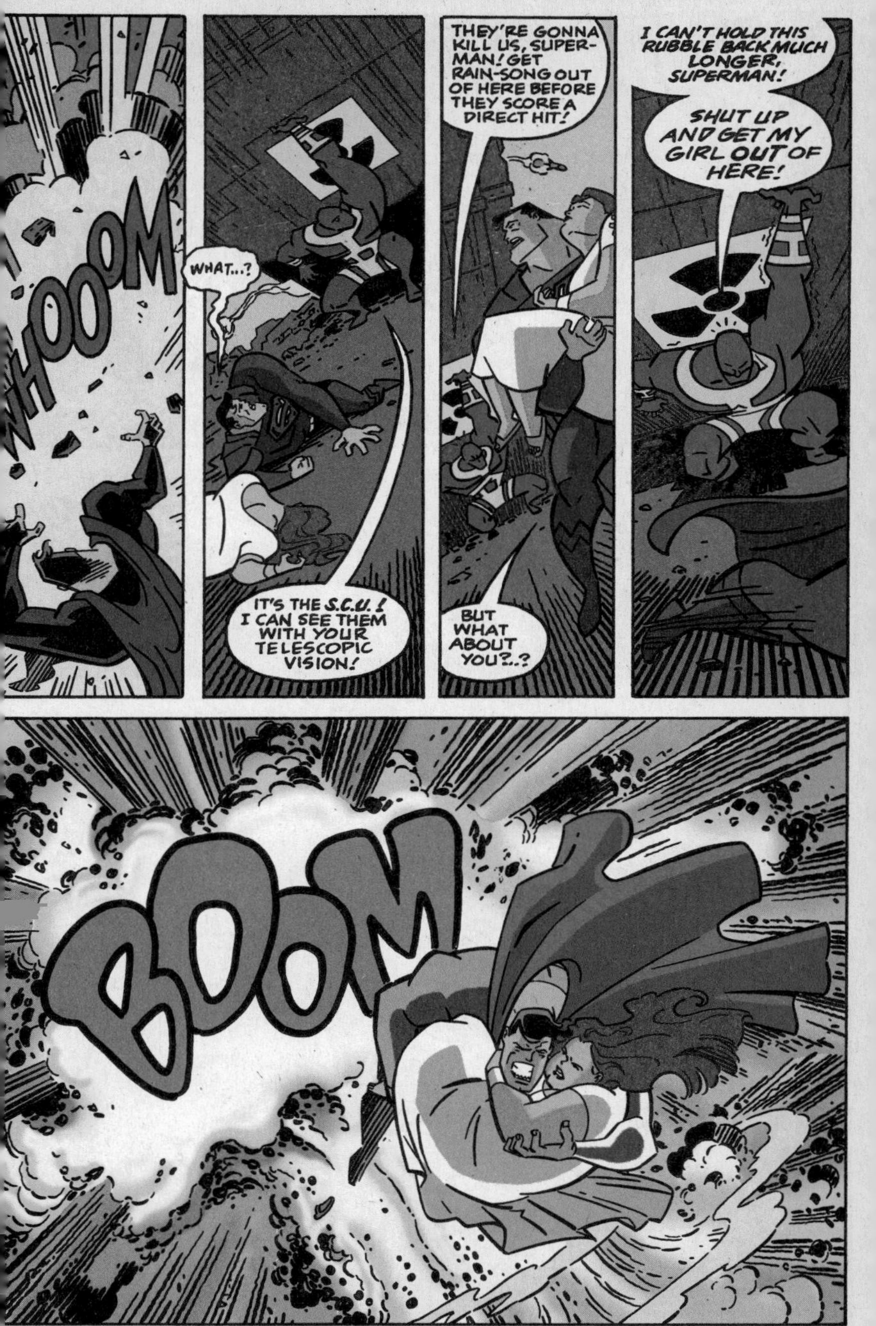
WHOOOOM
WHAT...?
IT'S THE S.C.U.! I CAN SEE THEM WITH YOUR TELESCOPIC VISION!
THEY'RE GONNA KILL US, SUPER-MAN! GET RAIN-SONG OUT OF HERE BEFORE THEY SCORE A DIRECT HIT!
BUT WHAT ABOUT YOU?..?
I CAN'T HOLD THIS RUBBLE BACK MUCH LONGER, SUPERMAN!
SHUT UP AND GET MY GIRL OUT OF HERE!
BOOM

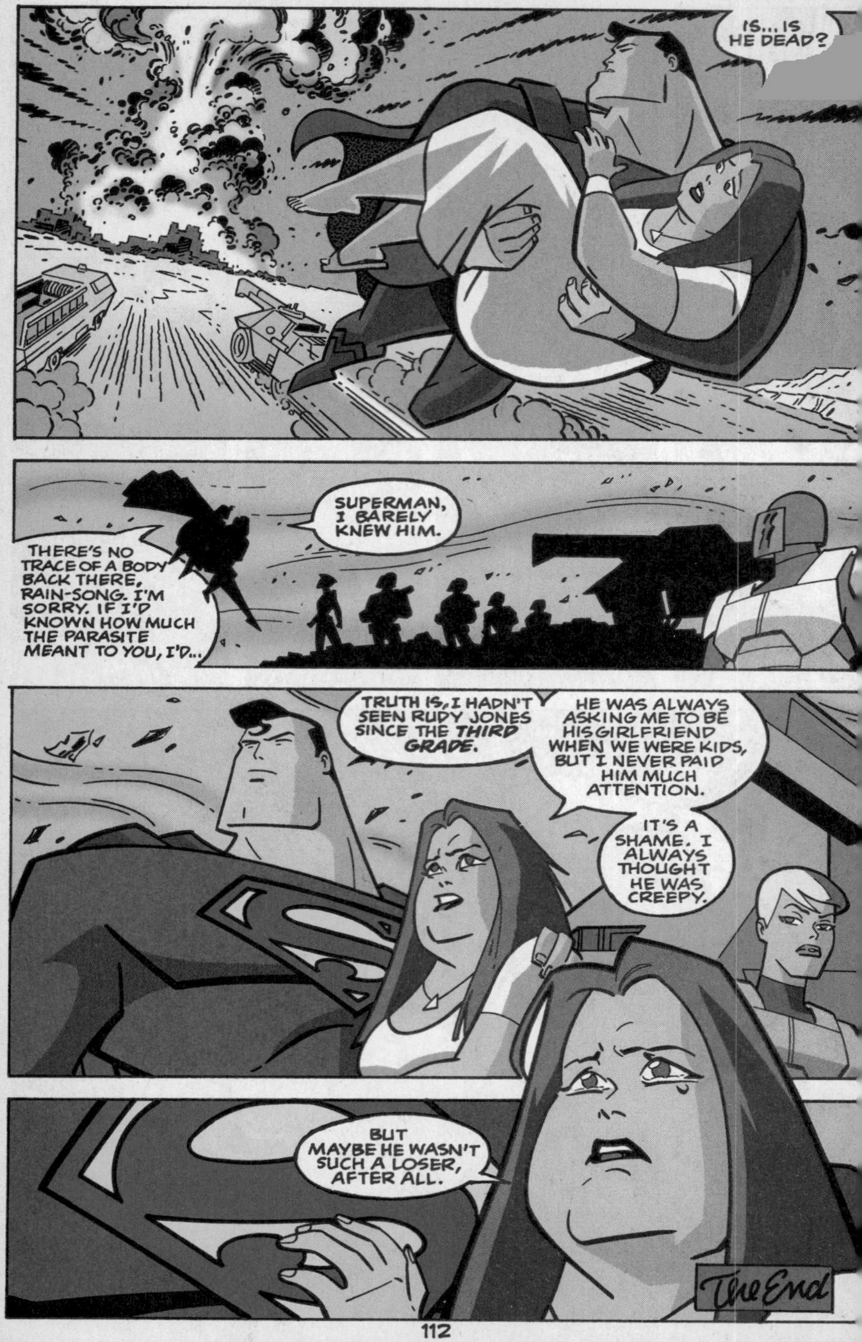
IS... IS HE DEAD?
SUPERMAN, I BARELY KNEW HIM.
THERE'S NO TRACE OF A BODY BACK THERE, RAIN-SONG. I'M SORRY. IF I'D KNOWN HOW MUCH THE PARASITE MEANT TO YOU, I'D...
TRUTH IS, I HADN'T SEEN RUDY JONES SINCE THE THIRD GRADE.
HE WAS ALWAYS ASKING ME TO BE HIS GIRLFRIEND WHEN WE WERE KIDS, BUT I NEVER PAID HIM MUCH ATTENTION.
IT'S A SHAME. I ALWAYS THOUGHT HE WAS CREEPY.
BUT MAYBE HE WASN'T SUCH A LOSER, AFTER ALL.
The End